JOSEPHINE BAKER'S
LAST DANCE

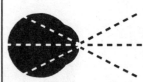

This Large Print Book carries the
Seal of Approval of N.A.V.H.

JOSEPHINE BAKER'S LAST DANCE

SHERRY JONES

THORNDIKE PRESS

A part of Gale, a Cengage Company

GALE
A Cengage Company

Farmington Hills, Mich • San Francisco • New York • Waterville, Maine
Meriden, Conn • Mason, Ohio • Chicago

Copyright © 2018 by Sherry Jones.
Thorndike Press, a part of Gale, a Cengage Company.

ALL RIGHTS RESERVED
This book is a work of fiction. Any references to historical events, real people, or real places are used fictitiously. Other names, characters, places, and events are products of the author's imagination, and any resemblance to actual events or locales or persons, living or dead, is entirely coincidental.
Thorndike Press® Large Print Historical Fiction.
The text of this Large Print edition is unabridged.
Other aspects of the book may vary from the original edition.
Set in 16 pt. Plantin.

LIBRARY OF CONGRESS CIP DATA ON FILE.
CATALOGUING IN PUBLICATION FOR THIS BOOK
IS AVAILABLE FROM THE LIBRARY OF CONGRESS

ISBN-13: 978-1-4328-6240-4 (hardcover)

Published in 2019 by arrangement with Gallery Books, an imprint of Simon & Schuster, Inc.

Printed in the United States of America
1 2 3 4 5 6 7 23 22 21 20 19

To Kate Dresser, editor extraordinaire.

Yes, I will dance all my life. I was born to dance, only for that. To live is to dance. I would love to die breathless, exhausted, at the end of a dance . . .

— JOSEPHINE BAKER

OVERTURE

Le Paradis du Music-Hall
1975, Paris

Sleep? How can she sleep when there's so much living to do? She's never needed much rest but it eludes her now and no wonder, her name in lights in Paris again, the first time in years, big stars filling the front rows night after glorious night, the critics raving like she's pulling off some kind of miracle, like she rallied herself from the grave to sing and dance her life's story across the stage. But she's just sixty-eight, not dead yet! She only looks it right now, running on fumes and just a lick of sleep after what might be the greatest performance of her life. How will she top it tonight? Never mind: Josephine Baker always finds a way.

"I heard you come in at five this morning." Lélia, her maid, stands behind her in the bathroom and pins Josephine's wig to the scant sprigs poking out from her scalp. Dear Lord, look at her in the mirror, the feed sacks under her eyes, she looks like a Saint Bernard. "Are you trying to kill yourself?"

"By dancing all night with Mick Jagger? I can think of worse ways to die." She has never had a wilder premiere, nor one as star-studded: Sophia Loren, Alain Delon, Princess Grace, Jacqueline Kennedy Onassis, Diana Ross, Carlo Ponti, and, of course, Mick. The standing ovation lasted fifteen minutes. She'd thought it would never end, her legs quivered like jelly as she'd staggered to her dressing room to collapse. Afterward, the reception in the Bristol Hotel with the cake like a tower to celebrate her fifty years on the Paris stage, the *50* on its top making her cringe, it would only remind Mick of her age. But the gleam in his eyes hadn't faltered for an instant, he'd made her feel like sweet cream in her silk Nina Ricci dress, and he the tiger licking its chops.

"The doctor said you need your rest," Lélia says as the doorbell rings. Josephine covers her unmade face with enormous sunglasses.

"There will be plenty of time for sleep when I'm dead," she says.

At the front door, the old doorman, Maurice, extends his arm. "Your car is waiting, madame." He walks her to the elevator and pushes the button and lets the door close. When she emerges at the bottom he is waiting for her, having run down the stairs. He's a little out of breath, which makes her grin: he'd never be able to endure the routine she'll be doing tonight, he'd drop dead before intermission.

Maurice hands her off with a bow to the chauffeur sent by the theater: French blue eyes and baby face, they get younger every year. He helps her into the back seat of a black limo, *like a hearse,* she'd told the director, Levasseur, making him laugh although she was dead serious. The chauffeur drapes a blanket over her legs, asking if she is comfortable. It's April, but the day is as rainy and cold as February; she wonders what he'd do if she said she was cold. Warm her up? But no — those days are gone.

As they roll down the Avenue Paul Doumer, the Eiffel Tower stands elegant sentry over her right shoulder, the embodiment of Paris that, unlike the Statue of Liberty, makes no promises and, therefore, tells no lies. Throughout the years, she has situated herself in hotel rooms and apartments where she could look out and see it.

Now, on the ride from her tiny borrowed apartment with no views of anything, it keeps her company on the way to the Bobino theater. She has fallen, yes, but not too far — she still has Paris.

The car pulls up before the theater, her name dominating the marquee in bold capital letters over the words *Un Grand Spectacle,* two and one-half hours of spangle and sparkle and froth — her life not as she lived it but as the audience wishes it to be, all sweet frosting and no cake. Her audiences don't want the truth. She's learned that lesson so many times she doesn't quite know anymore what's real and what isn't.

"Like hell, you don't," she mutters. "Don't start lying to yourself, Josephine."

The car door opens and she accepts the hand of her chubby chauffeur, his mustache like a paintbrush, a far cry from the elegant André who drove her for so many years, watching her life unfold in his rearview mirror. He once took her right here in the back seat, no, not this one, but a seat covered in snake-skin, the heels of her shoes punching holes in the ceiling, try explaining that to the upholsterer! But that was a long time ago. Everything, it seems to her now, happened so long ago.

She emerges into a crowd of fans holding

out records and programs and autograph books for her to sign, the driver trying to shoo them away until Josephine tells him to stop. These people have been waiting for who knows how long, and she isn't going to disappoint them. But as she is signing her name and petting the little dog in someone's purse and posing for pictures, M. Levasseur, the director, comes striding out the theater doors — pointed nose, cleft chin, he used to be handsome, but now, like her, he is getting old — and steers her through the throng and into the theater. She will take the stage in two hours, barely enough time to apply her frosting.

"You must enter through the stage door tomorrow, in the back, and avoid the crowds," he says, knowing that she won't, that she wants to see and be seen for this, "My last show," she has pledged to everyone, her friends, her children, her doctor, none of whom believe her. She does not believe herself.

They walk as fast as she will let herself be led through the red-and-gold lobby, into the red velvet auditorium where stagehands are arranging the staircase for her grand entrance, to her dressing room draped in blue silk, where two makeup artists whisk away her wrap, hat, and sunglasses, help her sit before the mirror, and begin smearing and dabbing and brushing and stippling layer upon layer.

She drowses in her chair and dreams of the night before: Mick twirling her and twitching his skinny hips, Grace's speech praising the show but saying it doesn't do Josephine justice — *You need a film, darling, or a novel* but who would dare? She awakens when they pin her hair tight under a wig, pulling back her skin to smooth the lines and erase the years. A pin pierces her scalp and brings tears to her eyes, which someone quickly dabs away, mustn't smear the makeup! — before the costumers rush in and stretch the white gown like a second skin over the body that she has starved for weeks. *Magnifique,* the costumer says as she turns this way and that to admire her slender arms and neck, her nearly flat belly. Sixty-eight years old, and she still looks groovy.

As they attach the giant feathered cart-wheel hat, the stage manager comes in to fetch her, bowing like a supplicant and exclaiming over her beauty. Josephine checks her reflection one last time in the full-length mirror, marveling anew at the transformation. No longer is she a tired old bag but a vibrant and youthful woman, propped up by feathers, pearls, four-inch heels, and force of will to capture once more the heart of Paris — her true love for fifty years, but just as fickle as every other lover in her life. She lifts her arms, ruffling the feathers on her sleeves.

"It's showtime," she says.

The stage manager takes her hand almost reverently, as though leading her to the altar. Behind the curtain, two beautiful boys in white tuxedos step up to escort her to the top of the staircase. There she waits for the first notes of the overture, poised in a gown the likes of which she never wore, one from the belle epoque, before Josephine's time, but so what? It's all the same to folks now.

People don't come to the theater for truth. Her fans want the dream, the candy coating: a face with no lines, a heart never broken, a life free of cares.

The first notes sound. The curtain lifts. The full house cheers. The spotlights and footlights dazzle. Josephine, blinking back tears, begins the slow descent to live her life once more.

■ ■ ■ ■

Act I
La Louisiane

■ ■ ■ ■

While the woman looks on, younger versions of Josephine cross the stage with a parade of musicians and dancers, confetti splashing the air, a NEW ORLEANS sign flashing. These girls look well fed and well clothed, nothing like her as a child. For one thing, they're wearing shoes.

These girls with happy childhoods are figments of her own fancy, characters she invented in the made-up stories she has told over the years — her real childhood being too miserable for anyone to stomach. Josephine's public life has always been illusion and spectacle, the shine on the star with none of the tarnish.

So instead of Saint Louis, Missouri, she gives them New Orleans, Louisiana.

A jazz band plays bright notes on its horns while dancers in green and gold strut in a Mardi Gras parade and toss strings of bright beads into the audience. Josephine sings an upbeat "Sonny Boy," not because it has anything to do with her childhood but because it shows off her voice, which has ripened with age to a rich contralto.

A succession of children walks on- and offstage: a swaddled "infant" cuddled by a Negro woman; a little girl in a nicer dress than she ever owned and pickaninny pigtails, which she never had; an adolescent playing the slide trombone — here, a kernel of truth — and at sixteen, leaving New Orleans for New York, as if her year in Philadelphia and marriage to Billy Baker never happened. That part of her story is best left untold.

But here it all comes like a cyclone, the bad parts and the good, picking her up and spinning her around, and there's nothing she can do to stop it.

CHAPTER 1

1913, Saint Louis

Her mama had kept saying what a nice lady Mrs. Kaiser was, but Josephine knew meanness. She'd seen it in the woman's clenched teeth, in the hard little black eyes giving her the up-and-down as though Josephine were her own great-grandmama on the auction block in Charleston, South Carolina. The way the woman talked, high and desperate-sounding, reminded Josephine of a yellow jacket buzzing around, frenetic and angry, looking for somebody to sting.

"Carrie, you didn't tell me she was so *pretty.*" Now there was a lie, right there: Josephine had buck teeth. "What's your favorite subject in school, child?"

She had to think about that one. School meant sitting still and keeping quiet. "Lunch," she finally said, and Mrs. Kaiser's narrow face sharpened like a razor honing itself on disapproval. Too mean to laugh at a joke did not bode well for Josephine, who rolled her eyes and turned her lips inside out.

Standing next to her mama, his ill-fitting Sunday shirt popping its seams on his big frame, Daddy Arthur stifled a snort. He loved Josephine's silly faces and acts, but he knew better than to egg her on in front of this white lady who thought herself fancy in the flowered dress that Mama had washed and ironed at the laundry where she worked. Some thought Josephine's faces funny and some did not, but everybody agreed that she looked like she had no sense, which she knew Mrs. Kaiser was thinking. With her eyes crossed, she couldn't see that face too ugly for even a mother to love — except for Josephine's mother, blinded by the glint of the twenty-five cents she was about to make.

"She's clever, too," Mrs. Kaiser said, pulling her lips across teeth even bigger than Josephine's. "Why, I can hardly believe she's only seven years old! She's mature for her age, just as you said. But I don't know. The child is a bit small. I need a strong one. I told you that."

"She's as strong as I am, ma'am. She hauls water from the pumps down the street every morning and evening. Show the mistress your muscles, Tumpy."

Josephine lifted a limp arm. No way she was going home with this stingy-looking witch, not if she could help it. But then her mama was dragging her out the door and down the steps and pushing her into the mistress's Model T, Josephine's first time in a car. She watched as if in a spell as Daddy Arthur cranked the engine and the vehicle sputtered and popped to life, and then they were moving and it was too late for her to get away. She pulled on her goggles and accepted her fate.

"She's a burden to us," she'd heard Mama murmur to Daddy Arthur last night, while her brother and sisters slept and Josephine stared into the dark, listening to the rattle of a tin can dislodged by a rat and then the creature's gnawing.

"I can't do it anymore," her mother had said. "She's driving me out of my ever-loving mind."

Josephine's face burned as though she'd been slapped. "It was an accident!" she wanted to cry out, but it wouldn't make any difference. Nobody thought she'd sent the old man's casket crashing to the floor on purpose. She remembers the scene: the garden snake she'd found outside clutched in her hand, a gift to old Tom, who loved snakes; the scream of the woman who knocked it from Josephine's hand; lunging under the casket perched on six dining room chairs to retrieve the poor little guy; the topple of the coffin and Mr. Tom's body rolling out. At home, as she'd whispered the tale to Richard, Margaret, and Willie Mae, they'd about split their sides from holding in the laughter, worried Josephine might get a whipping. Now, she wished she had. Maybe then, Mama might be satisfied, instead of sending her away to live with this pinch-faced white woman who, when it came down to facts, just wanted a slave. "She doesn't fit in here," Mama had said to Daddy Arthur. Or anywhere else, it seemed to Josephine.

"Stop sucking your thumb, you little heathen," Mrs. Kaiser snapped, knocking Josephine so hard she saw white dots. "I'll keep your hands so busy they'll forget where your mouth is." She kept her word, too, didn't she? Josephine almost forgot how to use a fork, so little did she get to eat.

A piece of leftover cornbread for breakfast with some molasses, another piece for lunch. After school, the rest of the cornbread, cold and dry as sawdust, with no molasses. She'd come home to a house smelling of food, her mouth watering, and get nothing but a boiled potato for supper while the mistress would sit with a full plate and eat it right in front of her: ham, collard greens, black-eyed peas, red-eye gravy, sugared tomatoes. The bone would go to the dog, Three Legs, who would take it to the box in the basement that he and Josephine slept in and smear its grease all over the straw, making her hair smell like ham for a week. When a breeze would stir up that smell and bring it to her nose, her stomach would clench and her mouth would fill with water, and all she had to swallow was ham-scented air.

Was it any wonder she fell asleep in school? Prodded by the toe of the mistress's shoe, she dragged herself before daybreak out of the box, stuffed coal from the basement bin into a burlap sack, and slung it over her shoulder to haul upstairs, the dog limping along behind. She'd open the door to let the dog out to pee and light the stove in the kitchen, then haul more coal upstairs and start that stove — quietly, so she didn't awaken the again-sleeping mistress and get a beating.

She and the dead mister's belt became close friends, kissing cousins, blood sisters. It came to know every part of her, almost: legs, back, bottom, and — when she'd turn to protect herself, begging the mistress to stop — arms and hands and stomach and chest. She felt its sting all over except on her face, because then she'd have to go to school with her bruises and welts in plain sight and her teacher, Mrs. Smith, might ask more questions than she already had: "What time do you go to bed, child? When do you get up? Do you have nightmares? Answer me, Tumpy, please, I'm trying to understand why you can't stay awake in class. Are you ill? If this keeps up, I'm going to have a talk with your aunt." Mrs. Kaiser had told the school that Josephine was her brother's illegitimate child, which, for all Josephine knew, might be the truth.

Not long before Thanksgiving, the mistress put the turkey, Tiny Tim, Josephine's only friend besides Three Legs, in a cage inside the kitchen to "fatten up for the feast." Unable to run around the yard with her now, he gained weight so fast that she hardly recognized him except for the way he cocked his head when she talked to him, his bright eye looking right at her as though he understood every word. "Don't eat this," she'd whisper while scooping dried corn into his bowl, but he devoured every kernel and gobbled for more.

A few days before Thanksgiving, the feed bag disappeared. Josephine knew what that meant: Tiny Tim would be slaughtered the next day. She curled in the box with Three Legs that night and held him tight, burying her face in the matted fur and trying to think only of the dog smell and not of her friend awaiting its fate in that cage. She imagined herself sneaking up into the kitchen and setting Tiny Tim free, but how? The doors to the house were locked, and the mistress had the key. Besides, if she let the Thanksgiving turkey escape, the mistress would probably cook *her* for dinner.

In the morning, her chores complete, she found the mistress at the counter with a mess of potatoes and a paring knife. She pulled her stool over to start peeling, but the woman handed her scissors instead. Then she picked up the cage and took it outside, telling Josephine to take off her dress and come on out.

"Mr. Kaiser used to take care of this, but he's gone, and so it's up to you," she said as Josephine stumbled out the door. "What are you shaking for? You afraid of a little ol' turkey?" She snorted. "It's about as big as you are, that's a fact, and as stupid, too, so it ought to be a good match."

She set down the cage at the edge of the chicken yard, motioning for the shivering Josephine to sit on the stool she used for killing chickens. She set Tiny Tim in Josephine's lap. The bird peered at her with one trusting eye. Josephine lifted her hand to her face —

"Don't be touching your eyes after handling that bird, you dumb little pickaninny." The mistress knocked her hands away. "I ain't sending you home sick, not with Christmas coming." Josephine wanted to jump up and push the evil woman to the ground and run with her friend out the gate and down the highway, but she couldn't go anywhere in just her panties. She'd freeze to death, or the mistress would catch her like she did the last time and beat her until she fainted.

She let go of the bird for a second to scratch herself — Three Leg's fleas again — and he flapped his wings and flew from her lap to the ground.

"He got away! Look what you've gone and done," the mistress said. "I told you about that scratching, but you just can't keep your hands out of there, can you, you little heathen?"

"Leave me alone!" Josephine shouted, scrambling to her feet. The mistress's gaze fell to the scissors still in Josephine's hand and her expression sharpened to a malicious point. *Go ahead and try it,* her eyes urged

Josephine.

"Put down those scissors or I'll wring *your* neck," she said.

"My mama will kill *you.*"

"Your mama will thank me. Now get that turkey and kill it, and do it quick. Call me when it's stopped bleeding so we can scald it for you to pluck. Hurry it up, or you'll be late for school."

"Stupid bird," she said to Tiny Tim when the mistress had gone inside, and she pushed his head into the killing cone. She decided to pretend the bird was just a big chicken instead of Tiny Tim, who used to come wobbling and gobbling whenever she walked into the poultry yard. She closed her eyes and, holding him between her knees, stretched his neck to snip the arteries as she'd done many times before but never to something she loved. Blood ran over the handsome purple head. His gobble sounded gargled and choked, like when Daddy Arthur would clamp his hands around Mama's throat and shake her, shouting, *Goddamn woman can't even cook a hot dog without burning it.* The bird kicked her hard in the tenderest part of her arm, then hung still and limp in her trembling clutch. As she waited for the blood to stop running, she averted her gaze from the

27

glassy eye, the open beak.

"Took you long enough," the mistress said, striding toward her from the house but making no effort to take the carcass. She led Josephine to the fire pit and gestured to the pot of water on the boil. Josephine lifted the heavy bird with both hands and lowered it slowly into the bubbling cauldron, averting her face to avoid the steam and hot water breaking in bubbles over the lip of the pot. Moisture beaded on Tiny Tim's legs, making them slip in her hands, but she managed to grasp the feet and hold on although every muscle in her body strained with effort.

"You're going to drop it, you idiot." The mistress snatched the bird and pushed Josephine backward, snarling for her to get out of the way, couldn't she do anything right? Laying the carcass on the grass, she told Josephine to start plucking and hurry up, she had to get to school, and stop that scratching or she'd get another thrashing. So Josephine plucked her friend, closing her eyes against its nakedness, and went inside to wash herself and put on her dress, which swallowed her too-thin body, but not as much as she would wish, not enough to make her disappear.

"Look at her itching herself! You got fleas down there?" The boy pointed at her crotch with an open, laughing mouth, summoning others on the playground to gawk. Josephine wanted to run back into the classroom, where the teacher had been helping her catch up on her studies, smelling so good sitting next to her, like a garden full of beautiful flowers, scents that made her feel like she was in heaven. At one point, the teacher's arm had brushed against hers, making her want to crawl into the kind woman's lap and rest her head and try to forget Tiny Tim's frightened screams.

"She's got critters in her crotch," the big boy cried out, and the other kids pointed at her, too, and danced around chanting, "Critter crotch, critter crotch." Josephine, having had enough meanness for one day, made her face blank and tuned out their taunts, thinking instead of the music she'd heard floating down the street last Saturday.

She'd gone home for the weekend, and Daddy Arthur had taken her to the Soulard Market to beg and scavenge for food. All that work had left her hungry, so he gave her an apple from the sack and walked her over to Market Street to see the new colored theater, the Booker T. Washington, a small brick building on the outskirts of downtown. Outside, a long line of folks from Union Station waited to watch the vaudeville show, passing the time until their connecting trains arrived. Only white people were allowed in the station restaurant, but for a nickel Negro folks could spend all day at the Booker T watching jugglers, tap dancers, poodles jumping through hoops, clowns in blackface, magicians sawing ladies in half, and men in dresses and high-heeled shoes singing in falsetto and prancing up and down the stage.

5¢ QUALITY ACTS 5¢

Josephine, on Daddy Arthur's shoulders, kicked her feet against his hips and begged him to take her inside, flying dogs and lipsticked men swinging through her mind, but he said they had to get home before her mama left for work. Outside the theater, a man with a trumpet, another with a guitar, and a woman with a tambourine played a song about gasoline, the people in line clapping to the beat; one couple broke out to dance, arms and legs in a blur and big smiles on their faces.

"Ouch, baby, my head is no drum," Daddy Arthur said, laughing as he trotted down Market, greeting by name folks walking to the beauty shop or the drugstore or the soda fountain, which was now selling ice cream wrapped in cone-shaped cookies. Josephine's mouth watered, but she knew better than to ask. There had never been money for ice cream, and maybe there never would be, but it wouldn't matter, anyway, because if she stayed at Mrs. Kaiser's house she'd be dead before long.

"The mistress hits me," she said.

Daddy Arthur laughed and said, "Welcome to the world." He reckoned that was why colored people were born: to give the whites someone to beat up on.

"I don't want to go back," she said. "Please don't make me, Daddy Arthur. I promise I'll be good."

"Best talk to your mama about that." Meaning: you're not my child. He loved his real children best, Margaret and Willie Mae, bouncing them on his lap and singing, "Ride a little horsey up to town, for to get him a plum." Plums. Josephine shuddered at the thought of all that sweetness, imagined the juice dripping down her chin. Daddy Arthur loved Richard, too, even though he wasn't Richard's daddy, because he had dark skin like his own. Josephine's light complexion served as a constant reminder that her real daddy was somebody else, someone whose name Mama would not say.

"That's because she doesn't know," Grandmama had said, her mouth puckering like she'd eaten sour fruit.

People speculated. Once, two women walked past her remarking, "Carrie McDonald likes cream in her coffee," talking about her mama. Another time, some kids in the neighborhood called Josephine and Richard bastards. Boy, that got Mama's goat.

"There are no bastards in this household," she hollered when Josephine asked her about it. "You all come from the same hole." While Richard's daddy came around to see him every now and then, nobody claimed Josephine except Eddie Carson, who looked like a flimflam man in his bright clothes and sneaky mustache. "Got a quarter for your old man?" he'd asked one day, offering her Mary Jane candies. She'd snatched the bag from his hand and run away, but inside her head was buzzing with questions. Was Eddie Carson really her daddy? That evening, she asked her mother.

"Daddy Arthur is all the father you'll ever

need," was all Mama would say.

Why, then, did he let Mama send her back to Mrs. Kaiser's? He still hadn't found a job, so maybe they really did need the money the mistress gave them, a quarter a week, but she had earned more from raking leaves, sweeping steps, and caring for the white folks' babies on Westmoreland Avenue.

She'd sent Josephine back even after seeing the marks the mistress's belt had made. "Maybe she'll teach you to behave yourself."

On the playground now, Josephine dug her fingernails into the heels of her hands and thought about that pain, nothing else, until the boy got in her face and cried, "Critter crotch!" Josephine wanted to shut him up, so she punched him in the kisser with both fists. He stumbled backward, and she hit him again, flailing, not stopping, because the minute she let up he would flatten her to the ground and she was sick and tired of being hit.

The whole playground came over to shout and scream as the boy fell, her on top of him, slapping and scratching and pulling his hair and snarling, "Goddamn, goddamn," until the teacher pulled her away and led her inside, into the faculty bathroom, where she closed the door and wiped the blood off Josephine's face, murmuring, "Poor thing." When Mrs. Smith lifted her shirt and saw the welts, she sucked air through her teeth and said, "My God, this can't be. This will not be!" Foreboding flooded Josephine's bones like a storm rolling in.

The next day was Thanksgiving, but Josephine could think of nothing to give thanks for except that Mrs. Kaiser was too busy to pay her any mind. A bunch of folks came over to eat poor Tiny Tim, kissing the mistress when they came in the door, smiling as if touching their lips to that ugly face were not enough to make anyone sick. Josephine took everybody's coats to the bedroom except for that of one man, who said flat out that he'd let no nigger handle his fine wool and cashmere. A woman thrust her baby into Josephine's arms as if wanting her to pile it on the bed with the coats and hats and scarves and handbags. Josephine kissed the infant's cheek, a boy with big blue eyes and skin like peaches. The mother shrieked and snatched the child away, her blond curls snapping accusatorily, glaring as if Josephine were the one now making the baby cry.

Luckily, Mrs. Kaiser missed that scene.

She was busy kissing the next guests and exclaiming how *glad* she was to see them; how *sweet* they were to compliment her dress, she'd had it for *years,* it was Mr. Kaiser's favorite, God rest his soul; and yes, didn't the turkey smell wonderful? Josephine's stomach turned.

The guests took seats around the table, and Josephine filled their glasses with sweet tea while the mistress brought in the serving bowls from the kitchen, steaming mounds of mashed potatoes, a sweet potato casserole, a mess of green beans, cranberry sauce, dinner rolls, and, making its dramatic entrance on an enormous blue-and-white platter, Tiny Tim, trussed and buttered and browned. Bile rose to her throat. She gripped the mistress's chair to keep from fainting on the floor.

Mistress ordered her to hold the plate while the man who'd called her a nigger sliced the meat and laid it down in layers, white meat on one side and dark meat on the other, the smell making Josephine gag, so that by the time everybody began to eat she had to hurry from the room. "Go ahead and make a plate for yourself," the mistress called after her, the first time in two months she'd offered her a proper meal. But how could she choke anything down with her stomach in a thousand knots from thinking of poor Tiny Tim, and her teacher's calling a meeting for Monday morning with the mistress and the school principal to talk about Josephine's welts? When she'd given Mrs. Kaiser the note and the mistress had pressed her for information, Josephine had played dumb.

She curled up in her box and cried until the mistress's voice cut in, calling her to come upstairs and wash the dishes. When she got to the kitchen, darkness had fallen, the room lit only by a gas lamp on a shelf and a few candles. "Make sure you get them clean this time," the mistress said, and headed up to bed, leaving Josephine to scrape and scrub the piles of pots and pans and bowls and platters and plates that she could barely see. If mistress spied even a speck of food on anything tomorrow, there would be hell to pay.

She lit the stove to warm a pot of water filled with dishes, then turned and confronted the carcass on the serving platter, the bones picked nearly clean except for the legs, which wafted a faint aroma of animal fat that made her whole body leap with hunger. She grasped a leg and wrested it from the joint, releasing pieces of dark, dripping meat that she lifted to her teeth to chew and swallow in swooning bliss. When she had devoured it and finished the other leg, too, she sat on the floor in a stupor, her cheeks and jaw shiny, her skin stretched like a drum over her bulging stomach, Tiny Tim heavy in her gut and in her heart. She lifted her hands to her face and began to cry.

"What in God's name are you doing?" The mistress emerged into the kitchen's dim glow like a haint, her unbound hair flying about, her arms waving, her shrill voice piercing the dull lethargic bubble of satiety and shame. The woman seemed to fly through the dark and swoop upon her, grasping Josephine by the wrists and yanking her to her feet so hard that her arms felt, for a brief, sharp moment, unhinged. Mrs. Kaiser cried out when she saw one decimated turkey leg on the counter and the other in Josephine's hand; she shrieked at the sight of the pot of water boiling on the stove, cracking her good china.

"My mother's dishes from Paris," she screamed, pulling her over to look into the pot at the ruined plates. The turkey leg fell to the floor. "Look what you've done!" And she thrust Josephine's hands into the boiling cauldron.

Pain, pain shooting up her arms like flames,

her hands on fire, a constant searing excruciating pain, her throat raw from all the screams she'd uttered without knowing what she was saying until, coming to her senses, she shrieked, "Jesus, help me," and then lay limp and sweating.

"Help me," she breathed. A bright light cast a shadow on a pale, chipped wall, and a face emerged, there an eyebrow, there another, and a mouth, and a beard flowing over a long white robe. She stared until eyes formed, looking into hers, infinitely kind and full of love, love glowing in that white light down to her. *Father.*

Itching, itching, itching. She slid one bandaged paw over the other, both of them fat and cushioned and as useless as if she had no hands, and a voice floated into her mind. *We had to administer a palliative, something to ease her pain.* Pain? Pain was a dull memory, a vague recollection of misery now passed, her hands were alive with itch. She rubbed one against the other again, grunting with frustration.

"She's awake."

Someone lifted her wrist murmuring, "Don't scratch."

She opened her eyes to see her mama clutching a bandaged hand, her eyes floating in tears.

"Mama," she said. "I saw God."

What? She saw God — where? In a dream?

"He came to me, Mama." She smiled, anticipating the pride on her mother's face. "He said he would pin a golden crown to my head with a star."

Her mother dropped her hand, which she began, again, to rub impotently against the other.

"What kind of fool business is that? You think you're special?" She stood and brushed herself off as if Josephine were a toad that had hopped onto the bed.

"Hmpf. You're the queen, all right — the queen of cracked plates. Who's going to hire you now, knowing you can't even wash dishes?" She lit a cigarette and blew smoke into Josephine's face. "God pin a gold crown to your head — hmpf. That French china was worth more than you'll ever be."

Her revue Joséphine à Bobino shows none of this, of course. She has never minded this omission; it's a fete, not a funeral. Privately, though, every time she sees the child cross the stage with a doll in her arms, Josephine wonders: what really happened in the hospital?

Maybe the pain medicine caused the vision, as the nurse later suggested. Maybe some trick of the lights and shadows created a bearded man's face, as Daddy Arthur speculated. Or maybe her own active imagination — the only way, sometimes, to escape from her misery — conjured the scene. "God's a white man, huh? That explains everything," her grandmama Elvira had said with a cackle. Or did Josephine get the idea from one of her Sunday school books? Did God even have a face?

There had been no mistaking the crown, though, gleaming and golden in one of God's own hands, or the star burning like a ball of fire in the other. Josephine has never doubted these memories, or the message: *I will crown thee and affix the crown with this star.* Said not in a booming voice, as a child might expect, but as a thought that filled her mind like a song.

That was the day when Josephine started to sing, music always in her mind, running like a soundtrack through every moment of her days and nights. " 'You're sent from heaven / And I know your worth / You've made a heaven / For me, right here on Earth,' " she sings now, on the stage, to the innocent girl dancing with her doll. But whoever said these words to her when she was a child? Confused, she turns her gaze into the spotlights shining down, looking for God, her bedazzled eyes filling with dark shapes as the song rolls from her open throat.

Deep within her, still, the note the Lord struck with his promise — the expectation that, someday, she would do something monumental, worthy of a crown — resonates and hums. She wonders: *When will God give me that crown? What must I do to earn it?*

CHAPTER 2

1914

Carl, the runt of Josephine's gang and scrappy like a little Chihuahua dog, came running up one day to announce that Josephine's mama liked white sugar. "That's what my mama says." His sneering tone made her face burn.

"So the hell what?" she said, and, knuckling down, flicked her shooter into Freckles's aggie, knocking it out of the ring. "Everybody loves sugar."

"He's saying your daddy is white," Freckles said, like he was breaking bad news to her.

"My daddy ain't white." Her gaze veered like a bee looking for something to sting: the circle in the dirt, the scattered marbles, the black ant that she now crushed with her thumb, the faint scar running from nail to knuckle the only remnant of last year's burns.

Freckles shrugged. "It don't matter. Carl's stupid."

She lifted her gaze to his. A bit of breeze fingered his soft-looking honey-red hair. Her pulse skipping, she took aim for what should have been an easy shot, but missed. With a fingertip she brushed away the poor little ant she'd killed. What did she do that for?

"Tumpy's the stupid one," Carl said. "She don't even know her daddy is white."

Freckles jumped up. "Don't you talk about her like that."

"You're on her side? You must be stupid, too," Carl said, elbowing Josephine's brother, Richard.

"Don't they teach anything in that white school?" said Richard, who, in spite of having finished the first grade, could barely write his name.

"Who's the stupid one, cracker?" Carl jeered, dancing around behind Freckles, kicking up dust and destroying the game. They were playing in the patch of bare ground in front of the paint-peeling apartment building where Josephine and Richard lived, all of them with nicknames except Carl. Josephine was Tumpy, a name her mama had given her when she was a fat baby, "like the egg that fell off the wall" she said, getting the name wrong but it had stuck, anyway; Richard was Brothercat because he was Josephine's brother; Skinny was from Puerto Rico and as tall as a sixth-grader; Sonny, whose broad, flat nose made him look like he'd been hit by a door, was one of seven brothers, all called "Sonny" by their dad; and Fatty, a white boy, had three chins but could run faster than any of them except Josephine. These were her friends now that she was home again, boys she could chase and holler with instead of sitting around and playing with dolls the way the girls liked to do, and who'd seen the wounds on her hands from that boiling water and thought Josephine was tough.

She scrambled to her feet. "Don't you call my friend stupid!"

"You like Freckles?" Carl grinned, showing the gap between his two front teeth. "Is he your *boyfriend*?"

Now the others chimed in, chanting, "Tumpy and Freckles sitting in a tree, *k-i-s-s-i-n-g.*" She told them to hush, but she was smiling on the inside when she sat down again across from Freckles, who was scooping up the marbles and putting them in his sack.

"I don't need a girl standing up for me," he said, and walked away with his hands

44

over his ears.

Josephine's eyes filled with tears. What had she done wrong? She and her friends fought all the time. "Roughhousing," Mama called it, and had told her not to do such things, saying it "wasn't fitting for a girl," and that she ought to be more careful with the blue middy dress her grandmother had made. But it wasn't like she had anything to change into: that dress was the only clothes she had, and getting too tight and too short to play in. Even so, Mama had said that if she ruined it, there'd be "hell to pay," meaning a beating with the birch switch or the handle of the fly swatter. Didn't Freckles realize how much she'd risked for his sake? Didn't he *care*?

"Aw, look at the poor baby cry," Carl said, pointing his finger at her. Richard pointed, too — her own little brother, whom she'd comforted more times than she could count, like when he helped Carl steal a bicycle and Mama beat him so hard he fainted, then locked him in the shed out back for a whole day and night. "You think that's bad? Keep thieving and see what the police will do to you," Mama had said when he'd crawled out, shivering and sobbing. Josephine had sat him in her lap and fed him cornbread and molasses, and look at him now.

45

Now he pointed his finger at her and jeered with the others, calling *crybaby* and *little girl* and *weakling.* She balled her hands into fists, wanting to knock them all down, but there were too many of them and only one of her. The whistle of the noon train pierced the air like a cry. How could they treat her this way, her own friends? She'd make them sorry.

"I'll show you who's a weakling!" she yelled, and took off running toward the tracks, the shouts of the boys like wind in her ears as she hurled herself through the dusty lots and across the cobbled streets in her bare feet. She ran, leaped, *flew* over shards of glass and broken boards with rusted nails, her legs propelling her into the air, as though the hand of God lifted her up and over all the danger and the pain, over the cutting gravel and the ditch full of stagnant, snake-infested water and the hot metal tracks, but when she arrived at the train yard, giddy and hardly even out of breath, the train had passed and now receded before her, its red caboose so small she could make it disappear with a wave of her hand.

She heard the boys' approaching shouts mingled with her own thumping heart as she stood in the silent yard, dreading their jeers when they found her standing there bewildered and lost. Then she heard a sigh, and the shudder and rumble of a starting engine, and the clank of a furnace door, and she saw that a train of loaded coal cars would be the next to leave. For one wild moment, she thought to lie down on the tracks so it would run her over, but the engineer would see her and call the cops, who would drag her home to be whipped. The humiliation would be worse than death. The boys' shouts grew louder as they neared. She looked around for a place to hide.

She ran over to a coal car, reached over her head to grasp the ladder running down the side, and hoisted herself up. By the time the boys arrived at the yard, she was climbing, up and up, another idea forming as she neared the top. She'd show them.

"What's she doing?" somebody yelled — Freckles! Here was her chance to win back his love.

From the ladder's top rung, she clambered into the bed of sun-warmed coal, which burned her feet. Puffs of gray and black dust arose as she stepped, gingerly now, fearing collapse into a hole that would suck her under the pile.

She picked up a black chunk and, seeing

the boys on the ground below, took aim and threw it at Carl, nearly hitting him on the head. "Look!" she cried, "Coal! As much as we want!"

And she picked up two more pieces and threw them, then two more, sending the coal down as fast as she could while the boys scampered below, picking them up and stuffing them in their pockets and then into a sack someone had found on the ground. She laughed out loud. Who was the baby now? Who was the weakling? She felt like a queen, like the queen of this coal car, of this rail yard, of the whole city. To see their upturned faces and mouths open in admiration, in *awe,* to feel their eyes on her, to mesmerize them — that was strength.

And then the car lurched, and she fell into the bin. As she slipped and slid in an effort to regain her footing, the train began to move. *Click click, click click,* faster and faster. She stood to see the boys staring and shouting something she could not hear over the squeal of the slow-grinding wheels and the hiss of the steam rising in a black cloud from the engine. Richard's mouth was a rictus of fear. Good. Let him worry. Maybe next time, he'd think twice before picking on his own sister.

She threw one leg over the side of the car

so her foot rested on the top rung of the ladder, and rode astraddle the car while the train flowed along in a lazy stream. With her free hand, she grabbed more coal, thinking how happy Mama and Daddy Arthur would be when she came home with it. Their home would be nice and warm this winter, thanks to her.

More and more coal hit the ground as the boys ran alongside to keep up with the train, which was picking up speed. They were waving their arms now, Richard's eyes so wide she could see their whites. She couldn't hear them but she knew what they were saying: *Jump, Tumpy!* She waited just a hair longer, just enough to make Richard cry, she could see him wiping his eyes, thinking she was gone forever, and then she scrambled down, not looking, as Daddy Arthur had warned when they'd descended the Eads Bridge's trestle to fish in the Mississippi. *Never look down and never look back.* He'd laughed like he'd made a clever joke, but Josephine knew it was good advice.

She got to the bottom and, wanting to give them just a little bit more excitement, waited until she saw a patch of soft green grass before finally leaping. When she hit the ground, she rolled around and around until she stopped. She would have liked to lie for a moment to catch her breath, to luxuriate in the shade of the maple tree spreading its limbs overhead and listen to the boys bleating like lambs, but she didn't want them to know she was winded so she popped up like a jumping jack and ran toward the tiny dots that they had become, laughing at them, stronger than they would ever be.

When she reached them, she was out of breath and didn't mind showing it, bending over with her hands on her knees, panting, allowing them to clap her on the back and exclaim over her courage and to call her a devil and an acrobat. Then Richard pushed a bag stuffed with coal at her, and she took it and came face-to-face with Freckles, whose eyes now glinted with admiration.

She looked right back at him, smiling like she'd seen her mama do with Eddie Carson once in Aunt Jo's laundry. "Love of my life," Mama had said to him right in front of Josephine, but later, when Josephine asked if he really was her daddy, she wouldn't respond. Freckles stepped forward, and briefly she thought he might kiss her on the lips the way Eddie had kissed her mother, but instead he knocked his fist against her upper arm.

"That was something else," he said.

She and Richard went home, lugging the bag between them, a canvas strap in each of their hands. As they walked, their neighbors stared. "Where did you all get that coal? Did Santy Claus come early this year?" Josephine grinned, imagining her mother's initial surprise followed by, as she heard the tale, amazement, then, finally, gratitude.

When they got home, though, they found Mama sitting at the table pressing her forehead into her hands.

"Look what we brought." Josephine yanked the sack from Richard and lugged it across the threshold by herself, then dropped it at Mama's feet the way a cat drops a mouse.

"What in God's name have you done to your dress?" Mama jumped up, her eyes wild.

Josephine looked at her dress. Covered now in smears of black from the coal and green stains from her rolling in the grass, it hardly looked blue anymore. Worse, the skirt had a long tear on the left side.

"You've ruined the only piece of clothing you've got," her mother yelled, yanking her by the arm and stinging her bare legs with her hand. "I ought to beat the shit out of you."

"I brought coal!" Josephine danced and

51

jerked to avoid her mother's blows. "Enough to keep us warm for months!"

"You brat! How could you do this to me, today of all days?" She grabbed a handful of Josephine's hair and jerked it hard, making the girl scream in pain. "That good-for-nothing Arthur has gone to jail, and now my sorry-assed kids are stealing coal."

Choking on a sob, Josephine fled from the house, ignoring her mother's commands to *get back here right now,* running as she did before, finding sweet release in the strength of her legs, the leap and soar, the feeling that, if she just jumped *a little* harder, she would go up and up, far from her mama's hateful words, never to come down until she was ready, landing only where she wanted to, which was at Freckles's house. She'd seen respect in his eyes today and needed to see that look again, to be reminded of the great thing she had done, coal-stained dress be damned.

She found him, as she'd hoped, in the yard in front of his house, a neat brownstone in the white part of the Mill Creek neighborhood, playing marbles by himself. "Practicing so I can beat you next time," he said as she sat across from him. She held out her hand for a shooter, but he suggested they go to the rail yard and play back slaps.

Outside the train station, he opened his sack and spilled the marbles between two tracks, clearies and shotsies and aggies and snots, and handed her a shooter to bounce against a rail so it hit the marbles in the center. Josephine wasn't very good at this game, but Freckles was, snickering with glee as he hit marble after marble and put them in his sack, while she got only a few.

He tossed his shooter against the rail. It bounced and hit one of the clearies, a purple one, Josephine's favorite, but she didn't care, how could she begrudge him anything? She would give him all the marbles in the world if she had them, and as she turned to offer him the three in her hand she saw his eyes smiling at her, teasing, and she flung her arms around his bony shoulders and, ducking a little, pressed her lips to his, felt his warm breath on her mouth and nose and his heartbeat jump against her chest before he yelped, "Hey!" and scrambled to his feet to stare at her as if he'd never laid eyes on her before.

"What the hell are you doing?" His voice squeaked, his face and neck now covered in red blotches.

She had gone too far, she realized. How could she be such an idiot?

"I did it for you," she said, slowly standing, too, but not meeting his eyes, unable to bear his disgust.

"Did what?" She looked and saw him lift his hand and wipe away the kiss, spitting for emphasis. He didn't aim for her, but he might as well have spit in her face.

"I jumped on that train for you," she said, pleading now. She stepped toward him, her hands outstretched. "Carl was right: I do like you. I'd be your girlfriend if you wanted me to."

He reached out one of his hands toward her. She started to close her fingers around his, lifting her gaze — as he snatched his marbles from her palm and stuffed them into his sack, then stepped backward again, more rapidly now, like that train picking up speed before she'd jumped off.

"You're not my girlfriend," he said. "And I'm not your boyfriend. Never."

"But why not?" she said. "We like each other, don't we?"

"Don't put your nasty mouth on me. You're a nigger," he shouted, and ran away, faster than she'd ever seen him go, so fast even she couldn't catch him.

"Freckles, come back!" she wailed. "I forgot to tell you something. You were right! My daddy *is* a white man, do you hear? My daddy is white!"

CHAPTER 3

1915

There would be no Christmas presents this year, Mama announced, not with Daddy and Josephine both out of work. The confusion on the children's faces made Josephine cringe. *What about Santa Claus?* they wanted to know, and Mama had snapped that they couldn't count on him, either. "We can't afford cookies to leave under the tree for Santa. Hell, we can't afford a tree."

Josephine saw the truth in an instant: Santa Claus was only a story, and Christmas was up to her.

So she went out and scrounged presents from the rich white people's garbage cans on Westmoreland Avenue and mended them with her grandmama's help: a yellow shirt for her mother; a colorful necktie for Daddy Arthur; a miniature train for Richard; doll babies with new yarn hair and sewn dresses for her sisters. She'd even wrapped up a couple of partially chewed steak bones for the puppies, so playful with their wagging whiplike tails and excited yaps that Mama had banished them to Grandmama's house, saying she had more than she could handle in the hyperactive Josephine.

Where did Josephine come by all that energy? Never sitting still, her nine-year-old self opening and closing kitchen-cupboard doors; kneeling on the floor for a solitary round of jacks; bumping on her rear end down the stairway; running back up two steps at a time to the rooftop; skittering back down to the apartment to bounce on the couch and twirl and reach for the ceiling with her outstretched fingers; grasping the hands of her youngest sister, Willie Mae, to swing her around in a dance; leaping into the kitchen to get some cornbread; running to the back to see if her other little sister, Margaret, had awakened; motoring back into the kitchen to dance in circles and sing "Jingle Bells" to Willie Mae, who laughed so hard when Josephine whinnied and crossed her eyes that crumbs fell out of her mouth and into her lap. Like a housefly zooming and careening. She must have inherited all that get-up-and-go from her daddy, whoever he was, because Mama complained all the time about being dog-tired, even though she often changed clothes after work and went out again with her friends in her red dress and flowered hat.

Daddy Arthur used to get so mad about Mama's gallivanting that he'd wait up for her at night to scream at her, but these days he did little more than snooze and lift the bottle to his lips, groaning as if that one act exerted him to the extent of his capabilities.

Sit down, Mama would snap at Josephine, *you're wearing me out.* Mama hated her constant motion, like a blur, she said, making her seasick, but she sure enjoyed the results: the chicken heads and feet brought home from the butcher, the nickels and dimes she earned doing jobs on Westmoreland Avenue, the sweet peaches and strawberries and fresh eggs begged, scavenged, or stolen from the Soulard Market. But all that wasn't enough, it turned out, to keep Josephine with her family.

She came home from her grandmama's house on Christmas Eve with a bound bedsheet tied around the presents and slung over her shoulder, just like the *real* Santa Claus, and topped the staircase to see Mama swaying outside their apartment, bottle in hand, staring at a piece of paper nailed to the front door.

"I don't have my eyeglasses. Tell me what

this says."

Josephine's reading was poor, but she'd known these words before learning to spell her own name: EVICTION NOTICE.

Mama cursed and punched Josephine's chest with the heel of her hand, nearly sending her tumbling down the stairs. "This is your fault for losing that good job." Mama had tried to talk Mrs. Kaiser into giving Josephine another chance, but the school principal had asked about the bruises and welts on Josephine's body and that was that.

"Running to teacher," her mama mocked. "I've got a mind to beat you myself. You going to tell on me, too?" Josephine stood her ground: her mama would have to catch her first, but she could hardly stand up. Mama lunged and slapped her face — the *pop* like a firing gun, the burn spreading across her cheek and neck, her ringing ears. She snatched at the pain, dropping the sack of presents to the floor, spilling the contents.

"You laughing at me?" her mother said as Josephine knelt to gather the gifts. "You think I'm funny? One smack of this bottle upside your head, you'll be laughing all the way to the grave."

Josephine knew better than to talk back. When her mother got herself into this state there was only one thing to do: get the hell out of her way.

"I've got a mind to send you to a home for juvenile delinquents," Mama slurred.

Josephine quickly tied the sheet around the presents again, laid the sack over her shoulder, and, ducking under her mother's upraised arm, stepped into the apartment.

"Ho, ho, ho!" she boomed, as loudly as she could. "Merry Christmas!"

The following week, Mama took her to the laundry to meet Mrs. Mason, a rich woman who wore silk from head to toe and didn't mind spending her husband's money. She didn't blink an eye when Mama charged her twice as much for Josephine's services as Mrs. Kaiser had paid.

Mama had made Josephine take a bath and put on a jumper and turtleneck shirt and a new wool coat, only a little too large, all dropped off at the laundry last September and never picked up by their owner. Having something new to wear usually cheered Josephine, giving her a special feeling like it was her birthday. Today, though, she gained no pleasure from the mustard-colored shirt of thick, soft cotton or the brown jumper with shiny brass buttons and large front pockets. Her red coat couldn't stop her shivering as she followed her mother, blinking back tears. Willie Mae cried and begged her not to go, but nothing could stop their mama when she'd set her mind on something. She and Josephine were just alike, which, Daddy Arthur said, might be why Mama was so hard on her.

When Mama pushed Josephine forward to shake the woman's hand, the blond, bright-eyed Mrs. Mason seemed like *she* might burst into tears. She looked like Josephine felt when she saw a stray kitten or puppy wandering around lost. "She's so thin," the woman said, not fooled by the layers of clothing, her blue eyes moist as she took in the legs like sticks protruding from beneath Josephine's coat, her bony knees like door-knobs, her spreading feet pushing at the edges of her too-small shoes.

Mrs. Mason reached for Josephine, who clung to her mother's pink uniform before Mama pushed her into the woman's grasp. But Mrs. Mason withdrew her hands and bent to bring herself face-to-face with the trembling Josephine, who didn't want to sleep in the basement with the dog, who didn't want to work from sunup to sun-down, who didn't want to be called "stupid nigger" and "pickaninny," or be forced to kill her friend or have her hands thrust into a pot of boiling water. *They made us slaves,* her grandmama Elvira always said. *That's everything you need to know about white folks.*

"Tumpy, don't you want to come home with me? Mr. Mason and I have always wanted a little girl."

Mrs. Mason's voice reminded her of whipped cream. Josephine lifted her gaze to the woman's face, looking for meanness.

"Of course she wants to go," Mama said, making Josephine want to throw her arms around her mother's legs. "We've talked all about it, and she is excited. She's just shy."

Mama's hands tightened on her shoulders, gripping like she was about to shake her. Mrs. Mason made little clucks of sympathy.

"Poor thing, she loves you so." Her voice was full of doubt.

"This is breaking my heart, too, Tumpy," her mama said. "But you deserve a better life than we can give you here."

Josephine burst into tears. "I don't want to go," she said. "Mama, don't make me go."

"I've got a nice house with a big bedroom, just for you, and lots of toys to play with. And new clothes and lots of good food. We're having spaghetti and meatballs tonight."

Josephine's mouth watered. At home, all

61

they had was a ham bone and cornmeal mush.

"Your favorite," Mama said. "If I were you, I'd go."

"Just for one night," Mrs. Mason said. "Come and try it. I'll bring you home anytime you say."

Josephine looked up at her mama, whose lips were smiling but whose eyes were saying, *You'd better not come back.*

"Please?" the woman said. Josephine wiped her eyes and shrugged. She might as well go where she was wanted. If things got bad, she would return home no matter what her mama said, and work twice as hard so she could stay.

But she did not ask to go back after her first night with the Masons, or the second, or in the weeks that followed. She passed the time doing simple chores for the mistress: keeping the floors swept and the furniture dusted, cleaning the toilet and sink, and washing the dishes after dinner each night before going to sleep in her own bed with linen sheets and goose-down pillows — a far cry from the misery she'd endured at Mrs. Kaiser's house.

The Masons were nothing like that evil woman. They lived in a nicer house, in town, and they treated Josephine like a person, not an animal. Sometimes she pretended that this was her home and these, her real parents: the pretty Mrs. Mason, who smelled of roses, sitting with her at the dining room table to do Josephine's home-work, her lilting voice cooing, "You're so smart"; Mr. Mason, with his balding head and fluffy brown mustache and pipe curling fragrant tobacco smoke as he held her in his lap in his big leather chair, calling her his "good girl." She felt like purring, fat with the evening meal, sated with hamburger steak and whipped potatoes and gravy and all the milk she could drink, sluggish with food, warm and dreamy under the nice man's stroking hands as he told her she was so pretty and soft that he just wanted to pet her all over. This must be what having a daddy was like. This was how it felt to be loved.

"Tumpy helps so much around the house, and she keeps me company on all those evenings when Lyle has to work," she heard the mistress say to a friend over coffee one day. "And it hardly costs us anything. I felt shocked by the low price her mother asked, to tell the truth. We might not have done this if we could have children of our own, but we'll keep her now, even if we adopt. Nannies are so expensive!"

Thinking of living there forever made Josephine a bit sad, until she went into her bedroom filled with toys and opened her closet and saw all the beautiful clothes, a different dress for every day of the week, dresses *she* chose, not the faded castoffs her mama brought home from the church charity box or from Aunt Jo's laundry. The dresses the Masons gave her were *new,* fresh and crisp and clean and pulsing with color. When she modeled them for Mr. Mason, he shielded his eyes, which made her smile. She wanted to razzle and to dazzle — to be *seen.*

For the first time she felt like she was Somebody, allowed by Mrs. Mason to decide when to do her chores, what to have for breakfast, when to do her homework — always with the mistress sitting next to her, and with cookies or cake provided by the round-faced cook, Geraldine, who fed her treats when she got home from school, warm gingerbread with lemon sauce, chocolate pudding, strawberry shortcake, saying her job was to fatten Josephine up. Then Josephine would do her chores until suppertime, and, after washing the dishes, homework — with the rest of the night free to play on her own until bedtime.

Josephine had always hated going to bed,

but at the Masons' house, she didn't mind. She loved to be in her room with its pink bedspread and flowered wallpaper and ruffled curtains and shelves filled with stuffed animals and toys and books, and her big, soft, warm bed, like her mama's lap, or even better, because wrapped in all those blankets and with those squishy pillows like clouds cushioning her dreams, she felt as safe and cozy as a caterpillar in its cocoon.

A couple of months after she arrived, Mrs. Mason mentioned that she'd gone to the laundry that day.

"Did you see my mama?" Hope blossomed like a flower on a wild vine. Had her mother asked about her? Maybe after two months, she missed Josephine and was sorry she'd sent her away.

"I did," Mrs. Mason said. "I saw your brother and sisters, too. They had so many questions about you! I could tell that they miss you a lot.

"I wondered if you might like to go home for a visit," Mrs. Mason said, setting a piece of chocolate cake in front of her. Josephine, suddenly afraid her mistress would snatch it away, crammed the whole piece into her mouth.

Josephine remembered her mother's glare. *You'd better not come back.* "Why?" she said when she'd washed the cake down with a swig of milk. "Have I done something wrong?"

Mrs. Mason laughed. "Of course not. I told your mother they could come to visit any time. Your little sisters jumped around as if it were Christmas morning all over again. So don't be surprised to see them at the door," she said with a wink.

That night, Josephine dreamed that the teddy bear she held tight was her mother, soft and warm and welcoming.

The following Saturday, Josephine was coloring in the living room when someone rang the doorbell. "I wonder who that could be?" Mrs. Mason said, smiling, and, rising from her sewing chair, took Josephine's hand in hers, telling her she had a surprise. Josephine hung back, but when the mistress reached for the door, she slipped under her arm and twisted the knob, and opened the door to her family.

"Mama!" she cried. As Willie Mae and Margaret threw their arms around her, nearly knocking her down, and Richard stared like he'd never seen her before, her grandmama stepped forward to give her a hug. Josephine looked past her, but saw no one else on the porch.

"Well, look at you." Elvira clenched her

corncob pipe between her teeth and looked Josephine up and down. "Fat as a little pig, and all dressed up. Are y'all going to church?" She frowned. "These folks ain't Seventh-Day Adventists, I hope."

Mrs. Mason rushed forth to greet Elvira, who looked so fierce with her scowl and her long hair that Josephine wanted to slam the door in her face in hopes that she would go away. What would her mistress think, knowing that her grandmother was an Indian? But Mrs. Mason declared in a voice breathless and lilting how *happy* she was to meet Mrs. McDonald, and to see Tumpy's brother and sisters again, would they please come in?

The family filed in, Grandmama and Richard and Margaret and Willie Mae, who hung on Josephine as though it had been a year since they'd seen each other. To a little kid like Willie Mae, even a single day lasted forever, unspooling lazy and dreamy as a kite in a slow breeze, but her life was not carefree. In the months before Josephine had left home, Willie Mae had started to irk Daddy Arthur. "She's intelligent," Mama would say. But Daddy Arthur said he didn't see what was so smart about asking questions all the time. *Why do I have to brush my teeth? Why can't I have money for candy when you've got some for hooch? Why can't I go to live with Tumpy?*

"I've missed you so much," Willie Mae said, kissing Josephine's cheek again and again, so close that Josephine hardly noticed, at first, the black patch she wore over her left eye.

"A dog scratched her eye out, your mama told me," Elvira said. "Arthur said it was a splinter. He tried to get it out and popped her eyeball right out of the socket. So he *said*." She grunted.

"A splinter! In her eye! Oh, how terrible." Mrs. Mason stared at Willie Mae. "How on earth did that happen?"

Willie Mae dropped her gaze to the floor.

"Don't try to get her to tell," Grandmama went on. "She won't say a word. I beat her with the fly swatter, and she still wouldn't talk about it."

"Poor thing," Mrs. Mason said. Heat rushed to Josephine's face as she imagined what Mrs. Mason was thinking, for neither she nor Mr. Mason had raised their voices against her, not even when she'd dropped Mrs. Mason's pretty china teapot and it shattered on the floor. Mrs. Mason had given her a broom and a dustpan to sweep up the mess, then showed her how to dry fragile things over the countertop or the table. "Accidents happen, Tumpy," she'd said, "and it's only a teapot. I know you'll be more careful in the future." Josephine still couldn't figure out why the mistress hadn't beaten her.

In her bedroom, where she took her siblings to play while Elvira drank a glass of tea with the mistress, Josephine heard the real story about her sister's eye. Drunk and resentful about having to watch Willie Mae while Mama worked, Daddy Arthur had flown into a rage when she'd cut her thumb on a can and awakened him with her crying. Telling her he'd "give her something to cry about," he'd knocked her upside the head so hard her eyeball had popped out. Then he'd passed out on the couch. Mama came home for lunch later that day and carried Willie Mae to the hospital, running, but it had been too late to save her eye.

"Richard and Margaret don't know," the baby whispered to Josephine. "Mama said not to tell."

Josephine lifted the black patch, saw the empty socket, and promised not to say a word. The last thing she'd want would be for the Masons to learn about the brutality in her home. Poor Willie Mae was just five years old.

When Richard and Margaret started fighting over her teddy bear, Josephine led them down to the basement "to see the best thing of all." She stood on a stool to light the lamps and hopped up onto the wooden stage Mr. Mason had made for her, with a red velvet curtain Mrs. Mason had hung for a backdrop. Then, she reached into one of several boxes on the floor — boxes full of Mr. and Mrs. Mason's old clothes — pulled out a purple hat quivering with black feathers, arranged it on her head, and sang, "By the Light of the Silvery Moon," which Mrs. Mason had taught her. Her sisters and brother sat in the old dining chairs lined up in front of the stage, entranced. Afterward, they clapped and stomped their feet, making Josephine wish she knew another song.

"You ought to try out for the Booker T. Washington Theater," Richard said. Daddy Arthur had taken the kids to a show there before Josephine came to live with the Masons. Josephine had laughed at the clowns, watched the acrobats with wonder, and loved the animals' tricks, but when the ladies in spangled dresses and feathered hats came out to sing, she felt like she was home.

"We went again last week, and it was even better," Margaret said. Josephine panged. Would the Masons ever take her to the Booker T? White folks had theaters, too, but she knew colored people weren't allowed.

That night, she fell into a deep, exhausted sleep, bad dreams gathering in her head like thunderclouds: babies with eyeballs dangling from their sockets and roaring monsters bearing down on her. Startled awake, she sat up, her heart lurching against her chest. Poor Willie Mae! She was Daddy Arthur's "sweet cake," his little "fart blossom," the "prettiest little girl in Saint Louis," with her big, luminous eyes looking up at him like he was some kind of god. And now because of him she had only one eye, and would have to wear a patch for the rest of her life, "like a pirate," Richard had teased, but the horrible violence of Willie Mae's loss was still too frightening for laughter.

Josephine lay back and stared into the dark. She thanked Jesus in her heart for sending her to the Masons' to live, out of harm's way.

And then, moving in the darkness, slowly taking form, a tall shape hovered beside her bed. She lay as still as she could, gripping the covers in both hands in case the apparition tried to snatch her up. Was it a burglar? Was it a ghost? She clutched her teddy bear and closed her eyes, feigning sleep, praying to God to save her as he once had done,

71

waiting for the intruder to realize that it was in the wrong room, that there was nothing there to steal.

But it took nothing, nor seemed interested in stealing, just stood beside her bed, moving its arm, was it scratching? The rustle of cloth turned frantic, and she heard its breaths coming in quick, sharp pants, and she peeked through her slit eyelids, but in the darkness she could see almost nothing, could only hear the movements and the breathing like a train building up steam. And then she heard a long sigh, and a moan, and a shaft of moonlight crossed the intruder's face. Josephine opened her mouth, a name trapped in her throat, unable to utter a sound.

The apparition turned and slipped out of the room, closing the door all the way instead of leaving it cracked open the way Mr. and Mrs. Mason always did. A strange odor — of sweat, mildew, and shame — filled Josephine's nose. She stared into the darkness, every nerve on edge, listening for its return — it was a "he," she'd seen that much — and praying to God that it wouldn't come back.

In the morning, hands trembling from fatigue, Josephine dropped Mrs. Mason's breakfast plate as she cleared it from the table. She watched in horror as it broke on the tile floor. Mr. Mason, reading his newspaper, may have glanced her way as she picked up the pieces and swept up the rest, but she did not look at him. She was afraid to see his face.

He came around to help her. "Are you all right?" he asked. "Is something the matter?"

"I had a nightmare last night," she said.

"What about?"

She said she didn't remember, daring to glance at him. At the sight of his face, she relaxed: surely, those were not the eyes she'd seen last night; his was not the face that had threatened to devour her. "It might have been a ghost," she said.

"A ghost." He cleared his throat. "Can I tell you a secret?" The house was haunted, he said in a low voice. He'd seen a ghost several times but had never told Mrs. Mason because he didn't want to frighten her. He was convinced the ghost was harmless — it had never hurt him, or even tried to. There was no reason to be afraid. Okay? And remember, this was their secret. He knew he could count on her.

After supper that night, Mr. Mason came into the kitchen, where Josephine was drying dishes.

"I'm concerned about you, Tumpy," he said. He stepped closer to her. His eyes narrowed, his face pointed now, like a fox's.

She opened a drawer and threw in a handful of silverware. Why was he looking at her that way? She felt like a small animal trapped in his hungry stare — a memory flashed — something clawed at her gut. "I'm fine," she mumbled, then turned and sped away, him following, saying, "Remember our secret." She made her way blindly to the bathroom, where she stared into the mirror. Big eyes stared back at her, frightened eyes.

Premonition trickled down her spine, slow and cold. That ghost would come back tonight. It would stand by her bed again and moan her name and clutch at itself and maybe it would devour her with its mouth instead of its eyes.

That evening, she could barely concentrate on her homework. When Mrs. Mason had asked the same question three times with no answer from Josephine, she put her hand on the girl's forehead. Was she not feeling well?

Josephine closed her eyes. Her dread of being sent home, to Arthur and his drunken rages, to Mama and her mood swings, to a bed filled with siblings and a house swarming with vermin, made her press her lips together and turn away. One word could break the spell of this fairy-tale life, might dissipate the sparkling mist and cause it to slip away like yesterday's dreams. But when the mistress said good night and suggested she go to bed early — "Let me tuck you in, poor thing, you seem so tired" — Josephine found she could not move.

"Mrs. Mason, is this house haunted?" She held her breath.

A crease appeared, like a tiny scar, between the mistress's eyes. "Why, Tumpy, what a question. Why would you ask such a thing?"

"No reason."

She gave Josephine's arm a squeeze. "You're ill, honey. Why don't you go to bed?"

Mr. Mason poked his head into the dining room. "That's where I'm headed. Want me to tuck you in, Tumpy?"

"No, sir."

"Are you sure? I'm on my way up."

"I have some homework to finish."

He gave the mistress a peck on the cheek. "Coming up, dear?" he asked. She said she wanted to read for a little while. Mr. Mason touched the top of Josephine's head as he passed, saying good night, and went up the stairs. *Doom, doom, doom,* went his heavy shoes.

"Tumpy, you really ought to go to bed. Don't worry about your homework. You can stay home from school tomorrow." Mrs. Mason stood. "Come on, sweetie. I'll take you."

"No!" She yanked her arm out of the mistress's reach.

"Tumpy! What is wrong?" She sat down again. "You can tell me, dear."

Josephine wavered. Would Mrs. Mason think she was crazy? Would she become frightened, as Mr. Mason had warned? Would the Masons send her home if she told what she'd seen?

"A ghost came into my room last night," she finally whispered.

"A ghost!" Mrs. Mason gave a little laugh. "There's no such thing as ghosts, Tumpy. It must have been shadows that you saw. It was a windy night, remember? And a full moon outside."

"It was a ghost. It stood by my bed and stared down at me."

"It did?" Hearing a note of doubt, Josephine told her the details: how the ghost had stared at her and moaned her name and panted like a dog.

"I thought it was Mr. Mason at first, but

then it went out and closed the door, and you and Mr. Mason always leave it cracked open for me."

"You thought it was . . . Mr. Mason? Why?"

"Because it looked like him. Except for the eyes. I have never seen eyes like that."

"It looked like *Mr. Mason?*" She sounded like she needed to swallow. She pressed her hand to her throat and stared at Josephine. "Why didn't you tell me sooner about the ghost?"

"Mr. Mason told me not to. He said you would be scared."

Mrs. Mason closed her eyes.

Please don't let them send me home, Josephine prayed. But also: *I just want to go home.*

When the mistress spoke again, her voice sounded different, more like a man's than a woman's, low and strong.

"Tumpy, thank you for telling me. It helps me a lot, to understand some . . . things. Now, I wonder if you will help me catch this ghost."

Mrs. Mason laid out her plan: she would linger, listening, near Josephine's bedroom door. If the ghost came into her room, she was to scream with all her might, at the top of her lungs, and the mistress would burst into the room and catch it.

"Can you be brave and do this for me?" Mrs. Mason said.

She took Josephine up to the bathroom to brush her teeth, then into her room and helped her change into her pajamas. She tucked her in, gave her a hug, and walked out the door, leaving it cracked open. Josephine lay in the dark and waited for the creak of the door hinge, for the shuffle of shoes on the floor, for the sounds of panting and the fierce glow of mad-hungry eyes. Mrs. Mason had not talked of sending her home — was that good or bad? She felt torn inside, and clawed by yearning for her mother. She folded her arms around herself and waited. . . .

And felt a sudden chill as the covers of her bed rose up and a dark shape slid between the sheets. "Tumpy," it murmured, and slid its hand down her body, fingers slipping under her nightgown and pressing into her thigh. She tried to squirm away, but its other arm clamped across her chest, pressing her into the mattress as its mouth began to suck at her neck. The ghost was devouring her! A shudder ran through her body and rose to her throat in a scream that pierced the night for just a moment before the ghost's hand stifled her mouth.

"Don't be afraid," it whispered. "I'm going to make you feel good."

The bedroom door crashed open, revealing Mrs. Mason standing in the doorway. The ghost leaped from the bed and flew out the door without even touching the mistress, who stood like a wraith, herself, against the backlight, her hair unpinned, her body frozen. Was she dead? Josephine began to cry.

"It will be all right," Mrs. Mason murmured, not dead, scooping Josephine into her arms and cradling her against her breast, holding her close and rocking her on the bed. "It will be all right. There's nothing to be afraid of now." And then she climbed into Josephine's bed next to her and held her tight while they slept, riding together the storm-tossed tides of night.

But what had bound them also tore them apart. The next afternoon, her eyes like dark holes in her face, Mrs. Mason took Josephine home, telling Mama that it wasn't safe for her at the Masons' house anymore.

Mama simpered and flapped her hands as she scurried about their little place, putting a pot of water on to boil for some coffee, offering the mistress a chair. Beside her, Josephine waited for a hug or kiss or even a

79

"Welcome home," but her mother never even looked at her, and Daddy Arthur just lay on the couch, not even bothering to sit up when she and Mrs. Mason walked in. She supposed it was a shock, seeing her like this, two suitcases in hand full of her clothes and two more in Mrs. Mason's grasp containing the costumes and props for her "performances," which the mistress had said she could keep.

"What has she done now?" Mama finally looked at Josephine, but not with the love she'd imagined, not even when the mistress assured her that Josephine had done nothing wrong. She pulled a handful of bills from her purse and thrust them at Mama. When Mrs. Mason had given Josephine a final hug and, her eyes full of tears, gone out the door, Josephine's mother turned to her, her eyes snapping.

"How could you let go of such a wonderful opportunity?"

Josephine told her about the ghost's nocturnal visits and how she and the mistress had captured it. Mrs. Mason had promised her it wouldn't come back, but when she got home from school the mistress was singing a different tune. She and Mr. Mason had talked it over, she said, and she now realized that she could not guarantee

Josephine's safety. "I'm sorry, but I have to take you home."

Josephine had all but danced her way out that door, thinking of her brother and sisters, her beautiful mother with the jasmine perfume, the bed full of kids with nowhere underneath for a ghost to hide. She would never have to sleep alone again — unless Mama sent her away to serve another white family. But she was nearly ten years old now, and tall for her age, and strong from her years of hard work, and she knew that she could make her mother glad to have her back. All she needed was money.

Now, under the glaring light of Mama's disapproval, she struggled to redeem herself.

"It looked like Mr. Mason, which scared me even more, but it wasn't him, I know. Because Mr. Mason never closes the bedroom door, but the ghost did."

From the sofa, Daddy Arthur snorted and sat up to laugh at her.

"A ghost?" he said, fumbling for his bottle on the floor, twisting off the lid, and taking a big swig. "A ghost? Girl, you are a damned fool. You ain't seen no ghost."

"Mrs. Mason saw it, too. She saw it in bed with me, and how it flew away when she got there."

"Ghost, my ass," Daddy Arthur said.

"What's a ghost doing opening and closing doors, when it could pass right through? Why's a ghost hiding under the bed when it can make itself invisible?"

Her face felt hot, to be laughed at. "What was it, then?"

"Mr. Mason, wanting some of what you've got." Mama crossed her arms. "And you too stupid to see it, and here we are again. With nothing."

■ ■ ■ ■

Act II
Il Était Une Fois
(Once Upon a
Time)

■ ■ ■ ■

"Josephine at twelve," as the program says, skips onto the stage, licking an ice cream cone and twirling around, smiling and carefree, looking nothing like the frizzy-haired, wild-hearted girl she used to be.

As a girl of twelve, Josephine worked for money every minute she could, not only cleaning houses for white women in the wealthy neighborhoods but also, more often, playing with the Jones Family Band on Market Street, blowing with all her might into a slide trombone while Dyer Jones and her trumpet made the crowds fall down in bliss like the walls of Jericho. At twelve, Josephine skipped school most days to spend her time at the Booker T, where she helped the female impersonators put on their makeup and clothes, played with the dogs and cats in the animal acts, learned from the clowns how to make funny faces, and watched Ma Rainey, Bessie Smith, Ida Cox, Ethel Waters, and so many other women with voices like heartache sing and wail and moan and shout audiences to their feet and to their knees.

Thirteen, though, was when life really started happening. Thirteen was the ticket to everything.

CHAPTER 4

1919

"You must be a rich girl, turning down free ice cream," Mr. Dad would say, looking none too happy. Girls would giggle as they sat on Mr. Dad's knee in exchange for a scoop of chocolate, vanilla, strawberry, or the exotic, weirdly green pistachio, Josephine's favorite. Even though she never had much money, Josephine always paid for her ice cream, ghostly memories keeping her far from Mr. Dad's hands.

Nothing was free. She knew that now. Not the pretty clothes Mr. Mason's money had bought her, not the toys, and certainly not the affection she'd accepted like a starveling, as if love were a gift instead of something she had to earn.

When Daddy Arthur took her and her sisters out for ice cream, he bantered with Mr. Dad and plopped Willie Mae onto the man's lap. When she tried to squirm free,

Mr. Dad's fingers clamped down on her skinny leg, holding her in place while he asked her what flavor she wanted. Showing his crooked teeth like the big, bad wolf, he sent Josephine behind the counter to scoop some strawberry ice cream into a dish and bring it over.

"I want some," he said, flaring his big nostrils — like holes poked by a child's fingers in his puffy face — when Willie Mae started licking her treat. "Give me some of that sweet stuff." Josephine could almost hear Elvira's snort. *It ain't ice cream he wants.*

After Willie Mae, Margaret sat in his lap for chocolate, and then he turned his eyes to Josephine. She resisted the urge to hide behind Arthur's broad back.

"Go on, Tumpy," Daddy Arthur said, nudging her forward. "You love ice cream."

"She sure does," Mr. Dad said. "I have never seen a child who liked it so well. Comes in three times a week and always for pistachio. Nobody else will eat it, but she laps it up like a pussy cat." Looking at his bulging belly and creased neck, Josephine could have told him he ought to lay off the stuff, but she knew better than to sass-mouth an adult. He eased Margaret off his leg and patted his knee, his gaze telling her he knew she would refuse, the same as she had always done.

"Stubborn child," he said when she stood motionless, her arms folded across her budding chest. "I reckon she loves her pride more than she loves free ice cream."

"I brought money for mine," she said, digging into her pocket for her last nickel. Margaret, meanwhile, had already gobbled her scoop and stood waiting by the door.

"That girl has always got money," Mr. Dad said to Arthur as he stood. "Where does she come by all that loot?"

"I work for it," she said, staring him down. The two years she'd spent performing with the Jones Family Band had shown her how to earn it — by giving people something to love you for. Their audiences swooned at Mrs. Jones's feet as she'd played that trumpet, making them feel so good with her music that they'd showered her with coins, cheered and hollered and gazed at her with adoring eyes. Someday, folks would do the same for Josephine — but first, she had to get good at something.

She had become a passable trombonist, but her heart wasn't in it. She wanted to sing, but Mrs. Jones wouldn't let her, saying they wanted to attract people, not send them away. Only when she danced did folks toss coins at her, and even then it was almost all pennies. But her mama didn't like her performing with the Jones Family Band, saying it wasn't "respectable."

"You work for it? Is that so?" Mr. Dad looked at Daddy Arthur, who said it was. "I tell you what, then. I could use somebody in my shop who can do a job, and who won't eat up all my merchandise. Why don't you come to work for me?"

And so here she was scooping ice cream until her hands turned numb with cold and her arms and back got sore. *Your dream job,* Arthur had said, slapping her on the back as they'd left the store. Did he really believe that? And Mama, so proud: *A real job, and you got it all by yourself!* As if she'd done something extraordinary by getting hired when really Mr. Dad was just looking for a way to get his nasty hands on her.

Pinching her earlobe, tweaking her nose, touching her waist as he squeezed through the narrow space behind the counter. Coming up behind her as she washed glasses and sliding his fingers down her arms. Tickling her ribs. And always, always, every time she walked past him, trying to pull her onto his lap. She pretended not to notice, because now she needed the job.

The Joneses had gone on the circuit, performing on the "Strawberry Road," so called because they picked up shows the way people picked strawberries: one here, one there. She'd accompanied them the previous summer, when she was twelve, traveling in Mr. Jones's horse-drawn cart from town to flea-bitten town, "gigging to the gig," he'd said. Mr. Jones's horse and cart were a sweet chariot coming to carry Josephine home, which was wherever the music played. Josephine practicing on her horn while they rattled along in the wagon; Doll bowing and plucking at her fiddle in the camps, sparking impromptu jams of "Shortenin' Bread" or "Old Joe Clark," people dancing in the sultry starlight. It was the most wonderful summer she'd ever known, music and dance and laughter every day and night until she'd fall into a ghost-less dream of sleep, lullabied by the music that pulsed in her body until morning came, and it was time to get up and do it again.

That was a dream job, not standing until her feet hurt behind a counter in a cramped, cold space and pushing a metal scoop against rock-hard ice cream until her arms ached. Making things worse was the cloth-ing she had to wear, a shapeless uniform shirt that she'd had to buy out of her first week's pay and that she removed as soon as she left the shop.

"Have a cone on me," Mr. Dad said, flashing his wolfish teeth, patting his knee. Josephine pretended not to hear him as she walked out the door, peeling off the ugly uniform to reveal her dress, drop-waisted in the new style, of navy blue with red and yellow flowers and a white collar accented with a big red bow — her Easter dress bought new with her own money, giving her such pleasure that it almost made up for Mr. Dad's dog breath and pawing hands. He couldn't touch her anymore today, and tomorrow she didn't work, and now the evening beckoned, offering music and dancing and flirtations as she and her friend Helen sipped their Coca-Colas and giggled at the Concordia Club Dance Hall.

But it was still daylight, too early for the Concordia, so they strolled down to Market Street. At Union Station, a crowd of folks cheered and waved flags in welcome to the men in military uniforms stepping off the train, home from the war at last.

"Look at that one." Helen pointed out a tall, broad-shouldered man with light skin and eyes like a cat's, green and slanted. He moved like a cat, too, slithering and sleek, shoulders leading his tapering waist and legs like every step was a dance move. Josephine had never seen anyone so good-looking and he had never seen a girl like her, either, judging from the way he was looking at her now.

"Let's go," she said to Helen, pulling on her arm.

"But he's coming toward us —"

"Now!" She broke into a run, and Helen followed, down Market Street, all the way past the Rosebud Café. Josephine knew how to run from trouble: Mr. Scott, her school's truant officer, hadn't caught her yet. Helen, panting, begged her to stop, but she kept going, knowing the man was still watching, that her red hair bow and Helen's white dress flashed like beacons among the green fatigues of the military men making their way to the red-lighted brothels and stride pianos, the dancing girls and festive riverboats with floating dance floors, where well-heeled customers fox-trotted and one-stepped and tried to do the Breakaway, rolling and jazzing down the Mississippi River. When the men reached the docks and the ticket sellers turned them away, they'd recall that it was Thursday, and that Colored Night on the riverboats was Monday. But there was plenty of fun to be had on Market Street any night of the week.

The stranger had surely lost them now in the crowd of soldiers, ladies of the night stepping forth from doorways, and musicians carrying their instruments on the way to play somewhere or already playing outdoors, banjos and trumpets and fiddles and guitars and washboards and spoons and coffee cans and harmonicas and blocks of wood and rattles and trombones and saxophones and even a piano that somebody had rolled out onto the sidewalk, making it feel like a party.

The stranger's face flashed in her mind: trouble. But he'd forgotten her by now, lost in the perfumed cloud that would have converged around him as soon as he'd arrived on the scene. A looker like that wouldn't be alone for a minute. She thought of those green eyes and a thrill ran up her spine. When she and Helen stopped to watch a fire juggler she scanned the crowd, and, not seeing him anywhere, felt her spirits drop. But no matter. It was time to head to the Concordia, where there'd be plenty of boys.

The hall was already jam-packed when they arrived and the dance band was in full swing, horns calling out their invitation to shimmy and jump. On the floor men lifted their partners into the air and swooped them between their legs; women snapped their fingers and did the splits and shook their breasts and wiggled their hips to the beat. Josephine and Helen watched from the balcony, then moved down for a closer look.

"That trumpet player is on the make," said Helen, trying to act sophisticated in her childish dress with eyelet trim.

Josephine had her eyes on the dancers, watching their feet, memorizing the steps, imagining how she would do the dance, what she would add: a twist here, a kick there, noting how a woman in a bright blue dress let herself be lifted and flipped over her partner's head before sliding down his back, how she kept herself completely relaxed all the way to the floor before springing up and spinning around to catch his outstretched hand.

The music rose and soared and shouted and hovered on the edge of exultation, throwing off facets of sound the way she'd seen water shoot sparks of light at night from the riverboat wheels. Was there anything more perfect? Josephine felt a quickening under her skin, and the current in her blood made her body quiver and jerk, her fingers snap, her feet shuffle.

"Let's dance." The voice in her ear, intimate and low, spun her around, and when she saw him she laughed: the tall, honey-skinned, green-eyed man she'd seen at Union Station, standing so close she could feel him touching her even though he wasn't, his fingertips poised at her elbow to escort her onto the floor, his eyes gazing into hers. He steered her through the tangle and began a jitterbug, asking if she knew the steps, and of course she did, but soon ceased to follow them as her feet found other, more interesting ones, kicking and flying and tapping and spinning.

When she saw him looking at her with that green intensity she crossed her eyes, playing, and enjoyed his baritone laugh. "Hot stuff," he said. And when the music slowed she let him pull her close, her head barely reaching the center of his chest, his hand on the small of her back exerting a small and pleasurable pressure.

"You found me," she said. He smiled, and she noticed a missing molar in his upper jaw.

"I never lost you," he said. "Willie Wells knows a good thing when he sees it. I laid eyes on you at the train station and been watching you ever since."

A shiver ran up Josephine's spine, and she pressed herself to him more closely. His arm tightened around her waist, and they stood nearly still, clinging to each other, until the music stopped.

A hand grabbed her right shoulder and yanked her out of his embrace, and there stood Mama in her red dress, pointing a wagging finger at her.

"What in the hell are you doing here? These dances are no place for a thirteen-year-old." Josephine glanced over at Willie Wells, but he had disappeared, thank goodness. Her mother went on, saying she ought to beat Josephine's ass right there and then. Josephine met her eyes, daring. She was as tall as her mother now. She could knock her right off those high heels, could rip that bursting-at-the-seams dress right off. She'd do it, too, if Mama dared to touch her in front of all these people.

"And who were you mashing up against?" Behind her, Helen stared at the scene, slack-jawed. Helen's mother would never confront her in a public place like this — but Mrs. Morris wouldn't be at the dance hall, anyway, not without her husband. Others were watching, too, now that the band had taken a break. Josephine wished the floor would crack open and swallow her mama whole, or Josephine herself.

"A grown man, and a soldier! And you

acting like a common tramp."

Oh, dear Lord, please make her shut up! Josephine rolled her eyes so everyone could see that Mama was crazy, her words not to be believed. She put a hand on her own hip, mimicking her mother.

"Like mother, like daughter," she said.

She should have expected the slap, would have known it was coming if she'd taken a minute to think before speaking. Instead, she cried out in surprise and pain, eliciting gasps from the crowd. She lifted her hands to catch the blood from her lip split by her Mama's ring, wary of spoiling her new dress as she walked through the room, her head high, looking straight ahead as she headed for the exit, avoiding all eyes in general and those of one man in particular, and so not noticing how he craned his neck and whistled at her ass as she stomped out the door.

Her mama followed her home from the Concordia Club and promptly kicked her out of the house, telling her to not even think about coming back.

"I'll turn you in to that truant officer. He'll send your ass to reform school so fast it will make your head spin."

Josephine rolled her clothes into a ball and wrapped them in her scarf, then walked, sobbing, for what seemed like hours before ending up at the ice cream parlor. She thought to curl up inside the doorway, out of the wind, until Mr. Dad came down in the morning to open up the shop. But as soon as she'd settled down, huddled under her thin coat, a light in the store came on.

She tapped on the window. He opened the door, his eyes gleaming. He took her by the hand and pulled her inside. "We need to warm you up," he said, and led her up the stairs to his apartment, where he pushed her onto the bed and put his hands all over her, tearing off her clothes and breathing like he was running a race.

In the morning, he stayed in bed while she scurried into the bathroom to wash her sore privates, and watched as she pulled on her clothes.

"Come on back to bed," he said. "I've got something for you."

"I'm late for school."

"Aren't you the conscientious student?" he said.

She didn't bother to answer. He knew she hated school, hated being the oldest kid in her class after being held back a grade for missing so many days, hated being talked to like she was stupid when really she didn't care, not even about history, she would

97

never be one of those fair-skinned queens with blond hair and fancy dresses like in the books. No books showed dark-skinned queens and kings, even though Mrs. Wilson had told them Cleopatra was a Negro. Her teacher was the only good thing about school, telling stories that the books didn't contain, reading aloud newspaper articles about America's sending its colored soldiers to fight with the French in the Great War so white American soldiers wouldn't have to mix with them. The teacher shared letters and articles she'd clipped from the *St. Louis Argus. Here, what matters is not what color you are, but the kind of man you are,* one letter had read, the author writing of whites and coloreds fighting together in France, sleeping side by side, eating together at the same table, sitting together in the theaters and nightclubs of Paris, using the same bathrooms. Josephine had listened, entranced: *We are equals here.*

Why couldn't they be equal in the United States? Two years ago, in East Saint Louis, Josephine had seen white people shooting Negroes for getting factory jobs they wanted for themselves. In Chicago, Arkansas, and Washington, DC, the newspapers spoke of the "Red Summer," smeared with Negro blood. "Oh, Lord, why didn't you make us all one color?" Daddy Arthur had moaned while the stench of burning buildings and flesh rolled over the Mississippi, while hundreds ran across the Eads Bridge into Saint Louis, escaping death. Hearing about France, though, Josephine thought Daddy Arthur wrong to blame God. The problem wasn't the darkness of Negro skin, but the blackness of the human heart — or, at least, of the white American heart.

But her current events class happened only once a week, when a new issue of the *Argus* came out. The rest of the time, school meant reading, writing, and arithmetic, Josephine's least favorite subjects. She got restless, her mind wandered out the window and down the street to the Booker T, where she wanted to be, where she was in demand: *Tumpy, I need you!* they called, and *Where's my Tumpy?* Ma Rainey called her "Miss Do-It-All"; Eddie Green said she was the only girl in the world funnier than he was; Bessie Smith paid a dollar for Josephine's massages. She fit in at the Booker T; she belonged.

Without a word to Mr. Dad, she went down the stairs and out the door. She wasn't going to school; she hadn't been in two weeks. She was headed to the boarding house room of Miss Clara Smith, the star of the current Booker T revue, for whom she had worked as personal dresser the past six weeks. Josephine's duties entailed putting Miss Clara's costumes in the right order and helping her get ready for each new scene. She knew which pieces of clothing went on first, and which next, and how to adjust the feather in Miss Clara's hair, and which jewelry went with what. When a button came off, Josephine sewed it on. When an earring went missing, she crawled like a bloodhound on the dressing room floor, backstage, and all over the stage until she found it. She'd tried to get into the Booker T when Mama had kicked her out last night, once she'd stopped sobbing and could finally think, but the last show was over and the lights were out, the theater looking as dark and cold as she'd felt inside.

She pushed open the door to Miss Clara's room and saw her lying dead to the world and snoring, her purple hair staining the pillowcase, orange-lipsticked mouth opening and closing like a fish's, yellow teeth clacking and grinding. Josephine's sleep-deprived body ached to join her, so she slid under the covers. Miss Clara opened her arms to Josephine, who fell asleep instantly in her idol's embrace and dreamed of following her around the world. With no home to chain her down and no mama to tell her what to do, she could go anywhere she pleased.

The thought cheered her until, after the show that night, everybody went out where she couldn't go, and she had to find somewhere to sleep. As she trudged up the stairs to the apartment over the ice cream shop, her stomach clenched like a fist.

She had no home now except Mr. Dad's.

Two weeks had passed with Mr. Dad when Josephine heard a banging on the door and her mother's voice calling her name. At last! Josephine flung the door open, ready to rush into her mother's forgiving arms, but Mama's face stopped her like a slamming door.

"I want you to come home. Now."

Josephine grabbed her clothes from a drawer in Mr. Dad's plus the wad of bills he kept in his underwear drawer, and followed her mother out. The cold snap that had taken everyone by surprise had covered the trees, grass, buildings, and streets with an eerie hoarfrost. Josephine stepped carefully to avoid slipping on the wooden sidewalks, but her mother grabbed her hand and yanked her hard, making her stumble.

"I don't have all day," she snapped, pulling her coat more tightly around her body with her free hand. "The whole neighborhood is talking about you. Thirteen years old and living with a man older than I am. A disgrace to our family." Mama clamped her wrist as though Josephine needed to be dragged away from the disgusting Mr. Dad. If not for Mama's grip, Josephine would run ahead of her, all the way home.

As they entered Mill Creek, people Josephine knew came out on their steps, some calling "hey," but most just staring as if she'd grown another head.

"You have ruined me," Mama said between her chattering teeth. "I was glad to see you go — glad, you hear? You're as wild as an animal. I can't handle you anymore, and Arthur won't, he says you're not his young 'un and that you come by your wickedness honestly." Josephine would end up pregnant, just like her mother, he'd said, making another mouth to feed in a household already stretched to its limits. But Mama and Aunt Jo and Grandmama Elvira had worked out a solution, and Josephine would do what they said or Mama would kill her, so help her God.

They found Aunt Jo and Elvira drinking Coca-Cola at the kitchen table and sharing a laugh that ended when she and her mama walked in.

"Y'all acting like somebody died," Josephine said, pressing her cheek into Aunt Jo's plump skin and smelling her scents of laundry soap and butterscotch candy, and imbibing the cool papery roughness of her grandmother's age-puckered cheek and the fragrances of tobacco and sage. Aunt Jo pulled a bottle out of her bag and handed it to Josephine, who joined them at the old wooden table.

"Why did you go to stay with that man, Tumpy?" Aunt Jo asked. "Why didn't you come to my house, instead?"

Josephine didn't know what to say. Why hadn't she gone to Aunt Jo's, or to the Morrises' house, or anywhere else but Mr. Dad's? She'd left the Booker T and wandered around, then ended up at the ice cream parlor. She'd wanted to sleep in the doorway, was all. But once she was there, she felt she had to stay, having given herself to him like the "trollop" her mama had said she was.

Now her mama was speaking Willie Wells's name, asking about him. These last two weeks, Willie had continued to meet her at the Concordia Club and buy her soft drinks and dance with her until the band stopped playing, then walked her almost, but not quite, to her mama's house, where he thought Josephine still lived. His arms were strong, but how gently he held her while they danced, scooping her up and over his head as if she were a cloud. His gaze licked a slow flame over her belly. He called her Tumptation and Tumptress and kissed her until she gasped for air.

After living with Mr. Dad, Josephine was probably "with child," Mama said, which was the last thing they needed, that man had young 'uns running all over this neighborhood and never lifted a finger or gave a dime for their care.

"That there is why they call him 'Mr. Dad,' " Elvira said. Josephine sat back in her chair and took a swig of Coca-Cola, sealing off the bitterness with sugar and fizz. She hadn't wanted to work for him, but Mama and Daddy Arthur had pushed her. And now Mama was fixing to force Josephine into something else.

"Tumpy, that Dad fellow has made a woman of you," Aunt Jo declared.

"Now every man in Mill Creek will be sniffing around, trying to get a piece for himself," Elvira said.

"You are on the wrong path, child," Aunt Jo said. "We've got to find you a husband."

Josephine would have laughed, but they weren't even smiling. A husband? She was in the sixth grade.

"I'm not getting married," she said. "I'm going be a singer like Miss Clara Smith."

"You're going to be a mama with a bunch of snot-nosed kids to take care of and no man to help you," Mama said.

"It takes one to know one," Josephine said before getting smacked in the mouth again, which was what had started this whole mess. As she pressed her fingers to her stinging lips, her mama laid out a plan. Josephine would go to the Concordia Club with Willie Wells tonight, as usual, but this time she'd let him take her back to his room. In a few weeks, she'd tell him she was pregnant. If he was a good man, he'd marry her. If not, Daddy Arthur would show him the barrel of his gun, and he'd marry her then.

Josephine felt like running away from this scheme, but to where? It wouldn't be right to lie to Willie, she said, but Mama laughed and said this was no time to start having a conscience. She wasn't pregnant, she insisted, but even her grandmama shook her head and told her it didn't matter, that if she wasn't carrying a baby now, she would be soon; that, having had a taste, she'd want more, and eventually some man would knock her up.

"The taste of Mr. Dad makes me want to puke," Josephine spat.

"If you hated it so much, then why didn't you come home?" Mama said. Josephine stared at her mother, speechless.

"I hear he's got a big one," Elvira said, grinning.

Josephine decided to try tears. She begged her mother not to make her do this and promised to be good if she could stay here. She would never let a man touch her again; she'd go to school every day; she'd find another job that paid more than the ice cream shop; she'd keep the house clean and help Grandmama cook supper at night and be the best daughter any mother could ever want.

"You won't be doing any of that," her mother said. "The truant officer came here today looking for you, saying you've missed school for a month. You'd better get married, or they'll put your ass in reform school. They're getting all set to do it, he said. Only one thing can save you now, and that's a husband."

CHAPTER 5

1920

You could have knocked her over with a feather boa when Miss Clara Smith came bopping into The Old Chauffeur's Club, puffing on her pipe and flopping into a chair and kicking off her shoes.

"What a night," she said, and looked up at Josephine with that familiar smile: all gums, small teeth. Josephine felt like she'd just stepped out of a dark hole into the sun. "And it's not over yet, is it, Tump?"

The table was littered with half-empty glasses sticky with sweet tea and the remnants of bathtub gin surreptitiously poured from sneaked-in flasks, but Miss Clara was settled, her feet up on the chair beside her. She introduced the man by her side: Mr. Phillips, her new piano player, who barely glanced at Josephine but hung on Miss Clara's every word like a pup eager for its master's next command. Her former piano player, Mr. Washington, had married a Philadelphia chorus dancer and quit touring to suit his new wife.

"Seems like whenever folks get married, they give themselves up," Miss Clara said.

Josephine wondered what Miss Clara had heard about her marriage to Willie Wells. She'd given herself up, all right, after the wedding that Daddy Arthur had forced. She'd tried to learn to fry chicken the way Willie's mama made it, spent her days washing and mending his clothes and knitting hats and booties for the baby she'd told him was coming, stayed home with him most evenings since he was too tired to go out, and succumbed to his nightly demands for sex even when *she* was too tired, knowing she'd better get pregnant before he learned the truth. Sorry for her deception, she tried to atone by loving him, getting up early every morning to fix his breakfast and pack his lunch, waiting on him hand and foot when he got home, giving him massages, kisses, and hugs, giving everything he asked for in the bedroom, too, no matter how unpleasant.

Then, not quite two months after the wedding, when they'd run out of money and had to move in with her family, he'd come home hollering about Mr. Dad. "I thought

I was your first, but he says he was fucking you the whole time we went around together. That probably ain't even my baby you're carrying." He looked like he might cry, and Josephine, who had begun to feel some tenderness for him, told him the child was his. He called her *liar* and *whore,* and punched her in the gut, right where the kernel of a baby had sprouted unbeknownst to her. She doubled over, catching her breath, and came back up with a Coca-Cola bottle in her hand, which she smashed into his face, gashing his forehead.

He went running down the stairs, a hand pressed to the bleeding wound, pushing aside Elvira, who'd heard the shouting and started up to see what was going on. Out the front door he went, slamming it behind him, never to be heard from again, which was just fine with Josephine. If he'd stayed, she'd have ended up killing him. People said she and her mama were just alike, but Josephine differed in one respect, at least: she would be no man's punching bag.

"The Good Book says, *A man will leave his father and mother and be united to his wife, and they shall be as one flesh,*" Mr. Phillips said, looking for all the world like he wanted to be one flesh with Miss Clara's bosom.

Miss Clara rolled her eyes and grinned at Josephine. "What time do you get off work, honey?" she said.

Soon she was spending her nights in Miss Clara's room in the Pine Street Hotel, not feeling November's bite in the warmth of the soft flesh enveloping her, and days in Miss Clara's dressing room setting out her gowns, which were even more beautiful now that she had become "The Queen of the Moaners," the star of Mr. Bob Russell's traveling troupe The Dixie Steppers. Exempt by her marriage from having to go to school, Josephine fell to her knees and thanked the Lord when Mr. Russell gave her a job as errand girl. The money wasn't as good as she had made at The Old Chauffeur's Club, but what she lost in wages she more than made up for in happiness.

When rehearsals began each day, she'd move to the auditorium and watch the dancers; laugh at Booth Marshall clunking around in his dresses and sagging "breasts" and enormous rear end; and admire Miss Clara in her bright red wig shouting bawdy songs and, yes, moaning, not sadly, but the way she did at night with Josephine.

One afternoon, performing with the Jones Family Band outside the theater, Josephine laid down her trombone and began to dance, as much to warm herself as for any other reason. To her surprise, the crowd of folks waiting to buy their tickets to the next performance clapped and cheered and dropped coins at her feet. As applause and Dyer Jones's trumpeting swirled around her, Mr. Russell emerged from a car at the curb and watched with his arms folded across his chest. When they had finished, he tossed a five-dollar bill into her trombone case, tipped his hat at her, and went inside.

When Josephine went to work that night, she found Miss Clara fully dressed — who had helped her? Josephine wondered jealously — and looking like she might bust open with excitement. One of the revue's musical acts had broken up the night before, and its members scattered. Mr. Russell wanted to hire the Jones Family Band to perform in its place.

"This means you'll be coming with us on the road," Miss Clara said. "I'm so happy, my love." Josephine hardly noticed her kiss. She was going to be one of The Dixie Steppers!

When the Joneses came to audition, Josephine led them into the auditorium and up onto the stage. Mr. Russell sat in the third row as they played "Won't You Come

Home, Bill Bailey?" Josephine hamming it up on her slide trombone, and Dyer Jones blowing that trumpet with all her might. The next thing they knew, Mr. Russell had leaped to his feet and was snapping his fingers and jiving to the beat. Josephine wiggled her knees and crossed her eyes and puffed out her cheeks, and hoped he was laughing the way the people did when she clowned on the streets. They finished with a big fanfare, the horns screaming, and were greeted by applause and whistles from the other troupe members watching in the wings.

"That Tumpy is a born comic," she heard Booth Marshall say, and turned to cross her eyes at him, too.

"Fantastic," Mr. Russell said as he ascended the stage. "Perfect." He shook Mr. Jones's hand. "Just what we need. Can you start right away?"

Josephine squealed and clapped her hands, but he frowned at her. "Sorry, Tumpy, but this offer is only for the Joneses. I've already got a trombone player. A good one," he added to Mr. Jones.

In the dressing room, Clara had to clamp her arms around Josephine to stop her from tearing everything apart.

"He doesn't hate you," Clara said, strok-

112

ing her trembling back. "He's a business-man."

"Well, I hate him."

Clara released her. "What kind of fool talk is that?" Mr. Russell had treated Josephine well, she pointed out. "But it doesn't matter, because you aren't cut out for show business." This dried Josephine's tears, that and her beloved Miss Clara turning her back. She reached out, but Clara shrugged her off.

"If you can't handle disappointment, you'll never make it as a performer." Miss Clara had been rejected more times than she could count, she said. At every audition, she'd heard a different criticism: her voice was too soft or too loud, too girlish or too masculine; her skin was too dark; she wasn't pretty enough; she was too young; she was too old. "But did I give up? No, ma'am. I kept on trying, and now I'm the star of this show, and I'm going to be a bigger star, too — because I don't cry and whine when things don't go my way." She picked up her pipe and began loading it with tobacco.

"What should I do?"

Clara struck a match and lit the pipe, sending a question mark of sweet smoke curling. "Me, I make the situation work to my advantage."

Josephine was flapping her wings and telling herself to stay calm and keep her head high, as Mr. Bennett, the stage manager, had advised: "Acrobats and angels never look down; you see that stage far below and think about falling and you're likely to get dizzy." Just as Daddy Arthur had said.

But it wasn't the height that she feared. She'd climbed too many coal cars to be afraid of falling. If she hit the floor she'd bounce right back up again, buoyant with joy over making her stage debut, playing Cupid in a pink leotard and glittering wings in The Dixie Steppers' production *Twenty Minutes in Hell*.

After Josephine's rampage over Mr. Russell's rebuff, Miss Clara had gone to him and demanded that Josephine get a part in the show. When he resisted, she threatened to quit, so he'd given Josephine a trial run in the role of Cupid and a spot in the chorus. His furry white eyebrows shot up when she'd run onto the stage and danced as though she'd been born in that chorus line. Did he think she didn't know the steps after all the times she'd watched rehearsals with him?

Some others might have been scared to

fly around on that flimsy wire, but Josephine knew the harness she wore was safe, held by a pulley now moving her in circles over the actors' heads. She pulled the strings in her hands, flapping the wings on her back as the horns blew and Clara sang "Someone Else May Be There While I'm Gone." She dropped to the floor to fire an imaginary arrow at two lovers on the bench just as a man walking by caught the stricken actress's eye. Her jealous lover chased the passerby away and went after Cupid, too. The wire lifted Josephine just in time, out of his reach — then set her down, then lifted her up, just beyond his fingertips again.

They'd rehearsed the skit many times but never with an audience, "a full house tonight," Mr. Bennett had whispered, winking, strapping the harness across her chest before she'd risen up, up, up to the rafters to perch, waiting for her cue and trying not to look at the crowd, knowing all those faces would terrify her.

She'd gotten the Cupid role because nobody else wanted it. Only a few among the cast had been small or light enough to fly, and none had wanted to try. Josephine had seen the gleam in Bob Russell's eyes when he'd offered her the part; he'd expected her to turn it down, too, and then he could tell Clara that he'd done all he could — but he didn't know Josephine. He'd never seen her shimmy like a lizard up the side of a train car and stand on the top throwing coal to the ground. He didn't know that, except for ghosts, there was nothing she feared. But he was about to find out.

On her final descent, the rigger set her down too close to the backdrop curtain. When the wire tugged at her harness, she flapped her wings as she had rehearsed, ready to fly all the way back up to the rafters and out of sight. This time, though, things didn't happen the way they were supposed to. Her wings caught on the curtain, and she tipped backward, off-balance. The rope twisted and she spun, her kicking legs pulling her too far forward. The auditorium swam before her eyes, a sea of upturned faces.

A gasp shuddered through the room, followed by the one sound in theater that no one wanted to hear: silence. The music had stopped playing. Clara no longer sang. The creak of the rafters, the squeak of the wire on the pulley wheel, the scream tearing at Josephine's throat which she choked back — these were the sounds of her career gasping to an end with her very first performance. She spun around and saw Mr. Russell in the wings, scowling, and without even thinking crossed her eyes, not wanting to see him and, even more, not wanting to be seen.

Titters arose from a crowd not certain whether it should laugh. Encouraged, she waved her arms, turned a somersault, and rolled her eyes around, dancing in the air, starting to enjoy herself. She turned the cry she wanted to make into a *whoop* as she reeled and veered, swinging from one side of the stage to the other, reaching behind to untangle the curtain from the wires attaching her wings to her wrists. From below she heard shrieks — of laughter or terror, she couldn't tell. She tugged and mugged and flung her body out this way and that, yanking and jerking until, with a rip, the curtain fell to the floor.

Suddenly freed of its restraining weight, she shot like a rocket across the proscenium, waving her arms as if trying to really fly, sticking her bottom up in the air, making every face she could think of, having the time of her life. When at last she ascended into the rafters, her elation turned to dread at the thought of the torn curtain and the anger that she knew would await her when she climbed down.

Her legs felt like rubber as she descended the ladder to the backstage area, her breath coming in shallow gasps. At the bottom, she saw Mr. Russell, his tall back turned to her, his shoulders shaking. She remembered the sound of ripping cloth: he would have to pay to replace the curtain. She should go over and apologize, and beg to remain in the show. Instead, she stood in place, staring at him, imagining his rage or, worse, scorn.

One of the technicians spoke to Mr. Russell, nodding in Josephine's direction. He turned, and she willed herself to return his gaze. *Don't be a coward, he ain't going to kill you* — although firing her would be its own kind of death sentence — and she saw that his eyes were full of tears. Bob Russell, one of the biggest names in vaudeville, was crying, wiping his eyes with both hands, his mouth open, laughing.

"You're a real clown, Birdy," he said, using the nickname the stagehands had called her in rehearsals. "You had me in stitches. Jesus, my side aches from laughing so hard." He strode over and grabbed her hand, squeezing it as he shook it — glorious pain — and slapped her back. "Welcome to The Dixie Steppers."

CHAPTER 6

1921, Philadelphia

The train pulled into Philadelphia with a sigh, or did that sound come from Josephine's fellow passengers, forty-two dancers, singers, comedians, jugglers, acrobats, female impersonators, animal trainers, actors, and actresses exhausted by the long days of traveling in heat-sticky cars whose windows wouldn't open?

At each stop on their circuit they'd stagger out, gulping for air and thirsting for an ice-cold glass of tea, to find a WHITES ONLY sign on the screen door of the only restaurant in town.

At night, they'd perform two shows to audiences of ten huddled in an open-air theater in the drizzling rain; or, in a theater that smelled like feet, to one hundred people who threw tomatoes and rotten eggs and, once, ran up onto the stage to attack an actor in a villain's role; or to drunkards fresh from the bars who broke out in fist fights that became messy, vomit-streaked brawls.

Afterward, they'd sleep in a ramshackle boarding house that swayed and creaked in the wind, or in a roach-infested flophouse with bloodstained mattresses and fist holes in the walls, or in rooms whose ceilings leaked rainwater onto the bed. In Mississippi, walking to their lodging at midnight, they passed a group of white-robed figures sharpening their knives and hissing, "Nigger," their eyes glinting hate through the slits in their hoods. The only good thing about the South, as far as Josephine could tell, was New Orleans, where everybody welcomed everybody, black and white, because the most important thing was the music.

Maybe that slow exhale came not from relief but from resignation, because, truth be told, none of them had wanted to leave New Orleans and nobody felt thrilled by what they saw now. If New Orleans was a buxom woman with her blouse undone, Philadelphia was a stern, prim aunt buttoned all the way up to her chin. Gray buildings, gray sky, gray sadness seeping into their bones: even the people on the gray sidewalks wore gray clothes.

Without Miss Clara, life had lost its color for Josephine, anyway. Clara had stayed in New Orleans, saying, "I'm the *South's* favorite coon shouter, not the North's." She didn't go north of the Mason-Dixon Line except to New York City. The North was too cold for her, even in the summer. No matter how hard Josephine begged, she refused to change her mind. "You've got to learn to sleep by yourself sometime, Tump."

Josephine cringed to think of sleeping in an empty bed where anybody might come in and get her. As unpleasant as her nights with Willie Wells had been — even though, toward the end, she'd started to enjoy herself — at least she could sleep with him, knowing that he'd protect her. Alone, she had only herself. Even with a locked door, a ghost might slip underneath and slide between the sheets. More than once in New Orleans she'd waited up for Miss Clara to come home, but that woman had other fish to fry — namely, a trumpet player she was sweet on in the Tuxedo Brass Band. On the nights when she stayed out, Josephine would lie awake until sunrise, sheets pulled tight to her chin so no one could slip in, listening for Clara's key in the lock. Only when dawn broke could she finally doze off.

In Philadelphia, she and Mrs. Jones shared

a room in a colored hotel with two other chorus girls: Pontop, half-Chinese, who wore her hair like a pom-pom on her crown, and Evelyn, who complained about everything Josephine did, said, and was. When she'd compared the darker-skinned Josephine to a monkey, Josephine had run crying to Clara, who'd laughed: "If you're going to be a star, you'd best get used to jealousy."

Without Clara, Josephine would have been miserable if not for Dyer Jones, who'd left Mr. Jones in New Orleans. "I tied him to the bedpost while he was passed-out drunk, and left his sorry ass," she said. "He ain't casting no more spells on me. I'll make my own magic from now on." Their daughter, Doll, had stayed behind, too, in love with a dwarf who thrilled her by tying her to the bedposts and striking her with a whip. Bob Russell, the manager of The Dixie Steppers, had frowned to hear that two-thirds of the Jones Family Band had abandoned the act, but Mrs. Jones coaxed him into letting her audition solo. "Wicked," is all he said when she'd finished her song, and he made her a headline act.

"A woman don't need a man to hang like a stone around her neck," Mrs. Jones told Josephine. "Don't you forget that, Tump."

The men weren't lining up to court Josephine, anyway. They went crazy over Mrs. Jones, with her lovely face like a heart framed by smooth, sleek hair. Josephine wasn't pretty, but, according to Miss Clara — who was no beauty herself — she wasn't ugly, either. "You're cute," she'd said, grinning with her pipe in her teeth. "Cute" didn't cut the mustard, but what could she do? She had knobby knees and buck teeth. Her chest was as flat as a board. Her hair sprang up all over her head like unruly weeds. Better ugly on purpose than cute on accident, so Josephine grimaced while she flapped around the stage, waggling her knees and wiggling her rump, ugly as a demon, ugly as sin, ugly as the duckling before it grew into a beautiful swan.

Her figure wasn't half-bad. At fifteen, she'd started to fill out, the contours of the body Paris would call "magnificent" just beginning to emerge, like buds on a tree straining to burst into bloom. Flapping around on a wire as Cupid had strengthened her arms, and all her squats and jumps and flips and breakaways and spins and leaps and hops were shaping her legs into thick, sturdy trunks, nearly as muscled as a man's. And the continual, frenetic energy that had caused her so much trouble at home worked, now, in her favor. Unable to sit still, she constantly rehearsed, dancing from the time she arose at noon all the way through the shows, and then, later, again in her room, perfecting her moves in the fresh-spilling light of new dawn before falling, exhausted at last, to sleep next to Dyer Jones.

"You work too hard," Mrs. Jones said one Sunday afternoon, sprawled on the bed, reading a newspaper and watching Josephine practice sliding down into a split and back up to standing without using her hands.

Josephine told herself not to listen to those devil's words. She intended to *shine* like the star she was meant to be, and that meant polishing herself with practice, buffing herself with work, learning everything she could by watching and imitating until she'd made her own every good thing she saw. Philadelphia was only one hundred miles from New York City, and now that she was here, she meant to stay.

"Play some music, Mrs. Jones," she said. "There's a new dance I want to try." She'd seen it at the Dunbar the night before: the Geechie dance, a lazy twist of the foot that became a frenzy of kicking legs and swinging arms, hands and knees crossing, a dance that looked like sheer joy to do and was about as much fun to watch. But Dyer had a different idea. She pulled a flier from her purse: *We've got yellow girls, we've got black and tan. Will you have a good time? YEAH, MAN!*

"A rent party? No thanks, Mrs. Dyer. I'm not in the mood."

Rent parties were a dime a dozen, thrown to help folks pay their rent. This one promised music, which sounded like fun, but Josephine had had enough of parties. In show business, every night was a party. People called Sunday "Doomsday" because businesses were closed, including the theaters, but for Josephine it was the best day. Sunday meant getting time to herself.

Dyer persisted, itching to go; she'd heard some good musicians were going to be there, and she wanted to play. "Why can't you go by yourself?" Josephine said, but Dyer said there was no better way to find trouble than to walk alone into a party full of men hopped up on hooch. That was how she'd met Mr. Jones, and she wasn't about to make that mistake twice.

Josephine demurred until Mrs. Jones turned the flier over and showed her the menu: hog maws, black-eyed peas, fried catfish, banana pudding. Josephine's stomach roared all the way to the party, in an apartment on the top floor of a pretty brownstone with wood floors and high ceilings, "a historic building," said the woman who met them at the door. Josephine kept her thoughts to herself. Having grown up in old places — crumbling, rotting, smelling of mildew and ash — she preferred the modern, the sleek, the shiny, the new. She walked straight to the long table slathered with good things to eat, catfish and creamed corn and collard greens and sugared tomatoes and cucumbers in vinegar, gumbo and ham hocks and grits and sweet potato pie and watermelon and banana pudding, and, at the table's edge, a beautiful boy whose eyes made her forget the food.

She looked away, disoriented, smiling at the catfish, but he knew she meant it for him because from the corner of her eye she saw him look away, too. He put random things on a plate, chocolate pudding and corn, hush puppies and mustard, still smiling, glancing at her as she helped herself to everything and moved to a chair by the window to devour every morsel.

As she finished, a handkerchief appeared, the boy pressing it to her chin, his smile shy but his eyes insistent, like he feared she might eat him next and also feared she wouldn't.

Her mouth watered. She stepped up to the boy, slid her arms around his neck, and pulled him down for a long kiss. She could tell from his awkward response that he hadn't kissed many girls, but when she pressed her body to his he had no trouble figuring out what to do with his hands. As she stepped back, she took the handkerchief and wiped his face, then her own, and kissed him again. He was a quick learner, out of breath, eager.

Music struck up in the front room — clarinet, bass, drum, banjo, fiddle, trombones, saxophones, trumpets, and little Dyer Jones making a sound bigger than all the rest put together, playing the "Black Bottom Dance."

Josephine felt the music stream like water into her body and she began to move, slapping her hips, snapping her fingers, throwing her arms over her head, consumed by the music and forgetting the boy again until he took her hand and began to dance with her, his legs swinging from side to side, hands reaching up, then down to the floor, his compact body not just mimicking her moves but anticipating them, his jacket coming off in one swift motion and landing on a chair, hands rolling up his shirtsleeves while she answered his challenge, improving on his dance, which was impressive but would pale against what she could do.

She held herself back, kept to the known steps although she longed to show off for the cheering crowd and especially for him, whose long-lashed eyes watched her with the appreciation of a contender who thought she was good but not good enough to beat him. He slapped his hands on the floor and jumped so high he might have taken flight, shimmying all the way back down, then broke into a twist and a spin, and sent a wink at her that said, *Sorry, honey, but I am the best and I know it, and now you know it, too.*

She slapped her behind in a fast rhythm, matching that of the drum, wiggling her black bottom as if it had inspired the dance, then bent over and bumped her elbows to the floor and flung herself nearly to the ceiling before performing her no-hands split. The whole party went crazy, shouting and screaming and shaking the floor. The music stopped, and she bowed, the undisputed winner, while he stood grinning like someone caught in a lie.

Dyer put down her horn and came over, frowning at Josephine. "You'll never get a fella with stunts like that," she muttered, and walked over to the boy, stuck out her hand, and congratulated him on his fine dancing.

"Not as fine as hers," he said, missing Josephine's apologetic smile, which was just as well because she didn't mean it.

"What did you expect? To win a dance contest against the Dixie Steppers' star chorus girl?" Dyer winked at her.

"Get out," the boy said.

"I'm at the end of the line. The comic." Josephine crossed her eyes.

He laughed as he reached for his jacket and slipped it on again. "The Dixie Steppers — I've been meaning to see that show. Now I will go, for sure."

"How about tonight?" she said, stepping closer and reaching for his hand again. He was taller than she was, but only by a little. "The next performance starts as soon as Sunday ends — at one minute past midnight."

Doubt crossed his face, making her wish she hadn't been so bold. She'd forgotten, for a moment, that boys liked to be the ones to ask.

"I've got to be at work at six in the morning, serving breakfast in my family's restaurant," he said, but in the next moment he laughed. "Listen to me, an old man at twenty-three. Sure, I'll go tonight, on one condition: that you'll let me take you to dinner this week."

Josephine kissed him again, on the cheek this time. "I'd be delighted," she said, as though a boy had ever taken her to dinner before. He caressed her hand with his thumb and her face with his pretty eyes, as though she were the most beautiful sight he had ever seen, and she wondered if he saw the same in her eyes, because *handsome, gorgeous, darling* kept running through her mind. "My name's Tumpy," she said.

"That's an awkward name for a graceful girl. Is it a nickname?"

He had a way of speaking that tied her tongue, using words like *graceful,* as though he'd actually gone to school and had even finished. For the first time, Josephine wished that she had paid mind to her schooling, too — but then, she'd still be in St. Louis, instead of here with this boy who was too lovely for words, anyway.

"My real name is Freda Josephine Wells," she said.

"Josephine," he said, and lifted her hand to his lips for a kiss — classy, that's what he was — that sent shivers up her arm. "That's the name that suits you, and it's what I'll call you, if you don't mind. Mine's William

Howard Baker — but call me Billy. If you think it suits me."

She'd have called him anything he wanted, but instead of telling him so, she tugged at his hand and led him out the door while the music played, down the stairs and up the street, to her room, upon which, finding it empty, she pulled him inside and closed the door behind, locking the bolt against anyone who might come home, knowing that Dyer was out for a long time yet, and laughing to think of giving her unhappy roommate Evelyn, at last, a real reason to complain.

The bride wore white, even though, having been married before (an event she'd kept to herself, *what folks don't know won't hurt 'em,* as Elvira said) and considering her condition, she was far from entitled to the color. Nobody knew the difference, anyway, not the clerk who filled out their license for them — to Josephine's relief but Billy's indignation ("Because we're colored they assume we cannot read?") — nor the reverend who pronounced them man and wife, although he did look Josephine up and down. As they left the chapel, Billy cursed.

"We've got to get married, that's what he's thinking, and what business is it of his?" he said. Josephine smiled and kissed her hus-

131

band's pretty bow of a mouth. The reverend was just thinking about their souls, she said. Maybe he figured she wasn't really nineteen, the age she'd given the clerk, or perhaps he could tell that she was pregnant.

"The reason for our marriage is not his concern," Billy said.

"You're marrying me because of the baby?"

"No, that's not what I meant." He put his arm around her waist. "I'm marrying you because you are the sweetest, funniest, most beautiful girl on the planet, and I am madly in love with you." Josephine wanted to fall to the ground and kiss his feet. Who had ever treated her so well?

He patted her stomach. "But I am mighty excited about Little Billy."

"We might have a girl," Josephine reminded him. "Would that be all right?" Her question was sly; she already knew the answer.

"As long as she looks like her mama, I'll be happy."

She'd made a good choice: Billy would take care of her. He came from a nice home, and his parents' friends were "well connected," as his mama liked to brag: bankers, businessmen, even famous people dined in their restaurant, often with the Bakers themselves. Josephine wouldn't have to work or worry.

Already he had applied to work as a porter on the Pullman trains, where he would make more money than he earned waiting tables. "I've lived a life of leisure until now," he said, "but soon I'll have a family to support." He'd rise all the way to the top of the company, especially with her to push him along.

On Sunday afternoons while he slept off their late Saturday nights, she explored the city's rich neighborhoods on her own, Rittenhouse Square, Chestnut Hill, the Main Line, gawking at the mansions the way she'd done as a child in Saint Louis's Washington Square, and dreaming of the future. She and Billy were going places: namely, to a mansion on a hill.

But Pullman porters didn't live in mansions, and Josephine would have to end her performing career. The Dixie Steppers were moving on, leaving for Chicago in a few weeks. She'd landed a job dancing with Sandy Burns's company, the troupe billed next at the Standard Theatre, but she'd have to give it up now, though, and her hopes for New York City. When the child started showing, she'd quit: there was nothing funny about a pregnant chorus girl.

Panic gripped her insides when she thought of leaving the theater. No more, for Josephine, a body filled with music — the drum, the fiddle, Dyer Jones's trumpet making her step and groove, spin and move, snapping her fingers to the dance in her head, the exuberance, the wildness, the doleful moan. After a while, even the music in her head would surely stop. How would she walk without timing her stride to "Crazy Blues"? How would she laugh without music? How would she live?

She'd live like everybody else, she supposed, in the audience instead of on the stage.

She'd be happy. She loved babies, their skin like silk, their talcum smell, their sweet blank faces unmarked by life's cruel stamp. Had Josephine ever been so innocent? It felt like she'd entered this world with a special sorrow: the taint of being unwanted, her bastard status imprinting her like the mark of the beast.

Billy would be a good father and a good husband to her — if he ever learned to stand up to his mother. Even now, with Josephine in the household, his mama reigned supreme, like some kind of matriarch. Tall, fine-boned, and oh-so-proper in her fine tailored suits, she'd looked down her nose at Josephine from the minute Billy had introduced her as "a performer in the show at the Standard, one of the stars."

"I see," she'd said, giving Josephine the once-over. She pursed her lips and turned to her son. "She's a *showgirl.*"

"The best dancer in the troupe," Billy boasted, oblivious, beaming at his handsome father, who cradled Josephine's hand between his and said he was pleased to make her acquaintance, yes, *very* pleased. She'd averted her eyes, afraid to see his man-hunger, but he just kept holding her hand until she looked up into a face so kind it made her want to cry.

No one could harm her, anyway, now that she was married to Billy. He'd promised to love, honor, and cherish, and she knew he would. He had treated her as gently as a kitten since they'd met, holding her close and calming her that evening when his mother had asked how, with a white father, Josephine had such dark skin. That had made her spitting mad, but Billy had loved all the hurt away, murmuring "sweetheart" and "darling" and "beautiful."

Beautiful? That was a first. Josephine had been called all kinds of things — monkey, blue gums, ferret face, buck teeth, coon, skinny, thick lips, darky, tar baby — but no one had ever said she was beautiful. In the bathroom of his parents' apartment one afternoon, standing before the big mirror over the sink, she'd glimpsed for the first time what he must see: luminous dark eyes, an oval face, clear skin. Her chest was pretty flat, true, but she was only fifteen, there was time to grow, and her body was lean and strong and her butt round and firm, "like two melons," Billy said, and when, onstage, she arched her back and shook it like a rooster wagging its tail feathers, the crowd cried out like she'd done something no one ever had before.

Mrs. Baker walked in and, seeing her preening, said, "Beauty is only skin-deep, but ugly goes clean to the bone." Josephine slunk out like a kicked dog but remembered that she'd set her glass of tea on the sink. Turning back to get it, she encountered her mother-in-law-to-be lifting the lid of her jewelry box, "checking to make sure it's all here."

Josephine wanted to run down the stairs and out the door, but instead she joined Billy and his daddy in the kitchen, where Pa Baker was stirring a pot of chili and saying with a grin that he bet Josephine didn't mind a little heat, being "hot stuff" herself.

"She isn't vain enough that you've got to

encourage her?" Mrs. Baker snapped as she swept past to the living room. Josephine looked at Billy, but he'd blushed like he had neither a tongue to speak with nor a girlfriend to stand up for.

Now, on their way to tell his parents about their marriage, she wondered if he would protect a wife better than a girlfriend from his mother's wrath. Mrs. B would throw a fit, for sure. Pa Baker would be all right — he loved her, and when he heard there was a baby he would understand — but Mrs. Baker had never said a kind word to Josephine.

"Will they be upset?" Billy squeezed her hand. "They might be, a little bit, but they'll get over it fast. Shoot, we'll be living with them. Seeing you every day, how can they help loving you as much as I do?"

Close your mouth, her grandmama would say, *or a fly's gonna fly in it.* But every time she closed her mouth it popped open again. Sitting in the fifth row of the Dunbar Theatre on Broad Street, Josephine felt like she'd entered another world, one that, when the curtain went down and the lights came up, she didn't want to leave. She had never seen anything like *Shuffle Along,* had never even imagined such a show, with Negro

137

folks acting and singing and tap-dancing —
tap-dancing! — not in blackface but just as
they were. "I'm Just Wild about Harry" was
as catchy a tune as she'd ever heard, someone whistling it as the audience filed out.
"As good as any white show," the woman in
front of her said, as if she or anybody in the
room had set foot in a white theater.

"Better than most, I'd wager," her companion said. "I read in the *Tribune* that it's
going to Broadway."

Broadway! Josephine was out of her seat
in a blur, leaving Billy as she headed backstage to see Wilsie Caldwell, her classmate
from Dumas Elementary School, whom Josephine had recognized in the chorus. Two
months had passed since her and Billy's
wedding day; one week since she'd discovered that she wasn't pregnant, after all.
She'd been blue ever since. Billy had
brought her out to cheer her up, and succeeded beyond his wildest hopes: motherhood was, suddenly, the last thing on Josephine's mind.

"If it isn't Tumpy," Wilsie cried when she
saw her, making Josephine blush at the ugly,
childish name. She smiled and said she was
glad Wilsie remembered her, and the girl
said how could she forget? "Teacher put the
dunce cap on your head, and you sat there

138

making faces. It was the funniest thing I ever saw." By the time Billy caught up, Wilsie was saying yes, she would be happy to arrange an audition for Josephine, that having her in *Shuffle Along* would be the "cat's meow."

Did Billy walk with her to his parents' apartment that evening? With her head in the clouds and her eyes so full of dreams, she had a hard time seeing anything else. She did remember Mrs. B's greeting them at the door, though, and linking arms with Josephine like they were best friends, and asking for her help in the kitchen. Josephine knew how to make cornmeal mush and that was about it, but she let herself be led, exchanging a smile with Billy as they parted.

"How are you feeling? Here — have a glass of milk. It's good for the baby," Mrs. Baker said.

Josephine struggled for an answer. She'd started her period the previous Sunday. How could it be? She had *felt* it growing inside her; it had visited her in dreams, a baby boy with Billy's eyes smiling up into hers. *I will never be lonely again,* that's what she'd thought when she awakened, and the baby whispered, *I will always love you, Mother.*

She'd kept quiet about the loss at first,

dreading Billy's disappointment. He'd gotten the Pullman porter job and talked all the time about all the "advantages" he was going to provide their child: a nice house, a college education. Every day he checked to see if she was "getting fat," but she never was; every night he'd pressed his ear to her belly in effort to hear the baby, whom he'd started referring to as Junior.

But when she'd told him the truth last night, he wasn't disappointed at all. He was "sort of relieved, to tell you the truth," he hadn't "felt ready" for fatherhood; he wanted some time to "get established" and to have Josephine "all to myself" for a while. Now here she sat in his mother's kitchen, feeling guilty because the woman still thought Josephine was pregnant. She ought to tell her, but to see how Mrs. B smiled, hear all the questions she was asking about the show, Josephine had never heard her talk so much, and when Josephine replied she hung on every word. When Josephine got up to go to the bathroom, Mrs. B stopped her, saying, "Oh, please tell me the rest of the story before you go, I don't think I can wait to hear the end," and as Josephine spoke she ladled out some of the snapper soup left over from dinner and insisted she have some right then and there. When the woman excused herself "for just a minute, to see if Billy wants some," Josephine followed, unable to hold her bladder a minute longer — but Mrs. B turned and extended her arms, blocking her way.

"You haven't finished your soup!" she said, her eyes wide and unfocused. "It's no good cold. Go on back in and eat it up. Go on!"

From behind Mrs. B, Josephine heard voices — a female voice, and that of a man not Pa Baker or Billy. "I have to use the bathroom," she whispered.

A woman appeared in a pretty, peach-colored dress and matching hat, her skin so pale that Josephine thought, for a moment, that she was white.

"Mattie, where *are* you?" the woman said.

"Get *in there,*" Mrs. B hissed to Josephine. The woman came up behind her and stared.

"Who is this?" she said.

"Nobody," Mrs. B said. The woman laughed.

"Mattie Gwendolyn Baker, I see right through your tricks. Everybody talking about what a good cook you are, when you've got help in the kitchen. Charles? Come here, and see what the Bakers have been hiding."

Josephine saw right away what was going

141

on, why Mrs. B had kept her for so long — she'd been hiding Josephine from her friends.

"Did y'all like my snapper soup, ma'am?" Josephine curtseyed, putting on her thickest Southern drawl. "It's my specialty; I've been cooking it all day."

The woman's mouth opened. "Mattie, who *is* this?" Mrs. B looked like a dog about to bite. Josephine crossed her eyes, blocking out that mean face. "My name is Tumpy, ma'am," she said, and pranced into the living room to dance the Black Bottom, singing "I've Got a New Baby" until she heard the whole apartment laughing and Billy's proud "That's *my* baby!" When she'd finished her performance she bowed, and everyone applauded, and she blew kisses. Pa Baker's eyes glowed with pleasure and Billy's with pride, the guests in their fancy clothes laughed and praised her — and Mrs. B's mouth twisted as if she had a shit smear on her skinny lips.

When they had gone, the church deacon in his flaxen suit and his peach-colored wife, smiling and thanking Mrs. B for the evening — "Your daughter-in-law is delightful, you must be so pleased" — the woman closed the door and rounded on Josephine.

"You little porch monkey," she said. "How

dare you embarrass me like that? If it weren't for that baby you trapped my son with, I'd kick your ass out on the street."

Josephine looked at Billy, who stared at the floor. She turned her eyes to Pa Baker, who was walking down the hall, calling to his wife to come to bed. It didn't look like anybody was going to stand up for her, not even her own husband. Coward.

Josephine felt the woman's insult coil around her throat. "Porch monkey" was what Mrs. Kaiser had called her. She reached out and grasped the woman's jaw, the way she'd wanted to do to Mrs. Kaiser when she was little, squeezing, relishing the pop of her eyes. Billy spoke her name, stepped forward to interfere, but she struck out with her free arm, knocking him back — Mama's boy, good-for-nothing of a husband.

"Take it back!" Josephine cried, restraining herself from punching the woman's mouth with her fist, with the very hand that Mrs. Kaiser had thrust into that pot of boiling water. No way would she quit her job now; she and Billy would have to find their own place. "Take those ugly words back, *Mattie Gwendolyn Baker,* or I'll force them down your throat."

CHAPTER 7

1923, New York City

The prod of a policeman's stick against her arm: time to get up. Josephine pushed herself up and off the bench, wondering if she'd slept, and pulled on the thin jacket she'd used as a blanket. Her hips, her ribs — every place where bone had pressed against wood — felt bruised. Shivering, she stomped her numb feet. A white man with stringy hair watched her from a bench across the sidewalk, taking sips from a paper sack once the officer had moved on. Now, it was just him and her out there: Josephine, and her observer, both of whom had spent the night in Central Park.

She picked up the bag of clothes she'd used for a pillow and walked across 110th Street and up Seventh Avenue into Harlem, where Wilsie lived. "We've barely got room to swing a cat, and three of us in my tiny apartment," Wilsie had said, explaining why she couldn't offer Josephine a place to stay. Josephine had shrugged, pretending she had other options, when, in fact, she'd had no idea what she would do. She'd spent all her money on train fare, thinking to audition yesterday and head right back to Philadelphia, but her train had been delayed and she'd missed her appointment. Today things would be different. She'd arrive at the theater early and be the first to audition for the new *Shuffle Along* touring company. If she got turned down, she'd sleep in the park again tonight and try again tomorrow.

Too young, too ugly, too dark, Mr. Sissle had said last fall. What would he say now? She'd grown some since her last audition, and she'd been working extra hard on her dancing with her new company, which performed with all the touring shows. Bessie Smith, now billed as the "Empress of the Blues," had taught her how to "project" herself on the stage. One of the chorus dancers had shown her how to lighten her skin tone by rubbing herself with lemon juice. She'd begun using straightener to tame the kinks out of her hair, and sported a sleek, mature style. She was ready.

If only she hadn't made that silly scene at the end of her last audition, looking back up at those men in the pouring rain like some kind of pathetic street urchin. She'd wanted them to remember her, but now she hoped they would have forgotten that awful afternoon.

Last October, Wilsie had kept her promise and gotten Josephine an audition with Noble Sissle and Eubie Blake, the men behind *Shuffle Along,* who, Wilsie had said, were "as good as gold," or at least that was true of Mr. Blake, she said. Mr. Sissle was funnier, always making jokes but also "sharp around the edges, and his words can cut." Josephine didn't fear either man, or that's what she told herself; she'd seen their musical five times and could do a better job than any of the hoofers they had. She knew the chorus dances by heart, had practiced them at least a hundred times, rising early to practice while her fellow dancers at the Standard slept off their hangovers from the night before.

Josephine was confident: she'd open the show in New York, which was scheduled to run off-Broadway, it turned out, but no matter. She'd have Mr. Sissle and Mr. Blake begging her to work for them, and throwing money at her to do it. Billy hadn't liked the idea at first, but she'd convinced him that he could come with her: they had Pullman trains in New York, too. If Wilsie's pay was any indication, she'd make better money than Billy did. They'd be able to live on their own, far from his mama, who hated Josephine more than ever now and tried in every way to make her life miserable. When she'd learned that Josephine wasn't pregnant, the woman had laughed and congratulated her for the "fast one" she'd pulled.

"You got what you wanted, didn't you?" she said.

"I don't have to lie to get a man," Josephine snapped back. "And if I just wanted to get married, you think I'd pick somebody who lives with his mama?"

As she spoke the words, their truth rattled her. She loved Billy, she reminded herself. But while leaving her own mama to live with Mrs. B hadn't exactly been jumping from the frying pan into the fire, it was still too hot in that apartment for her. She wanted out.

" 'I'm just wild about Harry,' " she'd sung as she'd walked to the Dunbar, picturing herself dancing for Sissle and Blake, the famous songwriting team. Would the men want her to make them laugh, or should she play it straight? At least she looked nice. When he'd heard about the audition, Pa Baker had taken her to a fancy dress shop.

"The first rule of success is, you've got to dress for it," he said, and bought her a green dress with a navy-and-green cloche, the "height of fashion," the proprietress said. Real Chinese silk, it felt like water against her skin, but when she said so, the woman told her not to get it wet or it would be ruined. Water dripped from an awning as she passed, and she dodged the drops. It had rained much of the day, but now the sky was clearing, in weather as in life, and some people carried umbrellas but they were folded up. " 'I want to spread a little sunshine,' " she sang, " 'I want to chase away the rain.' "

Just before she entered the stage door, a drop of rain hit her on the head. No, that was not a bad omen, only a reminder to do her best, to shine like the star she was, or would be. Wilsie came running up — Mr. Sissle was there, but Mr. Blake had yet to arrive. "You'll knock 'em dead, Tumpy. Just do your dancing and forget the rest." Josephine didn't need to be told that. She was ready.

She'd flexed and stretched her arms as she walked with Wilsie across the stage, past the musicians gathering, trumpets and saxophones and drums and a clarinet, down into the auditorium, where a slender man spoke to a white-haired man at his side. He turned his head very slightly and looked her up and down from the corners of his shrewd, hard eyes. His mouth pursed.

"How old are you?" he'd said before Wilsie had even introduced them.

The stage door opened, and a very dark-skinned man with a bald head hurried in, talking about "the damned rain," scampering down the steps, striding up the aisle, shaking water from his clothes.

"Eubie Blake," he said, smiling, holding out his hand to her.

"This is Tumpy, Mr. Blake, the one I told you about," Wilsie said. "She's here to audition for Clara's spot in the chorus."

The man with Mr. Sissle — the stage manager — motioned to her and she followed him up the stage steps. Did she know the songs? Could she dance to "I'm Just Wild about Harry"? Josephine wanted to jump for joy. She pretended to watch as Wilsie showed her the steps, which she already knew as if she'd made them up herself. Josephine stripped down to her dingy leotard, tossed her clothes on a chair, then ran and leaped to the center of the stage. This was it. She bent over to grasp her ankles, stretching her legs, then stood and pulled her arms over her head.

"Ready?" Mr. Sissle barked. The music started, and she began the dance, so simple she could have done it in her sleep. Practicing in the Standard, she'd gotten bored with it and had made up her own steps, throwing in a little Black Bottom, wiggling her ass and kicking her legs twice as high as they wanted to go, taken by the music, played by it, the instruments' instrument, flapping her hands, step and kick and spin and spin and squat and jump and down in a split, up and jump and kick and spin — oops, the steps, she didn't need no damn steps, she had better ones — and kick and jump and wiggle and spin. She looked out into the auditorium — a big mistake: Mr. Blake's mouth was open and Mr. Sissle's eyes had narrowed to slits. *Don't be nervous, just dance.* Only the music remained now, her feet and the stage.

When she'd finished, panting, and pulled on her dress and shoes, Wilsie came running over, her eyes shining. "You made their heads spin, you better believe it," she whispered, but when they went down into the aisle Josephine heard Mr. Sissle muttering.

"Too young, too dark, too ugly," he said. The world stopped turning, then, the sun frozen in its arc, every clock still, every breath caught in every throat.

Mr. Blake turned to her, smiling as if everything were normal, and congratulated her on "a remarkable dance."

"I can see that you are well qualified for our chorus, Tumpy," he said, and on his lips, the name sounded like a little child's. "You have real talent, and spark, besides. How did you learn to do that at such a young age? You are — how old?"

"Fifteen," she said.

Mr. Sissle snorted, and cut Wilsie a look. "Wasting my time," he said. Mr. Blake looked at her as if she'd just wandered in from the orphanage.

"I'm very sorry, there's been a mix-up," he said. "You must be sixteen to dance professionally in New York State."

"I'll be sixteen in June," Josephine said. Her voice sounded plaintive and faraway. (Why had she said that? It was April now — would they remember, and turn her away?)

"We need someone *now.*" Mr. Sissle folded his arms as if she were underage on purpose. Mr. Blake led her toward the stage door, an apologetic Wilsie saying she hadn't known. Mr. Sissle followed, talking to Mr. Blake about adding some steps to "I'm Just Wild about Harry," saying they should put in some kicks, that he'd been thinking about it for a while. Uh-huh.

"Come and see us in New York after your birthday, doll," Mr. Blake said. "You never know when we might have an opening." He opened the door and let the rain pour in before shutting it again. He looked at Josephine's thin, optimistic dress. Where was her umbrella? She hung her head. He stepped over to retrieve a black umbrella propped against the wall and handed it to her. She took it without even knowing, her thoughts colliding like too many birds in a cage. She would have to stay in Philadelphia, she had failed — *too young, too dark, too ugly* — she should have lied about her age, what had gotten into her? Showing off, that was what. And now Mr. Sissle disliked her, and she would never get into their show; it didn't matter how many times she went back. As she stepped out into the rain with that big umbrella in her hands unopened and felt the rain pour down her face; she was glad, for now they would think it was water instead of tears, but when she looked back, Wilsie was crying, too, in the open doorway. Seeing the men watching from a window, she stopped. They wouldn't forget her; she'd make them remember. She walked slowly, her silk dress dripping, while Mr. Sissle gesticulated with excitement as he stole her ideas — *authentic Negro dancing* were the last words she'd heard — and Mr. Blake looking as if he wanted to run out there, scoop her up, and carry her back inside.

She'd wanted them to remember her, but now she hoped they wouldn't. Maybe Mr. Sissle wouldn't recognize her with her new hairstyle, with the curl on her forehead, and the chorus costume she'd brought from the Standard instead of the dingy dance leotard she'd worn for the last tryout.

Mr. Blake, at least, would be impressed. She recalled how he'd looked at her in Philadelphia, his eyes moving over her body like a lover's hands. She would smile at him at lot, and lie about anything that needed lying about, and dance as if life depended on this audition, which it did.

She hadn't come all the way to New York and spent the night on a bench in Central Park to fail. She'd come to follow her destiny, which was *Shuffle Along*.

She'd gotten Wilsie's letter about auditions for a new, traveling troupe and begged Pa Baker to lend her the money for train fare, telling him she could stay at Wilsie's. At work, she'd done her shows and pretended, the night before last, to get sick.

How many performances could she miss before losing her job at the Standard? What if she failed the tryout and ended up with no work at all? Depending on Billy made as much sense to Josephine as trying to dance with her hands tied behind her back. One misstep, and she'd fall on her face, and then how would she get up again?

Billy's paltry wages from the Pullman Company couldn't pay the rent for a place of their own, and he wouldn't let her contribute her salary, saying it was the man's job to provide. Now he was always gone, leaving Josephine in bed alone and listening for ghosts, and enduring the merciless indignities of life with Ma Baker, a name Josephine had taken to using for the sheer pleasure of seeing the woman grit her teeth. (Billy called her Mother, a bloodless endearment if she'd ever heard one.) But who did Josephine need, really, besides the audiences who cheered for her every night? She'd escaped from that hard life in Saint Louis and made it to Philadelphia by using her wits and working hard, and she'd make it in New York on her own merits and her own terms.

The city was just waking up as she neared Wilsie's brick apartment building, horses pulling carriages among cars and streetcars honking and rattling up the street and filling the air with the sickly sweet odor of exhaust; shop owners rolling out their awnings and sweeping the sidewalks in front of their establishments; a grocer setting out fruits and vegetables on a rack; a florist filling buckets with flowers and taping a sign to his window (APRIL SHOWERS BRING MAY FLOWERS); a big dog leading two little ones in a zigzag across the busy thoroughfare and cars screeching to a halt and drivers honking their horns to avoid hitting the dogs; a grizzled man leaning against a doorway, smoking a cigarette and whistling at her as she passed, his eyes greedy.

"Turn a quick trick, baby doll? I've got twenty dollars for you right here." Patting his crotch, grinning at her.

"I wouldn't give you the time of day for that puny offer," she shot back. Twenty dollars sounded good to her right now — it would buy her a room if she had to stay in New York another night — but she quickly dismissed the thought. She wouldn't need a room tonight. She would *not.*

"You ain't seen what else I've got," the man said, his right hand fumbling with his fly. Josephine ditched her plan to wait on the steps until Wilsie had the chance to wake up. She pressed the buzzer once, twice, three times, holding it in the third time until Wilsie came down to let her in, scowling and pointing to her watch and asking Josephine what in the world she was doing here so early.

"I know you didn't get to bed until at least three o'clock this morning, because that's when I went down," Wilsie said. "Don't you ever sleep?"

"Cops turned me out when the sun come up," she said, telling Wilsie where she'd spent the night. Wilsie gasped, and her expression changed to guilt as Josephine had hoped.

"Lord have mercy, why didn't you tell me? I thought you had other friends in the city you could stay with."

"They weren't home," she lied.

Quietly, Wilsie let her into the apartment, as tiny as she had said it was, a single room with three twin beds and a kitchenette.

"Come on and get in bed, I don't care what the girls say." Josephine, still wearing all her clothes, crawled under the blankets and quilts with her friend and snuggled in her arms, drowsing off. But she didn't want to sleep, she whispered, she wanted to be at the theater when Mr. Blake and Mr. Sissle arrived, she didn't want to miss her chance as she'd done yesterday, she'd have to take the train back home this evening, she'd gotten her friend Mildred to lie for her once, but she didn't want to push her luck.

When Wilsie heard her fretting, she kissed her cheek and told Josephine not to worry. She was a good dancer, even Mr. Sissle had admitted it after she'd left that day last fall, telling Mr. Blake that if Josephine weren't too young he might have overlooked the rest. *Too young, too dark, too ugly.* She would show him; she would show them all.

"Just tell them you've turned sixteen," Wilsie whispered, but Josephine was already in another world, winding up her arms and kicking up her heels, throwing off sparks, spinning like a dervish, rising to the ceiling and shining there, filling the theater with light.

■ ■ ■ ■

Act III
Josephine Chante
La France
(Josephine Sings
France)

■ ■ ■ ■

A crowd of Negro dancers fills the stage, wearing grass skirts and dancing to a jungle beat: *La Revue Nègre,* the colored American revue that would have flopped like a dead fish in America — it was nowhere as sophisticated as *Shuffle Along,* or even the second Sissle and Blake show that Josephine toured in, *Chocolate Dan-*

dies. In Paris, though, Negroes were in vogue after the Great War, the colored soldiers having fought so valiantly with the French, and artists like Pablo Picasso now using African masks in their art to express man's "primitive" nature. Josephine didn't understand what Africa had to do with her — she was from Missouri — but she knew a good thing when she saw it, and let the good times roll.

Chocolate Dandies closed after just a couple of months on Broadway, a flop even though it was good, telling real stories of real Negro life. Not a lot of people went to see it, the novelty of an all-colored musical having passed, and white critics dismissed it as "too ambitious" and "not Negro enough." Although they heaped praise on Josephine, calling her a "star" when, in reality, she was only in the chorus, she could not break out into a real starring role. At the Plantation Room on Broadway, she auditioned to sing, but the manager said her voice was weak. He hired her for the chorus, instead, and made Ethel Waters his singer. It was Ethel whom Caroline Dudley Reagan, a rich white woman who always wore black, had come to see on the night she hired Josephine.

"Come to Paris and be my star," Mrs. Caroline beckoned. How could Josephine say no? She signed up on the spot, to hell with what Billy thought. He wanted her to quit show business and raise a family, but he couldn't get her pregnant again, so why shouldn't she go? She'd make more money in a few months than he earned all year, and she would be back by the spring to try again for that baby.

From the look on his face when she told him, he must have foreseen how it would all turn out. Confronted with his tears, she'd wavered — hadn't she promised "till death do us part"? But then Mrs. Caroline bought her the red dress she'd been eyeing in the window of a Fifth Avenue shop, and had smiled when Josephine told her she wanted to sing.

"Paris, queen of the world," she sings in *Josephine à Bobino,* the dancers in their grass skirts gyrating around her in frantic imitation of the moves that made her famous, the Eiffel Tower and the Arc de Triomphe and the windmill of the Moulin Rouge rolling out onto the stage. Little had she known, when she'd signed the contract for *La Revue Negre,* that she would become the Queen of Paris at age nineteen. Even her big dreams hadn't carried her that far. But Billy had known.

Nothing, in fact, had turned out the way Josephine had imagined. But if, like Billy, she'd seen into the future, she'd have done it all the same. No. If she'd known what would happen in France, she wouldn't have walked onto that steamship to Europe: she'd have danced.

CHAPTER 8

1925, Atlantic Ocean

On top of the world was how she felt on the deck of the RMS *Berengaria,* a triple-decker steamship as big as a continent. She felt small, surrounded by stars in the sky and their reflections glittering in the water, but also big, floating on the ocean fathomless and eternal and filled with possibility. Steam from the three stacks atop the ship dissolved like dreams into the warm September night, the crescent moon waxing, the smell of the sea filling her nose and mouth, music falling from the upper deck where the band warmed up for the show they were about to put on. The whole world moving under her feet, propelling her forward. She had never been so high, and tonight was only the beginning.

Josephine ascended the broad spiral staircase in her red Tappé dress, stepping carefully so as not to rip the stitches at the narrow hem. Everything must be perfect on this, her night to shine. Tonight, she would show Mrs. Caroline where her true talents lay — not as a "great clown," as the woman kept calling her, but as a singer.

Angling for a singing role in *La Revue Nègre,* she'd told Mrs. Caroline that she'd filled in for Ethel Waters at the Plantation Room, which was only almost true. Ethel had gotten sick for three days, and Tony, the manager, had almost let Josephine take her place. But then Ethel got wind of that scheme and said, "Ain't no goddamn way," no chorus dancer was going to get a crack at *her* job, and she came back to work.

Tonight, though, would be different.

In exchange for passage for her musicians and cast, Mrs. Caroline had promised a performance for the first-class passengers in the upper-level dining room. Featured would be the other star dancer, Louis Douglas, the singer Maud de Forrest, and Josephine. Unbeknownst to Mrs. Caroline, though, Josephine had decided not to dance, but to sing "Brown Eyes" as she would have done in Ethel's place in the Plantation Room. Then, for the rest of the voyage, the white people would be talking about her in their white lingo, how "marvelous," how "the bee's knees," how "the cat's meow" she was. They might even ask her to perform again, and Mrs. Caroline would realize that she ought to be a singer and not a comic.

She neared the top step, a pair of white shoes stepped down, and then she was in Claude Hopkins's arms, the bandleader's face so close she had to look away, not wanting to smear her lipstick. Her lips brushed his collar, just slightly. She saw the faintest, tiniest smudge of red, but when he let her go his shirt closed around his neck and there was nothing to see except his out-of-this-world handsome face: wavy hair, smooth skin, sensuous mouth that could kiss her until she turned to cream, heavy-lidded eyes telling her all the things he wanted to do to her right here and now.

"You look delicious in that red dress," he said, smacking his lips. "I ought to carry you back to your room right now and eat you up."

She lowered her head and pushed past him. "It's not a *room*. It's a *berth*."

The first-class dining salon, on the other hand, ought to be called a palace, with its domed, elaborately painted ceiling rising above an enormous, red-carpeted room with marble walls and a balcony running all around. There were white-clothed tables and green chairs upstairs and down, glowing sconces on the walls, and plants filling the room with more green. Josephine found Mrs. Caroline at the front of the room, on the small stage before a wooden dance floor, with Spencer Williams, the stocky piano player, and the baby-faced Sidney Bechet, who played clarinet and saxophone.

Dismay flattened Mrs. Caroline's tiny face when she saw Josephine. Her argument with Sidney came to a screeching halt as her mouth dropped open.

"How are you going to dance in that dress?" she said.

Josephine felt Claude on her neck like a hot breath. "I'm not dancing, ma'am. I'm singing. Claude and I have been working something up, and Sidney."

Mrs. Caroline looked up at Claude.

"We're doing 'Brown Eyes,' " he mumbled.

"Josephine. I had hoped this performance might inspire the audience members to come to our show."

"Yes, ma'am," she said.

Mrs. Caroline fingered the pearls circling her throat, giving Josephine a long look that she couldn't quite decipher. Josephine looked right back, unintimidated by the diminutive, doll-like woman.

She sighed. "Fine, Miss Josephine — you

finally get your way." Her expression hardened, though, before she turned back to Sidney and Spencer.

When the show began, Mrs. Caroline took the microphone and introduced Josephine Baker, one of the "stars" of the new Paris musical *Le Revue Nègre,* "making her singing debut." She did not sound enthusiastic. Josephine rankled: was she trying to hex the performance? Then Claude began at the piano, and Sidney blew his horn, and Josephine forgot all about Mrs. Caroline as she stepped onto the stage and began to sing. "Teardrops in the light, in your eyes so bright, just like raindrops in the window pane." How she loved this song!

But something was off. A ruddy-faced man at a front table lit a cigar; the smoke puffed into her face, nearly making her sneeze. She snapped her fingers, trying to get the beat — where was it? Her voice cracked. Someone laughed; she followed the noise and saw two women chatting as though she weren't even there. Soon everyone was talking. Josephine raised her voice, singing another off note that Sidney covered up with playing so good people began tapping their feet to the beat that Josephine had finally found, but then the song was over, and the music stopped, and the silence that followed rang more loudly than any applause.

The man with the cigar puffed away. His wife smiled blankly. Josephine wanted to cross her eyes, but how would that look in her slinky red dress? Not funny at all. Sad.

Could they hear her heart beating like it wanted to jump out of her chest and run away? Dazed, she looked at Claude, who began the next song, a peppy tune. Louis Douglas's little girl, Marion, whom Josephine had taught to dance the Charleston, got excited and ran out to join her on the stage. Why didn't her daddy call her back? The crowd applauded as the girl danced, knobby knees, white anklet socks, patent-leather shoes, her arms waving in a blur. Josephine knew she should dance with her, the audience would like that — but how, in this dress? Instead, she sang more forcefully, her voice warmed up, now, but no one was looking at her, they were watching the five-year-old. They wouldn't notice if Josephine walked off the stage, which she felt tempted to do. Mrs. Caroline stood at the bar talking behind her hand to Maud de Forrest, that old drunkard who'd looked down her nose at Josephine for begging to sing just one song. Both of them were eyeing her, Maud smirking and Mrs. Caroline's lips twitching in a shit-eating grin.

Mrs. Caroline knew this would happen. The realization hit Josephine in the chest so hard she couldn't find her breath for a minute, but then she ended the song with a long, low note, and little Marion bowed, taking all the love that should have been Josephine's. Marion's eyes shone as she skipped off the stage with her hand in Josephine's. Josephine remembered being her age, dancing on Market Street outside the Rosebud Cafe, Tom Turpin inside playing ragtime on the upright piano, Mexican Robert on the sidewalk playing his harmonica, Uncle Joe spinning her around, and Miss Sweety clapping her hands while Josephine did the Mess Around, the Shim Sham, and the Tacky Annie all at the same time, pennies falling at her feet, people calling her name, "Do it, Tumpy! Look at that girl go." Little Marion's daddy was a dancer; she'd be one, too, now.

Louis Douglas went on next, dancing while Maud sang, her raspy voice lubricated by the gin she'd started drinking as soon as they hit international waters. Josephine took the girl to bed, ignoring the narrowed eyes of Claude's wife, Mabel, and her friends. They were jealous, Mabel that Claude loved *her,* and the rest, because among the dancers, she, Josephine, was the only star.

"Just because she can cross her eyes and wiggle that ass. What kind of talent does that take?"

"She doesn't even do the steps. Just flaps her arms and crosses her eyes like somebody with no brain."

"Ever hear her talk? She ain't got no sense."

Oh, the chorus could be awful, brutal, everyone scratching to climb that ladder with so little room on each rung, clawing at one another, trying to push everybody else down as they strove for the top. Josephine didn't need to play that game. She danced her own dances, and people loved her: nobody could take that away. These girls would love to see her cry after tonight's humiliation, her head hanging down, her lips pooched out and quivering. Instead, she walked back into the lounge like the star she reminded herself she was, the star of *Le Revue Nègre,* chic and elegant and beautiful in her Tappé gown and diamond earrings and dancer's body.

She moved through the crowd gracefully, smiling as though she had triumphed, but no one would meet her eyes, not even Claude, who stood at the bar with Mabel and her friends; certainly not Maud, who murmured, "She set you up," as Josephine passed her table; not the dancers she liked, Evelyn and Mildred, sipping Coca-Colas and whispering to each other; not even Sidney, drinking a beer and sliding his gaze to the floor rather than look at Josephine.

Tears came to her eyes, and she blinked once, twice, and saw Mabel standing before her, arms folded.

"You stay away from my husband," she said. Bea Foote and Marguerite Ricks, her cronies, came to stand with her, their arms crossed, too, loyal to the bandleader's wife who'd gotten them their jobs.

"You'd better talk to Claude about that."

"I'm talking to *you.*" Mabel's voice rose. Josephine could feel people onstage and off-looking at them now. "You stay away from Claude, or I'll fix your ass."

Josephine laughed. "A few no-talent chorus dancers can't hurt me. I'm the star of this show."

"You'll be the star of nothing if we all quit. We'll go back to New York and take our husbands with us. I'll take Claude. Without a bandleader, you've got no show."

Josephine turned to Claude, who shrugged. Shrugged! All his good looks and sexiness drained away. "Claude? Didn't he tell you? I already ditched his ass. I'm through." She cocked an eyebrow at Mabel. "Don't worry, I left some for you."

She turned, her temples throbbing, a headache coming on. She walked as if she had all day to the piano, where Caroline stood talking to Spencer Williams as he ran his fingers over the keys.

"How could you do that to me?" she said in a low voice. Spencer began to play a song.

Caroline acted like she didn't know what Josephine was talking about. She'd wanted to sing, hadn't she? She flicked her cigarette over an ashtray. Josephine felt tempted to knock the burning thing from her hand.

"You're fixing to kill me."

"Ah, my dear, I don't think you need my help for that."

"You set me up."

Yes, the woman said, she supposed she had. "I wanted you to realize where your talents truly lie."

The weight of tonight's failure crashed down upon Josephine. No one had clapped. They had just sat there, their hands fidgeting, their eyes looking past her, searching for the next act.

"I'm going home," she said, trembling. "I'm headed back to New York tomorrow."

"That's fine." Again, she flicked her ash as if she had not a care in the world. "But we are in the middle of the Atlantic Ocean. You will have to wait until the ship docks at Cherbourg. I will pay for your return journey."

Adrenaline flooded her body, making her heart race. This was not the response she had expected. After her performance tonight, Mrs. Caroline now wanted to get rid of her. Pricked, she felt all her pride seep away. Her shoulders drooped, and tears filled her eyes. Did she have any talents?

"Why did you choose me, Mrs. Caroline?" Josephine sniffled, and brushed away a tear. "Why did you want me to come with you?"

"I chose you because you can dance," Mrs. Caroline said. "And because you are beautiful. My God, look at you tonight! You have a chic that will amaze even the Parisians. And you are funny. People love you, you make them laugh."

"But I want to sing."

Caroline shook her head. "Maud is our singer. You are a dancer, and a brilliant one. And you are our clown. *There* is where your talents lie, Josephine. Do not forget that."

"But I want to sing," she said again, and Mrs. Caroline laughed.

"See what I mean, Spencer?" she said to the piano player. "She's a natural comic."

"I want to yo-o-odel," he sang, winking at

Josephine. "Can you yodel, gal?"

She didn't want to, but she tried, her voice sounding choked, blocked by all the feelings stuffed there.

"You can do better than that!" he said.

She tried again, and her voice trilled. Still playing, he made up a verse: "I love dance time, dance-y dance time."

The music lured her; she took a step toward him, then another, and then she was shuffling, snapping her fingers, gliding to stand beside the piano and sing with him. Here was a song for her — "I want to yodel" — and she yodeled again, strong and pure and laughing. She saw the white people looking at her and did a little dance, and applause rang into the air, a struck bell — clangy-clang bell — and she yodeled and crossed her eyes. Shouts and cheers clamored into the infinite night; they loved her at last. She lifted her dress and hitched up her bottom and danced in earnest, kicking and wriggling and swinging her arms. The people cried out, *her* people, now, making a great noise to scatter the starry stars and send tremors through the ocean all the way to Gay Paree.

CHAPTER 9

1925, Paris

Listen to those Frenchmen argue! Lord, if they didn't love to hear themselves holler, louder and louder, faster and faster, all trying to outtalk one another, voices and hands rising, and what about?

"The jungle." M. Jacques-Charles, standing on the stage in the Théâtre des Champs-Élysées, lifted a fistful of feathers from a cardboard box. "Parisians want the jungle." The dancer he had brought in, Joe Alex, the blackest man Josephine had ever seen, had barely taken his eyes off her. The first thing he did when he saw her looking was shrug off his long-sleeved shirt and flex the muscles rising on his arms like mountain ranges. In the stage lights, his skin shone as he pointed to her again.

And then Mrs. Caroline gasped and clasped her hands to her chest, looking at

Josephine like she'd just seen a heavenly vision.

"*Oui*," she said. *"C'est parfait."*

"You are going to save us," she said to Josephine. The theater's owner, M. Rolf de Maré, and his friend M. Jacques-Charles disliked Maud's song at the end of the show. Parisians wanted to leave with their spirits lifted, not be put to sleep, they'd told Mrs. Caroline. They wanted a big finale — with Josephine at the center.

M. Jacques-Charles had come today to fix the "terrible chaos" of *La Revue Nègre:* its "too much tap dancing," which the French disdained; its light-skinned cast that would disappoint a city expecting "real Negroes"; and its preponderance of ballads. "You will bore them to death," he had said, and vowed to rechoreograph the entire revue in less than forty-eight hours. In ten days they would perform the dress rehearsal, to which the crème de la crème of Parisian society and the most eminent critics had been invited. And M. Jacques-Charles seemed not at all concerned about whether they could do it.

Mrs. Caroline, on the other hand, had gotten all ruffled up, her face red and her voice saying *non, non* as she argued in rapid French. *Monsieur* lifted from the box a fancy, velvet tricorn hat with a long white feather. He paired it with some overalls, grinning at Caroline, who rolled her eyes. Josephine and her fellow cast members huddled at the back of the stage like cattle in a pen.

None of them except Louis Douglas could understand a word of what they said, so as the three men and one woman bickered, he translated. Mainly, the Frenchmen thought *La Revue Nègre* stank to high heaven. Josephine had already figured this out: M. de Maré had rudely held his nose while they'd run through the show the night before.

Earlier, as they'd assembled for today's rehearsal — the musicians tuning their instruments, the dancers stretching, Josephine bending and twisting her body into provocative shapes, tilting her ass in Claude's direction and bending over to show her cleavage, reminding him of what he was missing — Mrs. Caroline had walked onto the stage and announced that M. de Maré was going to make some changes. In a few minutes he would arrive with his friends, including M. Jacques-Charles and a new dancer, from Nigeria.

"What do we need a new dancer for?" Josephine said.

"They want more . . . color," Caroline

said. *Too dark?* Not for them. The French were not interested in Negroes who looked white. *Vive la différence:* They wanted *exotique.*

Josephine's heart beat a little faster. They were cutting out most of Maud de Forrest's songs and, now, they were adding a dancer. That must mean they wanted her to sing! She saw herself on the stage in her red silk dress, draped in feathers and jewels, singing "Brown Eyes," the audience cheering and shouting for more.

"They want you to wear these feathers," Caroline said.

On her head? As a necklace? Josephine eyed the paltry bunch. From the back of the stage, she heard laughter. "Necklace, my ass," Mabel said.

"You are to wear *only* these, my dear. Feathers around your waist and nothing more, like savages in the African jungle."

Josephine took the feathers in her hands, wondering how they would cover her.

"Naked?" Josephine said. "They want me to dance with no clothes on except these feathers?"

"They want you to dance in them, with Joe Alex. The choreographer will create *La Danse de Sauvage,* the 'Savage Dance.' " French people were different from Americans, Mrs. Caroline said, as if Josephine had not already noticed this. "They are not so prudish about the human body. Women have been appearing topless in the dance halls for many years. But never a Negro. You will be the first!"

Josephine broke out in a sweat all over. "I ain't a stripper, missus."

M. Jacques-Charles said something in French, gesturing toward her.

"*Monsieur* wants you to remove your blouse," Caroline said. Josephine crossed her arms over her chest, her face burning.

"Choose somebody else," she said. "Please."

"The others are too light-skinned. They want *you*, Josephine."

Mrs. Caroline begged, and Joe Alex pled, and M. de Maré threatened to send her home unless she did what he commanded. Everybody watched her, including the musicians in the orchestra pit, even Sidney — everyone except Claude, who wouldn't meet her eyes. Was he feeling guilty for making her sleep with ghosts while he spent his nights in that sleazy brothel on the rue Pigalle? She'd slipped out after him and followed him there, had seen three white girls — two skinny ones with bad teeth and one with a butt as big as a mule's — welcome him at the door, greeting him by name like he was a cherished return customer. Had he forgotten the contours of her body, the breasts he compared to sweet apples, her perfect ass? Now was as good a time as any to remind him. Keeping her eyes on Claude, she whipped off her shirt and unclasped her bra, and let it all hang out.

One of the Frenchmen blew out his breath, as though the room had suddenly grown hot. Not knowing what to do with her arms — she wanted to cover her chest, but not from Claude, whose eyes were, now, just where she wanted them to be — she held them stiffly at her sides. In the auditorium, a man she hadn't noticed before sprang to attention in the fifth row, his eyes alert and focused on her body and his hand moving a pencil across a sketchpad in broad, bold strokes. Josephine forgot about Claude. Each mark the artist made enlivened her, as if he were caressing her skin. Her nipples hardened. She thrust out her chest and arched her back, posing. If she had to do this thing, she might as well make the most of it. The men talked excitedly, waving their arms. Joe Alex smiled at her, big white teeth ready to eat her up.

"Good, Josephine, good!" Caroline said. "Do you hear what they are saying? *Parfait.*

That means perfect. You've got the finale — congratulations, my dear. You will be a sensation — the first Negro to dance nude on the stage in Paris. The first in the world!"

Dance nude? Josephine shivered, suddenly cold. Forgetting the man with the pencil, she covered herself again.

"But — I'm a comic, miss. A clown? Remember?"

"Yes, you are. You will make them laugh, yes, even as they are adoring your wonderful dancer's body. They will desire and love you — and so, perhaps, the inflammatory Parisians will not riot. Although, if they did, that would be good for us, too.

"My God, Josephine, I hope those are tears of joy on your face! Because you are on your way to stardom, just the way you wanted."

On opening night she was a mess, worried that she might pass out the minute she appeared on that stage wearing almost nothing, praying the black paper cap glued to her head wouldn't fall off when Joe Alex lifted her onto his shoulders, turned her upside down, and began the Savage Dance. But if she hadn't fainted by now on such an awful day, she probably wouldn't.

She'd woken up with a shriek, the Mary's

Congolese left on too long, the dream of her hair on fire all too real. She'd run to the bathroom and fallen on her knees in the tub, sobbing under the running water as hair stuck to her hands in thick, wet clumps. Afterward, she screamed at her reflection in the mirror: What little hair remained frizzed in thin tufts around great bald patches.

She yanked a towel off the hook and wrapped it around her head. How could she have fallen asleep? She barely remembered lying down. Now, the clock on her bedside mocked her: in just a few hours, she'd have to go onstage looking like a badly plucked chicken.

Her roommate Lydia yawned in the doorway, saying she needed to pee. Josephine whipped off the towel, waiting for her response, but Lydia only asked her to hush so she could go back to sleep.

"Look at me," Josephine wailed. "I'm ruined." Lydia's face pinched itself together.

"If you hadn't stayed out so late this wouldn't have happened. *I* went to bed early. You should have, too, instead of gallivanting all over Paris with that artist."

Stung, Josephine formed a retort, *We didn't gallivant anywhere except between his sheets,* but it wasn't true, she and Paul Colin had gone to so many parties she'd lost count. She had slept with him, but it was nothing worth boasting about; she'd done it only out of revenge. She didn't normally go for bland-faced little men in round glasses, but Paul was a popular artist now, celebrated for the posters he'd drawn of her dancing nude. He would make her famous, he'd told her, but she knew it was the other way around.

Paul had taken her to meet every celebrity in the city, it seemed, his mouth shaping too many names for her to remember: Picasso, Man Ray, Cornelius Vanderbilt, Anna Pavlova, Mistinguett. She'd remember Mistinguett, of course, the star of the Casino de Paris. Paul had taken her to see the city's favorite lily-white dance-hall star perform to a theater full of whites who'd thrown flowers onto the stage and would have kissed her little feet if she'd offered them. Josephine could see why she was popular, the way she used her eyes as though every person she looked at were alone with her. "A great beauty," Paul had murmured as she took her bows, but Josephine couldn't agree. Her red hair was striking and her mile-high legs looked like they'd been sculpted from pale marble, but she was on the downhill side of her prime, her face starting to bulge and sag like dough left to rise too long.

"Mistinguett is the biggest star in Paris," Paul said as he introduced them backstage. The women looked down her nose at Josephine, who decided to take her down a notch.

"Not for long," Josephine said.

Mistinguett's face turned sour. Josephine had made an enemy, but she didn't care. Soon Paris would be at *her* feet, and Mistinguett would be a nostalgic memory of lace dresses and silly, girlish hats, and the occasional, titillating flash of leg. She had insured those legs for five hundred thousand francs, but Josephine's would be worth more, and also her ass and her *nichons,* her entire body revered along with, someday, her singing.

Paul was doing everything he could to help her succeed, including making sure she met the right people. He'd hitched his wagon to her star, knowing that she could make him a fortune. After that rehearsal when she'd first danced nude, he'd invited her to his studio to pose. She hadn't wanted to go, not alone, but Mrs. Caroline had encouraged her, saying it was all right, that he was the official artist hired to promote *Le Revue Nègre.*

She'd only been there a few minutes when

he'd told her, in French, to remove her clothes. She'd said no at first, and had started to leave; she'd seen that look in enough eyes to know what he had in mind. But he'd just kept babbling as though she'd agreed, as though a shake of the head meant yes in his language. He'd drawn a picture of a naked woman dancing and held it up for her to see, his voice rising with exclamations. Then he went to the far corner and opened up a phonograph and put on a record. The song "Copenhagen" transported her back to New York, where she had danced to Fletcher Henderson's orchestra, the clarinets and the cornets and the drums and the slide trombone moving her every which way, her shoes coming off, her feet slapping the floor, her dress too tight so that came off, too, until the next thing she knew every stitch of her clothing had fallen to the floor except her underwear. Paul reached out and unsnapped her bra with a flick of his wrist, and it slid to the floor. Then he'd picked up his pencil and drawn her for hours while she danced.

But she had not let him make love to her until last night.

He'd tried, she had to give him that, plying her with gifts, with introductions, with parties at the homes of rich people. Confused by the babble of words she could not understand, she'd spent most of those evenings at the food table, eating fish roe on little pieces of toast, meaty little frogs' legs, snails in butter, raw oysters, great chunks of lobster, until Paul would drag her away to meet someone new. At one soiree, in a gold-and-white penthouse apartment overlooking the Seine, the fashion designer Paul Poiret, full of himself in his goatee and pink silk necktie, had offered to make a dress for her — and Paul the artist had bowed as though the man were God Almighty. At Gertrude Stein's stuffy parlor crammed with ugly paintings, Picasso, a rumpled man whose mismatched clothes begged for a consultation with Paul Poiret, had invited her to pose in his studio. The jealousy on Paul's face when she'd said yes! She hadn't even slept with him, yet he acted like he owned her.

Last night, after the dress rehearsal, Paul had taken her to the home of Maurice Chevalier, whose greasy smile made Josephine want to take a rag to his face. He'd played the piano and sung his hit song "Valentine" for his guests, winking at Josephine until Mistinguett, glaring, sprang to the top of the grand piano and lifted her skirts to dance. Afterward, M. Chevalier had talked about Hollywood, asking if Josephine had been there and surprised to hear her say no, as if California were a short jaunt from New York. He was hoping to go soon; his agent was trying to get him a starring role in a moving picture — and now Josephine was the jealous one. While he boasted, preening back his sand-colored hair, Mistinguett clung to him like a leech and warned Josephine with her eyes not to come one step closer.

Josephine shrugged it off. The woman had good reason to worry, old as she was getting to be. She had more years on her than Chevalier did, and they showed, while Josephine, at nineteen, had skin as smooth and taut as a young girl's. She didn't want the smarmy actor, anyway — a man so vain would have little to offer in the sack, and she meant *little*. When he kissed Josephine's hand and gave her naughty looks, she played bashful while Paul nearly had orgasms on the spot. Did she know the favors Maurice Chevalier could do for her? Of course, he would want something in return, every man did — waving his hands as if he felt silly for stating the obvious. Josephine didn't have to ask what *he* wanted, the way he strutted around with her on his arm as if he'd already had her, like he knew something

187

nobody else did.

He didn't know anything, though, not yet. Claude was giving her all the love she could handle. After she'd taken off her shirt for M. Jacques-Charles, Claude had come back to her with a face full of hunger, as she'd known he would. This time, though, he was serious. He'd left Mabel, now slept with Josephine every night, and was even talking about marriage — she hadn't told him about Billy. And speak of the devil, here came Claude, striding into the party in his white tux, turning heads, definitely the best-looking man in the room, better, even, than Chevalier. As she approached him, she felt her insides turn to butter.

"Fancy meeting you here," she said, giving him a wink. "This party is fun, but not as much fun as we're going to have later."

He cleared his throat. "Josephine, I meant to tell you sooner. But with the dress rehearsal tonight, and now this party, I just haven't had the chance."

"What's the matter, honey?" She touched his arm — and he drew away.

"I'm not — I mean to say, I'm back with Mabel."

Josephine put a hand to her chest and choked back the sob trying to break loose, the emerging sound like a strangled laugh.

"Well, if that ain't a hell of a note," she said. "You and Mabel together again, two peas in a fucking pod."

"We've known each other since we were kids, Josephine," he said, dropping his voice and testing the room with his eyes, wondering if anyone could hear.

"You're shitting me." She laughed out loud, breaking the French code of decorum — even at parties the noise level never rose above a murmur — and drawing looks of distaste as if she'd cut a brazen fart. Claude's own nostrils flared as he asked what was so damned funny.

"I've seen you buck naked, but I've just figured out that you don't have any balls," she cried. Would you look at all the raised eyebrows! *L'Américaine, si gauche,* she heard a woman mutter. Claude's frown deepened.

"Better thank the Lord for that," she said. "Because if you did have any, I'd plant my foot in them right now."

Claude slinked off to his precious Mabel while she laughed some more. Josephine knew she'd hurt him, but she didn't care: he deserved it. That's what she told herself while downing one glass after another of Chevalier's expensive champagne, willing herself to get drunk, not caring that opening night was less than twenty-four hours away. She was finished with men. Willie Wells, Billy Baker, Claude Hopkins — they were all losers, not worth the salt in her tears. Well, maybe Billy was. What was he doing now? Did he miss her?

An hour later she'd been rolling with Paul in his silk sheets, then taking a taxi at sunrise to Le Fouquet, her hotel, nearly falling asleep in the back seat. By the time she got to her room she was wide awake again, her aching head buzzing with memories of the night. Claude had looked right through her, as though he'd hadn't murmured his love into her ear just the night before, their bodies naked and slick and intertwined, and whispered promises: *I left her for you.*

She'd wanted only to crawl into bed and forget the whole stupid mess — but then she'd decided, for some drunken reason, to put straightener in her hair and, while waiting to rinse it out, had fallen asleep. Lydia was right, she was paying the price — but for what? She'd committed so many sins since arriving in Paris, she couldn't remember them all.

"Nobody wants to see a bald-headed gal on the stage, whether she's wearing clothes or not," she said, and Lydia laughed, thinking she was being funny, which made everything worse.

While Josephine wailed, Lydia called Mrs. Caroline, who called her beautician friend, André, "the best in Paris," a small, fussy man with mirthful eyes who made a paper cap and lacquered it black and glued it to her head. Voilà!

She danced and sang her way through *La Revue Nègre* to more applause than she'd ever heard in her life, all the way to the last dance, the Savage Dance, which would either make her famous or send her home to New York.

Joe Alex wriggled his eyebrows suggestively, obviously looking forward to their duet. Josephine peeked around the curtain for a look at the audience packing the rose-and-gold theater. The carved wooden chairs on the main floor were completely filled, although, while Maud warbled out her blues like somebody on the brink of death, she spotted several yawns and one white-haired man completely asleep. She heard throats clearing, even muted laughter in the front rows. The boxes on the second balcony, where the very rich sat, were mostly empty, their occupants having left the auditorium to smoke and drink on the mezzanine behind the velvet curtains, confirming M. Jacques-Charles's prediction that

Maud's ballads would bore them. People milled about on the first and third balconies, too, but the boxes on the very top, for poorer folk, looked crammed to the gills, their inhabitants craning their necks to see as much of the stage as they could. Josephine, remembering when she and her family could afford only the cheapest seats at the Booker T, made sure to do all her dancing where those people could see it.

The evening had also featured acrobats; a celebrity impersonator; a strongman spinning on his head and using his feet to twirl a merry-go-round bearing six flying trapeze artists; and the revue: Sidney playing the sax, a solo so winsome it brought tears to Josephine's eyes; Josephine and the chorus dancing the Charleston in grass skirts; Louis Douglas in blackface and a top hat holding a flower and singing "Columbine"; Josephine's "I Want to Yodel," her rolling her eyes and cracking her voice to make them laugh. How would they respond when she reappeared, naked and spread-eagled, on Joe Alex's shoulders?

Maud's song ended to polite applause. She waddled backstage muttering and made a beeline to the dressing room, where she'd hid a bottle under a pile of wigs. Who wouldn't want a slug after that dismal performance? Now *La Danse de Sauvage* would wake them up again — but how could she go through with it? The Lord would strike her dead on the stage. She turned to flee, but Joe Alex had come up behind and put his arm around her, leaving her no escape.

The drums began their hypnotic beat, drowning out her frantic heart's pounding. Joe, wearing little besides feathers himself, lifted her up and over his shoulders. He turned her upside down, and she draped herself over him, the back of her head resting on his chest, bare breasts facing the audience, her legs split apart. He lumbered onto the stage, carrying his captive slung across his shoulders. The breath of the gasping audience shot over her skin. She smelled heat, smoke, perfume, and, underneath it all, sex.

Using all her strength, she held herself in position as Joe rolled her off his shoulders and over his head, her legs wrapping his neck, her crotch now squarely in his face. In the audience, a woman screamed. Joe rolled her down and placed her on her feet, and she saw people scurrying toward the exits, fur-draped women dragging their reluctant husbands up the aisles and out the doors as the men craned their necks around for another look. Was this the riot Mrs. Caroline had so gleefully predicted?

The slow, suspenseful beat of the drum summoned her back to the performance. She crouched, parting her legs. The trombone uttered a long blast and the music erupted in a frenzy. Josephine forgot, then, that she stood all but naked before hundreds of staring eyes, forgot her denuded scalp and the paper cap clinging tenuously to the few tendrils of hair she had left, forgot the treacherous Claude at the piano watching her slither and slide like a charmed serpent and lusting for her, or so she might hope if he were anywhere near her thoughts, but she had forgotten all except the music. It possessed her like a seizure, or a drug; it convulsed and flung her body.

She succumbed to the orchestra, the drums pounding her blood, stomping her feet, swinging her arms, the slide of Sidney's saxophone like a long sweet kiss over her skin, Claude's fingers on the keys playing her, too, more deftly than he'd ever done in bed, rolling her over, flailing her arms, oblivious, panting, laughing, dancing, *free.* And when it had ended, the final notes still tinkling the glass on the great chandelier illuminating the hall, she came back into herself and saw that everyone had stood, the audience bringing their hands together in a great crash of noise, cheering and shouting, raising their arms to her, their eyes shining, their mouths smiling.

Encore, the audience members shouted, tossing flowers at her, cheers surging and resurging like a wave that builds and builds and never crests.

"Thank you," she cried, and blew a kiss. "I love you all." And the wave crested again; it could carry her up to heaven, it felt like, but as she lifted her arms, the golden curtain dropped to the floor, and she found herself looking at Joe Alex, in whose sullen eyes she saw the bow they should have taken together.

Approaching her, M. Jacques-Charles tried to look stern, although the pleasure of success softened his face.

Did Josephine not see him gesturing? he asked. Had he not signaled for the curtain to fall she might have remained out there all night, capturing accolades until the audience fainted from exhaustion.

"Yes, sir," Josephine said. Meaning, yes, she would have. All night long.

CHAPTER 10

After the show, the theater crew set up a dinner party on the stage, sliding tables together end to end. Josephine and Claude and Sidney and Evelyn and Mildred and everybody else, all the colored singers and dancers and musicians and clowns, sat blinking their eyes at one another, incredulous, this the first time any of them had shared a table with white people.

Where had she learned to dance like that? asked M. Paul Derval, manager of the Folies-Bergère theater, a gray-haired man with a plump belly whose lips seemed always about to smile.

"You have no inhibition," he said. "You are wild, a — how do you say? — a true force of nature, *from* nature. When you dance, the audience sees one with the grace of a panther and the mischief of a monkey."

Josephine rankled: she knew what it meant when a white person called her monkey. But he went on: She seemed to have no bones. Was she double jointed? Where had she learned to dance that way?

She told him of her girlhood, the scene every Saturday outside the Rosebud Café, where those who couldn't pay to get in danced on the sidewalk and in the street. The Chestnut Valley was Josephine's church, music halls and brothels and taverns, music rolling out of every window, horns and banjos and fiddles and washboards and soup pots, music coming from snapping fingers and clicking tongues and stamping feet and voices singing, shouting, whistling, whooping, filling the air with melody and syncopated rhythms and happiness and jazz.

"Where was this? In New Orleans?" he said.

She mentioned Saint Louis, and the monsieur's face went blank. "Missouri," she added, and he drew his eyebrows together. These names meant nothing to the French, he told her. "It would be better if you said you are from New Orleans."

"My mama taught me not to lie," she said.

"When one is a performer, one trades in illusion."

"Dancing in nothing but a feather felt pretty real to me."

"Do you think we came here tonight in a search for truth?" he said. "After the war, we have become weary of reality. We do not know anymore what is true. Or, whatever it may be, we long to escape from it. If you want to be a star, mademoiselle" — he tapped his soup spoon against her bowl, as if to command her attention — "do not give us truth. Give us fantasy."

"I was raised in New Orleans, yes, by a . . . Creole mama who was a blues singer and a daddy from . . . Spain who danced and played the guitar," she said. "He taught me to dance when I was little, and took me on-stage with him sometimes. I loved him so much." She brushed away an imaginary tear.

M. Derval leaned toward her, his shrewd dark eyes bright as a bird's. "What happened to him?"

"He died," she blurted. "He was . . . killed, the victim of a, a . . . love triangle. The jealous drummer shot him right before my eyes." Her voice faltered — she was really getting choked up.

"The musicians of New Orleans took care of us. My mother had to get a job as a washerwoman, so they took me under their wing. I grew up dancing to their songs, and I've danced ever since in my daddy's memory. Every dance I perform is really for him." She lowered her eyes. "Except for today. That dance, I did for Paris."

"Voilà." M. Derval clapped his hands together. *"Parfait."*

Josephine laughed. With one phony story, she'd erased her past and created a new one. Just like that!

A waiter filled their glasses with champagne, and M. Jacques-Charles stood to propose a toast. "To *La Revue Nègre,* the new Paris sensation." But before the glasses could clink, M. Derval leaped to his feet and added, "And to the biggest scandal of them all, our city's new *nudiste,* Josephine Baker."

Josephine took a sip of the golden liquid, which tasted like magic bursting on her tongue. This "being famous" stuff was already a lot more fun than she'd imagined.

When she walked into *Le Rat Mort* a few nights later, everything stopped: the drunken writer's crude joke, told to a tableful of drunken writers; a railroad baron's hand sliding up his mistress's thigh in a private booth; the sexy dance-floor tango between a tuxedo-wearing woman and her buxom blond partner; the tug of the cork from the Prince of Wales's bottle of champagne. Even the music took a breath at the sight of Josephine blazing through the door, her hand in the crook of Paul Colin's arm, her pink dress shimmying with every step like a candle flame, as though she were on fire.

"Josephine!" the sexy American writer Hemingway called out. "Are you going to dance for us tonight?"

"You know it, sugar lips, I'll be dancing all over *you* by the time the night is through."

She shrugged off her fur stole, and the writer caught it, to her surprise as well as Joe Alex's, who'd been reaching for it — neither the first nor the last time he'd be disappointed tonight. Now, here came the prince, his eyes eager — not for her, but for Claude, who looked like handsome was made for him in his white tux, his skin like milk and honey. Mabel cut her eyes at Josephine and clutched her husband's arm like he might fly away, which he might, given how he smiled back at the prince. But he'd never leave Mabel, he was too much of a coward to be on his own. Not Josephine — she embraced life!

She released Paul's arm to stride ahead of the *La Revue Nègre* musicians and dancers walking into the club, spreading her arms wide to accept her acclaim, basking in the sound of her name echoing through the room. On the floor, she lifted her skirt to free her legs, generating whistles and cat-calls. "Get a load of those gams," a white man shouted. She wiggled her behind and a drum roll sounded, and cheers filled the room — cheers for her, a poor Negro kid with buck teeth and knobby knees! *Too dark, too ugly.* Not for Paris, she wasn't.

The house musicians set down their instruments and left the floor, making room for Sidney and Claude, who, with Josephine, had sent the house into an uproar the night before. She wasn't waiting for them, though, but danced to the song playing in her head while Claude headed for the piano, Sidney to the saxophone, and the prince to the drums. They launched into the song she was thinking of, all one with her, the players and the played. The music moved her, her muscles limbered up from tonight's show. It had been standing-room-only again, Sidney's horn drawing wild applause, Louis's song of longing evoking tears, the Savage Dance sending her audiences into paroxysms of lust and fear. People running for the door like she was the devil. Now, in the club, she bared her teeth for them and rolled her eyes like a demon, and danced.

And when they were finished, Sidney's notes rolling across the room like a sigh, she lifted her arms and they cheered, and she bowed all the way down to the floor and rose again, blowing kisses, calling, *Merci! Merci beaucoup!*

She stepped into the crowd again, cutting like a shark through the white-faced sea. *"Bonsoir,* monsieur, you haven't seen our show yet? Yes, it is sold out for two weeks but I will put your name on the list for front-row seats. Bring your wife! Oh, you have no wife? You want to marry me? Thank you for the invitation, I will consider it, maybe, perhaps, *peut-être."*

Peut-être had become her favorite word. She'd said it tonight to the blond youth who had sat in the front row at every performance. A pretty boy with blue eyes, he'd waited outside for her, stood on the edge of the crush of fans, and pouted his pretty lips until she'd noticed him, hers for the taking like a sweet peach dangling from a tree, never any question in her mind about whether she ought to pluck it. *Tomorrow,* she said, *peut-être.*

Now, as she moved through the club among the tables and the cloistered, curtained booths, collecting accolades, grasping hands — it still astonished her that these white folks *wanted* to touch her — Josephine scanned the crowd for Paul Colin, her escort tonight. Where had he gone? Although surrounded by adoring faces, she'd never felt so alone. Who among all these people was her friend, wanting nothing from her except herself? There was Sidney, but he'd taken to the French bottle like a fish deprived of water, and his sloppy drunkenness irritated her as a terrible waste. He was sitting with Claude and Mabel and their bunch, anyway. They wouldn't welcome her, and good riddance: she'd rather have her tongue cut out than speak with any of them.

But why fuss over a man she couldn't have? She ought to enjoy what was, now, hers — what she had wanted all her life. *We love you,* magnifique, belle, *superb*! Josephine wished she could fill a bathtub with that praise and immerse herself; roll in a field of it, covering herself with the fragrance; pour it down her throat and into her belly, slaking her hunger at last. *Peut-être.*

She spied her escort at the table with M. Derval, the manager of the Folies-Bergère theater whom she'd met at *La Revue Nègre's* opening night dinner. She'd hoped to stir his desire, for to sleep with one of the most important people in Paris could only work to her advantage — but he'd spoken only of the theater and show business. Now the linger of his gaze on her chest made her smile. It was only a matter of time.

"I see that you have brought a friend," he said, touching his throat. Josephine realized what he'd been staring at: the little snake she had curled about her neck, which, now that she had stopped dancing, was sleeping against her warm skin. Had M. Derval even noticed the dangerously low neckline, nearly to her navel, of her new Paul Poiret gown? The designer had brought it himself to her room today. It was a beautiful creation, covered in fringe, light pink at the top and deepening as it cascaded down to a rich rose.

"I heard he's all washed up," the jealous Maud de Forrest had said when M. Poiret had gone. "Now he wants to ride your coat-tails back to the promised land of fame." Josephine did not tell Maud that *she* had, in fact, designed this dress. Mrs. Caroline had taken her to an international exposition on the Seine where M. Poiret's designs had filled three barges. He'd strutted like an overstuffed peacock in his shiny silver vest and brightly checked necktie and waved his ringed hands as he'd exulted over her, "begging," she could have told Maud, "to design my clothes." But as his models trotted out one outfit after another — loose harem pants, a kimono-style dress that reminded her of potato sacks — she'd nearly put a kink in her neck from shaking it so many times before asking for a pencil and sketching this design. He hadn't liked it, she could tell, it was too much like the flapper clothes he scorned, but he'd rearranged his expression to delight and said he adored it: he would add it to his Spring 1926 collection. She'd held her tongue about that to Maud, not wanting to increase her jealousy now that she was Josephine's roommate. The disapproving Lydia had found someone "more quiet" to room with — Maud's roommate — and moved out. Maud couldn't afford to live alone and spend a fortune on booze, too, and Josephine couldn't sleep in an empty room, so she forced herself to be nice. She'd do anything to avoid ghosts, even suck up to Maud.

"I am happy you could join us," M. Derval said as Paul Colin left the table, his sketchbook already open to draw the Fitzgerald woman, who turned her head this way and that and slurred, "Which is my good side? My left? I always preferred the right, it's more symmetrical." She knew he'd walked away because M. Derval had shifted his focus to her. Paul didn't like to be ignored. He would be petulant for the rest of the evening. Why did she put up with that crap? Few things were worse than a pouting Frenchman! "I made you famous," he'd said to her — what a load of bull. She didn't owe him a damned thing. His posters might have drawn people to her shows at first, but Josephine's endless days and nights of work kept them coming back. Does the candle owe its flame to the one who lit it, or to the fine wax that forms it?

"Let me introduce you to my wife," M. Derval said, gesturing toward a dark-haired woman sitting on his other side, "and to Bricktop, your competition, just returned from a tour in Barcelona."

"*Not* your competition," Bricktop said. "You wouldn't catch me dancing naked in a million years." Josephine took in her red hair, not shining and golden like Mistinguett's but wiry and the color of bricks; her freckled face; her short, pudgy body. Who would want to see her naked?

Bricktop gave her a shrewd look. "You've got it, honey. I don't have your . . . daring."

Josephine crossed her eyes. "This is all it takes," she said. Everyone laughed.

Across the table, an elegant, curly-haired man in a tux and top hat made love to her with his blue eyes, as did the wild-haired older woman in a green silk sheath beside him.

"Meet Marcel Ballot, the automaker and race-car driver." M. Derval continued the introductions, "and Colette, France's greatest woman writer and most notorious lover." Josephine widened her eyes: the woman had to be fifty, at least, her amber cloud of hair streaked with silver, her lovely, long neck beginning to crease, tiny lines radiating from her mouth, bleeding her red lipstick. Colette read her thoughts, and leered.

"France's most notorious lover? *She's* my competition, M. Derval," Josephine said, making everyone, including Colette, laugh again.

M. Derval placed his hand on her arm, drawing her attention. "I saw your performance again tonight. *Fantastique!* We must talk. May I come to your dressing room tomorrow?"

Josephine widened her eyes. Was he propositioning her in front of his wife? She glanced at Mme. Derval.

"This is business," he said. "I want to do a show at the Folies-Bergère — with you as the star."

"*La Revue Nègre* is headed to Berlin in a few weeks," she said. "Then we're off to Russia. When that's over, I'm as free as a bird." The letter she'd received from Billy last night made her pang — *Hurry home, baby, my arms are aching for you, and I haven't laughed since you left* — but she brushed away that thought. She had to seize every chance that came her way while she was here, because there was nothing — nothing — for her in the States. Well, except for Billy. But if she made it big in Paris, he could join her here.

"My schedule is inflexible," he said. "You will need to choose."

"Berlin?" Colette shook her head. "I would not advise it."

"I've heard it's a lot of fun."

"It used to be. But I was there a few months ago, and things are getting weird," Bricktop said. "That Hitler fellow got out of prison last December, and his flunkies are going around like cops in their brown uniforms harassing people."

"My friend M. Jacques-Charles has read Hitler's book," M. Derval said. "It is the rantings of a madman, he said, full of hatred against Jews and Negroes." He gave Josephine a pointed look.

"Berlin is changing," Colette said, motioning for another bottle of champagne. "The last time we were there, some of Hitler's guys called my lover Maurice a *Juden* and shoved him off a moving streetcar. It may be worse for you and your friends."

"We are American Negroes," Josephine said. "There's nothing they could do to us that we haven't already suffered a thousand times."

"And there is your reason to remain in Paris, *non*?" said M. Derval. "We do not discriminate against the races here. Why would you want to leave?"

"That's easy." Josephine rubbed her fingers together. "Money."

"You of all people cannot argue with that, Paul," Mme. Derval said, laughing.

M. Derval's lips twitched as Josephine arose from her chair, but his eyes remained serious.

"We will talk tomorrow," he said.

"Don't forget your checkbook, M. Derval," Bricktop said, winking at Josephine. "I think you will need it."

"How is it that you and I have just met," Josephine said to her, "and you know me so well?"

CHAPTER 11

1926, Berlin

If Paris was a woman, with her gilded bridges and ornate buildings like jewelry boxes, Berlin was most decidedly a man. Even the *Berolina* statue in the Alexanderplatz, buxom and beefy, exuded a masculine quality. The Nelson-Theater, too, came as a study in contrasts: rather than a pretty showplace like the Théâtre des Champs-Élysées or the Folies-Bergère, the corner brownstone on a tree-lined boulevard didn't even look like a theater. The glass-topped atrium out front gave it the appearance of a restaurant or café, instead.

In front of the building, people crowded the patio, autograph seekers and journalists as well as men in brown uniforms handing out fliers and glaring at the *La Revue Nègre* cast members as they emerged from their bus. Some of the men began to shout as Caroline ushered the group to the stage

210

door around the corner from the main entrance. When Josephine asked what the men were saying, Caroline replied that she didn't know, but it wasn't good.

"I only hope they do not plan to disrupt tonight's performance."

Josephine worried about this possibility for just a moment, then brightened. If the men did come tonight, she'd give them her special attention, winning them over the way Miss Clara had done the men in her audiences, by going down into the seats to sing especially to them. She'd make funny faces, and they'd soften up: you couldn't dislike someone who made you laugh. Mrs. Caroline would be grateful to her for making *La Revue Nègre* a success in Berlin — and maybe she wouldn't be so mad when she found out what Josephine had decided to do.

Dancing that night in the intimate hall, dazzled by the uncommonly bright footlights, she couldn't see the auditorium or the audience. Were the men in brown uniforms there? Just in case, she gave her all and then some, opening her arms and crying out, *Ich liebe dich,* "I love you," at the end. Then, to her horror, a crowd rushed onto the stage. She cried out, but they snatched her up before she could run and lifted her onto their shoulders, hooting and hollering. She looked down and saw their smooth cheeks, their dancing eyes, their smiling faces full of joy: strapping blond boys, none wearing brown. As they carried her through the auditorium she heard cheers, and she arranged herself like royalty to wave and blow kisses and elude the hands grasping, always grasping, everyone wanting a piece of her — but without clothing, there was nothing for them to grab.

Afterward, she headed to her dressing room, where a reporter waited with questions about the protests she had encountered today. Had she felt afraid? Offended?

"I didn't understand a word," she said.

"They said you are *untermenschen*. Subhuman." Josephine flinched. "And immoral."

He was trying to rile her up, she could see it in the way he jabbed pen to notepad while she spoke, as though prodding a wound.

"Immoral? Me?" She gave a little laugh. "I rescued a puppy from a cardboard box today. Is there something wrong with that here?"

"They were talking about your nudity. They said you have no shame."

Josephine's hackles rose. Why should she be ashamed? Sure, she'd felt awful at first to have to stand before a crowd in barely a scrap of clothing, on display like her great-grandmother on the auction block. Josephine had heard the story many times, how Grandmama Elvira's mother had stood naked and chained while white people judged her flesh. One had pinched her nipple as he passed, and the auction master had told the man that if he bruised the merchandise, he'd have to buy it.

Josephine was "merchandise," too, she admitted that, but she was no slave, she had no chains binding her. She was a dancer, doing what she was meant to do with the body God gave her.

But she couldn't say all that, this man would quote only a few words and so she had to speak carefully. Her fans loved her nudity: she made them think of their childhoods, when nudity was innocent, natural, like Adam and Eve before the fall. They desired her because they imagined she was primitive, that her dance came from some African jungle or even from New Orleans instead of from Saint Louis, Missouri.

"I'm not immoral," she said. "I'm natural."

Inside her room, she opened the cage on her dressing table and pulled out her snake, which she had named Claude. It flicked its little tongue and she lifted its head to her cheek, letting it kiss her before she draped it about her throat. The serpent rested its head on her chest, calmed by the heat rising like steam from her body, and calming her, as well. It was a wonder that she didn't burst into flames; she never broke a sweat, no matter how hard she danced, just burned like a furnace until the fire went out, all night long until the dawn. That was why she kept herself apart from people, why she'd demanded her own dressing room. Folks thought she was unfriendly, but she was only reserving her energy for what she needed to do, for what she *had* to do. She couldn't trust people, anyway. They were two-faced, most of them, acting like they wanted to be her friend while they tried to figure how they could get something from her. Even in her mama's eyes, she was never worth more than the money she brought home. Josephine had sent her a check from Paris — what did Mama think of her now?

She hadn't responded to a single one of Josephine's letters. Willie Mae had written whole books, practically, telling her they were proud of her and asking when she was coming home. *Never,* Josephine would think, but then she'd read some news — Richard had gotten married and his wife was expecting a baby; Elvira had nearly died of dehydration and had to be hospitalized; automatic washing machines with wringers had put Aunt Jo's laundry out of business, and Mama had taken work as a house-cleaner on Westmoreland Avenue — and she'd feel empty inside, like her heart had a hole that only her family could fill. *Daddy has lost his mind, maybe for good, I don't know,* Willie Mae wrote. *He screamed so much that somebody called the police, and now he's in the asylum. I see him every few days, but he doesn't know me.* Their lives were the same chaotic mess as always.

A part of Josephine wished she could go back and fix everything, but she knew that was impossible. She'd be no good to any-body in Saint Louis. When she tried to imagine herself there, it felt like a bad dream. Her life in Europe, though, seemed just as unreal: the adoring crowds, the bow-ing servants, the eager faces of people beg-ging for her autograph, wanting their picture taken with her, Josephine Baker famous when, just a few months ago, she'd been invisible. Those people on the ship ignoring her while she sang, humiliating her — what did they think, now, when they saw her picture in the newspapers?

Josephine could hardly believe it, herself.

She felt like Cinderella, as if at any moment the clock would chime and her time would be up, the dream would end and she'd be back in New York or, worse, Saint Louis, a nobody with nothing.

She closed her eyes, banishing the thought. Success had not just happened. She'd worked hard for it. Tonight, the crowd had carried her like a hero: she'd conquered Berlin with a single performance. This was no dream.

She took a seat at her dressing table to touch up her makeup and gasped. In the mirror she saw a man behind her — wavy black hair, dark suit bearing the cut and weight of money — leaning against the wall. She leaped up, and whirled around to face him.

"Are you looking for someone?" She wondered if he could hear her banging heart. How had he gotten in?

A knock sounded on her door, and she yanked it open. A blushing youth thrust an armful of packages and flowers at her.

"Someone is in my dressing room!" she cried. She pointed to the man, and the boy's face brightened in a smile.

"Herr Reinhardt," he said, and bowed. Turning to Josephine, he blushed again, then rushed off with the tips of his ears as red as flames.

"Well, at least *someone* knows who you are," she said, closing the door.

"I do not know whether to pity the lad, or envy him," the man said. "Imagine coming to Josephine Baker's dressing room and having her answer in the nude! I thought he might faint, all his blood having rushed from one head to the other."

Josephine studied him, hair combed back in luxuriant waves, that beautiful mouth, deep-cleft chin, eyes like cobalt fire. She took a step toward him. The snake lifted its head.

"I am Max Reinhardt," the man said, exuding power. Mrs. Caroline had been all a-tither before the show, whispering, *Max Reinhardt is in the third row!* A famous director, she'd said, fanning herself with her hands, and Josephine could see why.

"That still doesn't explain what you're doing in my room."

"I am here to make you a star," he said.

Josephine laughed, giddy with choices already, *La Revue Nègre,* the Folies-Bergère, and now, Max Reinhardt.

"But I'm already a star." Would he kiss her with his luscious mouth? He shook her hand, and her spirits sank a little. She did not want to sleep alone again tonight. She slipped the snake back into its cage. "Did you see my ovation? Did you see how they carried me around?"

He lifted his eyebrows. "I saw a group of young men eager to set their hands upon your naked flesh."

"There's more to me than that, Mr. Reinhardt. In case you ain't noticed."

"I did notice — tonight and also when I saw *Shuffle Along* in New York. Anyone can take off her clothes and wiggle. It is a cheap entertainment." He raised his eyebrows. "But you are more than that, and, although you suspect it, you have not fully realized it yet. You have something special to give. And it is neither here" — he pointed to her breasts — "nor here" — to her crotch.

"I'm a dancer." She pulled on a robe. "I use my whole body."

"You do, and it is spectacular. The expressive control, the spontaneity of motion, the rhythm, the bright emotional color — these are your treasures. No, not yours only, these are American treasures, uniquely American, vulgar and powerful and true. In you, they come from here" — he pointed to her head — "and here" — to her heart. "With such control of the body, such pantomime, I believe I could portray emotion as it has never been portrayed."

218

What was he talking about? He wanted dance lessons? Charleston parties were all the rage in Paris — Bricktop had started giving them with her friend Cole Porter, and Josephine had done a few, too, teaching the steps to rich white folks with big bellies and trying not to laugh at them. Josephine couldn't picture this elegant man knocking his knees around and flapping his hands.

"Give me three years of your life," he said. "Enroll in my acting school at the Deutsches Theater, and when you are finished you will be the greatest comic actress ever known. I will make you a film star, with the entire world at your feet."

Her face larger than life on the screen, her name in marquee lights on Broadway, Hollywood producers begging her to be in their movies: the possibilities for this future rolled out like a red carpet. She could be a great actress, the best ever known, wasn't that what he had said? There was no such thing as a Negro movie star — but before Josephine, no colored women had danced naked on the stages of Europe, either. She would be the first. She'd be famous in America, too, and they'd love her so much they'd forget about her skin color. They'd love her for herself, because she made them laugh and cry, because she made them *feel,* like Gloria Swanson and Clara Bow. Josephine, an actress!

The only thing was, she wanted to sing.

He leveled those fiery eyes on her. "It will be a great opportunity for us."

She'd like an "opportunity" with him, all right. Look at him standing there like a mouthwatering treat, his expensive suit shimmering even in the thin gas light, his hair waving and curling like a dollop of meringue. She licked her lips and swayed toward him.

"I'll think about it," she said. She was already thinking, about her contract with Mrs. Caroline, to tour Russia next with *La Revue Nègre.* Then she thought of her contract with M. Paul Derval, to begin rehearsing for a new show at the Folies-Bergère in just a few weeks. Herr Reinhardt might be right: this might be a great opportunity, but he was wrong about the "us" part. Whatever Josephine did, she did for herself.

While she pondered his offer, she let him take her around the raucous, rambunctious city, even more exciting than Paris in some ways. Sure, men in brown tried to spoil the fun, even going into the clubs and drinking too much and interrupting the performances, but more pervasive were the all-night orgies, men with women, men with men, women with women, and people of indeterminate sex cramming all together like sardines. One night they'd gone to a "costume contest" that made Josephine giggle because nobody was wearing a stitch.

Everywhere they went, Herr Reinhardt introduced her as "my new star at the Deutsches Theater," even though Josephine hadn't said yes to him. When she'd gone into the Nelson to perform her second show, she'd heard Mrs. Caroline giving hell to the theater manager. "Those boys carted her around naked, touching her body while your security stood by with their heads up their asses. She is my star. You must protect her! If anything happens to Josephine, we are kaput." Josephine's conscience had panged like a plucked string.

Max was trying hard, though, she had to give him credit for that. After her final show one night, a friend of his, Ruth Landshoff, a beautiful dark-haired woman in a tux and top hat, took her to a dinner party to discuss a pantomime that her boyfriend wanted to write for Josephine. Max loved pantomimes, he considered it a "pure" art form, "stripping performance to its basic essence," whatever that meant. For the occasion, Josephine had changed into a vivid green

221

gown cut low in the back and an emerald-and-diamond necklace Max had given to her. "I want my stars to look like stars," he'd said. *My* star. The words thrilled her — but she reminded him that she hadn't decided, that if she broke her contract with *La Revue Nègre* the show would fold, putting everyone out of work.

"The show must go on — and it will," Max had said. "They will do fine without you. They can put your feathered skirt on another girl, and she will slide down Joe Alex's body, and everyone will love *her.*"

Josephine frowned. If that was how he saw things, then why did he want her for his theater?

"I see your potential, Josephine — potential that you are wasting in this revue. You are casting your pearls before swine. In Berlin, we will polish and present you as a shining jewel."

The dinner party was at the home of Harry Kessler, a count and also a writer working on a book about his life in Berlin. She and Fräulein Landshoff were among the first to arrive, joining the sleek, ermine-like count and other guests in the dining hall, a sumptuous room carpeted with rugs so beautiful Josephine hated to walk on them. Paintings crowded the walls; sculptures perched on tabletops and stood around the rooms, as in a museum. As a maid offered champagne, Josephine peered around for Max, who had sent Ruth to fetch her. Why hadn't he picked her up as usual? She would have preferred to arrive on his arm than with the decadent Fräulein Landshoff, who, at a party last week, had worn her tux shirt and tails without any pants. She'd kissed Josephine on the mouth, given her a toke of reefer, wrapped her in a pink apron, and pulled her down to kiss on a sofa as these same men watched. Josephine blushed to greet them, but the dour face of the fräulein's playwright, Karl Vollmoeller, sported a happy smile as if they were all one big family, and the count gave her a respectful bow. He escorted the entourage into a large library with all the furniture pushed to the walls.

"I have cleared a space for your dance," he said to Josephine.

She frowned. Dance? She'd already danced two shows tonight. Excited about the new "pantomime" play Herr Vollmoeller wanted to write for her, she'd shimmied and shaken twice as hard, falling to her knees at the end of the night and throwing open her arms, giving love or receiving it, she never knew, but it had left her drained and hungry.

At one o'clock in the morning, she had not eaten in more than twelve hours.

"I didn't come dressed for dancing, Herr Count," she said. "I thought we were going to talk about my pantomime."

"I thought you *undressed* for dancing, Fräulein Baker," the count said with a wink.

The doorbell rang and the servant announced Herr Max Reinhardt and Fräulein Helene Thimig: his mistress, Fräulein Landshoff whispered. "He has made her a famous actress in his films. He wants to marry her, but his wife won't give him a divorce." Josephine stared at Fräulein Thimig, pretty enough with those high cheekbones and that pale skin, but the set of her mouth gave her a pained look, like somebody had forgotten her birthday.

"You are heartbroken!" Fräulein Landshoff said. "But you must abandon any hope of love with Max. These men are Germans. They might fantasize about a girl like you, but they won't do anything." She kissed Josephine's lips, licking off the champagne. "I don't share their prejudice, dark skin is sexy. I adore you, so why do you care about them?"

Three women arrived, one from England telling her how much they looked forward to seeing her dance tonight. No, they hadn't attended her revue, they weren't allowed: their husbands were prominent men and Hitler's brownshirts had condemned Josephine. If they were seen in the audience it might cause trouble.

"Those who oppose you do not understand you," the count said. "They see your nude body and think you are decadent. They do not recognize the innocence of the savage race that you signify, the purity in your primitive dance." Josephine wanted to tell these folks where she came from, and that she didn't even know where Africa *was,* but she knew which side her bread was buttered on and kept her mouth shut.

"Did you see today's revue?" Max joined the gathering with his woman, who gave Josephine a frosty smile. "Josephine Baker embodies German expressionism." He beamed as proudly as if he'd thought up the idea.

"What are your thoughts on expressionism, Fräulein Baker?" the English woman asked. All eyes turned to Josephine, waiting for her to say something clever, but her mind was on other things: the woman with Max, his *mistress;* the expectation that she would dance on demand; the pantomime that no one had yet mentioned; Ruth Landshoff's hand on her ass; the smell of food slowly filling the house; her champagne glass, now empty.

Josephine shrugged. "Expression-what? I don't know what that is." A servant traveled through the room bearing a platter of hors d'oeuvres, and she untangled herself from Miss Landshoff's embrace to follow him. Why had she come? These people didn't care about her, they just wanted to gawk at the naked and savage dancing beast from the jungle. She'd thought Berlin was more advanced even than Paris, the cafés crowded with intellectuals who welcomed her to their tables and offered her glasses of beer and asked her questions about growing up colored in America, or for her thoughts on the popularity of jazz and who the next great stars would be. These snooty folks just wanted to be amused, to watch her perform like a circus animal, and Max wanted to brag as if he'd had something to do with her success.

Tears stung Josephine's eyes. Max had never led her on, but he hadn't mentioned a woman. Why? Josephine had never worked with a man she hadn't slept with — did he know that, too? She'd even given in to Joe Alex, her body tingling and alive after slipping and sliding across his skin so many times in rehearsal — that erotic moment when she straddled his face with her crotch still got her hot and bothered. She'd taken him home with her just once, partly out of loneliness and partly to get Claude's goat. Afterward, their dance had taken on a new sexual intensity, even Mrs. Caroline had noticed it, although she didn't know the cause. Josephine had made Joe swear he would not tell a soul. "I couldn't stand for people to whisper about us," pretending to be modest when in fact she didn't want Claude to know.

She filled a plate with sausages, sauerkraut, mustard, and dark bread, and took a glass of beer to the library, where people sat in chairs and spoke German. She found a seat in a corner, away from the babble, and gobbled down her food. When she finished, she went back to the dining room and heaped her plate again, then went back to her seat, ignoring the hopeful faces turned her way. Fuck them, fuck Max and his cold-as-a-witch's-teat girlfriend, fuck the count and his pantomime that didn't exist except as an excuse to get her dancing in his library, another story for his notorious, name-dropping diary. Harry Kessler had closed the eyes of someone named Nietzsche in his coffin, Max had marveled, his voice hushed as if they were in church; he'd gone joyriding with Igor Stravinsky and Jean Cocteau after the riotous premiere of *The Rite of Spring;* he'd loaned money to Auguste Rodin, who never paid him back; and Josephine Baker had danced naked in his library. Fuck him. She cleaned her plate and got up for more.

When she returned, Count Kessler was standing in the middle of the library describing a scene he wanted to contribute to her pantomime. The new piece would not be a jungle dance as she was doing now in *La Revue Nègre,* but more refined, a ballet of sorts, with music by his friend Richard Strauss. "The best composer in Germany," Fräulein Landshoff said. "You know his operas, don't you? *Salome? Der Rosenkavalier?*"

"Nein," Josephine said.

Herr Vollmoeller sat at the piano and began to play. The music would be half oriental and half jazz, the count said, and the music changed to a Chinese or Japanese motif with a syncopated beat — very catchy. The scene would involve King Solomon. Loosened by the music, champagne, and beer, Josephine set down her plate. So there really would be a pantomime — one made from a Bible story, what a good idea! Would she play the Queen of Sheba? No, she'd be a slave girl — a dancer, presented naked to the king. Josephine's spirits sank again. Must she always be nude? She'd thought Max wanted to free her from "casting her pearls before swine."

The dance would not be crude, the count said, as if reading her mind, but elegant, some of it *en pointe.*

"Josephine is not a ballet dancer," Max said. He grimaced, like she wasn't up to the task, but she'd show him. She slipped off her shoes and rose up nearly onto her toes. She arced her arms over her head and twirled a time or two, eliciting a few polite claps. She glanced at Max, but he was still frowning. The ice queen beside him wore a haughty look. Josephine decided to show them both what she could do.

"The slave girl is naked," the count said, "because the king wishes to dress her himself, with the gowns and jewels of his choosing. He presents her with gift after gift, each more splendid than the last." Josephine stripped off her gown and began to act out the scene in the nude, mindful of Max's gaze but not letting herself look at him now. Applause and murmurs filled the room.

"The more the king gives to his slave girl, the less he himself wears, and the more elusive she becomes. In the end it is the king who is naked, while the dancer disappears, ascending in a cloud composed of all the silks and jewels he has bestowed on her."

Parfait, Josephine said, she loved it, but who would play the king? She danced about the room in invitation, but no one dared. Still on her toes she glided, arms waving, to a large statue of a crouching, nude woman. Josephine bowed, bending low to the floor, and then began a pantomime of worship, picking up her gown and laying it at the sculpture's feet, then removing her necklace and presenting that, as well, finally sneaking a glance at Max who stood in the doorway watching her, his eyes glinting a look she knew well. At last! Encouraged, she changed the dance, becoming the goddess and making the statue her supplicant, asking for her gifts to be returned to her, pulling on her underwear, her dress, her earrings and bracelets and rings, and then clasping the necklace about her throat and opening her arms to the room, inviting applause. Cheers echoed off the walls. She had done it: she had won them over, and Max, too. He would be hers soon enough. She stepped into the gown and zipped it up, and smiled at the count.

"Got any more champagne?" she said.

■ ■ ■ ■

She went to work the next day in high spirits. Not even rain falling like nails from a box and snarling the traffic in slow-moving knots on the Alexanderplatz could daunt her. So what if she was late getting to the theater? What would they do — fire her? The thought made her laugh, as did the man holding an inside-out umbrella over his head as though it were keeping him dry; two women scolding some children for jumping in puddles and splashing passersby; and, in front of the Nelson-Theater, several brownshirts braving the torrent in a most manly fashion to hand out soggy fliers that called Josephine more awful names. She hoped they would provide such great publicity when her film debuted!

After her dance at last night's party, the library had buzzed with ideas for her first feature film. Excited, Josephine had made an announcement: she had decided to stay in Berlin and study at the Reinhardt school. Cheers and applause filled the room, and Max proposed a toast, in German. She couldn't understand a word, but the delight on his face told her what she wanted to know: lily-white girlfriend or not, he'd soon be in Josephine's bed.

Outside the theater, a little man huddled alone at a table on the patio, shivering and wet under the leaking atrium. When Josephine emerged from her car, he stood and she recognized M. Lorett, who worked as the booking agent for the Folies-Bergère. Josephine's spirits sank. His coming here meant only one thing: trouble.

"Your timing is perfect, monsieur," she said breezily after rushing him to her dressing room. Thank the good Lord, no one had seen him. She patted him with a towel as lovingly as if he were her child, or her lover, soothing him as she broke her news. "I'm not returning to Paris, after all."

"But you signed a contract," he sputtered.

Josephine shrugged. "In Saint Louis, we made agreements by slapping hands."

"Mademoiselle, you must return." His voice rose; his face reddened. "M. Derval has already spent thousands of francs on your show. He will file a lawsuit."

Josephine threw the towel down onto her dressing table. How dare he tell her what she "must" do? She would do what was best for *her*, and why not? Everyone else looked after themselves. Herr Reinhardt had offered her acting lessons for free, she told him, and had promised to make her a movie star. How could the Folies-Bergère compete with the best director in the world?

He sighed, switching tactics, and his face returned to its normal color. She was making *un grand erreur,* he said. Did she not know what a wonderful opportunity lay before her at the Folies-Bergère? M. Derval had pulled out all the stops, commissioning the most beautiful and elaborate sets, paying the best designers for twelve hundred costumes, very extravagant — she should see them before she decided, they were breathtaking, covered in jewels.

Josephine gasped. Her show had twelve hundred costumes?

"*Bien sûr,* it must be, when you have a supporting cast of three hundred dancers and singers."

A cast of three hundred? Josephine's heart beat a little faster. "And they have saved the best costume for last," he said, "to be designed . . . by Josephine Baker."

Josephine imagined herself onstage in a costume of her own design. She would create something completely new, something that people would talk about for years to come. Hadn't M. Poiret made a fortune from the gown that she'd drawn for him that day? He'd sold so many that she'd had to stop wearing hers. This new gown wouldn't be for sale, it would be hers alone, an "exclusive," maybe even her trademark.

"Why do you need a school?" M. Lorett said. "Herr Reinhardt will not make you a star — because you already are a star. And you are in the prime of your life. As a woman, you will never be more desirable than you are now. Should you waste your best years toiling in some dreary classroom when you could be onstage at the Folies-Bergère, bedecked in splendor, accepting the accolades of your adoring public and making lots of money?"

He was a smart one. Josephine could see right through him, but he did have a good point. She'd heard what a demanding teacher Max could be, even more so, she imagined, if he was letting you in his school for free. He'd work her day and night for three long years. By the time she got out, she'd be twenty-three. And then, if she succeeded — and she would — she'd have to spend her days in movie studios instead of theaters. She'd gone with Max to the set of his new film, wanting to see how things worked. She'd gotten an eyeful of people standing around doing nothing but tugging at their costumes under hot lights and trying to keep the sweat from ruining their makeup. They missed out on the best parts of show business: the applause, the tossed flowers, the leap to its feet of an entire room in adulation and thanks.

"What about the music?" she said. "Does M. Derval have anything lined up yet?"

"Mais oui," the man said. *"Magnifique.* All new songs, written for you, by Spencer Williams and Irving Berlin."

Josephine caught her breath. The great Irving Berlin was writing music for her? This could mean only one thing: M. Derval was going to let her sing! Her childhood dreams, the hours playing dress-up in Mrs. Mason's clothes, it was all coming true. She would, at last, be a chanteuse.

Seeing her expression change, the little man pressed on, his face eager at the prospect of closing the deal. He thought he had her in the bag, but Josephine knew it was the other way around: *she* had *him.*

"It sounds tempting, but I've already given my word to H. Reinhardt," she said.

"But you gave your word first to M. Derval!" Now he looked like he was going to burst into tears. How much was M. Derval paying him to bring her back?

"Movie stars make a lot of money," she said.

"M. Derval is paying you a large sum. You

will earn nearly as much as Mistinguett." It was a gross exaggeration, of course; she could not compete with the highest-paid performer in France. Not yet.

"It isn't enough," Josephine said. "I'll need a raise, four hundred more francs per show." Irving Berlin! "If M. Derval agrees, I will leave for Paris next week. If not . . ." She shrugged.

"But he has already spent so much." Whining again. Josephine knew that she had won.

"Then a little more won't matter. But if he prefers, he can hire Mistinguett to replace me." She opened her dressing room door, her face impassive, feigning indifference while, inside, she was jumping with joy. To sing the songs of Irving Berlin at the Folies-Bergère!

As the monsieur hurried toward the exit, though, Mrs. Caroline came around the corner and stopped just short of running into him.

"M. Lorett, what a surprise to see you in Berlin," she said. Josephine slammed the door shut, her heart beating like a big bass drum. She didn't know what the man would say, but Josephine didn't want to be around to answer any questions. She pressed her ear to the door, trying to hear the conversation, but they had moved away. Lord have mercy, she was in trouble now. Mrs. Caroline was going to be hopping mad. M. Derval might get angry, too, if he knew she hadn't told Mrs. Caroline about her contract with him. Nobody liked a double-crosser, not even one who'd grown up like Josephine did. And if Herr Reinhardt knew she'd changed her mind on *him* today, he might get upset, too. She'd be left with nothing. She'd have to go back to the States.

Dancing in the sheeting rain, in the smothering heat, in piss-smelling theaters, in rat-ridden juke joints, the sleepless nights in roach-riddled rooms, the nights sleeping upright on seedy "coloreds only" train cars, the crick in her neck when she woke up, the meals she couldn't afford, her stomach cramped with hunger, her heart cramped with loneliness, her seasickness on the RMS *Berengaria* and her catarrh that stunk up her breath, her pregnancy, the pain, the infection and her delirium, the baby she'd given up, the ones she hadn't been able to carry since, all her dreams for her life, all her striving to make something of herself, to be Somebody, all of it might go to hell in a hand basket right this very minute. One wrong word from M. Lorett, and she would lose everything. She shouldn't have shut the door; she should have pulled Mrs. Caroline inside and told M. Lorett to go; she should have confessed the truth right then and there.

She touched the rabbit's foot Mrs. Jones had given her when saying goodbye in Philadelphia. *Everybody needs some good luck now and then.* She'd carried it ever since, and it had worked thus far.

"Lord, whatever you do," she prayed, "please don't send me back to New York unless it's in a casket." She'd rather die than go back to that sorry life where she couldn't eat in restaurants, couldn't use the bathroom, couldn't even take a drink from the water fountain. She remembered the flames burning the homes in the East Saint Louis riots, the fires of hell blasting across the Mississippi, the shrieks of the children running for their lives, their burning hair, the sweet smell of burning flesh rimming her nostrils with every inhale. She'd rather die here, or anywhere else, than live in America.

She heard a knock on her dressing room door and Mrs. Caroline calling her name. She fumbled with the latch, opened the door, and saw the woman looking like she wanted to cry or kill somebody, or both.

"You are going to harm your soul with this decision," Mrs. Caroline said.

As if Mrs. Caroline had been thinking of Josephine's soul, telling her she'd be the star of *La Revue Nègre* when she'd already hired Maud de Forrest as her singer, letting Josephine bomb on the *Berengaria* just to teach her a lesson, coaxing her to dance naked onstage so she, Mrs. Caroline, could make money. Everybody wanted something from Josephine, as much as they could get. No one had her interests at heart — except herself. And that, she realized, was plenty.

"But, missus," she said, "I'm feeling just fine."

CHAPTER 12

1926, Paris

It didn't take long for her to wonder what she'd gotten herself into. During the first dress rehearsal for her Folies-Bergère revue, she crouched on the mirrored floor inside an egg-shaped cage that, upon touching down on the stage, had opened to reveal Josephine dancing nude except for a belt of bananas — the costume she'd designed as a joke, but the joke was on her — and then closed again to lift her up, up to the rafters. When it had nearly reached the top, though, the contraption lurched to a halt and Josephine fell over.

The world under her shifted and tilted, and the cage swung open. Josephine slid sideways. Her fingers slipped against the smooth glass as she tried to find something to grasp, to stop herself from plummeting to the stage so far below. The winch turned, jolting the contraption again and she screamed, sliding in earnest now, before clutching with her fingertips the mirror's edge to which she clung, dangling. If she fell, she'd hit the stage. The impact would kill her.

Arrêtez! M. Derval cried, running up to the rafters. She could see him up there, so near but too far away to help, his face as white as death. From below she heard pandemonium, a cry for a doctor, feet scurrying, shouts in French. Her arms trembled. Sweat ran from her scalp into her eyes, stinging, but she couldn't wipe it away, she had to hang on.

Stay calm, she told herself, *you ain't come all this way to die before opening night.* They'd find a way to rescue her, and she could hold on until they did, her arms muscled and toned from her daily exercise, "the new woman," she'd been called, strong on the outside *and* on the inside instead of weak and limp like most women, like Mistinguett, even, whose half-a-million-franc legs looked like fifty cents next to Josephine's. Squats and splits and lunges and pull-ups and push-ups and even barbells. She sweated and worked to shape her body like a sculpture, like one of those statues in Count Kessler's house, because, like them, she was on display.

When she'd begged to sing, M. Derval had made her audition and then turned her down, saying her voice was *trop mince* — too thin. And when she'd given him her costume design, a spangled dress that would reflect the colored stage lights, he'd shaken his head. "Where are your *nichons*? You have covered up your *fesses.*" Tits and ass, ass and tits, that's all people wanted from her, so M. Derval thought, but Josephine knew better. It wasn't just her body that set her apart but also her spirit: the affection she showered on her audiences and the adoration they gave back to her. Her dancing differed from everyone else's the way that sex differs from lovemaking.

Annoyed, she'd drawn another costume as a joke, a belt of bananas jutting saucily upward. "I call this one 'Circle of Dicks,'" she'd said while slapping it spitefully on his desk. What good were tits and ass without dicks? She'd watched him with her arms folded, waiting for him to reject the vulgar design, but instead he'd cried, *Voilà!,* and sent it down to the costumers. Now, clinging to the slippery mirror, hanging on for dear life above the gawking, fainting cast and crew, that crazy belt was all she wore. Be damned if she was going to die in it.

"Josephine!" M. Derval called out, and

she stretched her neck to see him dangling upside down, two stagehands holding his feet, his arms reaching toward her. "Can you pull yourself into the open lid? Then we can join hands, and I will pull you up."

Stop shaking. One wrong move might tilt the whole contraption again, and send her tumbling down. M. Derval dangled so close, his face red from the blood rushing to his head, his forehead a wrinkle of fear, his voice as quiet as a funeral telling her to reach for him, to clasp his wrists if she could, and the crew would pull them both to safety. Josephine crawled into the lid and stood slowly and steadily, calm, her head clear — she'd dangled like this before, hadn't she, as a girl of thirteen in a Cupid costume falling on a wire? Here, at least, she had some control.

Someone from below cried out as she shifted her grasp, again, from the cage to M. Derval's hands, then swung free to hang high above the stage, bananas waving, legs bicycling as if to speed her ascent. Little by little they rose, inch by inch, each heartbeat a lifetime, each thought a prayer. Sweat slicked her palms, or maybe his, or both. She thought her arms would come loose from their sockets before the final heave pulled her up and onto a rafter, where she lay — shivering and wet, tears on her face — and clung to the rough-hewn beam.

M. Derval called for a doctor but she said no, and struggled to her feet and raised her arms, smiling at the musicians and cast members and crew gathered in a crowd far below. *"Ça va,"* she called out. Everyone applauded and some cried, "Bravo!" Josephine blew kisses as if she had just given a great performance, when in fact she was giving one now.

M. Derval's eyes twinkled as though they'd pulled a fast one on everybody, as though they would now share a laugh together. He reached out to help her descend the steep, narrow stairs.

"You'll need to come up with a different act for me," she muttered, her teeth chattering, as she rejected his hand. "I ain't going up in that fucking egg ever again."

The audiences loved her at the Folies-Bergère, filling the house night after night and selling out performances weeks in advance to see, first, the long opening act in which eight nudes strolled through Paris shop windows and put on clothes, jewelry, hats, and shoes, a strip-tease in reverse, like the German playwright's idea that Josephine had shared with M. Derval. *"Trés genial,* brilliant," he had said, and added the skit, saying it would "make the audience feel better when the clothes come off again." After a short intermission, Josephine came out in her banana skirt, ass in the air, walking her hands and feet backward on a tree limb, *jungle ape,* one of the Russian dancers, Olga or Helga, hissed when the scene was finished. As the girl danced onto the stage, Josephine stuck out her foot to make her stumble right in front of the crowd.

The egg dance was a triumph, an easy Charleston for Josephine, her image reflected by the mirror and broken like shards by the lights, which threw her shadow this way and that. The crowd went wild; she'd never heard anything like it: they loved it better than her Savage Dance with Joe Alex, they loved *her* more than ever. During intermission, when the comic Benglia came out in his own banana skirt poking fun at Josephine with a jangly elbow-swinging knee-knocking Charleston, they screamed with laughter and shouted for Josephine to join him on the stage. Laughing and crying, she blew kisses to the crowd and pretended to catch the ones they blew back, the footlights hot on her bare skin, her body taut with energy, her skin flush with love. How could she have ever thought to leave

Paris? She would not make that mistake again.

The critics were not all as adoring as the crowds. For every writer who called Josephine the "black Venus" there was another who said she was a devil. The writer E. E. Cummings said she was the most beautiful star on the Parisian stage — surely making Mistinguett gnash her teeth — but the music-hall critic Gustav Fréjaville mocked the revue as "trash." Josephine, he said, was debasing the Folies-Bergère and Paris by pandering to foreigners, who had no taste. Josephine had cursed when she'd read it, angered not only by the review but also by the one who'd slipped it under her door out of spite. It had to be that Russian girl, Olga or Helga, Josephine never could remember, the chorus dancer M. Derval had sent up and down in his precious egg twenty times to satisfy Josephine's concerns about its safety. She'd given Josephine the evil eye for a week after that. After getting that awful review, Josephine saw the girl out with the snooty ballerina Anna Pavlova, the two of them waltzing into Le Grand Duc like they owned the place. As Josephine danced on the little stage that night, they arose from their seats at a front table and walked out, Olga-Helga openly yawning.

Josephine had to laugh: she didn't care what Pavlova thought of her. When she'd met the prim little dancer at last year's Grand Finale Ball of *L'Exposition Internationale des Arts Decoratifs,* Josephine could tell that she thought her shit smelled better than everybody else's. Some genius had put them on the same bill, the ballerina and the dance-hall star, clearly a bad idea. The floor manager had scheduled Pavlova's performance first, during the hors d'oeuvres. Pavlova had argued that *she* was the star, she had danced in the Ballet Russes under Diaghilev, and so ought to be featured during the main course — but Josephine said she was fine keeping things the way they were. Pavlova pouted until the manager told her the appetizer was very small, that the audience would finish it quickly and have more time to give their full appreciation to her dance. When he'd left to speak with the bandleader, Pavlova arched a perfectly plucked eyebrow at Josephine.

"I will perform first because ballet is a complex art form, requiring the audience's attention," she said in French, the interpreter beside Josephine translating. She turned to her manager and added, in English, "She is completely untrained. Anyone could dance as she does. A child could do it."

After the ballerina tottered on her toes and waved her arms around for a while, Josephine took the floor. "It's time to wake y'all up." She peeled the long gown from her body to reveal a skimpy leotard. The prime minister of France, Paul Poiret, the Prince of Wales, the king of Sweden, the head of the Banque de Paris, the dashing motorcar-racer Marcel Ballot all ogled and cheered. "Voilà," she said, and told the crowd they'd saved the best for last — making everyone laugh except Pavlova.

"It seems like everybody in Paris wants Charleston lessons," she went on. "Folks pay me big money to teach it, but you know, it's one of the easiest dances to learn. I can teach anybody to do it in three minutes. I could probably teach Pavlova in thirty seconds." And she invited the ballerina to the floor.

Pavlova tried to refuse, but the crowd wouldn't let her. They demanded to see her do the Charleston, their applause and scattered cheers pushing her into Josephine's cunning hands. Mindful that the meals were on their way, Josephine sped the lesson along, teaching only the basics, *forward, tap, back, tap,* then showing her how to twist her feet so her knees went in and out, then adding arms and then kicks, increasing the difficulty until the ballerina flailed and her legs got tangled up, to everyone's delight but her own.

Afterward, Mrs. Caroline had warned her: Russian girls were tough. Josephine laughed. Should she be afraid of a ballerina? "She'd better be worrying about me, missus." Back at the theater, though, she now noticed that Olga or Helga had replaced her icy glare with a smirk, and that all kinds of things were suddenly going wrong: one of her shoes went missing right before the curtain, so that she had to dance barefoot; her rabbits got out of their cages and into the costume box, shitting all over the fabric; one of her wealthiest fans stopped sending her gifts, and when she saw him in Le Grand Duc said he'd received an insulting letter from her that she hadn't sent. Josephine knew that Olga or Helga and Pavlova had cooked up a plan to make her life miserable, but when she went to M. Derval, he'd shrugged and said his "girls" had to work these problems out among themselves.

Was it any wonder that, for her birthday, she wanted only to get away? As her gift, M. Derval rented a little Renault two-seater, a convertible the color of lemon chiffon, and had it delivered to her apartment. Josephine, who'd just learned to drive, took the wheel with only one thought: escape. The car's top was down, letting the noontime sun warm her and the breeze caress her arms through her white silk jacket as she drove along the winding road to Deauville, the seaside resort where M. Derval had urged her to go. "It is good for my stars to be seen in fashionable places," he had said, but she just wanted the beach, where she might relax in the gentle, early-summer heat; take off her shoes and walk in the sand. No one would bother her there, they were used to seeing folks far more famous strolling on their boardwalk and lounging on their shores. She had a room reserved at the hotel Le Normandy and cash for the casino and anything else — or anyone — that might come along.

When she'd traveled about forty-five minutes out of the city, a car came barreling behind her so fast that she thought it might run her down. It tailed her until she finally pulled over, cursing, to let it pass. It whipped around her and zoomed ahead, but once she steered back onto the road to follow, it slowed down almost to a crawl. What the hell? Had Pavlova sent someone to harass her on the road, too?

The road opened up and she shifted down, grinding the gear. Intending to pass, she pressed the accelerator and jerked the wheel to the left, too hard: the Renault veered all the way across the opposite lane and nearly into the trees. By now, she had passed the red car and was speeding away, her pulse wild. She gave a whoop, letting her laughter fly away on the wind, her sleeves flapping like wings, her hat fluttering, straining against the scarf tying it to her head. She was free. After just a few lessons from M. Derval, she could *drive.*

The road began to wind again and she slowed to navigate the narrow, twisting curves. When she glanced into her mirror, the red car had caught up and was again bearing down on her. The driver was doing something with his hand — waving to her. How childish! It looked like he was grinning, too, a very nice grin, she could see now. He looked familiar — she'd met him at the Dead Rat last year, and seen him in the audience at the exposition. She recognized the Ballot insignia emblazoned on the car's hood, and laughed out loud.

She'd beat Marcel Ballot, the race-car driver, in a race.

She floored the accelerator and took off. She'd show him: she'd keep him behind her for as long as he cared to follow. She didn't have a fancy race car, but there were more ways than one to skin a rat. When he caught up with her again, she swerved her car to the left, the right, and left again, taking up the whole road until they reached the curves, where he didn't dare try to pass. When the road straightened out, she swerved again, only moving back into her lane in the face of oncoming traffic. Whenever she looked in the mirror at him, he was laughing. She wondered where he was going, and wished she were going there, too. When they'd nearly reached Deauville, Josephine decided to hit the gas and leave him in the dust. But he stayed on her tail. Her eyes on the mirror, she forgot to watch the road ahead, but M. Ballot's horn alerted her just in time to avoid hitting an oncoming car. She turned her wheel too sharply, though, and careened off the road and, this time, really did hit a tree.

M. Ballot was by her side in a split second, his face full of concern as he asked if she was injured. "Just my pride," she said as he opened the door and helped her out of the steaming, hissing car. Josephine felt like a princess in the fairy tales she had once loved, rescued by a handsome prince in a bandbox hat and a cream linen suit with a pale-blue silk handkerchief in his pocket.

"You should feel very proud," he said. "You nearly won the race."

Standing next to him, she gazed up into his eyes and nearly had to sit down again. He smelled of cigarette smoke, musk oil, and mint.

"I think your car is finished for today," he said. "But it can be repaired, do not worry. And for your next automobile, I suggest a Ballot. They are faster cars, as you would have seen had you raced me fairly." Lord, she had never seen such perfect teeth except on movie stars.

He was headed to Deauville, too, it turned out, and would be more than happy to offer her a ride. Her luggage in hand, he escorted her to his car, then took off his jacket and tossed it into the back along with her suitcase — and his. Josephine could not believe her luck. His waist was as trim as a dancer's, his shoulders wide, his body sleek — but the way he carried himself was what made her blood sing. Like he'd won every race he'd ever driven in; like he'd had every woman he'd ever wanted.

Then, to her surprise, he opened the door to the driver's side, and motioned for her to sit behind the wheel. "Now," he said, "you may experience for yourself the charms of the Ballot." His palm pressed into the small of her back.

"Yes, please," Josephine said, smiling into his eyes. *Thank you, sweet Jesus, thank you thank you thank you.* "I do want to learn the Ballot charms."

CHAPTER 13

Two months after *La Folie du Jour* opened, Josephine's longtime friend Florence Mills came to Paris. Florence had sung in the New York production of *Shuffle Along,* and "I'm Just Wild about Harry" had made her a big star. She'd never gotten a big head, though: she gave everybody a smile that came from her heart. Now she was starring in *Blackbirds,* a hit New York revue touring Europe, in Paris to open the new Hotel et Restaurant des Ambassadeurs.

Josephine gritted her teeth to think of having Florence as a rival here: Florence's innocent beauty captured hearts. That sweet face, that valentine mouth. She didn't cross eyes or dance naked; she didn't need tricks to draw the crowds. (But then, neither did Josephine, as she kept insisting to M. Derval.) Flo had a voice like an angel and she danced like the devil himself, or like she'd made a deal with him to give her all that grace. Even while Josephine told herself that this was *her* town, that *Blackbirds* was just Lew Leslie's attempt at a *Shuffle Along* knockoff, she wondered, too, what Parisians would think of her after they'd seen Florence perform. Would they say that Josephine had no training and no talent, that folks only loved her for her *nichons* and her *cul*?

A part of her dreaded seeing the revue, but she had to go: Flo had reserved the VIP table for her on opening night. Her own second show finished at eleven thirty, and after removing her stage makeup, redoing her face, and changing clothes, she walked into the opulent, gold-and-marble lobby a half hour late. She didn't mind waiting until intermission to take her seat: she'd make a little party with the twelve escorts in white tuxes she'd brought in a sort of tribute to *Blackbirds* and its chorus of men dancing with Flo. But Florence, it turned out, had held the curtain for her. Josephine felt bad, but what could she do except walk in and claim her seat so the show could begin? She swept in with her train of men, everyone eyeballing her, to the most ostentatious table in the room, right beside the stage and topped with a model-ship centerpiece alight with little bulbs. Later, she'd be criticized for trying to upstage her friend, people always being so quick to judge. She heard whistles and applause — this wasn't her night, she wished they wouldn't — but what else could she do but wave and throw kisses?

To tell the truth, it did feel good to have some love coming her way tonight. Marcel, her lover since their race to Deauville, had declined to come to *Blackbirds* with her. In fact, he hardly went anywhere with her any more. He'd moved Josephine into a fancy apartment and spent every night with her, but he kept her apart from other aspects of his life. Tonight he'd gone to another of his many business dinners, which he never invited her to attend. Fool! Any man in this club would give his right arm *and* his left to be with her, but after only a few months together, Marcel took her for granted, or worse.

"Josephine, épousez-moi!" a man's voice cried out, making everyone laugh as one of her escorts took her ermine coat and another pulled out her chair, and a waiter poured champagne for them all. Her jitters melted away: Florence might be the Queen of Happiness and the Queen of Jazz, but Josephine Baker was still the Queen of Paris.

When she'd settled in, two men in tuxedos walked onstage carrying a giant cake and Florence emerged from it, her sequined dress flickering like a lighted candle. Singing "Silver Rose" in her girlish voice, she gave a warm smile to Josephine, who lost herself in the show. Flo's dancing mesmerized her — she moved with an easy grace that belied the complex routine, never missing a step, something Josephine had never been able to do. Dancing came as naturally as breathing to Josephine, and to follow someone else's choreography felt stifling, like being bound in a corset.

And damn, could that woman sing — about the hardships of being a Negro and a woman, songs that struck deep within and rang all the way to the ends of Josephine's fingers and toes. "Though I'm of a darker hue, I have a heart the same as you, building fairy castles the same as all the white folks do." Josephine looked at the table of frowning Americans beside her and wondered, did they understand any of this? But then the "Three Eddies" came out in corked-up faces and white lips, serving up darky songs with their wild tap dances, and sucked the meaning right out of the show. Josephine saw relief on the Americans' faces; order had restored itself.

After the show, she hurried backstage to visit her friend, wanting to get there before a bunch of people crowded in. On the way she saw Johnny Hudgins in a doorway, smiling like he expected a hug. Well, he could stand there all day. Last time she'd seen him, when he and Mildred, his wife, did *Plantation Days* with her in Atlantic City, Johnny had lorded it over her, telling her that if weren't for him, she'd be a nobody. "You've stolen every gag I've ever done," he claimed. As if he hadn't borrowed everything in his act from the comics on the circuit they'd toured with in the States. Crossed eyes, pantomime, funny shuffle: she'd seen it all long before Johnny came along.

"Hey, Jo, it's good to see you," he said as she approached.

She craned her neck around him to peer into his empty dressing room. "Mildred here?"

"She stayed in New York with the baby." He opened his arms to her.

"Flo!" Josephine called out, hurrying toward Florence's dressing room. Mildred had a baby? Josephine panged. Mildred might have an asshole for a husband, but she also had a soft, warm child to hold and love. A memory hovered like a phantom at the edge of her mind, and a twinge of remorse for what might have been, but then the door at the end of the hall swung open and Flo gave a shout loud enough for the whole city to hear.

"Look at you," she said, her eyes shining as she spun Josephine around, "in that beautiful velvet dress, every bit the star."

"Not as big a star as you, Flo. Can't nobody compare, and that's a fact."

"It's a good show, isn't it?"

"The best." From down the hall, she heard voices. She'd given the security guard a hundred francs to hold people back, but they'd bust past him in a few minutes. "You touched my heart with those songs, Flo. I felt like you were speaking for me."

Flo started to answer but lifted a handkerchief to her mouth and succumbed to a powerful fit of coughing. Josephine waited for her to catch her breath, but she coughed and coughed, so deeply and violently that it seemed like her lungs themselves might come out. Josephine helped her onto the divan, where she sat and wheezed for a few minutes while Josephine poured a glass of water from the tap. While she composed herself, Josephine took in the room: a lone painting of two ballerinas at the bar; a dressing table with a wooden stool; a blue rug on the wood floor; a sink; an armchair, and the divan, both upholstered in yellow with blue fleur-de-lis. Pretty bare bones: Josephine would have insisted on more.

"I was speaking for you, and for all colored women," Flo said when she could. "For all Negroes, in fact. It's too bad so few of them see our show. In the States, most of our people can't afford a ticket to Broadway, if they could even get in."

"Whites are the ones who need to see it," Josephine said. Except for the Three Eddies routine — they hardly needed to see that, but how could she criticize when she wore a grass skirt and wiggled her ass onstage, the white man's wet dream of savage conquest? "Are you going to do those songs in the Ziegfeld Follies?"

Flo shook her head. "I turned the Follies down." Josephine couldn't believe her ears. If she'd accepted, Florence would have been the first colored woman to appear in that popular Broadway revue.

"I couldn't do it, Josie. Get up in all those feathers and parade around like a white woman, so they could cut me down for not being one? They don't even let Negroes attend their shows."

"You could have shown those crackers that you're just as good."

"But I'm not — not at what they do. And I don't want to be. I'd be miserable, trying to pretend. I want to make life better for

261

our people, not worse. Doing Negro revues, like *Shuffle Along* and *La Revue Nègre* — that's the best way to change people."

A knock on the door brought Josephine to her feet. Her time with Flo was over.

"Come with me for a ride tonight?" Josephine said. "I've got a fancy car, a cabriolet upholstered in snakeskin. It's a dream of snakeskin, an indigestion of snakeskin!" She forced a laugh as she helped Flo struggle up. Although only ten years older than Josephine, Flo looked, now, like she was pushing a hundred.

But Florence didn't feel up to a ride, so Josephine left alone, her mood pensive even while her men poured champagne and laughed, spilling it on the exotic upholstery. "Every time you get in that thing I think of a snake swallowing you up," Bricktop had once said. Tonight, as the car pulled up to Le Grand Duc, Josephine thought the opposite was true. Those *Blackbirds* songs and her talk with Flo tonight had touched something in her so profound that, getting out of the car, she felt like a snake shedding its skin and starting anew.

No longer, she decided, would she be merely a clown who played a fool to make the white folks laugh, or only a nude dancer who excited them — all this making her no better, not really, than the Three Eddies with their blackface and darky songs. Things were going to change — *she* would change.

Flo was wrong about one thing, though. Turning down the Ziegfeld Follies had been a mistake, not only for her own career, but for their people. So what if the audiences were whites-only? It wasn't Negroes who needed to see Florence Mills perform, to hear her heart-wrenching songs, to witness for themselves that a colored woman could play the same part as a white woman. Flo couldn't see it, but Josephine could. Maybe, then, it was up to Josephine to show the world what she wanted it to know: that skin color meant nothing, because people were the same inside, all wanting love.

She returned home at five in the morning, just when Marcel was waking up. Good: she had a bone to pick with him. He had another dinner tonight, and would receive an award, but when she'd asked to go, he'd said no. When she'd pouted, he said she was ungrateful, pointing out the apartment he'd remodeled for her. How could she complain about being left at home in such a beautiful place?

Overlooking the Champs-Élysées, of marble and glass and elaborately frescoed ceilings with cherubs, grapevines, trumpets — it was a stunning apartment, Josephine had to admit. Technically speaking, the place belonged to Marcel, but he had given it to her, and had even installed a marble swimming pool surrounded by aquariums of colorful tropical fish.

He'd thought Josephine loved to swim because she'd said, "Animals who live on the ground will never be as elegant as fishes." In fact, Josephine had a fear of the water dating back to her childhood, when Daddy Arthur had thrown her into the Mississippi for a "swimming lesson" and she'd nearly drowned. Now, though, she'd hired a swimming coach with blond hair and blue eyes who'd held her by the waist as she practiced her strokes first in the water, and then on him. Marcel had guessed something was going on between them, and when she'd admitted it, he'd shrugged. "Frenchmen are not like American men," he'd said, which made Josephine wonder if he loved her.

But he'd let her decorate the apartment, and paid the bill for Paul Poiret's tapestries, curtains, and rugs; for the telephones she had installed in the bedroom, living room, and bath; and for the shockingly expensive bed, an elaborately carved antique made hundreds of years ago for an Italian doge.

"I thought we needed an extra sturdy bed," she'd said, sly. But she was only half joking. Josephine had the energy of three people, but she'd been put to the test during those early, wild nights with Marcel — marathon nights of sex that seemed, now, like a distant memory.

They'd seemed perfect for each other at first. As she'd driven his car to Deauville, shyness had tied her tongue, but he'd filled the car with talk about the Ballot automobile and its "superior engine" and "luxury design." He'd compared the 2LS sports car they were in with the Renault M. Derval had rented for Josephine, a good-enough model but it could never endure the 24 Hours of Le Mans race in which he would push the 2LS to its limit for twenty-four hours. He had also raced in the Indy 500 and the Grand Prix, he'd added, glancing over for her reaction. Josephine had no idea what he was talking about but she tried to look impressed, although she could barely focus on the words coming out of that sensuous mouth curving so beautifully around his perfect smile.

In Deauville, they'd first gone to a service station, where he'd given the attendant a fistful of bills to repair her car and drive it back to Paris. Then they'd gone to Le Normandy, their hotel, and taken a table in the tea garden blooming with roses and silks, women in chiffons and short dresses and long strands of pearls, their lovers in summer suits and hats of cream and dove gray, and a little jazz band in the front, trumpet and saxophone and clarinet and drums and a singer whose rich, lush voice Josephine might have envied had she not been too entranced by Marcel to notice much else.

A waiter in a black tuxedo escorted them to a table in a far corner, at Marcel's request, nullifying Josephine's choice of seats near the stage where everyone would see her with the most eligible bachelor in France. "I do not care for the spotlight," he said, a strange sentiment for a famous racer. But if he wanted her all to himself, would she argue? And when they'd been seated and she noticed the whispers and sidelong looks their way, she realized that he'd made the right choice. In the front, they'd be fair game for autograph-seekers and hangers-on, but people wouldn't bother them back here. When people started to dance, she'd looked at him inquiringly, but he'd said he'd rather dance alone with her and took her up to his room.

Later, spent on the mangled bedsheets, she'd suggested they go back to the tea garden, but he'd said, again, that he didn't want the attention. Josephine thought about the people downstairs enjoying the music, the warm spring day, the delicious food, and the tea in those beautiful cups while she hid on the top floor like Rapunzel in the tower. When he'd pulled her back down to the mattress for more, though, she'd forgotten about wanting anything else. Now she understood that that day had been only the beginning. For months, Marcel had kept her from his family and friends like a secret sin.

Hiding their affair, she realized, was why he'd installed her on the Champs-Élysées.

When they saw each other, now, it was in this apartment: Marcel never took her to his place or out to dinner with the business partners whom he saw so frequently. She would find those gatherings boring, he'd claimed, the discussions banal: the women talked about household affairs and gossiped while the men held forth about cars, business, and football, and little else. It did sound terribly dull, she'd had to agree.

Now, though, she'd be damned if she was going to miss his awards banquet, especially if he was excluding her for the reasons she suspected.

He was reading the morning paper in his robe and drinking coffee when she got home the morning after Flo's show. She joined him at the breakfast table and told him that she wanted to go with him that night. He looked at her as if she'd broached the subject again just to get on his nerves.

"What is the matter, don't I give you enough?" he said.

She looked around at the cold marble, the glassy pool, the frowning maid picking up the droppings her pets had left behind. What *was* the matter? Why, in six months together, had she never met any of his friends? She knew the answer, but couldn't even think the words. He could not simply add her at the last minute, he said, his table was full, would she want him to eject his mother or sister to make room for her?

"You've got somebody else," she said wildly. "A wife." Her face grew hot when he laughed, but she continued. "You have another mistress, then." She looked around as if to find this other woman, seeking any reason for his behavior besides the one whispering like the devil in her ear. He smiled as though she were a foolish child. He'd be patting her on the head at any minute. When did he have time for anyone else? he asked. He spent every night with her.

"You're ashamed to be seen with me, then." Her voice snagged on the truth still locked in her throat. "Because I'm a performer."

"Do not be ridiculous. How can you say this, when the reason I must work so hard is to support your extravagant habits? No, your accusations do not make sense. You have come home in a mood and want to fight."

He yanked on his swim suit, grabbed his towel, and stomped out of the room to the pool that might as well be filled with her tears. Was it because she performed at the Folies-Bergère? At that theater, *vedette*, or star, had long been synonymous with *cocotte*, or prostitute. The famous women whose photographs hung in the lobby — Liane de Pougy, Odette, Yvonne Printemps — had earned cash, jewels, cars, houses by sleeping with wealthy men and even kings. Some became royalty, themselves. If kings weren't ashamed of these women, why should Marcel, a mere businessman's son and racer who had not yet won a contest, want to keep her hidden away? The answer sprang to her tongue; she bit down so hard the taste of blood filled her mouth.

There was no need to get carried away. He loved her, didn't he? What more *did* she want? Why couldn't she ever be satisfied?

She crawled into bed and buried her head under the covers in case he came back in, not wanting him to see her cry. Unhappy thoughts whirled like a cyclone, wreaking havoc in her mind. No one had ever loved her, not her mama or her grandmother or even Billy Baker. No, Billy hadn't loved her, not really, or he'd be in Paris now. She'd sent him a letter begging him to come, she missed his sweet smiles and gentle touch and the way they used to laugh together, they'd been like best friends and lovers at the same time. And he'd always supported anything she wanted to do, instead of pressuring her like his mama did to quit the theater and become "respectable." He hadn't liked it when she left for Paris, but she'd promised to return. She'd planned to — but how could she now? "How you gonna keep 'em down on the farm, after they've seen Paree?" When she'd written and asked him to join her here, though, he'd said no. *Not unless there's a job there for me. I don't want to be a kept man.* She'd cried on that day, too, reading his letter. Where was the love in such selfishness?

Bobo, the little monkey Marcel had given

her, pushed open the bedroom door and leaped onto the mattress, crawling under the covers to cuddle. The thump of his heartbeat against her chest, his arms around her neck: *This* was love. This was what she used to do when her mama cried, her mama whom she loved with all her heart even as she was slapping Josephine in the face and screaming that she was "good for nothing."

Maybe only animals and children had the capacity for love. Maybe over time, people's hearts got knocked around and beaten up and bruised and broken so many times that a kind of scar tissue formed like a shield all around until love couldn't penetrate either way, going out or coming in. The idea made her tired. Bobo patted her face and, feeling tears, whimpered as he wiped them with his monkey fingers. How she wished Bobo were a child, hers and Marcel's baby. Then she would have the love she'd always wanted, and Marcel wouldn't be ashamed of her anymore, because she would quit the stage — she was sick of dancing nude, anyway.

The scenario presented itself: Josephine with an infant in her arms and Marcel lean-ing in to admire the child, his son, his eyes turning tenderly to hers. They would go on picnics together, and to the beach, where Marcel would swim like a dolphin with their little boy on his back while Josephine squatted on the shore with their girl and made sand castles that the tide washed away, and if the little girl cried, Josephine would tell her that everything in life changes, that nothing is permanent, that all we build are castles in the sand except for love, which is the only thing that lasts.

She'd wrapped a colorful kerchief around her head and a silk robe around her body when Marcel stepped back into the boudoir, toweling his damp hair and skin. When he pulled off his swimming trunks she placed her hands on his hips to pull him close, murmuring her apology. She hadn't meant to upset him, she loved him, was all, and wanted to celebrate his success with him. She pressed herself to him, felt his cock stirring against her belly, and offered her mouth for a soft kiss. *"Je t'adore,"* she whispered, feeling him growing and hardening in her grasp.

His kiss felt hot on her mouth and he pressed into her, pushing her toward the bed. At last; at last. *"Je t'adore,"* she said, emotion carrying her away like a tide, her mouth gasping. "Oh, Marcel, I want to have your child."

He softened and withdrew, his face white. "A child? Are you pregnant?"

"You look like you seen a ghost, baby. What's the matter? I'm not pregnant, but would it be so bad if I was? We love each other, don't we?"

"Illegitimate children are messy."

"Let's make it legitimate, then." She'd ask Billy for a divorce. After refusing to join her here, he wouldn't say no, would he? She softened her voice, her eyes, every part of her as she pressed herself to his damp body once more and kissed his beautiful mouth. "Oh, baby, I love you so much, I'd marry you in a heartbeat, don't you know?"

He got out of bed and went to the closet. She walked up behind him and reached around to stroke him some more — but he pulled away.

"What's the matter, Marcel? You don't want a family?"

He moved out of her reach and took up his clothes.

"Is it because I'm in show business? I'd quit to raise your babies, and I wouldn't mind it a bit. I'd be the happiest woman in the whole world, in fact."

He yanked on his trousers. "I don't want to get married."

But all men say that, don't they? Willie Wells sure as hell wouldn't have married her if she hadn't pretended she was pregnant, and Lord only knows what Billy Baker would have done if she hadn't been, and if *Shuffle Along* hadn't been leaving Philadelphia. Marcel, though, was rich and good-looking and could fuck anyone he wanted. And so she told him now, her heart feeling like it might fly out of her chest, that she wouldn't tie him down, she'd be a French wife in every way, she'd even get her citizenship. He could have a mistress.

He sighed as he buttoned up his shirt.

"I want things to remain as they are," he said.

"Even if I quit? It's because I'm a dancer, ain't it?" As he looked in the mirror to knot his tie, she tried to meet his gaze but couldn't bring herself to hold it as she added, "Or is it because I'm colored?"

He turned around to face her. "It is both."

A deadly calm fell over her, then, as though the cyclone had shifted and she stood in its eye. This was what she had dreaded to hear, not just from Marcel but throughout her life: that the color of her skin made her unlovable. And then the storm moved in her again and her thoughts whirled and her blood raged. She looked around the room for something to throw, seized a pillow, hurled it at him. He ducked it, his face a closed door that all the pillows in the world wouldn't open.

"That's why you won't take me to your dinners," she said, her voice cracking. "That's why I'm not invited tonight, isn't it? Because I'm a Negro."

He shrugged again, and now her blood rose. She must know, he said, that her music-hall life was a fantasy, that not everyone in France embraced *le jazz hot* or its lifestyle.

"I must consider my family. And my position, which I will lose if I disgrace my father."

"Disgrace?"

"He does not see life the way you and I do. Nor do his friends."

"I will charm him!" She'd won Pa Baker's heart so easily.

Marcel came over and put his arms around her waist. He smiled into her eyes. She melted a little. "You cannot change the world, *ma petite chou,*" he said.

"Yes, I can!" she cried, and slapped him in the mouth, wanting to strike out that ugly, negating word, *disgrace.* Plenty of men richer than Marcel or his daddy would love to marry her. She got proposals every day from men who were rolling in dough. He touched his hand to the place where hers had struck.

"No," he said, "you cannot."

His blue eyes mooning at her now, he looked like he might cry, but she didn't care. He didn't love her. He had only been using her, and as soon as he got tired of the same pussy every night he'd be giving some other woman his come-hither looks and moving *her* into this place. Josephine saw what might have been their future unraveling like a piece of cheap cloth. All the animals he'd given to her, the mice with their little pink ears, the parakeets, the champagne he brought, the flowers he sent, the tender kisses, the nights spent holding her while they slept — it had all been lies. So why should she believe anything he said?

"I *can* change the world!" she shouted. He touched a finger to his lips, which made her scream.

Goddamn him and his phony morality, him and his fucking "class." Goddamn him and his family and his high-society hypocrites. She spat the words, he flinching as if every one were a blow.

"Yes, I'm talking about you! You go along with it, don't you? Looking down on people because of their skin. You're no better than . . . *Americans*!" There — she'd done it, compared him and his lot to the people he disdained. "At least Americans don't pretend."

His eyes drooped. "You hate me."

"You're the one who hates *me.*"

"Josephine, I adore you." That sad face! He looked like he'd just lost his best friend. Maybe he did love her, after all. But — he said "adore." He had never said "love" to Josephine. She crossed her arms over her breast, covering her heart.

"Not enough to have a child with me." He said nothing. She pushed past him into the bathroom, where she locked the door and turned on the bath, the sound of the water drowning out her sobs, which drowned out the sound of his knocking, so tentative that she wasn't sure whether he wanted to talk or to use the bathroom.

"Josephine," he called, more loudly now. "Josephine, open the door. Please."

Let the bastard stand there all day if he wanted to. If he had to piss, he could use the sink, or his stupid, pointless pool. She didn't care what Marcel did, not anymore.

CHAPTER 14

"Frenchmen don't marry foreign girls, colored or not." Bricktop, reclining in a booth and glistening with perspiration after her set, sat up straight when she said this, as if making an announcement to the group at their table: Cole and Linda Porter; Sara and Gerald Murphy; Elsa Maxwell; the Prince of Wales; Josephine's friend Bessie, visiting from New York; and the rakish journalist Georges Simenon. Sim was the only Frenchy, but they all nodded, the insistence of Frenchmen on having French wives being something everyone knew, it seemed, except Josephine. And this after listening to Sim complain about his miserable marriage to Tigy, a Frenchwoman with that closed-up look so many of them had, like they'd just stepped out of a cold bath.

"You knew this and never told me?" Her best friend had seen heartbreak coming and never said a word. "Damn, Bricky, if I can't trust you, who can I trust?"

The first time she'd met Bricktop, before leaving for Berlin with *La Revue Nègre* last year, Josephine had felt like she'd found the big sister she'd always wanted. Besides being a fellow Southerner and Negro, Bricky worked as a dancer and manager of Le Grand Duc, and had started her career, like Josephine, performing on the "chitlin' circuit" in Negro vaudeville shows. Being with her was like being home.

"It's no wonder you're a hit," Bricky had said that first night. "You look like a French-woman, the way you carry yourself." But Josephine hadn't felt like she fit in, so Bricky had helped her, choosing her clothes from the piles the designers sent every day and teaching her the words and phrases she needed to know: *Voulez-vous dancer? Donne-moi un bisou. Combien ça coûte?*

When Josephine had confided one of her most shameful secrets — that she could barely write, even her own name, the result of skipping all that school as a kid — Bricky had given her a stamp to use for signing autographs. She took care of Josephine and asked for nothing in return: a first, in Josephine's experience. But Bricky hadn't warned her about Marcel Ballot, hadn't told her about all the many women he'd moved into that apartment who'd moved out again because he wouldn't marry them: a Congolese maid, an Algerian student at the Sorbonne, a Russian dancer at the Casino de Paris. "He loves foreign women, but his family does not," she said now — too little, too late. But if he'd loved Josephine enough to spend all that money on her, why not tell his snooty family to take a hike? She earned almost as much as he did, and would happily take care of him, but he wouldn't even think about it. Men and their pride.

"All the Parisians I know love me," Josephine said. "Don't they?"

"I love you," Sim said with a wink. Josephine pretended not to hear. It would be a cold day in hell before she wasted herself on another Frenchman.

"Loving somebody is one thing," Bricky said. "Marrying them is another."

"You should have warned me," Josephine said. "I wasted all that time."

"Ain't no way you would have listened to me," Bricky said.

"You've heard that love is blind?" Cole said. "Guess what? It's deaf, too."

"A good friend tells the truth. Bricky, I don't know how you could watch me making a fool of myself without saying a word."

"I like my eyes, and don't want them

scratched out," Bricky said, and Josephine, on cue, lifted her long, gold-painted fingernails and aimed them at her friend's face, lightening the mood instead of pointing out that Bricky, her best friend, knew she would never attack her. Blinding anybody was the last thing Josephine would ever do. She still had nightmares about the day Daddy Arthur had knocked out Willie Mae's eye. Poor little thing had spent her life looking for a man who could love a woman wearing an eye patch and had gotten a venereal disease right off the bat. Somebody should have told her to be careful, to guard her heart and her body. Somebody should have told her that a man would say anything for pussy, that he'd do anything, too, even spend a fortune on a swimming pool that you didn't want.

"Bricky, the next time you see me doing a fool thing like that, you'd better say something. You ain't my friend if you don't."

Speaking of people who weren't friends, Johnny Hudgins walked into the club and Bricktop went to greet him. "Don't bring him over here," Josephine muttered, but she must not have heard, because in a minute he was standing in front of her with a big smile.

"I've just spoken with Mildred, and she

281

asked me to give you her love," he said. "I'm sorry you had to rush off the other night — I wanted to show you these."

He opened his wallet and pulled out two photographs of Mildred, looking somewhat pudgy in the neck and arms and holding as ugly a baby as Josephine had ever seen, its eyes protruding from an outsize head.

"How sweet," she murmured, handing the photos back to him. "He's the spitting image of his daddy, I must say."

"Thanks, Joe," he said. "That means a lot." Josephine's insides seemed to bunch up and twist. Why had God given Mildred a child and not her? Maybe she'd been with the wrong men. Marcel didn't have any bastards running around that she knew of. He was probably sterile! Thank the good Lord he'd refused to marry her, as badly as she wanted children. Maybe Sim would get her pregnant tonight, wife or no wife. That was all she needed a man for, anyway. She could take care of a child by herself, she had plenty of money to give and even more love. And a child would love her back — it would have to, wouldn't it? She loved her mama, mean streak and all, had just sent more money even though she still hadn't received a word of thanks. We love our mothers no matter what damage they do.

She slid her hand under the table and across Sim's thigh; he was a journalist who "must be discreet," he'd said when they'd danced together at Le Chat Noir, but the lust on his face now was open and raw. Should she?

But no, she ought to blow this joint now, before she got herself in trouble again. Standing up, she said her goodbyes: she and Bessie were going over to Zelli's to get the caricaturist Zito to draw their picture.

When they got there, though, Zito was packing his pencils and pens and easel and blowing his nose, saying he was *malade* and going home. Then, a dark-haired man wearing a monocle was standing beside him, bowing to Josephine and Bessie and kissing their hands. A thrill ran through Josephine's blood. He was the spitting image of Adolphe Menjou, the movie star, but he was even better than that: bowing, he introduced himself as Count Pepito Abatino, from Italy.

"A count? With a castle and all?" Bessie said.

"Of course that's what he means," Josephine said, straightening her back a little more as though she were royalty, too. *Forgive my friend's ignorance,* she tried to say with her eyes, and in his gaze she read a response that had nothing to do with Bessie.

Not only was he a movie-star-looking Italian count, he was also a dancer who taught the Argentine tango. Josephine and Bessie watched from the bar as he steered various women through the sexy dance, then Josephine put up money for their turns. If he was a count, why did he need their money? Bessie wanted to know. Josephine explained that, in Europe, a lot of nobles walked around as poor as church mice, run out of their castles and their countries by all the politics going on. Josephine saw the old French *comptes* and *comptesses* all the time in the clubs and tea gardens, their tiaras, silk sashes, and coats of arms faded testaments to past glories, their families having lost everything to Napoleon except their titles. The same thing was happening in Italy under Mussolini, she told Bessie.

"So is he a real count, or a has-been count?" Bessie said.

"I can spot a phony a mile away," Josephine said, watching an older woman slide her foot down his calf. "He's the real thing."

By the time their tango had finished, Josephine didn't care whether Count Abatino was real, fake, or imaginary. The press of his hand to her back, of her breasts to his chest, of his cheek to her cheek, of his thigh against her thigh as they moved on the crowded floor, all made her body and mind yearn for one thing only: this man in her bed as soon as possible.

But first she had the throbbing heart of Paris at night to present to her friend. She'd promised Bessie they'd paint the town red, and so off the three of them went in Josephine's snakeskin dream, her chauffeur André driving them up and down the Champs-Élysées, to the bulldyke bar Le Monocle in Montparnasse, to Le Chat Noir in Montmartre, and, finally, back to Le Grand Duc for breakfast, to end the night, as always, with Bricktop.

But Bricky wasn't in her usual good mood when they walked in. She looked at Pepito as though the sight of him made her queasy. Josephine felt, for a minute, like she'd lost her way. Had she failed to see something, a deformity of some kind? Slender, elegant hands; sleek, dark hair and mustache; slight figure barely taller than she; deep-set eyes as black as coal; nice smile with a crooked front tooth.

"Your handsome man looks familiar." Colette's shrewd eyes followed Pepito and Bessie to the dance floor.

"That's Pepi," said Elsa Maxwell, giving him the same breathless looks every other middle-aged woman had sent his way this evening. "He comes to my tea garden every afternoon and dances with the wealthy widows. I'm told he's a gigolo, but I don't mind — he's very popular."

"He's an Italian count," Josephine said. "And a dance instructor."

"He doesn't speak English, does he?" Elsa said. "Maybe I've misunderstood."

Josephine smiled, feeling like the cat that swallowed the canary. *She* had understood Pepito perfectly before he'd said a word.

After an obligatory dance with Bessie he took Josephine in hand, steering her through the fox-trot, Charleston, shimmy, and the Brazilian samba to the Argentine tango, Josephine jazzing up each dance with moves of her own. The floor cleared and a crowd formed around the perimeter to clap and cheer. Josephine laughed, giddy, the room spinning although she'd hardly drunk a drop. She was dancing with an Italian count, and her blood was racing like music in her veins. This would be Pepito's night if he wanted it, and tomorrow night, and the next.

As he turned her this way and that, his hand sliding across her bare back, their legs intertwining, flashbulbs popped like fireworks around them. Josephine turned her face to the left and the right, striking poses. By the time she found the photographer, though, he'd stopped taking pictures. Bricktop stood next to him, a restraining hand on his arm. What the hell? *La Folie du Jour* wasn't doing well, and the publicity might help. She didn't have time to think about it much, though, not with all the footwork and handwork and eyeball work and heavy-breathing work she and Pepito were doing.

When they returned to the table, Pepito excused himself and Bricky rounded on Josephine.

"What on earth are you doing with that creep?" she said.

Josephine felt like she'd been slapped. Creep? Did she mean Pepito? He was no creep, he was an Italian count; he treated Josephine like she was royalty, too, hadn't Bricky noticed how he'd pulled out her chair every time she got up from the table and sat back down again, how he'd kept her glass filled —

"He fills it with champagne you paid for," Bricktop interrupted.

"We've hardly had a thing to drink, Bricky, we've been so busy dancing. Did you notice what a good dancer he is?"

Bricky snorted. "He ought to be good, as much practice as he gets. You heard Elsa.

He hits her tea garden every afternoon, dances with rich women for money and does who-knows-what with them at night. He's a gigolo, Josephine. Ain't got a dime to his name, if I'm lying I'm dying. You take a look at his collar and cuffs, and those cheap cuff links?"

"I told you, he's a count."

"And I'm the Queen of Sheba."

"Are you calling him a liar, and me stupid for believing him?"

"I'm saying he knows how to charm the ladies into paying his way." She opened her fan and began fanning herself. "I've seen him here these past couple of weeks, always with one woman or another, wining and dining and never picking up the tab. Don't look at me like that. I'm your friend, remember? You told me to warn you when I see you headed for trouble, so I'm doing what you asked. And what I've got to say is this: count, my ass."

Josephine felt the blood rush to her face. "You're jealous."

Bricktop laughed and rolled her eyes.

"Jealous? Of what? Of that no-account count?"

"Jealous of *me*," Josephine said. "Ever since we had that night together in Deauville, you act like you own me."

"Honey, you can let go of that fantasy right now. We had fun, but I'm not into jelly roll. I honestly prefer meat with my motion." She laughed again, sending Josephine's blood pressure through the roof. She'd like to punch Bricktop in her ugly, freckled face. *Jo Baker's French is bad, but her English is worse,* she'd teased earlier tonight, laughing. How could she be so hurtful?

"Well, you ought to lay off the jelly rolls and the bread basket, too."

Bricky's face turned as white as a ghost's, but Josephine wasn't stopping. Every bad thought she'd ever had about her friend came tumbling out. Her string of expletives and insults started low and ended in a high, screaming fit about how Bricky had a hard-on for Cole Porter, everybody could see it, "but he wouldn't fuck you with a ten-foot pole, you're just his passing-for-white Negro prop so everybody can see how modern he is," and a lot more that the whole room might have heard if the band hadn't started playing just when she was getting wound up.

When she had finished, Josephine went to the table and announced that they were leaving. Bessie came running after her asking what was the matter. Josephine looked at Pepito, her eyes taking in his frayed collar and cuffs and worn shoes, and said she was tired of Le Grand Duc. She was thinking, though, that maybe he *was* penniless, like the duchess who made the rounds at night and got everybody to buy her drinks. But how could she find out, when he didn't speak English?

On the way to her car, it started to rain. Josephine cried out — her dress would be ruined. But Pepito pulled her under an awning and wrapped his arms around her and gave her a kiss that mixed up everything, and when they'd finished, all the pieces of her life had settled in a different place from where they'd been. And when the downpour stopped and the long kiss ended and they joined Bessie, who asked again what had happened with Bricktop, Josephine laughed.

"Bricktop who?"

CHAPTER 15

1926

Josephine screamed and hurled a vase against the mirror, shattering both. "Honkies! White crackers!" With each shout, Bric and Brac screeched and rattled their cages. She unlatched the doors, setting them free.

Pepito walked in to find the monkeys swinging from the chandelier; the goat chewing the tablecloth; the birds flying in circles, spattering the rugs and upholstery with their scat, and Josephine cursing. But for once, he didn't try to calm her down, didn't even warn her about the bill the hotel would send her for this destruction although she could read that worry on his face.

"This crappy-ass hotel ain't getting a thing out of me," she said. "If they even think about collecting, I'll sic the gendarmes on their asses. Hell, I'm going to do that, anyway." France had laws against discrimination. Slapped with a fine, maybe the management would think twice before giving a customer the boot for being colored. Pepi didn't say a word, not that there'd be much he could say. Not even a week here, and she'd been asked — no, *forced* — to leave because some Americans had complained. They didn't like sharing the hotel with a Negro! Maybe they felt bad that she had the fanciest suite, four large rooms with a fountained terrace and a view of the Arc de Triomphe. When the manager came to see them today, his face red and his eyes shifty, Josephine had stood right there as he'd told Pepito, not her, what was going on. Only Pepito's hasty slam of the door had stopped her from lighting into the coward.

"Stupid bastards," she muttered, putting on her makeup in the bathroom while the maid, Yvette, packed their clothes and Pepito made calls to find them a new hotel. "They don't know their asses from a hole in the ground." She'd thought this kind of thing couldn't happen in Paris. They had *laws* against this shit — she could walk, ride, shop, eat, and sleep anywhere, or so she thought. Parisians loved her skin color, they called her a "bronze beauty" and a "black pearl." She'd never felt disrespected in France until today.

American crackers. She'd endured two weeks of seasickness on the *Berengaria* to get away from their prejudiced bullshit, but she couldn't go far enough, it seemed. What kind of man would ask her to leave because of their complaints? Pepito said the hotel had plenty of white Americans and only one colored one, so she had to go. They would never do this if she were French, he said, startling her, because she felt more French than American these days, more at home in Paris than anywhere she had ever lived.

"They don't hate us in Paris like they do in the States," she'd said to Florence when they'd finally gone out together, to the Ritz to feast on oysters, foie gras, and duck and talk about old times. Florence agreed that folks were friendlier in Paris, but she wouldn't say, as Josephine did, that they were color-blind.

"They think we're all Africans, or they want us to be," she said. "That's its own kind of prejudice."

Josephine winced.

"I've worn grass skirts and blackface, myself," Florence said, guessing her thoughts.

"You've got blackface in this show," Josephine blurted.

"Sometimes, you've got to sweeten the pill."

While Parisians treated Negroes better than people in the States did, things weren't perfect here, Florence went on. "Look at the people protesting the colored revues, warning that jazz — 'Negro music' — will corrupt French culture. Look at the French government invading Africa."

"How do you know these things?" Josephine said.

Flo gave her a long look. "I read the news," she said.

Their talk hadn't settled easily in Josephine's mind, especially after reviewers called her "savage" and Florence "civilized." What did they know about either Flo or her, except what they saw on the stage?

But Florence did have one precious possession that Josephine did not: a singing voice that people loved. Lord, how Josephine had cringed to hear herself on her first record. If she sounded half as good as Flo, she'd be on that Follies stage in New York in a feathered headdress, singing white songs, showing the world that a Negro could do it.

"When are you coming home to the States, Jo?"

"It ain't my home, not anymore. If I go

294

back, they'll make me sing mammy songs."

"And you'd turn those songs right back around on them. You'd have the white folks laughing at mammy songs and laughing at themselves. Look what you do here, wiggling around in that banana skirt. You think I don't know what you're up to?"

She winked as though she and Josephine shared a secret joke, although Josephine wasn't entirely sure what she was talking about. What was she "up to" besides making people happy? Making good money, sure, but she worked hard for it. She would never have to live on the streets again, not even if a spineless jellyfish threw her out of her hotel suite because he couldn't say no to some lily-white, stick-up-their-ass bigoted fools.

Pepito strutted into the bedroom, he'd found another hotel, one with no Americans, him beaming like this was a great achievement, like he wanted a medal for his efforts. Josephine held her tongue. She hadn't wanted to come to *this* hotel. Her apartment near the Parc Monceau was plenty big, but Pepi had complained, saying her pets took up too much space. She'd put her feelings aside and agreed to move because of all he had done for her: straightened out her bank accounts; put her apartment into his name and most of her money in his accounts to shield her from Paul Poiret's lawsuit — the bastard had given her all those clothes, but now that she was famous he wanted to be paid for them — gotten her name on a new hair straightener, Bakerfix, that had already made her a bundle in sales; enrolled her in voice lessons and French lessons and English lessons and even a kind of charm school where she learned to walk like a lady; negotiated her recording contract with Odeon; arranged photo sessions and interviews and modeling sessions in famous artists' studios; put on charity events in her name for publicity. He kept her busy, but she made sure to take time for herself, too, learning to play the ukulele, working out new dance steps, strengthening her body, taking long baths, and making love — not always with Pepito.

For all his energy elsewhere, he couldn't keep up with Josephine in the bedroom. She was starting to think no man could. But she kept her side affairs to herself, dreading his jealous temper that she'd already glimpsed. Last night, he and her friend Dr. Gaston Prieur had come up with a scheme to open a Josephine Baker nightclub. When Pepito found out that she'd signed a one-year contract to dance in L'Imperial every night for no pay, he saw red. Josephine, who went to several clubs a night and danced at every one for free, thought she'd gotten a good deal: L'Imperial gave her a meal every night and their spaghetti was the best in Paris. And besides, the owners had put her name in lights, changing the sign out front to JO-SEPHINE BAKER'S IMPERIAL. What advertising! But Pepi said she shouldn't do anything for free, and Dr. Prieur, sitting at their table, agreed. She went to dance, and when she came back Pepi had talked the doctor into financing a club for her and had even decided on a locale, near Le Grand Duc.

Without thinking, she'd thrown her arms around Dr. Prieur's neck and kissed him in thanks. Pepito hadn't liked that.

"Dr. Prieur was your lover?" he said on the ride home, scowling.

She shrugged and asked what did it matter, as long as he was willing to put up the money for her club.

"Trop d'amours," he fumed. "Too many lovers. Have you sexed all the men in Paris?" His voice rose. "This one?" He gestured toward André, who, to Josephine's relief, looked straight ahead.

"Don't be ridiculous, Pepi. Other men don't matter. I'm yours now."

"You are mine," he said, and seized her and buried his face in her bosom.

"Yes, baby, all yours. Nobody else's." Did André keep his eyes on the road as Pepito lifted up her skirt and had his way with her in the back seat? (Josephine hoped not.) Now, with her arms around his neck and her lips at his ear, she hoped he'd do it again, here in the bathroom with Yvette outside the door. *Take me,* she whispered, but his thoughts had moved on, and now so did he, stepping into the parlor to help Yvette marshal the animals back into their cages.

When everything was ready, Pepito rang for the bellhop and they marched into the lobby with Yvette and two hotel maids, André, and two bellhops carrying her trunks of clothing and cages of animals. Josephine and Pepito led them, she in her yellow crepe de chine dress, pearl-seeded cloche, and ermine stole, holding her billy goat Toutoute on a diamond leash and clasping the arm of Count Pepito Abatino in his tan suit, red-and-yellow shirt, and two-toned leather shoes, shocking the Americans with the sight of her black hand wrapped around his white Italian elbow and his white hand on her Negro ass.

"We're moving out," she announced

loudly as she led the group through the lobby, her strappy high heels rapping on the marble floor. "Be forewarned, you all: This hotel is filled with rats."

She walks onto the stage in a skintight dress covered in silver spangles that reflect the blue lights, reminiscent of the mirrors that lined her first club. A marquee descends, flashing CHEZ JOSÉPHINE. Dancers surround her in shimmering silver leotards and blue-feathered headdresses: a parade of peacocks, which is how Josephine felt at the time, preening, adored, beautiful. She gives a shimmy and runs her hands down her torso, eliciting cheers. She has kept her figure or, rather, starved herself to get it back, any extra flesh reined in by a girdle so constricting it's a miracle that she can sing "J'ai Deux Amours." She'd rather not, anyway, but people expect it now; it's become her signature, performed so many times that she has to muster all her acting skills to pretend she's enjoying herself. "I have two loves, my country and Paris." Later, she changed the lyrics to sing, "My country is Paris," but only after her native country betrayed her, or, rather, revealed itself as the unfaithful lover she'd always known it to be.

Paris could be fickle, there was no doubt about that — but it never abandoned her. And from 1926, when she debuted at the Folies-Bergère, until 1928, when she left on her world tour, the city belonged completely to Josephine Baker. Even while the audiences dwindled for her second Folies show, they crowded her nightclub in the after hours. If you were famous; if you were chic; if you were beautiful and rich; if you loved to have a good time; if you dug jazz and wanted to hear the best in town play it; if you had a bundle to spend on champagne; if you wanted to see and be seen in the most fashionable club in the city; if you were white; if you were colored; if you didn't mind a venue that mixed the two onstage and off-; if you didn't mind flashbulbs; if you were willing to wait in a long line until the wee hours to see Josephine Baker make her grand entrance; if you wanted to get your picture taken with her; if you wanted a night that you would never forget unless you wanted to, then *Chez Joséphine* was the place where you wanted to be.

Her first nightclub was only the beginning. Chez Joséphine clubs opened in New York and Berlin, as well, dazzling with stars: Astaire, Hepburn, Davis, Gable; Dietrich,

Grosz, Brecht, Weill; in Paris, Sartre, de Beauvoir, Kiki, Buñuel — and in 1939, Frida Kahlo, that enigmatic, beguiling vixen whose tongue imprinted Josephine's body with secrets she never told.

She'd met Frida in the "pussy palace" version of her club, as Sim called it, the Chez Joséphine she opened in Paris after her disastrous time in New York, damn Pepito for talking her into that mistake! She'd come back angry and determined to push back against the rising tide of racial prejudice in Europe. The pink motif — pink walls and carpet, pink leather furniture, pink bathroom sinks, pink linens, and pink lights — embodied life in the cold shadow of the Nazi threat.

None of her clubs, however, could compare with her first, opened in 1926 on the Montmartre hill and pulsing with music and craziness and fun. Every night after dancing two shows in the Folies-Bergère, she'd make the rounds of the hottest spots in the city to end up at her *boîte.* Those were the golden years for Josephine. Her picture in the newspapers every day; famous artists painting and sculpting her; her face on posters all over the city and in magazines; fashion designers sending her expensive clothes, her name in lights over her own Paris cabaret: Josephine had always dreamed big, but never had she imagined all this!

Chapter 16

1927

Chez Joséphine was the most elegant boîte in Montmartre; she made sure of that. The cut-glass mirrors around the stage reflected her dances in what seemed like a thousand angles, and its stage could hold a full orchestra, not just a few instruments as in other Paris joints. Its dance floor was big, too, with enough room for the whole club to join her there. She'd put a mirror on the back wall to make the place look twice as big, filled the club with little tables all crowded together, and had the white walls and pillars trimmed in gold paint. Most of the patrons were white, too, and many of them Americans, which made her laugh as she, the great-grandchild of slaves, charged them outrageous prices for dishes whose ingredients cost almost nothing. Forty-five francs for a dozen oysters!

People paid in part because the food was

so good. She'd hired Freddie, her chef, away from L'Imperial — gee, were the owners mad about that! They'd filed a lawsuit for breach of contract, but Pepi said they wouldn't win since the club had never paid Josephine a sou. Her clientele didn't come for the food, though. They filled her club night after night to enjoy an evening of unadulterated class. Blue chandeliers bathed the room in cool light that accentuated the curls of cigarette smoke swirling up and around and made Josephine's skin look like café au lait. A mural depicting a dancing Josephine covered one wall, painted by Paul Colin, now the most popular artist in Paris, thanks to her. And she always made sure to enter the club in high style, delaying her arrival until one in the morning so folks would keep eating and drinking while they waited for her to burst through the doors amid a fanfare from the stage, wearing outrageous designer fashions and leading a train of maids and animals.

Aware that she was the star attraction — and seeing how little good it did him to complain — Pepi didn't protest her new clothes anymore, even though he'd yelled plenty when he'd first taken over her accounts. She'd commissioned tonight's outfit, of blue snakeskin and tulle, for an exorbitant sum, which would make Pepito holler but she didn't care. Reflected like a glittering sapphire in all those mirrors, she could hardly take her eyes off herself, and neither could anyone else.

She swept into the club with her white servants, and no one batted an eyelash. She still couldn't get over it. In the States they'd have strung her up, afraid of their own history, scared that colored folks might make slaves out of *them.* Her servants were hardly slaves, though: Josephine paid her maid Yvette more for a week's work than her mama earned in a whole year. Tonight, the girl caught Josephine's wrap as it dropped from her shoulders, then led Arnold, Josephine's potbellied pig, into the kitchen. André walked in leading Miss Blanche, her Great Pyrenees, on a leather leash. On the stage, the orchestra dragged though "Dinah," the Ethel Waters version: were they trying to send folks home? In a booth in the back, a man had nodded off to sleep. That would not do! Signaling to the orchestra to speed it up, Josephine went over and gave him a kiss on his bald head to awaken him, then moved him to a table in the front, next to hers, and ordered him a bottle of champagne on the house.

Pepito should have been looking after

these guests, but he was nowhere to be found. And where was Sim? He was supposed to be her night manager, but she found him at the bar with a red-haired chorus dancer. Josephine strolled over and laid an arm across his shoulder like she owned him, saying *"Bonsoir, chéri,"* and took the dancer to sit with the bald man, who perked up instantly.

Pepito appeared, carrying tennis rackets and paper balls.

"Sim's drunk again," she said. "I need to have a talk with him."

He scowled. Pepito didn't like Sim, not only because Sim hung around with prostitutes and in opium dens, but also because he suspected something was up between him and Josephine. Pepito was a professional, though, and played his role before the club's patrons, exclaiming loudly over her beauty and pointing out her new dress, getting her to turn around and show it off before she went on her way.

Sim was waiting in her office when she stepped in and locked the door behind her, and then they were on the desk, her fingers unbuttoning his trousers while he lifted her dress, the pleasure of him unbearably sweet like a candy toothache until she gasped and his hand covered her mouth and she cried out against it and he shuddered, and then there was a knock on the door and Josephine went to open it, her clothing rearranged and Sim sitting in a chair. In the doorway stood Pepito, his nostrils flaring.

"Why did you lock the door?" he said.

"I didn't want to be disturbed. Sim and I have serious business to discuss." Josephine went to her desk and took a seat as if the air didn't reek of sex. "Sim, did you hire this band? They ought to be playing in an old folks' home."

Sim, sitting with his back to Pepito, looked like he might explode with the laughter he was holding in.

"Is this a boîte or a mortuary?" she said. "Go tell them to play something lively, Pepi."

"The people are waiting for you. *Tout le monde.* Come." The eye behind his monocle glared. Josephine went to him, took his arm, and let him lead her out into the crowd, winking at Sim behind her.

Seeing Josephine, the band launched into the fast version — her version — of "Dinah," a song she'd recorded last October. As she stepped through her club, the bandleader gestured and the crowd burst into applause, clamoring for her performance — but first, there were heads to be rubbed, beards to be pulled, gowns to be admired, champagne to be ordered for this table or that. Josephine knew how to play to the men; in white couples, they were the ones with the money. Pepito handed her confetti packets and she tossed them about. Soon the room swirled with confetti, as if they were in a snow globe.

"C'est une fête," he announced from the floor, spurring cheers. *"C'est toujours une fête par Joséphine."*

She joined him as part of their nightly routine, him kissing her hand and then her cheek, calling out, *"Bella, bella,* what a beauty," even as, tonight, his eyes winced with pain. She felt bad — but what was she supposed to do? Pepi didn't satisfy her and he knew it, but he still got mad every time a man looked at her straight. *It's only sex,* she'd say, but he insisted that if she loved him, she'd be faithful. Josephine had never heard anything so ridiculous, but she didn't mind his jealousy: it made her feel special.

"I don't deserve you, Pepi," she said, this also a part of their routine, their little joke, but he didn't smile that night. Josephine touched his cheek and told him with her eyes that she was sorry. She would change.

He eyed her dress, wondering how much she'd paid, knowing he wouldn't like the answer. Pepito had become a tyrant with money, parsing an allowance so puny that she often ran out of cash and had to use credit. He had control of her finances now, and of everything she owned. His jaw ticced with suspicion as he appraised her diamond-and-sapphire necklace and long, glittering earrings, her huge diamond ring, her gown. He would have to learn to live with it; designers didn't give away their best stuff, and Josephine wanted nothing less for her audiences. In her new Folies-Bergère show, she didn't get to wear much except that damned banana skirt and some patched overalls left over from her last show. She'd grown as bored with it all as her audiences were coming to be. One critic had written of this revue, *Un Vent de Folie* ("A Wind of Madness"), that "it would take a hurricane to make Mademoiselle Baker stop wiggling in the same old way."

Had she worn out her welcome in Paris? She had become ubiquitous, appearing daily in newspapers and magazines; at tea houses where she danced in the afternoons; at charity events; in paintings and sculptures by Picasso, Alexander Calder, Paul Colin; in fashion shows; at ribbon cuttings, at parties, in boîtes every night, making the rounds, advertising her club, before heading to Chez

Joséphine. People would lose interest unless she gave them a spectacle. They wanted glamour from their stars, not the same face and hair and clothes day after day.

She flounced onto the stage, swishing her blue-skirted rear in the blue light, and sang, forgetting about Pepito and his clenching jaw and fishy looks that told her he knew exactly what she'd been doing with Sim behind that locked door. She sang "Dinah" and forgot about him, forgot everything but the music and the crowd come to see her. She pulled the no-longer-nodding-off man onto the floor and they danced, and soon the whole hot club was running out to join them, laughing and shaking and singing, confetti swirling in the blue light and legs and arms flying.

When she'd finished the number and rejoined her table, Pepito brought over Colette, whose tux and tails only made her look more feminine. With her was a tall, puckish man who, with his looping bow tie and goatee, reminded Josephine of the snake-oil salesman from her Saint Louis days who'd awarded her the dollar prize in a dance contest. This guy was no huckster but Luigi Pirandello, "the most famous writer in Italy." He bowed and kissed her hand and said, *"Enchanté, bellisima,"* in a way that made her forget his age.

"I have brought you my new book," Colette said, pressing it into Josephine's hands, her fingertips stroking Josephine's, her brown eyes glinting promise.

"My French is awful bad. Maybe you could read it to me sometime soon," Josephine said, glinting back. A shriek sounded from the floor; a woman stood laughing as a man used his racket to whack her full champagne glass, soaking her and everyone around them. It was just two o'clock, and things were already getting messy.

Sim interrupted their pas de deux, slipping an arm around Josephine's shoulders. "Take care, Jo," he said. "Madame Colette is a notorious seductress."

"Qui se ressemble s'assemble," the woman said. Sim translated for Josephine: "It takes one to know one." Madame, looking pleased with her repartee, placed a cigarette in an ivory holder and waited for Sim to light it.

"And Mademoiselle Baker is easily seduced." Sim, flipping shut his lighter, grinned at Josephine. "She would make love with all the world if she had the time."

"Qui se ressemble s'assemble," Josephine said. Everyone laughed except, she noticed, Pepito.

312

"Chérie," Colette said, taking Josephine's hand and leading her away, "why do you waste your time? Sim bores you, I can tell. If that Italian count of yours isn't keeping you satisfied, I can do much better. Let me show you the delights of a mature woman."

A hand grasped her arm: Pepito.

"We must speak," he said, and turned a stiff bow to Colette, asking for her pardon.

"What the hell? Pepi, what is the matter?"

Pepito clenched his jaw as he steered her to her office, where he shoved her inside.

"Hey," she said, stumbling. "What the f—" And then the door slammed shut and his hand came down across her face in a stinging slap.

"Putain," he was saying, his hands on her shoulders now and shaking her. Josephine cried out, but no one could hear, the music jaunty and jangling and people laughing and drinking champagne by the bucketsful while she wrested herself out of his grip and cradled the hurt place with her cupped hand.

Pepito was saying something — "Look at me," it might've been — but Josephine closed her eyes and made herself smaller and waited for the ringing in her ears to subside. The burning of her cheek, the shame: she felt seven years old again. He touched the top of her head, but she ran to a corner where she curled up in a ball with her arms over her face. A long time later, she heard the door open and close. He'd walked back into the club, and she should, too, folks had come to see her and she mustn't keep them waiting for too long. But she didn't move.

She heard a knock on the door, a woman's voice speaking her name. The door opened, and Colette came over to kneel beside her. She touched a hand to Josephine's still-stung cheek.

"Italians," she said. "Such violent people."

"Take me home with you, Colette, please," Josephine said. "Now."

CHAPTER 17

Josephine waved her left hand, shooting facets of light. Sixteen carats. "Ain't it the most beautiful ring you've ever seen?" Flashbulbs popped, making Pepito blink so hard he nearly dropped his monocle.

They were in her and Pepito's apartment, telling a gaggle of reporters and photographers about their "marriage." For the press conference, they wore wedding-type clothes: Josephine, a demure dress of black velvet with a white lace skirt; Pepito, a tux. He'd also brought one of the new Josephine Baker dolls to include in their pictures together, no occasion too sacred to make a buck.

Pepito never stopped scheming for money. He'd be showing off the merchandise — including Josephine — even if they really had tied the knot, which he wished were the case but never would be, not if Josephine had any say. Maybe this announcement would satisfy him at last, and he'd stop bugging her to really get married; hopefully, it would distract the press and keep them from digging into her past and discovering Billy Baker.

A reporter asked for details of the wedding. Josephine, beaming, recited the story she and Pepito had concocted: They'd had a private ceremony on her birthday a few weeks ago. Where? At the US consulate. The ambassador, yes, had officiated: Mr. Herrick, a friend of hers. Had he been heartbroken to marry her to someone else? Gee, what a funny question, but you know, she has had thousands of proposals. Mr. Herrick would just have to get in line, ha ha!

Pepito twisted his mustache, their secret signal that she was going too far. The last thing she wanted was for anyone to call the ambassador, whom she'd spoken with once at a party for about two minutes. To change the subject, she clutched Pepito's arm and said no man was his equal as far as she was concerned, just look at the beautiful ring he'd given her, too heavy even to wear.

"That ain't all he gave me, either. I got all the jewels and heirlooms that have been in the Abatino family for generations." There went Pepito blinking again, what was his problem? He was the heir to the Abatino

316

family fortune, wasn't he? He hadn't given her any heirlooms yet, but he didn't carry them around with him. Locked in a vault somewhere, she imagined. She'd get them when they went to Italy to meet his family.

One reporter asked about Pepito's title. He had not been able to find any record or genealogy of an Abatino noble family. Was her husband truly a count?

"There ain't no fake about that title," she said, remembering to breathe, to smile, to flirt. "I had it looked up and verified by a private detective in Rome before I signed on the dotted line. The count has a big family there and lots of coats of arms and everything. I understand they live in a big swell château, and as soon as my contract with the Folies-Bergère is finished, I'm going to visit them."

She squeezed Pepito's hand, wondering how much he'd understood. "His English is worse than mine, and mine is pretty bad," she told the journalists, all American reporters for newspapers, magazines, radio programs, and newsreels. Pepito, meanwhile, had stopped paying attention. What was on his mind? More ways to make money from this charade, most likely. Josephine-and-Pepito bride-and-groom dolls for wedding cakes was one of his crazy ideas. They wouldn't like that in the States, though. She'd tried to explain this to Pepito, saying that, with the American press, maybe he should keep his distance from her, but he wouldn't listen.

"I will have my arm on you. *Ton mari!*" Her husband. Thumping his chest.

"It's a good thing we're just pretending," she said.

He shushed her. "If the press learns the truth, our fish is fried."

For a moment, she slipped into regret: she shouldn't have shot her mouth off with that magazine writer yesterday. The interview had gone well and, when it was over, Josephine had asked about the diamond the writer was wearing. It was an engagement ring, the young woman said, her dark eyes misting over; she and her fiancée planned a spring wedding.

"With a cake and a white dress and everything? You are so lucky," Josephine said. "I wanted a real wedding, but we eloped." The reporter stared at her.

"You are married?"

Josephine's heart seemed to fly right up into her mouth as she tried to think of an answer that didn't involve Billy.

"I guess I just gave you a scoop." She pressed her fingers to her lips, oops! Thinking fast, she added, "Me and Pepito got married on my birthday." Conjuring the scene in her mind: herself in a white gown studded with pearls and diamonds; him in a top hat and tails.

Why had they kept it a secret? Out of respect for Pepito's mother: Josephine wanted the Countess Abatino's blessing before telling the world that she'd married her son.

"I thought we would wait to get married until our Italy trip, but Pepito wanted me as soon as I turned twenty-one."

This was partly true: He'd proposed to Josephine months ago, on his knee, the gaudy ring winking when she'd opened the box. Bought with her money, no doubt. So far, she had avoided giving him an answer, saying, what if she couldn't have children? Counts needed heirs. As he'd held her in bed that night so tightly she could hardly breathe, she'd wondered: should she tell him about Billy?

The very word *divorce* struck her heart like a fist on a drum. At least Pepito wanted her, though, while Billy, ultimately, had not. Pepito didn't mind her success but wanted to increase it. Instead of pouting in the corner as Billy had done, he'd stepped into the ring, fighting alongside her and for her.

But he also fought *on* her, another reason why she hesitated.

A week went by. Pepito started to grumble, pressing for an answer. After two weeks, smelling Sim on her breath one afternoon, he'd surprised her with a punch in the gut. "Now you know how I am feeling, not very good," he'd said as she'd doubled over trying to catch her breath.

Josephine knew why he was upset — because she hadn't accepted his proposal. But what could she do? Tell him the truth? Pepito was old-fashioned, "traditional," he called it, and she didn't think he'd cotton to her having a husband back in the States. In Europe, a man could have a wife and a mistress and no one minded, but women were supposed to be "pure." Josephine had laughed the first time he'd said this — *you're pulling my leg* — but he'd meant every word.

If he knew she was married, what would happen? She'd have to divorce Billy, and the papers would find out. Her fans would learn the truth about her, which nobody wanted. People preferred the fairy tale, the rags-to-riches story, Cinderella but with a loving family, a grandmother with a warm lap, a mother who worked hard to support her, and a stepfather who tried to help but was too sick. That was the tale her new book would tell. Marrying an Italian count would be the perfect ending, "happily ever after" — and she could have it, she could have everything, she'd realized. Pretending to be married would satisfy Pepito for now, and also give them the chance to talk about her memoir and her movie, both coming out soon.

After her slip and hasty cover-up with the magazine writer, she'd wrung her hands, at first, then decided not to worry: the story wouldn't appear for several months, giving her and Pepito time to cook something up. But she'd started hearing from reporters that very night. The magazine writer, sabotaging her own "scoop," had blabbed the news of Josephine Baker's marriage all over Paris.

Marcel Sauvage, the writer of her *Memoires,* was in her apartment at the time, going over the manuscript and translating passages she couldn't read, which was most of it. He had gotten quite a few things wrong, which worried her, but he was a storyteller, as Sim had said. When she'd protested, Marcel had seemed offended, saying, "Surely you trust me, after all the hours we have spent together." Did she?

She hadn't told Marcel about her marriage fib, but when reporters came to her door with questions, he acted like he knew all about her and Pepito's "secret" wedding. Thank goodness, because Josephine was at a loss for words. She'd been so flustered after almost spilling the beans about Billy that she barely remembered, now, what she'd said afterward. Yes, she told the journalists, they had married on her birthday, but she didn't want to say more until Pepito could be with her. Then she'd gotten busy setting the scene for breaking the news to him, making spaghetti and giving him a Bugatti watch, and making love to him in his favorite way. Then, in the languid warmth of after-sex, she told how she'd accidentally announced some very surprising news, ha ha ha! It was a joke at first, but the writer had become so excited and Josephine got caught up in the story and the next thing you knew, she and Pepito were hitched!

She couldn't believe her luck when he smiled. *"Et voilà,"* he said. He reached out for her but she pulled away, wary of the punch line — or the punch.

"Why should I be angry, *amore*? To make you my wife has been my desire, no? And this way, we avoid the expense of a wedding. Who needs a ceremony?"

Well, *she* did, but Josephine didn't say so.

She'd made this bed and now she would lie in it, no complaining. But Pepito must have read her mind, because he kissed her and said they would have a ceremony if she wanted one, and a reception, too, an enormous party, one that the entire city would talk about all year. He forgot to mention that Josephine's money would pay for it, but that hardly mattered now, she supposed; if they were to really get married all her earnings from now on, lawsuit or not, would belong to Pepito: that was the French law. She rubbed the gooseflesh on her arms, reminding herself that none of this was real. Now that they were "married," Pepito would have what he wanted, which was Josephine, and he'd stop throwing fits at her. She'd be his and he'd be hers, and, like Cinderella and Prince Charming, they'd live happily ever after.

At their press conference, Josephine used her acting skills to play the joyous bride as she maneuvered the discussion to her upcoming film.

"Your husband has been deeply involved in your career," a reporter said. "Will he join you on the stage, as well?" This was a silly question, Pepito couldn't dance or sing.

"No one gets to wear the banana skirt but me." That made them laugh, good.

"But we are making a movie together," she said. "The first film ever to star a Negro woman. It's a comedy, set against a background of nobility."

Would Pepito play a sheik, like Rudolph Valentino?

"He's handsome enough, don't you think? But he only has eyes for me, so he wouldn't know what to do with those other women."

Now it was time to pose for a few loving shots. "I'm just as happy as can be," she said, gazing into Pepito's eyes — for the cameras, yes, but also out of love.

"I didn't have any idea that getting married would be so exciting," she said as the shutters clicked. "I am just so thrilled." At last, she had a family — or a husband, at least, not a mama's boy like Billy but a real man. And who could tell? Doctors didn't know everything. Maybe she *would* have a baby. Pepito hadn't gotten her pregnant yet but he might. Or maybe someone would — a backup plan that she kept to herself.

"Now that you are my wife, you must be faithful to me," he'd said to her last night. He was such a jealous man. Was that bad? "I love you, and if you love me you will do as I say."

Warmth had spread like hot, sweet syrup through her veins. Who else had ever loved her? Not her mama, who'd resented her for being born; not her grandmother, who'd married her off at thirteen; not Willie Wells, who'd left after their first fight; not Billy, who was too much a baby to love like a man; not Marcel, who was ashamed to be seen with her. In all her life, no one had loved her except Pepito. For all his flaws, she had to give him that.

Chapter 18

1928

Josephine had come to expect big crowds wherever she went, but she cried out to see the line at her book event, hundreds of people snaking around the block and crowding Elsa Maxwell's Acacia Gardens tea room and spilling into the lushly blooming garden in back. As a counterpoint to the foliage, she'd worn a dress, coat, and hat with a black-and-white chevron pattern — her new favorite outfit, very modern — for the outdoor signing. One by one her fans approached with copies of her memoir and some with her records, too, wanting her autograph. Some brought their children, whom Josephine embraced, kissing their soft cheeks and breathing in their fresh smells, lotion and talcum and chewing gum and candy. Using her new stamp with her name spelled the French way, *Joséphine,* she put her imprint on everything placed in front of

her, including a man's bald pate, Josephine
Baker dolls, and a baby's behind.

Sitting next to her was the writer, Marcel
Sauvage, wearing a cheap suit but who
cared with those doe eyes? Nobody asked
for his autograph but he looked pretty
pleased, anyway: thinking about all the
money he was going to get, most likely. Josephine had agreed to split the royalties and
didn't begrudge him, as hard as he'd
worked, interviewing her for hours on end
and translating all her stories into French
— well, not *all* of them. Once she started
talking about the past, sometimes, she
couldn't stop, and would tell secrets she
didn't want him to write: the real story of
her childhood, for instance, including her
two marriages, Mr. Dad, and the child she'd
gotten rid of — stories he'd agreed, against
his inclination, to leave out of the book. She
should let him write it all, he'd said, pointing out that they were thin on material.

Josephine refused. And she had warned
him, hadn't she? She'd laughed when Marcel had suggested he write her memoir. She
was only twenty-two, she'd pointed out. "I
ain't done enough living to fill a book." And
a lot of what she had done and seen, she
didn't want to tell. So to fill in, she gave
him recipes and beauty tips, and got Paul

Colin to do some drawings. Even so, she'd been surprised to see all the pages in the finished book. What had he put in there? She couldn't tell for sure because it was all in French.

A murmur arose, and a shout. A group pushed its way in, men on crutches and canes, one in a wheelchair. A skinny fellow with yellow teeth hollered right in her face. He wore a military uniform and his breath smelled of sweaty feet and cheese. Someone waved a crutch, nearly striking Marcel, who stood up and cried, *"Assez!"* — enough. They were veterans, he told Josephine, come to protest.

Turning toward the men, she said, *"Pourquoi?"*

"Pourquoi? Pourquoi?" The man in front looked like he might faint. He talked so fast Josephine couldn't pick out a word. He reddened and his scar turned white and twisted like a worm. The man in the wheelchair, legs amputated at the knee, glared at her like his injuries were her fault.

A reporter from *Le Monde* came in, a blond boy with serious black eyes, scribbling notes in a pad. "How will you explain yourself to these men?" he said.

"Have I committed a crime? They're the ones who should explain. Their rude behavior is appalling."

The man in the wheelchair asked a question in a jeering tone. Josephine looked at Marcel, who had jammed his hands into his trouser pockets.

"He asks if he disgusts you," the reporter said.

"Of course he doesn't. What kind of question is that?"

"In your book, you say that you are disgusted by veterans who are disfigured or maimed."

"That's not true." Behind him, a little girl stared and clutched a Josephine Baker doll by the hair, making Josephine's head hurt.

The reporter picked up a copy of the memoir and read aloud, creating more of an uproar than before. Josephine wanted to cover her ears. She snatched the book from his hands and stared at the page.

"I never said this." She rounded on Marcel. "What did you do?"

"They are your words." She remembered the conversation differently. In Chez Joséphine one afternoon, she and Marcel had talked about the Great War, in which he had fought. An explosion had torn his leg nearly off, but the doctors had saved it. Marcel told her he would rather have died than live as a cripple, weak and pitiful or, worse, reviled.

"When I see a man like that, I cannot bear to look at him," he'd said, "perhaps because it might have been me. Is that wrong?"

Josephine had curled her fingers around his hand — at last, they were touching! — and told him she understood. "Is it wrong? I don't know. I feel the same way. When I see anything that's crippled, I feel sick." She hadn't meant it, of course — she was just trying to make him feel better.

"What the hell did you write? I trusted you," she muttered now.

"Josephine saw the proofs, and approved them," Marcel told the reporter. "She even made changes, which I can show you."

"They were all in French," she cried. "I couldn't read a word.

"Monsieur, this is a mistake," she said to the poor little wheelchair man. He must think she was a monster. "I'm not disgusted or reviled by you or any man who has given so much for our country. In fact, I'm grateful." She kissed her fingertips, then touched them to his amputated knees. She walked to the tall man and kissed the scars on his face, and greeted each of the veterans in the same manner, kissing and touching their hurt places and saying *desolée*, sorry, until they smiled, some with tears in their eyes. They loved her still.

"I'll sue your ass," she said when she'd sat down beside Marcel again. "I'll give your royalties to somebody who deserves them — to these fellas here."

Marcel smiled as if they were exchanging pleasantries. "A lawsuit? Be my guest. I will gladly provide the notes from our interviews — *all* the notes. A jury will find them enlightening. And your public —" He chuckled. "Your public will find them fascinating."

She was nearly late for her first show that evening, the book signing having lasted many hours, but what was she supposed to do, walk away from people who had waited in line to meet her? Marcel had grown impatient, telling her to stop talking, to just sign the books "or we will be here all night," as if he had something else to do. She'd be damned before she'd disappoint her fans.

"*I* don't let people down," she'd said. "But you can leave if you want to."

She wished he would. She could hardly stand to look at him, knowing what he'd done. Putting shit in her book that made her look bad. It didn't even matter whether she'd said those things, he should have known better than to quote her.

He'd admired her honesty, he'd said. To hell with him.

At the Folies-Bergère that night, picketers carried signs denouncing her: JOSEPHINE BAKER HATES VETERANS. André let her off at the stage door in back. When she stepped inside, M. Derval rushed up, wild-eyed: she was due onstage in five minutes.

"Don't worry," she said, "my costume only takes one minute to put on."

The theater was half empty, the same as when Florence's *Blackbirds* had been in town. Josephine didn't get much energy back from the sparse, half-hearted audience and so, when the show ended, she took a single curtain call and headed to her dressing room. It had been one hell of a day.

And it wasn't over yet.

At her dressing room door, several members of the press waited.

"I've apologized to the veterans for my mistake," she said. "I'm going to dance a benefit for them next month. I don't know what else I can say."

"We are not here to talk about that old news," one of them said. "We want to ask about your so-called 'marriage' to M. Abatino and his supposed title. It seems, mademoiselle, that you are not the countess you claim to be."

Pepito came up at just the right moment and steered her into her dressing room and locked the door behind them. "And so our trick is discovered," he said. "You must tell everyone that we did it for the film."

So Josephine had another press conference, in which she confessed that she and Pepito had not *officially* wed, but that to get publicity before the debut of her movie, *La Sirène des Tropiques,* they'd pretended to get married. "We got carried away," she said — but none of the journalists seemed amused. They looked bored, in fact, and none of them asked questions. The story came out in all the newspapers, but no one in Paris seemed to mind their prank. From the States, though, she had some letters.

We adored you, Josephine Baker. We threw parties in the streets to celebrate the wedding of one of our own sisters to a count. You made us believe. But it was all a lie.

She'd made them believe what? That a colored woman could marry a nobleman, that a Negress could become a countess? Her *success* should inspire them, not her choice of husband. Look at her on the screen, the first Negro woman film star! That was important, wasn't it? No matter that the movie was awful — so bad that, at the premiere the following month, she had to close her eyes.

"This is terrible," she wanted to whisper, but to whom? Beside her, Pepito wore a big smile, like he'd never seen anything so good. Elsa Maxwell, sitting on her other side, kept patting her arm and saying, "Marvelous, darling, just marvelous." When, on the screen, she fell into a flour bin, the theater erupted in laughter. Mistinguett had tears rolling down her cheeks. Dr. Prieur held his sides, which jiggled with mirth. Was Josephine the only one who thought it was crap? She felt like calling out, "The emperor has no clothes."

Of course they couldn't see the truth. They thought this shit was funny, the stupid jungle girl running around like she didn't have a lick of sense. *The French have their own kinds of prejudice,* Florence had said. Josephine had thought herself so high and mighty because she'd gotten away from mammy songs and blackface, but how did this differ?

The entire movie was foolishness. She longed to share her thoughts with Flo, and wondered if she might be watching, too, from her seat in heaven. She'd died so young; it didn't seem right. They'd dipped a plane at her funeral and released a thousand bluebirds, but no one could replace the happiness that left the world when Florence Mills died. How could Josephine not have seen it coming? She'd noticed that Flo seemed ill, but had never dreamed her friend had tuberculosis.

Florence's final letter had opened Josephine's eyes to some things. She'd read in the newspapers about Josephine's humiliation on the night Charles Lindbergh had landed in Paris. Josephine had interrupted that night's performance to announce that his plane, the *Spirit of St. Louis,* had successfully made the first transatlantic flight. She'd cried as she'd cheered with the audience, proud for the first time to be American, proud, even, to be from Saint Louis, "Lucky Lindy's" hometown. After the show, she'd gone to the celebration at L'Abbaye de Thélème and performed a dance in Lindy's honor before taking her seat with Pepito. In the quiet moments between songs, when the murmur of the diners and celebrants rose and fell, a man's voice — an American voice — punched through like a carnival barker's.

"Where I come from, nigger women belong in the kitchen," he said.

A hush fell over the room. Josephine, the only colored woman in the place, buried her nose in her menu, pretending she hadn't heard while wanting to crawl under the table.

"You are in France, monsieur," the waiter said. "Here, we treat all the races the same."

"Well, I don't like looking at 'em while I eat." With all those chins, he could stand to miss a meal or two — but she glanced away before he caught her looking.

"I think I'll get either the fish or duck," she whispered to Pepito.

"You may depart, or stay, as you desire," the waiter said. "But if you remain, you must respect our rules." No longer proud to be American, Josephine wanted to kiss the feet of France. The cracker stood up so abruptly that he knocked over his chair and bumped Josephine's seat as he barreled his way to the door, his wife running behind to catch up.

I felt so bad to think of you enduring that humiliation, Florence wrote. *And I also wondered what you replied to him. I'm sure it was a humdinger.*

She'd sat for a long time with that letter in her hand. Why had she let that ugly man insult her? She should have stood up for herself instead of cringing. She remembered Flo's words on their last evening together: "Won't nobody respect us if we don't respect ourselves."

Even Johnny Hudgins did a better job of fighting back. When Mildred had come to join him in Paris and the three of them had walked to Chez Joséphine one night, an American mistook the light-skinned Mildred for a white woman and called her a "nigger lover." Johnny had punched the man, spilling blood and a piece of the man's tooth on the sidewalk. A pair of gendarmes stepped in, but when Josephine and Mildred explained what had happened, they let Johnny go.

"I see what you mean, Jo, about Paris being a better place for us," Johnny said when the cops had gone, wiping the sweat from his face. "If this had happened in the States, I'd be bound for the gallows."

"Why did you stir up trouble, then?" she said, her voice trembling. He looked at her like he'd never seen her before.

"It wasn't me causing the trouble," he said. "What should I have done?"

"Ignore them," Josephine said. "Who cares what they think?"

"That's easy for you to say, living here," Mildred chimed in. "But we deal with this shit all the time back home. And believe me, honey, ignoring it won't make it go away."

"Doing nothing makes it worse," Johnny

said. "We've got to help our people."

Was she helping her people with this movie? Josephine watched herself roll her eyes and play the naif, an overgrown child, and wondered if she'd done more harm than good.

When the film ended, she wanted to tell the people to stop applauding, that the movie was trash — but instead, urged by Pepito, she took a bow. He was already working with producers on a new script for her, but there would be no deal if *La Sirène des Tropiques* didn't do well — and she would never become a Hollywood star. The next movie would be better. She would play a dramatic role, and do it so well that people forgot her color.

"Très magnifique," Pepito said as the house lights went up, and everyone around them agreed. Josephine had never felt so alone.

"This film will increase your audience at the Folies-Bergère," M. Derval said. Pepito bragged about the distribution: it would be shown throughout Europe and, next year, in the United States — as if showing the world how ugly and stupid she could act were something to be proud of. What in the hell was she doing with him? What had she seen in Pepito?

She'd seen his title. His good looks. His

flattery. His promises to make her the richest woman in the world.

Now, at thirty-eight, he looked old, the creases in his forehead deepening and lines forming around his mouth. His compliments, once so effusive, had turned like sour milk into criticisms and commands: *Hold your fork like this. Straighten your shoulders when you walk. Do not talk with your mouth full of food.* She didn't even have his title anymore. The only way to get it back would be to legally marry him, and she'd be damned if she'd do so.

Of course, that's not what she told the press. She and Pepito didn't need a ceremony, she'd said, because they were married in their hearts. She'd never seen so many eyes roll.

"Pepito is still going to give me the family jewels," she'd said. This was no lie: he'd get them when he took her to Italy in February, after her show *Un Vent de Folie* closed and after her "Farewell to Paris" show at the Salle Pleyel. They would leave Paris to tour Europe and South America. Pepito had arranged it. He was a great manager, which was why she stayed with him. Of course, he had a temper, but, truth be told, so did she. She'd thought about leaving him, but decided against it every time. He helped her succeed. He pushed her harder than she had even pushed herself. Bricky and others looked down on him, but even they had to admit: Pepito had made her rich.

And if his twisted English that she had once found endearing now made her want to strangle him? If she found his monocle no longer dashing but an affectation? If his kiss — the rare times when he parsed one out to her — left her cold? It was better than being out *in* the cold, wasn't it? For excitement, she had plenty of offers, in the clubs and in the wings, in the bedroom and the dressing room, in the back seats and the back alleyways.

"We will transform you," Pepito had said in proposing the tour, his eyes fairly flashing with dollar signs. No more naked *nichons;* no more banana skirts; no more jungle acts. "You will depart from Paris a primitive caterpillar and return a sophisticated butterfly."

In her farewell performance, Josephine sang. Perched atop a grand piano in a red gown, she sang her heart out for Paris, this city that had given her respect and love and money and dreams of a better life in a new world.

She sang her farewell to Montmartre and

Pigalle and the Champs-Élysées and Montparnasse, to the Les Halles market and the beautiful gilded Pont Alexandre III, to the Parc Monceau with its ponds and statues and Roman-style colonnade and sandpit full of playing children, to the gold-and-green Place de la Concorde fountain, to the Arc de Triomphe and the Eiffel Tower, to Le Chat Noir and Le Grand Duc and Chez Joséphine.

She sang to M. Derval and Bricky and Paul Colin, to Mistinguett and Chevalier, to Edith Piaf and Colette and Pirandello and Fernandel, to her hairdresser and furrier and shoemaker and clothing designers, to the men she had loved and the women she had loved, including to Sim, whose heart she could not help breaking, who had begged her to marry him (he would divorce Tigy, he swore, but Josephine knew it could never work out; she and he were too much alike). He had forgiven her and come to her farewell tonight to read his homage to her, eliciting sniffles and a thunder of applause from the sold-out house.

Most of all, she sang farewell to nude dances, banana skirts, and crossed eyes. Paris was ready to be rid of that girl, and so was she. She could all but hear the yawns these days as she danced the Charleston.

For her to come out in a gown and sing was risky, especially with the city's most popular chanteuses in the audience, but it was working, she could feel the energy rising. No one cared that she struggled to reach the highest note and hold it. When she'd finished on a long, low moan, the room fell silent for such a long time that she thought she might faint from holding her breath, but then came the reward: a standing ovation. She blew kiss after kiss, especially to Pepito, in the front row beaming at her, looking like he might break into light. Their experiment had succeeded. When they returned from her world tour, Paris would welcome the new Josephine Baker. She hoped. She prayed.

Europe was good to her — at first.

She adored Copenhagen, such a beautiful city and the people so welcoming; Oslo, where she went fishing under the midnight sun; Amsterdam, where she danced the Charleston in yellow wooden shoes; Stockholm, where the prince of Sweden took her to his palace, covered her body in jewels, and made such ardent love to her that she'd cried for days after leaving him. In Prague, an enormous crowd greeted her at the railway station, forcing her to climb on top of her car until the legions of hands swept her away, floating her on their outstretched arms like a cork on the water. The reception in Budapest was even more frenzied, the Hungarians grasping at her clothes, tearing at them, wanting to see her naked, forcing her to take refuge in an ox cart — an ill omen, she feared, and she was right.

Budapest was when things started to get ugly.

On opening night, young men threw ammonia bombs on the stage while she danced. "Go back to Africa!" they screamed. She ran off the stage, weeping from gas and grief, straight into the arms of a different André, a tall, blond cavalry officer who'd rushed backstage at the first sign of trouble, vowing to protect her. When he spoke to her, Josephine found herself, suddenly, able to comprehend French (although with Pepito she would still, sometimes, pretend not to). She'd thought her knees would buckle when he told her she was *la reine de la nuit,* "queen of the night," and *le soleil noir de la cité de la lumière,* "the black sun of the city of lights." He sent her love poems that she folded and tucked into her bra, next to her heart.

Pepito found out about their affair, of course, and the next thing Josephine knew, he'd challenged André to a duel. Josephine gave Pepito hell: he'd better cancel this foolishness! Pepito talked about *l'honneur,* which made her suck her teeth in disgust. What honor was there in getting himself killed? André was an officer in the Austrian cavalry, and surely knew how to use a sword. What would she do if Pepito ended up dead? Who would take care of her?

"I hope you've named me in your will," she said.

Pepito's face turned white, and he sat down to write another note. By the time the "duel" happened at dawn the next day, he and André had reached an agreement. As a gaggle of reporters snapped photos and took notes, Pepito parried and thrust, dancing and waving his sword like a dandy; Josephine screamed, playing her part, until André reached out almost casually with his blade to nick Pepito's shoulder, the "first blood" making him the winner.

That evening he sent Josephine another poem, inviting her to his bed, and of course she went.

"Joséphine à Bobino" doesn't mention any of the bad stuff in these around-the-world scenes. As she sings "Give Me Your Hand," the chorus takes the stage in red jackets and fur hats to do a Russian dance, although she never set foot in Russia. The audience loves it — the upbeat music, the spinning and kicking, Josephine smiling as though three years touring Europe and South America didn't teach her that racial hatred isn't just an American illness, but a plague that disfigures people everywhere. That tour changed her forever.

She kept her spirits up, at first. Although

glad to leave the ill winds of Budapest behind, she'd hoped the mood would improve as the tour continued. It didn't. As she danced in Zagreb, a group of young men stood and shouted, "Long live Croatian culture! Down with vulgarity!" She knew what that meant: "Croatian culture" didn't include Negroes.

Vienna, thank goodness, welcomed her with open arms, or so she thought when she stepped off the train and into a throng of admirers cheering and tossing flowers. The theater director drove her and Pepito in a gold-and-blue horse-drawn carriage through a light-falling snow along the Ringstrasse, the ringing of church bells coming from near and far. Were they for her? she asked the director, who nodded, looking grim. Later, she learned that the bells tolled to ward off the evil her "satanic" presence had brought to the city.

They passed buildings that looked like frosted cakes to arrive at the Grand Hotel Wien, a magnificent building of white marble, tall and broad, with velvet curtains framing the covered entryway. She felt as though she were in a fairy tale until she noticed the fifty white men on the sidewalk, none looking like he'd ever had a good day.

Josephine stared, feeling like she was in a recurring dream. Many wore brownshirt uniforms. Some carried posters for her show, a red *X* smeared across her picture. *"Negers-mach!"* some of them shouted — an ominous-sounding word if ever there was one. It seemed like a mile from the carriage to the hotel door.

"You are the scandal of Austria," said Pepito, twisting his mustache. "We will sell many tickets. That is good, no? Why are you sad? Your success grows with every protest. You are getting stronger."

In their room, Josephine looked out the window at the commotion, at the rage-red faces of blond-haired men shouting and calling her "black devil." The Viennese were more snobbish than Parisians, Pepito said, putting his arms around her. They resisted anything new that might "pollute" their culture. A jazz opera had debuted here last week and caused riots in the streets. Josephine extricated herself from his embrace and turned to face him. He knew this, and yet he'd brought her here?

He rubbed the fingers of one hand together and grinned, looking like *he* was the devil.

"Money," he said.

Throughout her tour, Josephine worked to improve herself, studying French, German, Spanish, etiquette, posture, piano, and voice, some days locked in her room by Pepito until she had finished her lessons. "You must work, and grow stronger in every way," he said. The day after she'd spent the night with Gustaf, the Swedish crown prince, Pepito locked her in the bedroom of their hotel suite for twelve hours. When she heard him come in the door she began to scream. "Dirty wop," she snarled. "Phony count." In an instant, the door flew open followed by Pepito's fist. Josephine fought back until he lay on the floor, cupping his balls.

"You were right," she said, standing over him. "I am getting stronger, and it feels damned good. You ever hit me again, I'll bite your fucking hand off."

CHAPTER 19

1928, Berlin

It seemed like every time she'd mentioned Berlin, folks had to issue a warning. Germany, they said, had become a dangerous place for anyone who wasn't an Aryan, meaning white. In Budapest, her lover André had urged her to cancel her Berlin performances, saying she might not get out alive. The Nazi Party was gaining influence; poverty had increased in Germany, and Hitler blamed the Jews. Those same people hated Negroes, too.

Josephine took the doom and gloom with a grain of salt. Hadn't she heard the same bleak warnings before her Berlin tour three years ago? With the exception of a few annoying brownshirts, though, she'd had little trouble. Au contraire, the people had loved her there. Of course she would return.

Knowing how popular she'd been in Berlin, Pepito had booked her for a six-month run in the Stage Theater des Westens, a much bigger venue than the Nelson, where she'd played before. The Westens reminded her of a palace, with an ornate white facade sporting seven arched doorways and seven huge windows. The auditorium didn't seat as many as she'd expected, though; the massive brick-and-marble balconies on either side of the stage took up a lot of room. Still, it was an improvement over the Nelson. No one was likely to rush onto the stage here, thank goodness. After six months' excitement in Eastern Europe, Josephine hoped for an uneventful time in Berlin.

One night about three weeks into her run, her old friend Max Reinhardt came to her dressing room door, his intense eyes hooded by a new, wary expression.

"Congratulations on your film," he said. "I look forward to its German debut."

"Oh, gosh, no, please don't see that garbage," she said. She should have enrolled in his school and learned to act, she told him. "I went there last week looking for you, but nobody would tell me where you were. Are you in trouble?"

"Life is not the same here, Josephine. Germany is not the same, especially for Jews like me and Negroes like you. I am certain

350

that you have noticed the changes."

She had: Berlin looked grayer and more squalid than before, the faces grimmer. The merriment and freedom that had buoyed the city three years ago had disappeared, clamped down by an oppressive hand and choked by squalor. She'd been shocked to see streetwalkers on the sidewalks at all hours of the day, eyes empty, faces gaunt, three of them clawing one another over a coin someone had dropped. She'd also noticed many more brownshirts, now with swastika symbols on their sleeves and glaring at her with a disgust that made her want to scuttle into the nearest hole, as though that were where she belonged.

The brownshirts were bullies but they wouldn't hurt her, Pepito had insisted. Her show was sold out for weeks, and he'd found a venue for a Chez Joséphine, where she could perform after hours. The club was a hit, the "toast of Berlin," someone had written. She'd enjoyed herself until the Nazis had started showing up, poisoning the room and sucking all the pleasure from the night, taking the best tables, pounding their fists to demand more beer, eating like pigs and strewing food on the floor, shouting insults with full mouths while she sang. Fräulein Landshoff came to see her, too, not in a tuxedo as before but in a blue evening gown. Josephine hadn't recognized her at first.

"When some Nazis called me 'boyfriend' and asked if I liked it in the ass, I changed my look," she said.

"Berlin has become a treacherous place," Max said now. "Promise me that, as soon as you feel a threat, you will flee. The Nazis are . . . unpredictable. You should be ready to leave at a moment's notice — as I am."

When uniforms filled the front rows that night, she wondered if Max had been trying to give her some kind of signal. These weren't the rowdy youths she'd been dealing with at the club but grown men, more disciplined, with disapproval chiseled onto their faces. Their hoots and whistles started while Lea Seidl, a popular, blond-haired German actress, was singing. Why were they picking on her? Then they began shouting "Rotter," the name of the show's producers, and *Juden* — the Rotters were Jewish. Josephine felt sick. Lord knew what they would do when she took the stage.

Lea staggered into the wings, her face full of fear. Josephine put her arms around the poor girl, and Lea leaned on her for a moment or two. "Kaput," she whispered, sliding a finger across her throat. She'd thought the Nazis were going to kill her.

"Not you," Josephine said. "I'm the *neger.* Me kaput."

Her legs shook so bad she could hardly stand up, let alone dance. Her voice stuck in her throat, not that it mattered, anyway, because they hollered so loudly no one could hear her. She danced in the banana skirt and a bra for the censors, ignoring their shouts of "Take it off!" Their laughter sounded like the barks of vicious dogs. A man with a scar on his nose and the hardest eyes she'd ever seen spread his legs and fondled a large pistol in his lap. His eyes seemed to see right through her clothes. Josephine had never felt so naked, or so vulnerable.

Fuck them: she was there for everybody else. She took a breath and started to dance, trying to let the music carry her away. Where was it? She couldn't hear a thing over the noise they made.

There: a note.

She danced and kicked, imagining the Nazi in the front row at the receiving end of her foot. Kicked him away, then stepped back and kicked another one. How dare they? Dancing harder now, faster, her feet keeping time with the beating of her heart, her racing pulse carrying her through the dance, faster and faster, running in place for dear life while fear like a fist attacked her chest, her arms and legs, her entire body. The sneering brownshirt faces became a blur, their voices twisting and screeching, *schwartze* — fuck them, she'd be dancing and giving love to her audiences long after their hatred had poisoned them to death. The music played faster and faster, spinning and whirling and jerking her in furious circles, her breath gasping, water streaming down her face, pouring from her eyes, she never sweated, this was something else, this was every pore in her body crying. As soon as she left the stage, she dropped to the floor.

They did it. They killed me, she thought. And fainted dead away.

Someone carried her into her dressing room and lay her on the couch. A nurse had revived her with smelling salts and was checking her pulse when Pepito came running in, his face as white as a sheet. From his usual seat in the third row he'd seen everything, including the pistol in the Nazi's lap.

"Do you believe I'm in danger now?" she snapped.

"Yes, the jug is up," he said. He sent the nurse away, handed Josephine's fur coat to her and stuffed her belongings in a sack, and led her out the stage door to a waiting car. The two of them lay on the seat, holding hands, all the way to the train station. Twenty long minutes later, their train pulled out of Berlin, and Josephine released the breath she'd been holding for weeks. The city streamed past her window, lights streaking the panes, her tears blurring the lights.

It would be a cold day in hell before she returned to Berlin, but she'd get those Nazi bastards back somehow. They hadn't seen the last of Josephine Baker.

For the BROADWAY—USA scene, a plaster-of-paris Statue of Liberty comes rolling out. Huh. Give me your huddled masses? Your tired and poor? America isn't the "land of the free," not for people like her. In America, liberty is a privilege reserved for white people, and the rest is a lie they tell themselves.

"You must go to America and show them what you can do," Pepito kept saying. The man never gave up, no matter how many times she said she didn't want to go back, that she knew how she'd be treated. But he could see only dollar signs. For a while after the stock market crash, the United States economy collapsing, folks jumping off buildings, he let up on this talk. In a few years he started up again, America this and America that. She would become a more popular singer than the Boswell Sisters, he said, a bigger movie star than Greta Garbo, more famous than God himself. Josephine snorted.

All of them white, even God. There was no way.

His enthusiasm could be catching, though. Sometimes, she'd let herself dream with him, of her name in lights at the Ziegfeld Follies, her face on the screen in a Hollywood movie, her book a bestseller in bookstore windows from sea to shining sea. First, though, she had to conquer Paris again after several years away.

Would the city embrace her now? She'd fretted all the way home from South America. Aboard the *Lucretia,* posing naked as her lover, the architect Le Corbusier, sketched her, she sang the Negro spirituals of her youth and told him how God had promised her a crown. He'd smiled and said that Parisians were not as forgiving as God.

Pepito begged to differ. "They will adore you as I do," he said, and took her to a Paris radio station to announce — in French — that she'd become a chanteuse, the naked, clownish caterpillar transformed into an elegant singing butterfly. Then she'd gone to sign a contract at the Casino de Paris to star in *Paris qui Remue,* "Paris that Spins."

"You will become the new Mistinguett," M. Henri Varna said.

"Being the new Josephine Baker keeps me busy enough," she said.

He opened the bottle of champagne cooling in a bucket on his desk. "Congratulations, you got everything you wanted," he said as they toasted the agreement. "But the best part is mine: Josephine Baker will be my new étoile."

Josephine laughed, feeling so light she might just float away on a champagne breeze. She'd bargained hard for her salary and would now, at last, earn more than Mistinguett. But when Josephine raised her coupe, she drank to an accomplishment far more precious: she would be the first Negro star at the Casino de Paris, not a dance hall with nude showgirls but a real theater that featured the city's biggest celebrities, chanteurs and chanteuses, including Maurice Chevalier and Mistinguett. At last, her lifelong dream would finally come true. Let Paris call her "savage" now.

Speak of the devil: Mistinguett swept into the room on the arm of a man with thin, dark hair, and heavy-lidded eyes. The great star had dyed her hair platinum blond, but there was no mistaking the ravages of age: deepening shadows, a hint of jowl.

"Oh, it's *La Négresse*," she said.

"Have a coupe, *La Vieille*," Josephine said. "We're celebrating my new show at the Casino de Paris."

If looks could kill. But Miss was a pro; see how she pulled herself together. She marched over to the bucket and lifted the bottle, turning it to see the label.

"I get the good stuff for *my* contract signings," she said, and swept out again.

Josephine poured herself another glass. Miss was worried and she ought to be: everything had a season, and Josephine's was on the rise. After *Paris qui Remue,* Parisians would struggle to remember what Mistinguett looked like. Anything she could do, Josephine could do better. Hell, she could outdo Pepito, too, she was finding. He'd be shocked to discover how much she'd gotten M. Henri to pay her.

Maybe it was time to make a change. Walking back to the hotel she thought that maybe Pepito's season, like Mistinguett's, was on the wane.

When she walked into their hotel room, though, he stopped her bombshell with a few of his own.

"Good news, darling: I have signed a producer for another film for you. The famous Marc Allégret will be your director. He made *Fanny,* and you will have your choice of costar. He suggested Jean Gabin, what do you think? It will be a sensation."

Josephine threw her arms around his neck. *Fanny* was the most popular film in France, and a good one. A real writer! No more falling in flour bins and coal bins and wearing fur coats in the tropics.

"Oh, Pepi, you've made me so happy." She kissed his neck and pressed her body to his, but he pulled away to smile into her eyes.

"Hold that thought, darling. I have another surprise for you, too. Come with me."

André drove them to Le Vésinet, a suburb just outside the city, steering the car through a gate and down a long, tree-lined driveway to a breathtaking house.

"Le Beau Chêne," Pepito said then they'd stepped out of the car. "The Beautiful Oak. What do you think?"

"Who are we visiting?" she said.

"Not visiting, *ma chère.* This is ours." She widened her eyes as he added, "I purchased it today for us. Do you like it?"

Josephine forgot, then, about leaving Pepito. She had a home! As he showed her the great stone fireplaces, the polished wood floors, the sturdy beams, the sweeping staircase, the ten bedrooms, the atrium for her birds, the stables, and the flowering gardens, she marveled at the luck this day had brought to her. A contract with Henri Varna, a film with the director of *Fanny,* and now, a home of her own. All her dreams were coming true. Now she only needed children.

"Let's consummate our new house," she

said, spreading herself like a meal on the downstairs mantel, letting her dress fall away, parting her legs.

Pepito walked over and gave her a peck, but his eyes barely made contact with hers. He stared beyond her at some unseen delight.

"What furnishings will you desire, *mafleur*? We must order them soon. In only one month we begin your performances in Spain, and soon — *chérie,* I have been saving the best for the last — I have had a call from an agent in the States who wants to book you on a national tour. Imagine, Josephine: America, the greatest country in the world, and you are going to take it with wild horses."

CHAPTER 20

1935, New York

She should not have come back. Why had
she? As the white clerk — white hair, white
eyebrows, skin like paste, white shirt — in
the Hotel St. Moritz shook his head, Josephine stared down at her fists, blood singing in her ears.

"Je suis Josephine Baker," she said softly,
and turned her back so he couldn't see her
tears. The exquisite lobby done all in gold
— curtains, ceiling, chandeliers — seemed
to mock her now, like the beautiful dolls in
the windows of Saint Louis department
stores that Negroes weren't allowed to enter.

Her friend Miki Sawada, who'd brought
Josephine from the airport, tapped her
fingers on the counter.

"Do you know who this woman is? She's
Josephine Baker, a world-famous celebrity
and the new star of the Ziegfeld Follies."

"This hotel is for whites only," the clerk

said. "I'm sorry." Josephine spun around.

"You bet your ass you're sorry," she said in French. "A sorry excuse for a human being." And she told him, still in French, where he could shove his hotel and every cracker in it, including Pepito, who stood holding his brass room key and looking confused. When she gathered her fur and strutted toward the door, Pepito followed, asking her what had happened.

She rounded on him. "You said we were all set to stay here." He'd announced the hotel's name as if it were the Taj Mahal: "The most elegant hotel in the city, with a reservation for the Count and Countess d'Abatino." Josephine had jumped up and down at the news. The St. Moritz! Things *had* changed in America.

"I do not understand," Pepito said. "The manager said that everything would be ready for you."

"Did you tell him I'm a Negro?" He gave her a blank look. "I didn't think so. This hotel will never be ready for me." She narrowed her eyes at the clerk, who watched her with a hand on the telephone as though he might have to call in reinforcements.

Pepito looked crestfallen; he'd waxed rhapsodic over the suite with its terrace overlooking Central Park. She'd looked forward to inhabiting the swankiest rooms in the fanciest hotel in New York, but she'd dreaded having to deal with the controlling Pepito again. Now she saw her opportunity, and seized it.

"Don't worry," she said. "I'll find a place. Maybe in Harlem." Harlem, her ass. No way in hell would she let them shunt her off to "colored town," but Pepito didn't have to know that, did he? The farther away he thought she was, the better. He wrung his hands, saying he felt bad — as well he should, putting her in this situation.

How it had happened still made her teeth hurt. The comedian Eddie Cantor had come backstage at the Palais Garnier after seeing her in the opera *La Créole* — Josephine, an opera star! When, he asked, would she return to the States? She'd given her ready answer: "Never."

"But you've gotta tour America," he said, rolling his bug eyes at her. "You'll be a huge hit. Listen, doll, you've conquered Europe and South America already. Why not try the good old U.S. of A.?"

Josephine could have told him why. But Pepito took over, and with the help of Mr. Cantor's interpreter they had quite the gabfest. Josephine slipped out to her car and sped away to Montparnasse, where Sim awaited at La Coupole.

When she went home the next morning, Pepito wasn't there. When he finally did come in, he was singing, tipsy with grappa and pulling her out of bed to dance her around the floor. Eddie Cantor had promised to connect them with the booking agent at the Ziegfeld Follies. Josephine would become the first colored woman to headline there, her name in lights for all to see. She didn't think it could happen? Why not? Hadn't they once invited Florence Mills? And she, Josephine, was now singing opera, *mon Dieu,* in the crown jewel of Parisian theaters where no colored person had ever performed. No one had thought she could do it, but she'd shown them. She'd sung Offenbach, stretching her voice, learning all her parts in spite of worrying that she'd never be able to. She became one of the first colored divas not only in Paris, but anywhere: another barrier for her race knocked down by Josephine Baker.

She'd won the hearts of the French, Pepito said. Now, she must impress the Americans, not just for herself but for all Negroes.

She'd wanted to say yes, thinking of all the good she could do for her people, but something told her not to go. "They'll make me cork my face," she said. "They'll make me wear a bandanna on my head. They'll put me in chains."

Worse, she said, what if she couldn't come back to France? Being stranded in America would be worse than dying and going to hell.

Pepito had laughed. He would never let it happen, he said. While in the States, she would divorce her husband and they would marry, and she would be an Italian citizen.

Josephine shivered to think of tying herself to Pepito. He wasn't even a count. She'd admitted the truth on her first trip to Italy, upon meeting his mother and sisters and seeing their cotton clothes and their modest stone house built, his mama had boasted, by Pepito himself. There were no family jewels, not even a crest, only the stonemason's tools he'd inherited from his father. He'd gone to Paris to meet a wealthy socialite. Josephine was all he had.

In spite of her no, he'd written to the Shubert agency without telling her, and booked passage for himself to New York for a meeting. "I'm not going back there," she squeaked, not sure anymore that she meant it. Pepito waved her protests away, telling her to let him see what he could arrange. He would commit her to nothing, he'd promised, then sailed away with a copy of her movie *Zou Zou,* which had been a hit in Paris but still left Josephine dissatisfied.

Once Pepito had gone, freedom! After nine years with him, she'd forgotten what it felt like not to have him watching her every move, tracking her like a shadow. Didn't he realize that the harder he squeezed, the more he strangled her love? Maybe he did, and that was why he clung to her more and more desperately, as a drowning man claws at a piece of driftwood floating farther and farther out to sea.

She bought herself an airplane. Without Pepito to hold her back, she took to the skies like a bird. She'd needed only six hours of instruction. Flying was so easy a child could do it, what was all the fuss about?

When Pepito returned home he fumed over the airplane, his jaw ticcing as he asked about the cost, but then he'd forced a smile and said she would earn it all back and plenty more as the star of the Ziegfield Follies. Josephine could not believe her ears: he had pulled it off! With the help of Miki — a dear friend whom Josephine had met at a salon in Paris, and who now lived in New York with her husband, the Japanese ambassador — Pepito had made contacts, including a film producer who wanted to make a Hollywood movie starring Josephine, and the owner of a café that would make a perfect Chez Joséphine. Pepito had used the power of attorney she'd given him to sign a contract for her; rehearsals would begin in October. Josephine didn't know whether to laugh or cry.

They'll kill me over there, she wrote to Miki.

Now here she stood outside the St. Moritz Hotel, looking up at its jumble of floors, at the very top suite Pepito had reserved for them, terraced, fountained, beautiful, too good for a Saint Louis bumpkin. Her cheeks burned as she remembered the curl of the clerk's lip, as if he smelled something rotten. Only her respect for Miki had stopped her from having a "good old McDonald fit," as her grandmama used to say. Longing for the sharp-tongued Elvira pierced her like a blade. What would she think of Josephine now?

Miki's driver steered the Rolls-Royce along the pristine, tree-lined streets of midtown Manhattan, a part of the city Josephine had never seen in spite of calling New York home for two years. How scrubbed and gleaming the skyscrapers appeared compared to the grit of Broadway and the poverty in Harlem. Even the older buildings looked stately, not shabby: the stone-and-brick Saint Bartholomew's Church; Grand Central Terminal, with its golden clock and statues, almost as elegant as the Gare de Lyon in Paris. On Park Avenue they stopped at the Waldorf Astoria, where the clerk said they had no rooms. Miki suggested the Astor, which was also full. They tried the Pierre, the Sherry-Netherland, the Ritz. At each she was turned away; after each, she hunched in her seat, her head hanging lower each time. Then Miki asked to go to the Plaza, and the driver protested, saying they had already been to Central Park.

"How does it look, for me to be seen chauffeuring a Negro all over the city?" he said.

"Driving an embassy automobile," Miki said, her voice cold.

"I didn't sign up for this," he mumbled.

Josephine slouched down as far as she could go. "I'll put a blanket on my head, if that's what you want," she said. Then, cursing, she rolled down the window and stuck out her head. "No, I'll tell you what, let the whole world see who you're carrying around. Josephine Baker!" she shouted. "The world-famous opera star! The Black Venus!" A double-decker bus filled with

369

tourists — men in suits and fedoras, women in pencil skirts and little hats tipped over one eye — pulled up next to them at the light, and everyone stared.

"Damn you!" the driver cried.

"Riding with the daughter of the richest man in Japan," Josephine shouted. "He founded Mitsubishi! Her husband is the Japanese ambassador!"

"Josephine," Miki said. "It's okay. Roland, let's take Mrs. Baker to my studio."

Josephine rolled up the window. In the rearview mirror, she saw the driver's frightened eyes.

"Mrs. Sawada," he said. "I didn't know she spoke English."

The car pulled up to a town house of limestone and marble with large windows and a set of marble steps flanked by onyx vases of white flowers. As they topped the stairs, a manservant in a black suit and white shirt opened the door and bowed. Miki sat on a bench by the door and slipped off her shoes, and Josephine followed suit, both putting on slippers that the servant handed to them.

"I am so sorry for my driver's rudeness. I will have him fired," Miki said as they walked through her sparsely furnished home into a courtyard, past a gurgling fountain where a flock of pigeons bathed, and into a small studio also made of limestone and marble. She walked to her telephone and picked up the receiver, and spoke in Japanese.

Josephine looked around her, at the white furnishings, the colorful vases, the easel by the tall windows, the drawings on translucent paper. Miki invited her to take a seat, then handed her sake in a little ceramic cup painted with cherry blossoms, begging Josephine to accept her apologies again. She pulled her easel over and began to draw.

"This relaxes me," she said. "Please, my friend, relax yourself, and let us decide what to do."

They sat in silence for a while, Josephine drinking and Miki drawing. Then Josephine asked to use the phone. She pulled her address book from her handbag and found the number for *Paris Soir,* a Paris newspaper that had invited her to write a column.

"I've got a story for you," she said.

The next day, she sat on a sofa with a creaky spring and drank coffee from a cracked cup in the lobby of the Hotel Bedford near Grand Central Terminal. *Paris Soir* had sent her there to meet her old acquaintance Curt Riess, a good-looking journalist she knew from her time in Berlin, with

371

coffee-colored curls and intelligent green-gray eyes fringed with thick lashes. He'd fled Germany the previous year, he said, seeing the writing on the wall for Jews — "Hitler will kill us all" — and getting death threats for his reporting on the Nazi Party.

"Adolf Hitler is a madman," he said. "Worse than Mussolini." He paused, waiting for her response. He'd seen her comments in *Paris Soir* praising the Italian fascist for invading Abyssinia. How had Josephine come to think of him as a liberator? Haile Selassie had modernized the country as never before, building roads, schools, and hospitals. Mussolini had invaded with no provocation, wanting to have African colonies as France and Britain did.

But Josephine disagreed, saying she'd heard Mussolini speak when she and Pepito had visited Italy. "Selassie maintained slavery," she said, "but Il Duce promised to end it. If he called on me, I'd raise an army to fight for him."

Riess focused his gaze on her for a long moment. "If I were you, I would keep those sentiments to myself," he said. "America hates dictators."

"And it hates Negroes." She told him about her experience at the St. Moritz and the other hotels. She wanted to write a series on racism in America — well, actually, she would do the research, and he would write it. Riess leaned toward her, running a hand through his thick hair, saying her idea was brilliant. As his knee grazed hers, Josephine had another idea.

"Say, I still need a place to stay. Do you think this hotel would let me in?"

They inquired at the front desk, Curt translating Josephine's French to the ruddy-cheeked concierge whose eyes took in her emerald necklace and earrings and her silk Dior dress before booking her in the hotel's penthouse, the "honeymoon suite," he said.

"What a coincidence," she said, slipping her hand into the crook of Curt's elbow. "We are on our honeymoon."

She paid in cash and, the elevator being out of order, led Curt up the stairs to her room. Why, he asked her as they climbed to the third floor, did Josephine speak only in French? Had she forgotten her English in the years she'd been away from the States?

"Oh, Curt, I know it seems foolish, but my English is so bad, I'm embarrassed to speak it. At least if I mangle French, no one here will know."

The following day, after spending the morning with Curt in her penthouse — with a terrace, take *that,* St. Moritz! — Josephine dressed in a blue Chanel suit and matching hat and went to meet Pepito at the Ziegfeld offices. Pepito, who'd remained at the St. Moritz, looked haggard, like he hadn't slept since she'd seen him last. He only had a bit of indigestion, he said, pressing his hand to his stomach. Had she found a place to stay? She was still at Miki's, she lied, but would send someone for her trunks of clothing and her maid.

"You have not found a hotel? You are not in Harlem?"

"Harlem," she said with a snort. "You know me better than that."

A phone rang, and the receptionist led them into an office, where a red-faced man with a paunch walked around his ship of a desk to greet them, shaking Pepito's hand and bending over Josephine's, but not touching his lips to her skin. He introduced himself: Lee Shubert. She saw ruthlessness in those eyes.

When his phone jangled, he picked up the heavy black receiver and talked excitedly into it, leaning back in his leather chair and waving a fat, fragrant cigar, spilling ash on the polished wood desk. Shubert gestured toward the carved wooden chairs uphol- stered in dark green leather, and she and Pepito sat, their seats so low that she felt like a child peering over the top of the gargantuan desk. Mahogany shelves filled with books covered the wall behind him. Josephine breathed in the scents of furniture polish, tobacco, and leather.

He slammed down the phone with a final *ring,* opened the manila file on his desk, and rifled through its pages, then began reading aloud from her contract: first-class passage on an ocean liner (Had her journey been pleasant? Josephine assured him that it had); $1,500 per week in pay, increasing to $1,750 if the show ran beyond June of next year; her name featured on its own line on the marquee. Josephine imagined her name in lights on Broadway, her dream all those years ago when she'd first come to New York, sleeping on benches in Central Park, praying it didn't rain.

"About my dressing room," she said. "There seems to be a mistake." She'd gone yesterday with a decorator to take measurements — she wanted everything in blue — but the space was too small. How would she do interviews and entertain her visitors? She would need a dressing table and mirror, a divan for resting, a small bar, tables and chairs for entertaining, and a sofa to hold any overflow. She expected a lot of visitors, some very big names. She'd already heard from Cole Porter, who'd promised to attend on opening night, and Paul Robeson, did he know the famous Negro singer? And her old friend Lily Pons from *La Revue Nègre,* now a well-known soprano, and many others, she assured him: the first Negro star of the Follies would draw lots of attention.

Confusion shadowed his face. He leafed through the contract and shook his head. There was no mistake — at least, not on his end. Her contract stipulated the number two dressing room for Josephine.

"Number two?" She laughed. "But I am the star. Who gets number one? You?"

He cleared his throat. "Fanny Brice is the star of the Ziegfield Follies."

Josephine's throat constricted. She glared at Pepito, who pressed a hand to his stomach again.

"Mr. Shubert, are you telling me that I'm not the lead in this show?"

"We have many stars," he said. "Ms. Brice, Eve Arden, the Nicholas Brothers —"

"The who brothers?"

"I thought you would know them. Negro dancers. You ought to see them; it's incredible what they do. Very popular. And then we've just signed Bob Hope, a real up-and-coming showman; he's the leading man."

"Up-and-coming?" Josephine stared at him, agape. "I'm the most highly paid performer in Europe, Mr. Shubert, the biggest Negro star in the world. I've headlined Paris and Berlin and Vienna and Rio de Janeiro, Rome and London and —"

"I am sorry, Miss Baker," he said, looking anything but. "We are not in Paris or Brazil. Most Americans do not know Josephine Baker. On the other hand, they adore Fanny Brice."

Josephine reached over and snatched the contract off his desk. Everything he said was right there. She flipped to the last page, her pulse racing. Pepito would never have signed this — but there was his name, written in his hand.

She turned to Pepito, his yellowish face rimmed with sweat like a cheese left out on a warm day. Quickly, in French, she told him what was going on.

"America does not know Josephine Baker, but they will soon," Pepito said, his voice ragged. "On the stage of the Ziegfeld Follies, you will sweep New York like a storm. Fanny Brice will be forgotten, the same as Mistinguett."

How could he have signed that contract? Josephine Baker always got top billing — he knew that; it was *his* damned policy. Pepito's explanation annoyed her more. The manager had barely negotiated, saying he was not authorized to alter the terms. His only concession was to insert a paragraph allowing her to perform after hours — but even then, he had stipulated that she must appear in a "smart east-side cabaret." Keeping it white. She ought to sign up at the Cotton Club; it would serve them right.

She didn't let Shubert see her temper over that sorry contract, though, but saved it for Pepito once they'd left the office and the elevator operator had taken them down to the first floor. How could he have brought her all the way across the ocean to a place she'd dreaded returning to, for this? She wanted to pummel him. Pepi had known she wouldn't be the star but had lied so she would make the trip.

"It is for your benefit," he said, herding her quickly into a cab lest she erupt in a full-blown tantrum on the street. Tucking himself in after her, he began peppering her with news, trying to distract her, she knew. He had now heard from two American film producers, a radio show, and a playwright, all interested in working with her. She had already captured the imaginations of important people.

"You will take them by tornado," Pepito

378

said. "You will break their windows. You will shatter their glass." America waited to be seduced, he said; it wanted novelty. It wanted Josephine Baker. She might not have entered New York a star, but she would leave as one.

Josephine turned her head to stare out the window at New York, her past and present and, if she played her cards right, her future. The Paramount. Loews. The Palace. Norma Shearer, Dean Martin, Judy Garland. And now, at the Shubert, Josephine Baker.

Pepito was right: America was her nut to crack. She'd gotten too big for Paris; after starring in an opera and making three films, what more could she achieve there? She needed a challenge, and New York was it. Without realizing it, Shubert had spelled out exactly what she must do. Second best? Like hell she was. The Ziegfeld Follies were in for a big surprise.

Chapter 21

Billy looked just the way she'd remembered him, slender and boyish, high cheekbones, eyes so pale they looked almost green, skin so light he looked almost white. His black porter's uniform, starched to stiffness, crackled when he stood to greet her, his face hopeful as he stepped forward for an embrace that she averted by offering her hand. Disappointment moved in, then, as they took their seats at the table in this inconspicuous Harlem diner where she'd proposed to meet. She'd dressed down: a dark suit, sunglasses. Avoiding notice.

"You're a big star," he said. "Just like you always wanted. I've got every newspaper story ever written about you, baby, a big box of them. I'm so proud of you."

She ordered coffee, glancing around at the red linoleum, the pictures of prizefighters on the walls, the man sitting across from her whom she barely knew any more. A stranger to her now, looking at her with a face as open and full of hope as a child's.

I couldn't stand to be "Mr. Josephine Baker." I'm sorry, but I can't come to Paris without a job.

"What are you so proud of? I did it all without your help," she said, the chill in her tone surprising her.

His hand trembled as he sipped from his Coke. "I wanted to come."

"Then why didn't you?" Two men sitting at the bar turned their heads at the sound of her rising voice.

"I should have." He set the drink down quickly to wipe a tear from his eye, nearly upsetting the bottle. She watched in disdain. She'd cried her heart out when she'd gotten that letter: Now it was his turn.

"I should have gone to Paris," he said, weeping in earnest now. "I've never stopped loving you, Josephine, and I've never loved anyone else. I've kept every article I could find about you, bought a dozen papers every day. It broke my heart when I read that you were married" — he smiled, blinking — "but of course it was all a joke, you couldn't have married that count because you're still married to me."

"That's what I've come to talk to you about."

"I'm ready now," he said. "I've learned to play the drums. I'm pretty good, too. I can come to Paris and be a real husband to you. Maybe I can play in your band." He reached across the table for her hand, which she moved to the dossier on the seat beside her.

"I know you'll make more money than I can," he said. "I'll never be a star like you, but I don't care about that now. I just want to be with you, Josephine. No more foolish pride, I promise."

"It's been ten years!" she cried. "You think you can just —" She stopped and closed her eyes, blocking out his face, which, she told herself, was not as handsome as she'd remembered.

"It's all over with us, Billy." She pulled a sheaf of papers from the file and laid them on the table before him. "I want a divorce, and I've come to ask you to sign."

His crumpling face almost made her cry, as well, until she remembered sobbing into her pillow those years ago, his letter in her fist.

"You're going to marry him, aren't you?" he said. "That Italian. The count."

Josephine closed her eyes again, thinking of Pepito, how sadly he, too, would someday look at her. Someday soon.

"No," Josephine said. "I am not."

■ ■ ■ ■

"Let's try it again, Josephine."

She had to bite her tongue every time. She'd heard this man address Fanny Brice as Miss Brice, Eve Arden as Miss Arden, Bob Hope as Mr. Hope. The only performers he called by their first names were the chorus dancers and her. She wondered what names he used for the Nicholas Brothers, the dance team — every bit as remarkable as Shubert had said — she'd seen perform at the Cotton Club. A revue this vast rehearsed in three groups, each in a different theater, and without the special effort she might never have seen their gravity-defying act: leaping from the floor onto tabletops without their hands, tap-dancing on every surface in the club except the ceiling.

Josephine might have liked working with the Nicholas Brothers. Instead, she had the snotty Fanny Brice and the dismissive Bob Hope to endure in frenzied, grueling rehearsals that went from two in the afternoon until midnight with nary a whit of levity, lightheartedness, or fun. Performing was supposed to be enjoyable — didn't these people know that? If the players onstage weren't having a good time, the audience sure as hell wouldn't. In Paris, rehearsing meant time singing and dancing half the time and laughing the rest. Her Follies sessions left Josephine stiff with inaction and boredom. She had just three scenes, which she'd quickly learned, but she had to lead the chorus through the numbers many times, their parts more complicated because, while she sang, they never stopped moving. When she'd danced in the chorus, she'd made up her own moves. In the Ziegfeld Follies, steeped in tradition, the longest-running revue in New York — just about as old as Josephine — people didn't improvise. They followed the steps.

As she pushed herself through the punishing routine, she reminded herself of the rewards she sought. Fanny Brice lived in a Central Park high-rise and had a Long Island summer home as big as a palace; Josephine wanted that for herself, and more. Why shouldn't she have it? She possessed more talent in her pinky than Fanny Brice had in her entire body. She could do anything — even be a Hollywood film star. She had three French movies to her credit now: in addition to *La Sirène des Tropiques* she'd made *Zou Zou,* her favorite, in which a colored girl working in a laundry becomes a famous theater star, and *Princesse Tam-Tam,*

Josephine playing an Arab urchin whom a wealthy Frenchman transforms into a socialite. Her films were big hits in France. Why shouldn't Hollywood give her a chance?

"What the hell is going on? These scenes won't work. She's Josephine Baker, not a frigging mannequin, for Christ's sake." John Murray Anderson, the producer, came into the theater in an Italian dove-gray suit and purple tie, a stylish look that she admired even as he destroyed her costumes, her dances, and her songs. She would need to start over again. Her smile froze in place, so that she *felt* like a fucking mannequin.

But she reminded herself of her goals. Money, yes. Also: to show America that a colored woman could do anything a white woman could do. She had proven it in Paris; she had proven it all over Europe. She could outdance Fanny Brice on one leg.

She would never be able to demonstrate her talents with the dull routines originally given her. They wouldn't let her do the Charleston: the choreographer had called it passé. And when she'd tried to spice things up by making faces, the director had asked what in the hell she was doing. Fanny Brice was the clown in this revue.

Josephine had some ideas for dance steps, but the choreographer had struck them down, too: "I won't tell you how to sing, okay?"

So while the chorus grumbled about the producer's changes, Josephine thanked her stars that someone was finally paying attention. She got a conga dance, much more exciting, in which Gertrude Niesen sang, "There's an Island in the West Indies" and Josephine knocked over a line of chorus boys with a swivel and thrust of her hips. This suited Josephine well except for the costume: a variation on her banana skirt but with spikes instead of bananas jutting from her breasts and bottom. She looked dangerous, not sexy, like she might gore someone if they got too close.

Ira Gershwin and Vernon Duke, the songwriters, penned a new number for her: she'd sing "Maharanee" while wearing a bright, printed-silk sari. Mr. Anderson brought in her old friend George Balanchine to choreograph "5 A.M.," her favorite number, in which she would wear a shimmering gown of real gold mesh that weighed a hundred pounds. It would take all the dancers' strength — six white men — to lift her into the air. Let Fanny top that!

"You will conquer America," Pepito said every time she saw him, and Josephine had started to believe it. New York offered opportunities that, in Europe, she could only dream about — such as starring in *Porgy and Bess,* the first Negro Broadway musical, not an off-Broadway revue as *Shuffle Along* had been. Josephine, there on opening night, wondered if she'd been wrong about her home country. Almost turned away from the Cotton Club until one of the Nicholas Brothers had recognized her; refused entry to the whites-only Stork Club restaurant late one night; not even allowed to use the toilet or take a drink from the water fountain in many places, she'd found that America treated colored people worse now than when she'd left. But *Porgy and Bess* gave her hope. Anne Brown came into "Summertime" on a note so high it made Josephine's ears ring, and her acting conveyed a dignity and grace that made her seem natural for the role. She *was* Bess — but Josephine could be her, too. She'd sung more challenging arias in *La Créole.*

After the show she and Pepito went backstage to meet the star, who did not speak French, unfortunately, since Josephine dared not use her poor, pidgin English around all these high-falutin white folks. She might as well speak French, hell, and a good thing she did, because the magazine publisher Condé Nast, a tall, white-haired man wearing little round spectacles, stepped in to translate. When they discovered that they'd both lived in Saint Louis, he invited Josephine to the cast party at his home that night.

At her hotel, the excited Josephine tried on six different outfits with the help of Yvette, who smoothed her spit curls and touched up her makeup, and chose jewelry and a white fur to accompany her yellow silk gown. Pepito picked her up in a cab and they rode to 1040 Park Avenue, a limestone building with a tortoise-and-hare frieze encircling the third floor and an awning over the entrance where, at first, Josephine expected the doorman to turn her away. They rode the elevator to the penthouse suite, Pepito murmuring, "Make them notice you, *chérie.*" She stepped into the drawing room, all pale blue and green and with a fire in a green marble mantel at the far end. Over the fireplace hung a large mirror in a gilt frame, reflecting a large floral rug and furniture that Josephine recognized, from decorating Le Beau Chêne, as Louis XV. She spied Mr. Nast on an embroidered canapé chatting with George Gershwin, and, letting her fur drop into a maid's waiting hands, went to them immediately, leaving Pepito to his own devices.

"Bonsoir, Mr. Nast," and then he was introducing her to "the great George Gershwin," and Josephine said, *"Oui, très genial."* Mr. Nast interpreted and sneaked glances down her cleavage. She told Mr. Gershwin that she had loved his "folk opera" more than anything she'd ever seen, that it had made her cry, that she felt as though the role of Bess had been written for her, that she hoped to have the honor of singing it someday, having already been the first Negro to star in an opera, Offenbach's *La Créole,* had he heard of it? He had not, he was sorry, would she please excuse him? And he stepped away to greet his Bess, Anne Brown, who had arrived not in fur but in a stunning blue silk dress with an emerald wrap and matching shoes. Her skin looked even lighter without her stage makeup, fairer than Josephine's. Why cast a Negro opera with a diva who could pass for white?

But even the star of tonight's performance could not hold the spotlight for long. When Fanny Brice walked in, every eye turned to her and remained fixed there. She gave Josephine the once-over but otherwise acted as though she didn't know who she was. Josephine hoped they wouldn't be seated together at dinner, but she needn't have worried: Mr. Nast had Josephine and Pepito sit at the head of the table with him, where he translated her French into an English much better than she could speak, making her sound lively and witty. When Mr. Nast had stepped away near the end of the meal, Fanny walked by and heard Josephine ask the maid for *plus de café, s'il vous plait*. Fanny laughed loudly, drawing everyone's attention to where she stood, pointing at Josephine.

"Honey, you is full of shit," Fanny said in a shrill Southern drawl. "Why don't you talk the way your mouth was born?"

Florence Mills had hit the nail on the head: it would take more than one woman's success to change people's minds about Negroes.

"How do you compare to Ethel Waters?" a reporter had asked, as if she and Ethel had anything in common except their race. Folks compared them because Ethel had her own show at the Majestic, the only Negro leading a cast of whites, and because she'd once sung in a Josephine Baker costume, an ironic twist if there ever was one. Irving Berlin, who'd written the music for her show, said Miss Ethel had done a good job, or so he'd thought until he'd seen Josephine perform.

"How do we compare? I'm a soprano," she told the newsman. When his story came out, he called her a "colored soprano."

Americans did not adore her, as she had hoped. Hell, they didn't even like her. On opening night, she went to the cast party and made her usual entrance, this time wearing diamonds, sapphires, and emeralds dripping from her ears, throat, arms, and fingers, and the great comic Beatrice Lillie — a white woman — had turned to the rest of the room and said, "Who dat?"

Josephine felt so delighted to meet her that she forgave the racial slur, seizing the opportunity at dinner to gush over the woman's films.

"I've seen every one, and love them all," she said in English. "You are the greatest comedienne in the world, Miss Lillie."

The women sent a sly, quick glance to Fanny Brice — Josephine noticed the exchange — and arched an eyebrow. "Honey chile," she said, affecting a drawl, "you ain't so bad yo'self."

Unfortunately, the critics did not agree. Mr. Anderson went out for the reviews and returned beaming, reading the praise for

Fanny who crossed her eyes at Josephine and curled her lips, making Josephine's face.

Fanny is marvelous. It is her evening. Her delicious mimicry, her occasionally crossing eyes . . . and her knees that often are not on speaking terms with one another . . . her ever-hilarious presence.

Josephine crossed her eyes and curled her lip back at Fanny. The woman's eyes widened and she snatched the notices from Mr. Anderson's hand.

"Let's see what they think of our little French performer," she said.

After her cyclonic career abroad, Josephine Baker has become a celebrity who offers her presence instead of her talent . . . her singing voice is only a squeak in the dark and her dancing is only the pain of an artist. Miss Baker has refined her art until there is nothing left of it.

"Oh, honey, how awful! I never liked this writer, anyway," she said, rifling through the papers for another.

In sex appeal to jaded Europeans of the jazz-loving type, a Negro wench always has a head start, but to Manhattan theatregoers last week she was just a slightly buck-toothed young Negro woman whose figure might be matched in any nightclub show, whose dancing and singing could be topped practically anywhere outside France.

"Imbecile!" Fanny shouted, and everyone laughed because she didn't mean it, they all knew she despised Josephine, but they didn't know why. Josephine knew; she'd heard Fanny call her nigger under her breath.

Josephine snatched up her stole and stormed out of the party. Pepito ran after her, grimacing with indigestion.

"This is your fault," she said. "You used to be a good manager, but I'm fed up. You are fired, Pepito, you understand? The doorman at my hotel could do a better job than you."

"Terminée?" He looked stunned.

"That's right," she said. "You're finished, and so are we. I put up with your jealousy and your abuse for too long, because you were the best manager I could imagine and you've got all my money. But I don't care anymore. Go back to Paris and take everything I've got. I can always make more. Which is more than *you* can say, you no-account 'count.' "

He didn't say a word, just got into a cab and rode away.

Chez Joséphine in New York kept her busy singing and dancing nightly to a packed house, getting away with things they wouldn't let her do in her Follies revue. When audiences had complained about white men touching a Negro woman, for instance, the producer had cut the scene in which the male chorus lifted her up. She added the routine to her nightclub show, and folks loved it. The critics loved her, too, saying she was "in her element" in the club. She made good money. She didn't need Pepito.

And she found a lover, too, right away, or, she should say, found him again. Josephine went with the cast to a cabaret on the East Side one night and the bouncer turned her away, saying it was a segregated club. Josephine flashed a hundred-dollar bill, but he suggested she try Harlem.

Harlem again? Was there nowhere else they could send her? Did Harlem alone house the Negro folks, a veritable cage of colored people in a whites-only zoo? Josephine walked into the street to hail a taxi. Fuckers. If they wanted her in Harlem, she'd go to Harlem. She'd put on the clothes Curt Riess had helped her pick out for her *Paris Soir* series in which she went out pretending to be just any Negro on the streets and then wrote about her experiences. At her hotel, she slipped on the cotton dress with a missing button, the ragged hat, the old shoes. In the mirror, she saw how she might appear had she never gone to Paris — if, God forbid, she'd stayed in New York. Why had she come back?

She walked to the nearest subway stop, where a skinny white man with bad teeth leered at her. She went to a bench and sat next to a colored woman who gave her a dolorous once-over. The woman wore a shabby cloth coat that had once been red, and a tattered blue dress. She looked tired. She averted her gaze to the little boy tugging at her knee. *You're richer than I am,* Josephine wanted to say.

She got off at 125th Street and saw a line of people standing outside the Apollo Theater, illuminated by rows of lights strung under the big marquee. What was going on? she asked a young man with a music case in one hand and a pretty girl in the other.

"It's Amateur Night," he said. "I'm going to play the saxophone, and she's going to sing." Josephine paid the fee and went in, directed by the doorman to a sign-up sheet. She wrote, *Gracie Walker, singing "J'ai Deux Amours."* Then she went backstage to wait for her turn.

When the emcee walked onto the stage, her heart turned over in her chest: it was

Ralph Cooper, her old love from her pre-Paris years in New York, who'd kept the ghosts away many nights while Billy worked. He was still so handsome it made her eyes hurt. They called him "Dark Gable" and anyone could see why: that wavy hair, those wide-set bedroom eyes. He welcomed the crowd and announced the first contestant, a tone-deaf crooner who hadn't made it through the first verse when people started to holler. A shot rang out, making Josephine jump in her seat. "Dead," Ralph cried, smoking cap gun in his hand. As the crowd jeered, the poor little man removed his porkpie hat and bowed as though he'd received a standing ovation.

Next up were a pair of jugglers who did a decent job of keeping balls, batons, and fire sticks in the air, but the audience grew restless, shouting, "Juggle something good," and the gun fired again. Josephine almost wished she hadn't signed up. This was a tough crowd; what if they booed her? Would Ralph recognize her after all these years and refuse to fire the gun, or would he send her slinking offstage?

A tap dancer whose feet flew so fast they might have thrown up sparks. A couple doing an acrobatic Lindy Hop. The saxophonist and singer she'd met in line, performing

"Dinah." A young woman singing, "Was I Drunk?" A comedian with the raunchiest mouth she'd ever heard — he didn't last three minutes. And then Ralph was peering into the wings, calling the name of the next performer, who didn't show.

"Somebody got cold feet," he was saying. "Gracie? You here?"

Someone nudged her and she stepped out and rubbed the famous tree stump on the stage for good luck, and sang "J'ai Deux Amours" with all her heart — "I have two loves, my country and Paris," even though, at the moment, she felt less than enamored of her country. The audience never made a peep, and the gun didn't go off, and when she'd taken her bow she glanced at Ralph, who looked at her like it was Christmas morning, and she the present under his tree.

"This is a special treat, folks, and a real surprise," he said. "I wonder how many of you recognized the great Josephine Baker on our stage?"

It was almost like being in Paris, then, applause rising and cresting in great, crashing waves, but no restrained Parisian audience made half as much noise as this cacophony of stamping feet, whistling, shouts, shrieks, roars. This, too, was nothing like the polite applause she heard at the Follies shows, the gold dress weighing her down, the masked dancers keeping their hands to themselves. She knew the reason for the difference: here, as in Paris, as in her nightclub, she performed naturally, as herself. The Ziegfeld Follies routines felt artificial — because, for her, they were. She'd been given the costumes, the songs, and the steps, all devised by others, with not a single bit of Josephine Baker in any of it. She might as well be a wind-up toy going through the routines. She'd hated the rehearsals and she dreaded every performance, and everyone — critics and audiences alike — could tell.

God, how she wanted to leave New York. She wanted to go home, where she felt like a human being, where she had dignity. But how could she? Pepito owned everything — Le Beau Chêne, her bank accounts, her royalties and income. She'd gone to the Shubert Agency and told them to write her checks out to her, not him, so she had that to live on, as well as her Chez Joséphine earnings. But she had nothing in Paris — no income, no house, no work. She couldn't even afford passage back to France. Her worst nightmare had come true: she was trapped in New York.

Perhaps she'd lashed out at Pepito too harshly. Certainly she'd been hasty: she should have waited until they'd gotten home. Her temper had gotten the best of her again.

What was done was done, though. She'd save her money and get back to France eventually. No matter what happened, she was still Josephine Baker.

Removing her stage makeup after the show one night, she heard a knock on her dressing-room door and a familiar voice speaking in French. Pepito! For a minute, she thought not to answer. But here was her chance to go home, and so she opened the door — and let out a scream.

M. Paul Derval dropped the bouquet he held as she flung herself against him, kissing his face and weeping.

"Josephine, you are being underutilized in this revue," he said as she pulled him inside.

"They are wasting my talent, yes. M. Derval, I wish you could tell the director what I am capable of. You know I'm better than Fanny Brice!"

"I am sorry, but I cannot help you succeed here," he said as he reached for the champagne chilling in a bucket on her dressing table. "If anything, I would like to hasten your failure."

Josephine frowned. Why had he come, then? To gloat, like everybody else? She had a mind to snatch the champagne bottle from his hand and break it over his head.

But this was M. Derval, who had given Josephine her first show, who had been her friend for ten years. "You want me to fail?" A tear rolled down her cheek. "Why?"

He turned to hand her a coupe, grinning: She had fallen for his jest.

"Because I want you to return to Paris with me and star in my new show this fall at the Folies-Bergère."

■ ■ ■ ■

ACT IV
VIVE LA RÉSISTANCE

■ ■ ■ ■

CHAPTER 22

1939, Le Beau Chêne

If there was one thing she hated, it was being underdressed. Josephine was having that sinking feeling right now outside her castle, Les Milandes, as she watched her visitors emerge from their car. Her theatrical agent Daniel Marouani was the picture of chic, as always, swarthy and slim and wearing a woven silk suit of pale taupe with a blue necktie. But it was his companion, in a military uniform, who made her want to run indoors and change clothes. He was a rogue, she pegged him in an instant: hair the color of sand falling over his brow *on purpose,* he probably thought it made him look rakish (and he was right), muscles like hard candy (and she with such a sweet tooth), a swagger that boasted of conquest. She'd forgotten how beautiful eyes could be, wasted on a man, some would say, but not when that man was lying under her, which was where she imagined him until his gaze took in her battered garden hat and old cotton dress, her grass-stained knees, and the jar of snails she'd been collecting to feed to her ducks.

Why hadn't she dressed up? She hadn't felt like taking the trouble, not for the old, fat-bellied coot she'd expected. "He does not trust you because you are beautiful and in show business," Danny had said of the *capitaine* he had proposed bringing to meet with her. The man hadn't even wanted to come — the meeting had been Danny's idea. Who but a codger with nothing going on between his legs would turn down Josephine Baker?

She whipped the hat off her head so fast the jar dropped to the ground, scattering the snails but she'd forgotten all about her ducks now. *Lord, let me work with this man.* What he was cooking up Danny wouldn't say, "the officer" would explain, something against the Nazis, which was all Josephine needed to know to say yes. Now she wanted to know everything else, too: his name, rank, and serial number, the feel of his hands on her skin, whether he liked it rough or gentle, and which of them on top.

"You must be the youngest commander in the history of the French army, Captain," she teased as her maître d' led them indoors to the parlor, a masculine room of stone and wood with an enormous fireplace in which a fire roared. Three Louis XVI chairs had been arranged in front of it, as well as several small tables, one of which held a bottle of fine champagne on ice. Settling into a chair, Josephine smiled as if she were wearing a silk sheath rather than an old cotton dress. "Do your men obey that sweet baby face?"

How anyone could pack so much contempt into a single glance she would never know.

"Captain Abtey does not give orders to soldiers," Danny said. "He works in the Deuxième Bureau."

"Intelligence?" She poured a flute of champagne and offered it to the captain, but he declined. "That must be so interesting."

His frown deepened; he still had not said a word. Josephine gave a coupe to Danny and took one for herself, saw the officer's eyes take note as she nervously gulped down the contents. She set her glass on the table.

"One of Captain Abtey's duties is to recruit volunteers," Danny said.

"Spies?"

"Honorable correspondents," Abtey said. His voice sounded like warm honey, just as she would have imagined. He shifted in his seat, crossing one leg over the other and looking uncomfortable.

"His correspondents travel around, observing and gathering information," Danny said. "Then they report what they find to Jacques."

"I'm very observant," Josephine said. "I remember details that escape most people. Like the flecks of gold in your blue eyes." Captain Abtey looked unimpressed, and so she added, "And the color of your socks."

"What color are they?" he challenged, daring her to look down at his feet, but she didn't need to.

"You aren't wearing any," she said. "In spite of the fact that the weather is cool. You must have known that you'd be sitting before a warm fire with me."

He cocked an eyebrow and regarded her. Her hand more steady now, Josephine poured herself another coupe.

"That is quite observant. What else have you noticed?"

"You are left-handed," she said. "At least, that's the hand you used to turn away my very good champagne."

He uncrossed his legs and sat up straight, glancing over at Danny. Ha! She was right.

"And as much as you want me to think

that you don't drink, I'm guessing that you do. I saw you eyeing my liquor cabinet. Would you prefer a snifter of cognac?" She rang for a servant, who presented a glass, which he took with, yes, his left hand.

"Your eye for detail is good," he said. "But will it be so when you are frightened or nervous?" He set down the glass and gave her a defiant look.

"Why, monsieur, I am surprised that *you* are not more observant," she said. "Otherwise, you would know that I am frightened nearly out of my wits right now."

"*Non,* you are not," he said, and the smile he finally offered made Josephine want to melt all over her chair. "The great Josephine Baker is fully aware of her power over men. Far from quaking in your boots, you have felt only confidence that you will get what you want from me."

"What do I want from you, Captain? Money?"

"If that were the case, your confidence would be misguided, since I have no money to give. Perhaps, madame, you ought to ask what *I* want from *you.*"

And then, he told her: the bureau needed volunteers — patriots — who could move across borders, from country to country, without suspicion from the Nazis.

"We must deliver information to our military and our allies — in person."

"That would not be a problem for me," she said. "I go on tour all the time, and I never get searched. If someone starts giving me trouble, I can make him forget all about it with just a smile."

"As I said — you are well aware of your powers. To what extent would you use them to help France? I am aware that this is not your native country. Will you run away to the United States as so many have already done?"

"Josephine is a French citizen," Danny said. "By marriage to the businessman Jean Lion."

"Yes, I renounced my American citizenship two years ago." At least something good came out of that disaster. "I've filed for divorce from Jean" — looking at Danny, but the words were for the captain — "but my heart belongs to France."

"She is more French than the French," Danny said.

"I would do anything for France. Anything."

"Even risk your life? We need sensitive information — German plans and secrets of Nazi allies. We need someone who can entice the generals to talk, and convince the diplomats to give us access to them."

"That would be no problem." She laughed and refilled Danny's glass. "One kiss from me, and they'll babble like schoolboys. One tickle on the chin" — grinning, she reached out her hand to demonstrate, making the captain flinch — "or a rubbing of their bald pates" — she ran her palm across his forehead, tousling his hair, and he didn't pull away, good! — "and they'll promise me the moon. They'll deliver it, too, because, as you have observed, I get what I want." She leveled him a gaze fraught with promise.

"This is not a game or a time for jokes," Abtey said. He picked up his glass and set it down again, then rose to his feet. "It is as I feared: she is not serious," he said to Danny. "Let us go."

Josephine stood, too. "A laughing demeanor can be an effective disguise, monsieur." *You should try it sometime,* she wanted to say.

"I have not come for a flirtation," he gruffed. "I seek dedication and passion for the cause, which is to save our nation from a monster."

"I was demonstrating my techniques," she said innocently. "Did they work?"

"You could be killed, don't you know that?" Josephine took a step back, expecting him to hit her — but he had already turned away from her to walk circles on the antique carpet, his hands folded behind his back.

"I am aware of the dangers," she said.

He walked right up to her, then, standing inches away, not touching her although she wanted him to. She could feel his breath on her face. A log shifted on the fire; sparks flew onto the hearth.

"You might be sent to a concentration camp to die a slow death," he said, biting off the words one by one. "Or, if you are fortunate, the Germans will shoot you in the head. Before doing either, though, they would torture you. They will do anything to make you talk. Tell me, madame — how much pain would you endure before betraying us?"

She did not break their gaze. "I would not say a word."

"Even as they pulled your teeth out one by one? Or pushed you under freezing water until you thought your lungs would burst?"

"I would swallow the water and drown myself."

"Do you think they would allow it? No. They hold death before their victims like a cherished prize, then yank it away before you can succumb. They are masters of pain."

Danny cleared his throat, and the captain

pressed his lips together. His face had *no* written all over it.

"That would never happen to me, Captain. You do not understand how the people love me, even the Germans."

He cursed under his breath and motioned to Danny with his left hand. "We are wasting our time."

Josephine reached into her cleavage and pulled out the cross she had worn since the Nazi threat to France had emerged. She'd gotten one for herself and one for her husband, Jean Lion, a Jew, hoping wearing crosses might fool the Germans into thinking they were Christians — Josephine had converted to Judaism for Jean's sake — and provide a way out if the ruse didn't work. "Do you know what this is, Captain?"

He sneered. "If the Nazis arrest you, your God won't save you."

She twisted the arms of the cross and pulled it apart. "Inside, there is poison," she said. "I wear it in case they do arrest me. If that happens, I'll swallow every grain. I would rather die than go against my people." His eyes widened. Good! She had impressed him.

"As you can see, I am serious. I can do this. It would be the most important performance of my life."

"Josephine is *une femme courageuse,*" Danny said, bless his heart. "She has already been working for the cause, with an anti-racism organization, is that right, Josephine?"

"And the Red Cross," she said. "Also, I have been entertaining the troops on the Maginot Line. I will do whatever it takes to defeat Hitler." The image flashed in her mind of the man with the scar at the Stage Theater des Westens in Berlin, fondling the heavy pistol in his lap and leering at her.

"You will make love to generals and ambassadors, enticing them to tell you their secrets, and then betray them?" He folded his arms. "This 'technique' has proved the downfall of the Deuxième Bureau before. You have heard of Mata Hari. How do I know you will not fall in love with the enemy and betray us, instead?"

"I already have two loves, Captain — France and Paris. To sweet France I will be eternally grateful, for it has been my refuge."

What would it take to convince him? She wanted to fall to her knees and weep. Instead, she sank back into her chair, blinking back tears. Far from intimidating her as he had meant to do, Jacques Abtey had only strengthened Josephine's resolve. Even if he turned her down, she would find a way to do more to beat those bastards.

"France made me what I am today." She sat erect, babbling now, but who cared? She would talk all night if that was what it took. "And did I not become the cherished child of the Parisians? They gave me everything, especially their hearts." She thumped her chest with her fist and pressed it against her own wild, twisting heart. "I am ready, Captain, to give my life to France. You may dispose of me as you wish."

"Bravo." His tone was wry, but she thought she saw respect in his eyes. Encouraged, she played her final card — one she'd remembered when Danny had spoken of the Red Cross a moment ago.

"I forgot to mention that I have wings," she said. "Or did you already know? I am a pilot, with my own aeroplane."

It was like switching on a light, the way his expression changed.

"An aeroplane?"

"A DGA-Eleven, yes. I deliver supplies for the Red Cross twice a week." Look at his beautiful smile! "I can fly you anywhere you want to go."

Abtey turned and gave Danny a pat on the back. "Now we are talking," he said. He resumed his seat, and reached for his glass.

■ ■ ■ ■

A party was in full swing inside the Italian embassy, a three-story building on the rue de Varenne fronted by an impressive array of marble columns. Inside, the decor was every bit as breathtaking as one would expect from Italians: even the ceilings were covered in art. How ironic that, amid all this beauty, men did the dirty work of Benito Mussolini, now in cahoots with Hitler.

Josephine craned her neck, pretending to be entranced by the colors of at least a dozen different kinds of marble adorning the spacious lobby. All the while, she was listening to the conversations of politicians and diplomats and men in military uniform who mingled and drank their vile grappa and congratulated themselves on the Germans' success. The pretty attaché — curly dark hair, winsome eyes, narrow hips — strode across the floor to her, licking his full lips.

"La Divina," he said, kissing her in greeting and following with a lingering hug, lightly pressing his erection into her thigh. She did not move away; in fact, the sensation was vaguely pleasant. How long had it been

since she'd fucked a stranger?

"Bella," he said, and followed with a stream of ardent declarations about her beauty, her talent, the honor of having her here as his guest. Josephine apologized and said her Italian was very poor although, in fact, she understood every word, having learned the language from Pepito and his chatterbox mother.

The youth switched to French but she shook her head again. Did he speak English? She knew, of course, that he did not. Captain Abtey had given her a complete dossier on the attaché: thirty-five years old; newly appointed in place of the pro-Nazi radical Angelo Parona; fluent in Italian, French, and German; and a farm boy drafted into service whose loyalties could not be discerned, as he kept company with all types. He gazed at her with mooning eyes.

"You've come a long way since Parma," she said, deliberately butchering her French. "You speak no English? None at all? How will we talk?"

"Love knows no language," he said in Italian, squeezing her waist. Josephine pretended not to understand.

His ardor was genuine; she had no doubt. She'd first seen him when she'd done a show in Parma — could it have been ten years ago? He had a face she could never forget. He and a half-dozen other boys had commandeered her car, ejecting the rented chauffeur and Pepito, and driven her through the cheering crowd to the theater. Josephine hadn't been frightened, but she'd resented Pepito for letting it happen. The attaché had sat in the back seat with her, holding her hand and giving her the same looks he was giving now. She'd been surprised to see him last week, in uniform, at her Casino de Paris show, *Paris et Londres.* She'd sent him a note inviting him backstage, and wrangled an invitation to this party. Now she batted her false eyelashes and let him put his hand on her ass and pretended not to comprehend a word as he and his colleagues spoke, in Italian, about how Mussolini was going to let Hitler take France so that Italy could focus on invading the Balkan States.

"The French have built a formidable barrier with the Maginot Line," her attaché said, asking exactly the right question. "How will Germany overcome it?"

The general in the group cackled. "Hitler has a plan," he said, "one so secret that even I do not know what it is. Il Duce says it will not fail."

When the talk turned to football, Josephine tugged at the attaché's sleeve and, brushing his ear with her lips, asked if he'd show her to the ladies' room. Immediately he excused himself, steering her with one hand on her waist and his fingertips on her hips, out of the beautiful reception room with its blue walls and velvet drapes and into the corridor where, unable to contain himself any longer, he covered her mouth with his. She resisted only a little, squirming against him to increase his arousal, and reminded him that she needed a toilette. When she came back out, she took his arm and asked for a private tour of the embassy.

He led her past a sumptuous dining room of gold and blue with chandeliers and long rows of white-clothed tables, and up the vast, multicolored marble staircase. Speaking in very slow French, which she made him repeat, he showed her the Chinese room; a library; a Sicilian theater with a small stage; reception suites in green, blue, and rose — and then, at last, the ambassador's office, all cherry wood and bookshelves and a heavy desk with a leather chair where he took a seat and looked as satisfied with himself as if he belonged there.

Josephine perched on the desk, picked up a pen and a notepad, and pretended to be his secretary. As he "dictated" his love letter to her, he roamed his hands up her thighs and, at last, pulled her into his lap.

"This is much more exciting than that dull party," she said between kisses, her blood heating up.

"You might have found it more interesting if you understood Italian."

"Why? What were you talking about?"

He shrugged and smiled into her eyes as he pinched her nipple. "Nothing important."

She pushed him away and stood. "You are making fun of me."

"No!" He went to her and slid his arms around her waist to nibble the back of her neck. "I would never do that."

She turned to gaze into his eyes. "I understand a *little* Italian, as I said. Your country is preparing to invade France, is that what I heard?"

He chuckled. "You really don't know Italian, do you? Never fear, my little bird, our plans have changed."

"You're just trying to make me feel better."

"No, I insist. Il Duce has commanded our generals to reposition our troops. Our men will head east, to the Balkans."

"Ah, the Maginot Line is too much for you," she said, slipping her hand down to his crotch. Should she try to get more information first? But he was already unzipping his fly, and she was squirming.

"Have I eased your fears?" He kissed her neck, sending shivers along her spine.

"I am very relaxed, thank you," she said, and let him lay her on the ambassador's desk.

When they had finished, she slipped into the adjoining restroom and washed up, pulling a pen from her purse and hurriedly writing down everything she had learned. Then she stepped out, and he went into the toilet. As soon as the door closed, she rushed to the desk and began opening drawers. A bottom drawer held files, but there was no time to read anything, so she looked in the top drawer, which held office supplies — a stapler and staple pull, paper clips, a bowl of loose change. The toilet flushed as she pulled the middle drawer, her heart racing, and saw a small book titled "German-Italian Codebook." *Voilà!*

When the attaché came out again, he found her reclining on a green-and-red-striped divan, her purse on the floor beside her, stretching her arms toward him. "Come and kiss me."

But he had grown nervous, his eyes darting toward the corridor. If they were caught in here, he would be in trouble.

"I understand," she said, and stood, picking up her bag and slipping the strap over her shoulder, feeling the satisfying heft of the little book within. "Let's go back and drink with the big shots. Do you have any champagne?"

CHAPTER 23

1940, Paris

To ensure there was enough food for all the soldiers at the Maginot Line, the French government issued ration cards, and restricted the sale of meat. "This occurred during the last war," M. Varna said. "You had better move your clothes to your city house, Josephine. Soon they will ration gasoline, as well."

Josephine told the staff at Chez Joséphine to save champagne bottles for her, as many as they could collect. She walked out that night with two cases, into which she poured fuel from the five-gallon gas can she had her driver fill at a different station every day to avoid drawing attention. She sealed the bottles with the corks she'd had her cooks whittle down to fit. She could always grow vegetables in her garden, but without fuel for her car she'd be trapped in Paris — a death sentence for her if the Nazis took over. Collecting gasoline became an obsession, almost like a game: how much could she gather before rationing began?

She wasn't the only one living like an animal preparing for hibernation. Secrecy pervaded the city, hooding eyes, shuttering mouths. Gone was the gaiety that had made Paris the most vibrant city in the world. No longer did laughter fill the clubs; no longer did cars race up and down the Champs-Élysées until four in the morning; no longer did crowds jostle and bump elbows cheerfully on the café terraces, or walk with brisk, joyful steps up and down the Montmartre hill.

The city subdued itself, the Parisians speaking in hushed tones, gathering inside the cafés and bistros if they left their homes at all, walking with shoulders hunched against the pall that coated everything like ash, faces etched with gloom. The bright colors of spring gave way to gray and black, as if the whole world were in mourning. Even the birds didn't sing that year, or if they did they could not be heard over the commands and replies of soldiers practicing defensive maneuvers in the streets, over the clang of shovels and picks as city workers dug trenches around the *places* and parks and built bomb shelters. When the city gave out gas masks, models wore them on the runway, adding a touch of macabre to the spring fashion shows. Signs appeared directing citizens to the nearest theaters, in case of emergency. Workers removed the stained glass windows from the Sainte-Chapelle cathedral, took down statues, and crated the major artworks in the Louvre. Anticipating bombings, the city, aided by the Red Cross, moved thirty thousand children out of the city to the suburbs — which the Germans then bombed, each sickening blast like a kick to Josephine's stomach.

Government officials began to leave the city for southern France, and many citizens followed, making Paris a shell as hollow and brittle as the laughter of those who remained. Josephine supervised the packing of her most precious belongings in her city townhouse and Le Beau Chêne, sending everything away by train or car to Les Milandes, the castle in southeast France she'd bought five years ago: carpets, light fixtures, the golden baby grand piano, medieval armor, the Marie Antoinette–style bed, all her clothing, curtains, linens, art, gold bathroom fixtures, jewelry, tables, chairs, figurines, carved Okimono ivories, Fabergé eggs, music boxes from Switzerland. All this she accomplished with a limited staff, for many had fled — aided by Josephine, who gave money and bottles of gasoline to those who needed it and put the rest on trains, buying their tickets and seeing them off: Nicolas, her butler, and Michel, who cared for her birds; Yvette and André, both in tears; Paul, her wine steward; Cecile, her cook, and all their husbands and wives and children, Josephine crying because they were like family but also because she wanted to leave, too. But she must await orders from Jacques.

She had not seen him in months. He had his duties for the Deuxième Bureau, of course, and a wife and children in Alsace. And she kept plenty busy with volunteering and flights for the Red Cross; her performances in the Casino de Paris and for the soldiers at the front; running Chez Joséphine; recording; making another film, and attending endless parties to gather information for Jacques. For once, she had no time for men, except for those she seduced in her spy work, but those liaisons were brief. Now, she slept alone — her nights haunted no longer by ghosts but by memories and dreams of her times with Jacques.

Her new maid, Paulette, a Parisienne with a pouf of dark curls and a small, knowing face, surely noticed the pouches under Josephine's eyes from lack of sleep and her frequent, obsessive queries about whether the mail had arrived. Her shrewd eyes saw too much, watching Josephine's every move. The girl always appeared wherever Josephine happened to be. Sometimes, Josephine locked herself in the toilet just to escape that piercing gaze. Was she a German spy? If so, the Nazis ought to fire her ass, because she didn't know the meaning of the word *discreet.* She was always pointing out news reports about this anti-Nazi group or that one, leaving articles around for Josephine to see, presenting her breakfast tray with the newspaper folded so that she was sure to see every story about the Maquis, the rogue group that slit Nazi throats, shot them in their sleep, and set off bombs where they gathered.

"Aren't the Maquis exciting?" she would say while combing straightener though Josephine's hair. "Hiding out in the mountains, shooting guns, becoming stealthy. One story said they imitate nature, learning from jaguars and panthers how to creep about without making a noise."

"Jaguars and panthers! Hmph," Josephine said. "You won't find those anywhere in France, except in a zoo."

"They keep the animals as pets, to guard

their hideouts."

"They'd better watch out, then, because those creatures get bossy when they get big." And then, Lord have mercy, she was chattering away, regaling Paulette with stories about the cheetah she used to have, Chiquita, her costar in a Casino de Paris show. She'd taken that creature everywhere, up and down the Champs-Élysées on a diamond leash, turning heads. But then, one day in a movie theater, it sprang from its seat next to Josephine and ran down the aisle and into the orchestra pit, sending everyone running for the exits. Paulette's eyes grew bigger and bigger as she talked, until Josephine, thinking they might pop right out of her head, started to giggle, and then the two of them were laughing together as Josephine, gasping, told how the cheetah had snarled at Pepito while he was driving and nearly caused them to hit an oncoming car.

"It was his own fault for shouting at me and calling me names," Josephine said. "I took that shit plenty, but Chiquita wasn't about to."

"What happened to Chiquita?"

"He died in the zoo." Josephine's voice cracked. "Pepito made me take him. He said Chiquita was unsafe, and that it was either him or the cat. Looking back, I made the wrong choice." And then the laughter again, and Paulette was rushing Josephine to the sink to rinse the conk from her hair, time flying so that she'd almost burned her scalp.

Loose talk aside, Josephine was a good spy. She knew how to get people to spill their secrets, and how to play innocent — and she knew better than to agree or disagree when Paulette started her treacherous talk. It was hard to be on her guard every minute, though, so from time to time, she slipped. One time, the girl piped up, "Wouldn't it be wonderful if everyone in France joined the Resistance? No one would do anything the Germans said."

"No one would do business with them," Josephine said, caught up in the notion.

"Or give up their homes."

"Or get on those trains."

"Instead, everyone would fight back. The Germans would always be in fear for their lives."

"The Nazis would have to leave," Josephine said, then stopped herself. What was she saying? Maybe Paulette was a good spy, after all.

"But that would only happen if everyone joined the Maquis." The maid became animated, waving her hands. "They are the

427

fighters, the trained killers. Krystyna Skarbek is the most wanted woman in Europe. And Michael Trotobas — ah, Trotobas! Have you seen him? So handsome." She placed her hands over her heart.

"Watch out for handsome men," Josephine said. "They know how good they look, believe me, and they'll use it. They don't even think about you."

"Yes, but all men are that way — children who never grow up. I would rather be with a pretty baby than an ugly one, wouldn't you?"

And then in June, the inevitable happened: the Germans blew into Paris like a terrible storm, a thunder of jackboots, a rumble of tanks and cars, an ominous dark cloud descending on the City of Light. Josephine and Paulette watched the invasion from the window of the apartment overlooking the Champs-Élysées, the streets completely empty except for the ugly invasion of green and gray, no one allowed outside, a curfew announced over loudspeakers that morning by their own government. They heard no shots fired in opposition, not a word shouted, nothing but silence and cringing from a people whose own leaders had betrayed them in the worst possible way.

"Like taking candy from a baby," Josephine said. "They just waltz in and invade our city, and what do we do? Roll over and play dead."

Paulette's eyes widened. "But some of us are only playing. Isn't that right?"

Josephine sucked her teeth. The girl had to be a German agent, sent to entrap Josephine.

"Why do you keep saying things like that?" Josephine snapped. "Are you recording me?" She gripped the maid's arm and patted down her childish body, apron pockets, all over her little chest, up her thighs to her crotch, everywhere. All she found was lint and loose change. When she let go, Paulette whimpered and rubbed the red marks on her arm.

"I'm sorry, madame. I feel like I am in a bad dream and I cannot get out. I want to join the Resistance, myself — there, I have said it, so fire me if you must. My beloved Paris. I can't bear it!" She burst into tears.

Josephine put her arms around her. "I'm sorry, Paulette. I can't bear it, either. Dear Lord, what will happen to us all?"

The next morning, she went to the theater to collect her final check from M. Varna. The previous evening, before the curfew began, he had told the cast and crew that he was closing *Paris et Londres*. As she walked down the Champs-Élysées, the sight of the Nazi flag flying from atop the Arc de Triomphe made her want to hit somebody. A pair of Nazis approached on the broad sidewalk, machine guns at the ready as if they expected the city to suddenly wake up and start fighting. The battle would come soon enough, but not in the way they expected. As they passed, Josephine lowered her gaze. If they saw what her eyes held, they would shoot her on the spot.

The dark hand on her heart squeezed more and more tightly as she walked. The Germans were defacing the beauty of Paris with their ugly handmade signs. LUFTWAFFE. The German army had claimed the Luxembourg Palace as its headquarters, degrading that noble place. And, most sickening of all, NO JEWS. Josephine wondered how her ex-husband Jean, a Jew from a Jewish family, would feel when he saw them. They made her think of the NO COLOREDS signs posted on the doors and windows of shops, hotels, and cafés in the South. How ashamed she'd felt, seeing those awful signs, as though she'd done something wrong.

After a tearful farewell to M. Varna and the rest of the cast, she took a cab to the bank, which was filled with Nazis. Their stares lifted the hair on her neck and made the teller's hands tremble as she cashed Josephine's check. Josephine wondered where the city's Jews were doing their banking today. Though she'd converted to Judaism when she'd married Jean, she kept that bit of history to herself.

At home she hid her money, sewing it into the hems of her clothes, and prayed for a letter or message from Jacques. *Deliver me from the valley of the shadow of death, O Lord.*

Late that night, she awoke to a banging so loud she thought bombs were dropping. She flung open the shutters and saw a Nazi soldier hitting her door with the butt of his rifle. Crying out for him to stop, that she would be right down, she threw on some clothes and called out for Paulette. Where was that girl? Josephine's pulse raced so fast she had to gasp for air. The banging resumed, and she ran down the stairs to open the door. A man with colorless skin and angry eyes held the gun still poised as if to smash it into her. Her blood ran as cold as ice water.

"Good evening, monsieur," she said. "What can I do for you?"

"The Jew who is your husband," he said.

"We want to see him."

"He isn't here," she said.

"Where is he?"

"In Marseille, on business," she lied. When the Germans had crossed the border a month ago, Jean had disappeared. She didn't even know whether he was alive. But Jacques had warned her never to say "I don't know" to a Nazi. *Do not make them suspect you of lying. Make up a story if you must, and speak it with authority.*

The man looked over her shoulder. "Why didn't you tell us, *fraulein*?" he said.

She turned to see Paulette standing behind her, her face flushing a deep red.

"Do you want me to have him get in touch with you when he returns?" she said to the soldier as sweetly as she could force herself to.

"There is no need. Herr Hermann Göring, president of the Reichstag, will be waiting for him. He has chosen this house for himself. You must vacate immediately."

When he had gone, Josephine shut the door and, leaning against it, closed her eyes. They had not arrested her. She was safe — for now. She heard a clatter and looked to see Paulette dropping to the floor. She rushed over to revive her and, when the girl awakened, asked her what the hell was going on.

"You're a German spy," she accused.

"No, madame. They paid me to spy on you, and I took their money, I admit. My father had died and left me penniless, and I was desperate. But what I really wanted was to join the Maquis. The officer told me they suspected you of working with them and wanted me to report. But I have had nothing to tell them — and if I had, I would not have said a word."

Josephine stood, letting her drop back to the floor. "That's where you belong, in the gutter," she said. "Get out of my house."

The girl struggled to her feet, and Josephine saw the butcher knife lying under her. "What's that for? Were you going to kill me?"

"No, madame, it was not for you but for him. If he laid a hand on you, I would have stabbed him to death."

"He would have killed you."

She lifted her chin. "What is my life worth compared to yours?"

The next morning, a man phoned and asked her to meet him at a café on the Place Pigalle. *I have a message from M. Fox.* Josephine, who'd relented and allowed Paulette to stay, slipped out without telling the maid where she was going, only that she would return soon. She left the girl packing Josephine's clothes in trunks, the only servant she had left: no one wanted to wait on the notorious Hermann Göring. The idea of that monster living in her home and writing out his evil decrees at her Louis XIV desk made Josephine want to set the place on fire.

She sat in a back corner table on the café terrace, sipping one café crème after another, lifting the cup to her lips with both hands to hide their trembling. Across the street, a grocer arranged oranges on a tray as if this were just another day. Citroëns and Renaults, French cars, crowded the street along with, now, the black Mercedes-Benzes the German officers favored, as well as green and gray military trucks. Men and women in business attire — suits and ties for the men, women in V-necked dresses that fell just below the knee — milled about as they had before the invasion, filling the sidewalks again, except that, now, most wore the colors of mourning in spite of the heat. Josephine herself had put on her navy Chanel suit, which fit her dark mood. The men at the table beside her chain-smoked Gauloises, and for the first time in her life

Josephine felt tempted to ask for one, wanting something — anything — to calm her nerves.

Where was the mystery man with news of Jacques? Why hadn't Jacques come himself? Now that Philippe Pétain, France's sorry excuse for a prime minister, had rolled over for Hitler and had to move his whole army to southern France — the only part of the country left for him to "govern" — Jacques was most likely helping with that transfer. Or maybe he was dead, and this new man would take his place. Tears filled her eyes at the thought, which she banished. The Germans would never vanquish the wily Jacques Abtey.

The terrace filled with men in uniform, then emptied, then filled up again. Two older officers stared at her, openly hostile, one muttering *neger.* From all around her, the German language ricocheted against her ears like machine-gun fire. She pretended to read a book, tried to imagine what Jacques's message would be. *Get the hell out of Paris,* most likely. She didn't need a messenger to tell her that. She had Les Milandes, her château in the Dordogne, far from Nazi rule. Thank the Lord for leading her there! She'd fallen in love with it at first sight, as they'd driven through the French countryside and it had come into view, a fairytale castle high on a hill above the sparkling Dordogne. The FOR RENT sign had only confirmed what she'd known from the start: she was destined to have it. Jean had tried to talk her out of it, pointing out that medieval stone buildings lacked heat and hot water. But Josephine didn't let any man tell her what to do, except, now, Jacques.

Would he send her away? The murderous hatred on the faces of the men beside her made her want to run. Now that Hitler had taken Paris, what was the point of spying? What was the point of anything?

She leaped up — and collided with a passing waiter who dumped coffee all over her dress. *"Merde,"* she cried, in surprise rather than pain since the coffee was cold (a detail she would recall later). A swarm of café staff surrounded her and ushered her inside, into the kitchen to clean the stains. "Voilà," they said, maneuvering her toward the very back of the room, where someone opened a door and pushed her into a closet. Her senses reeled. She raised her fist to pound on the door but felt herself pulled backward, through the wall. She lost her footing and would have fallen but for the arms that caught her. Shc tried to scream, but a hand

436

clamped over her mouth.

"Vive la Résistance," a woman's voice whispered.

Josephine relaxed. This was not the Gestapo. Her abductor released her, and she took a steadying breath.

When her eyes adjusted, she found herself in a secret world, surrounded by stone walls. The dark-haired woman replaced the panel she had removed from the wall and led Josephine down a steep staircase dimly lighted by tiny bulbs, into the bowels of Paris. Josephine walked carefully, unsteady on her heels. In the chill, gooseflesh rippled over her arms.

At the bottom, the woman unlocked a heavy door, which she led Josephine through and locked behind them. The stench of excrement filled Josephine's nose; a rat skittered near their feet; the drip of water made her think of blood, turning her stomach.

"Where are we?"

"Only in the sewer. We are safe," the woman said.

And then — thank the Lord — there was Jacques, sitting at the head of a table made from a wooden door piled on some stones. Gas lanterns cast flickering shadows across his face. It was all she could do not to run to him and throw herself, weeping in gratitude, around his neck. He was alive.

He strode to her and greeted her with a kiss on each cheek. He introduced her to his companions, uttering the names that she had read in the papers: Krystyna Skarbek, Michael Trotobas, La Besnerais — the most wanted people in France, the heroes whom she and Paulette had marveled over.

Skarbek, the famous freedom fighter — if only Paulette could see her, in a leather jacket and men's trousers! — turned to Josephine and placed a pistol in her hand: metallic, heavy, lethal, cold.

"Josephine Baker," she said, "welcome to the Maquis."

CHAPTER 24

The Casino de Paris had gone dark when the Nazis marched into Paris, but Chez Joséphine remained open. No music filled its hall now, for Josephine would not allow it: Music was for happy times. Still, the fine champagne flowed freely, supplemented, now, by good German beer, for Nazi soldiers and officers crowded the tables for her autograph — not all of them hated her, it turned out. Often they requested a dance, but she begged off, saying she had gotten too old. The fact was, she would not entertain these men. While a single Nazi remained in Paris, Josephine Baker would not dance.

Folks whispered about her keeping the club open, but she didn't care: she had her reasons. In fact, the gossip about her being a Nazi sympathizer was the best cover she could ask for.

Wearing a red dress cut nearly to her navel

and glittering spike-heeled shoes — her assignment, after all, was to seduce — she moved from table to table, pouring champagne, *No empty glasses, that's the rule,* and slipping past grasping hands while she kept an eye on the entrance, where, at last, the handsome blond *capitaine* with the smirking mustache sashayed drunkenly in with a group in military uniform. The chisel-faced Trotobas, handsome as the devil himself, followed arm in arm with two slender Nazi youths and winked at Josephine behind their heads; Krystyna Skarbek tossed her black hair and clutched Jacques's arm possessively, her eyes slanting a warning to every other woman to stay away. They put on this charade in case the Germans were watching, which, of course, they were, their eyes on Krystyna instead of on Jacques, which was the plan.

Josephine ordered champagne and beer for them. The Maquisards would only pretend to drink the bubbly, but the hard-drinking Nazis would slurp down the beer like it was soda pop, which was also the plan. Josephine slipped her hand inside the purse dangling from her shoulder and felt for her cigarette case. The microfilm inside held a copy of the German-Italian Codebook she'd filched from the Italian ambassador's desk. She'd wait for the handoff until the Luftwaffe were good and drunk — which, at the rate they were sucking down the juice, wouldn't be long.

After making the rounds at all the tables and settling a new crowd of guests, she went to the bar and ordered four bottles of German beer, which she carried to the high, round table where Jacques and his companions smoked and laughed as if it were New Year's Eve instead of doomsday.

"With my compliments," she told the delighted Nazis as she handed them their bottles. They hoisted them in a toast of thanks and guzzled down the contents, Adam's apples rising and falling like hammers. While they were occupied, she glanced at Jacques, who gave a quick nod. She reached into her bag for the loose cigarette and lifted it to her lips.

"Allumez-moi, Capitaine?"

Jacques pulled a silver cigarette case with a built-in lighter from inside his jacket and handed it to her. She lit the cigarette and closed the case, then called to a passing waiter, slipping the case into her purse as she hurried away to pursue him.

"Madame!" Jacques called, and in a moment he was tapping on her shoulder. "I would happily give you my case, but it was a gift from a special friend."

"Oh, excuse me," and, reaching into her bag, handed him the duplicate case containing the microfilm. "I hope your friend is not *too* special. I have long been wanting to meet the famous *capitaine* Jacques Abtey."

"Then we must arrange such a meeting," he said, slipping the case into his pocket and giving her a lecherous smile. "As soon as possible."

Josephine felt a pang: she wanted to pull him close right then and there, to feel the beat of his heart and to say goodbye — for he would leave with Pétain for Marseille tomorrow. Josephine would have left the city, too, by now, but she had to finish her mission. After three days' training with the Maquis, she had emerged with a camera, the cigarette case, and Jacques's instructions to make the film and bring it to him here tonight.

Paulette had already gone to Le Beau Chêne, not knowing what had become of Josephine during those three days. Josephine had joined the girl there this morning, the poor thing weeping in relief, she'd thought Josephine dead. Josephine had laughed and said she wasn't that easy to kill. But now, under the bloodless stare of the Nazi officer blocking her way to her office, she wondered if she'd pushed her luck just a bit too far. His cold blue eyes and scarred nose had haunted her for years. This was the man from Berlin who had fondled his gun while she'd danced, and sent her running out the stage door.

"Excuse me, Officer." She kept her eyes downcast. "A customer has fallen ill, and I must attend to her."

"Frau Baker," he said. "Don't you remember me?"

She shook her head. "I'm sorry, I am needed elsewhere."

"From Berlin?" he pressed, stepping to the side to prevent her passing. "The Stage Theater des Westens?"

"I was in Berlin a long time ago," she said. "Please excuse me." How did her voice sound so strong when she felt like she might collapse?

"But surely you remember Max Reinhardt, the *Juden.* Your good friend, wasn't he?"

"If you want information about him, you've come to the wrong place," she said. "We haven't been in contact in years."

"When someone does not look at me, I wonder what that person is hiding."

Josephine forced her gaze upward, to the man's face and saw, again, the mix of lust and hatred his eyes had held as he'd stroked the gun in his lap. The urge to run shot through her, but she knew better than to try.

"What can I do for you, monsieur?" She refused to use the German honorific "Herr." If they wanted to live in Paris, then let the fuckers learn French.

"That captain has been lighting cigarettes for women all night," he said. "Why didn't he light yours?"

"His hands looked pretty busy to me," she said.

He narrowed his eyes. "Give me your bag." He reached out a hand to take it but she jerked away from him, stepping back.

"What for, monsieur? I have done nothing wrong." The officer lunged and grabbed the strap, yanking it so hard that he broke it. Josephine's blood thrummed in her ears as he opened the clasp and pulled out the cigarette case.

"I see that you have a cigarette lighter of your own," he said. "And it matches the captain's case exactly."

"It is a common item." She folded her arms. "Unlike the bag that you have just broken. It's a Givenchy."

She held her breath as he opened the case, praying that she had not made a mistake and handed the wrong one to Jacques. If he found the microfilm, he would arrest her.

"It is empty," he snarled.

"Of course, monsieur." Her pulse slowed its wild ricochet. "I carry the case as a courtesy for customers who need a light. Everyone knows that I do not smoke."

"Then why did you ask the captain for a light?"

She took the broken bag, and the silver case, from his hands. "To lure him from his woman. Surely you saw how she clung to him? I took his cigarettes so that he would come after me. And as you saw, my plan worked."

The German's head snapped around as he looked for the captain — but the table where Jacques and the other Maquisards had sat with their drunken German "friends" was now empty.

"Where is he?" he said. "I want to inspect his cigarette case."

"Do you want to smoke? Let me get some cigarettes for you. I will return in a moment." She went to the bar, grabbed her wrap, and slipped out the kitchen door, for the second time in her life running away — this time, wondering if she would ever be able to stop.

Before the sun had risen the next morning, Paulette awakened her: The *capitaine* had come. Josephine ran down the stairs and into his arms.

"You are dressed," he said between kisses.

"For a quick getaway, Foxy. I didn't like the way the Germans were looking at me — or at you — last night."

"I am on my way to Marseille now. And you must leave, as well." She should not bother to pack her things, he said, but should go right away. If she were stopped she should say she had a performance in Sarlat, the village near her castle.

"Sarlat? Do they now have a theater?"

"Your concert will be in the cathedral." Posing as her agent, Jacques had arranged a benefit to help Paris reimburse the Germans for the cost of the invasion — a Nazi demand intended to further humiliate the city. "I could not believe how excited the priest became when I suggested you perform there. One might have thought the gates of heaven had opened."

As indeed they had: under normal circumstances, Josephine would never perform in such a tiny town as Sarlat. At any rate, she was ready to go, and so was Paulette. Most of Josephine's wardrobe and valuable furniture had already gone to Les Milandes, and Paulette had a Swiss passport and a train ticket to Zurich, where she would deposit Josephine's jewels in the Suisse Bank.

"She will wear my bracelets and necklaces under her clothes. With the passport, they will not search her. Then she will return."

"She ought to remain in Switzerland," Jacques said. "It is a neutral country, and she will be safe there."

Josephine had tried to convince her of this, but Paulette would not hear of it. "Paris is my heart, and without a heart, one cannot live," she'd said. She wanted to work against the Nazis; that was evident from the shine in her eyes when Josephine had confided her underground adventures.

"It is an enormous risk," Jacques said. "If she is apprehended . . ."

"She would rather cut out her tongue than inform on me." But Josephine had a plan to deflect the Nazis' attention: before leaving the castle, she would call the police and report that her maid had absconded with her jewels. Since the Germans had hired Paulette to spy on Josephine — and she had been cooperative, feeding them trivial (and false) information — they would expect the girl at their headquarters. By the time they realized she was not going to appear, she would have crossed the border as Marise Delaunay.

"She will keep the name when she returns — as a Maquisard. I will teach her to shoot." Josephine was a natural marksman, it turned out. After three days of firing at rats in the sewers, she could shoot out a candle at twenty yards.

"But she must not come back here — and neither, Josephine, should you. Göring received orders for your arrest a week ago. He has delayed detaining you to give the Parisians some time to adjust to the new regime."

"They will never."

"I am afraid you are wrong about that." He sighed. "But Göring has now sent his soldiers to raid your club. La Besnerais says they have shut it down, and will come to Le Beau Chêne for you soon. You must leave for Les Milandes right away."

"Taking my Paris house wasn't enough, huh? What grounds do they have to arrest me?"

"Conspiracy to commit murder." The previous night, five German soldiers had been found dead in a dingy apartment near the Place Pigalle, in their underwear, their throats slit. "Their uniforms were gone, but the Nazis are keeping that quiet. They say the men were in a homosexual party, with some Frenchmen." He curled his lip. "We decadent Parisians are such bad influences on the pure Aryan race."

"But what does that have to do with me?"

"They were seen in your club last night."

"In my club? But what would I know about it?" Chez Joséphine had crawled with Nazis. "Which Germans are we talking about? Who were they with?"

He grinned. "To their great misfortune, they were with me."

Paulette left for the Le Vésinet train station immediately with Josephine's driver François. While they were gone, Josephine fired her staff, telling them she was closing Le Beau Chêne and giving them their pay and bonuses in cash, and went to the stable to collect M. and Mme. Laremie, Jewish refugees from Belgium whom she had met through her work with the Red Cross and hidden in a horse trailer.

When Francois returned, they all piled into the car with her dogs, a box of food, and the champagne bottles of gasoline, and headed east to join the long stream of refugees headed for Pétain's "Free Zone" in the south. The line of people and automobiles stretched to the far horizon, thousands upon thousands on the road to Bordeaux, fleeing hell. The slow crawl made her want to scream — what if Göring's men had discovered that she was gone, and were now pursuing her? On the open highway, she'd outrun them — Jean had taught her to race at the Montlhéry track and she'd gotten pretty good — but stuck in this molasses she wouldn't have a chance.

"I can't stand it," she said when the car had stopped for the ten thousandth time. She threw open her door and jumped out to walk, joining the motley parade of cars and trucks and vans and wagons, taxicabs and horses and motorcycles and bicycles, a girl on a unicycle, an entire family on roller skates, a man walking a Great Dane with a small child clinging to its fur, a hearse with its back open and people crowded inside and sitting on top, everyone weary and dazed, so many in the city without any means of transportation except their legs or, in some cases, wheelchairs.

Josephine would have liked to carry them all, but she had a carload, including her two dogs whom she ought to bring outside with her. The buzz of an airplane drew her attention upward. A Heinkel aircraft sped toward them, careening from the sky as if to crash into their midst. Screams filled the air as it swooped over their heads, strafing the ground with gunfire, sending up puffs of dust and clods of dirt and exploding the hearse in a burst of flame. The blast toppled over the girl on the unicycle, and Josephine started to run toward her, toward the burning car, wanting to help, but a hand grabbed her wrist and Mme. Laremie pulled her back. "Get in the car, don't let the Germans see you." She followed the woman and crawled, shaking, into the front seat, where she lay down and sobbed, her cries mingling with the wails and moans of injured children and grieving mothers, wringing tears from her body, her mind stained with visions of death like blood that would never come out, until, numb, she slept.

And was awakened by a loud banging noise that, when she opened her eyes, became that of a German fist on her window.

"Madame, we have arrived at the border with Free France," François said. "The Germans want to see our identification papers, I think, but I cannot understand."

The poor boy looked scared to death, his knuckles white on the steering wheel. "*Bon courage,* François. God will protect us." As she rolled down the window, she forced herself to smile.

"*Bonjour, monsieur.*"

"Your documents," the soldier said in

German. He wore the uniform of a common Wehrmacht infantryman: gray jacket and pants, green collar and shoulder straps. Josephine handed him her identification card, gritting her teeth. If he asked to see her passport, she'd be in trouble. Jean had it; he'd kept it for her during their trip to Argentina, and when she'd told him she'd decided not to leave show business, after all, he'd left off in a huff, taking her passport with him. *You are incapable of being a wife to any man.* That had stung, but when he'd been injured on the Maginot Line, he'd begged her to come back to him. Keeping her passport was a way to pay her back, she supposed, for turning him down.

As the soldier took her card, he peered into the back seat, where M. Laremie was reading a newspaper, his white eyebrows furrowed over the page, and Madame knitted a sweater in such a frenzy that one hardly noticed the trembling of her gnarled hands — or so Josephine hoped.

"I want to see the old couple's papers, too," he said. "I want to see everyone's." Josephine glanced at the couple, who, continuing with their reading and knitting, either didn't understand German or were very good actors. The boy stared at Josephine's ID for what felt like hours. She could almost read his thoughts: *Why is this name familiar? Is it on my list of those to detain?* He mouthed her name and looked into her eyes. Josephine held her gaze steady as she gripped the armrest on her door.

"You are the famous singer?" He looked like he'd just found a treasure chest. "Josephine Baker. I have always wanted to see you perform."

" 'J'ai deux amours,' " she trilled, giving him a coy look. He called out, his voice excited, and three other soldiers came over, all boys, one holding out a pen and a notepad and begging for her autograph. She signed the back of another's hand, and to the first soldier gave a page of her sheet music with her signature scrawled across the front. Autograph in hand, he asked her to sing for them, and she opened the door and stood, and sang "J'ai Deux Amours" and "Mon Coeur Est Un Oiseau Des Iles," adding verses, singing them twice, watching the traffic stream past, unchecked. She might have distracted them all day but for the call crackling over the radio, and their realization that they were neglecting their duties. The soldiers applauded and kissed her hand, waving the car along, forgetting about M. and Mme. Laremie in the back seat, who embraced each other and did not release their clutch until, when the car had crossed over the line of demarcation into the free zone, they joined Josephine in a champagne toast to freedom.

They all knew, though, that the absence of jackboots and checkpoints was only temporary, free zone or not. Adolf Hitler's aims could not have been clearer: he planned to conquer the world, and a line drawn in the sand by a government that had so readily capitulated would not hold him at bay for long.

CHAPTER 25

They arrived at the castle midafternoon, after more than ten harrowing hours in the car. As the Laremies marveled over the budding trees, the brilliant green landscape, the blooming flowers, the bright ribbon of the Dordogne below, and the birds swooping down to fish, Josephine and François threw open all the windows, letting air and warmth into the chilly stone rooms. Josephine hummed as she removed the covers from the furniture, as she fluffed pillows and swept floors and wrote out a list of items for François to buy in the Sarlat market, and as she remembered the kisses Jacques had given to her before leaving that morning. Would she ever see him again? She hadn't dared to ask.

How could anyone think of love while the world burned? On the other hand, how could anyone *not*?

She cooked steak and *frites* for her little

group while they fiddled with the tabletop short-wave radio Jean had set up in the kitchen. At last they found a BBC broadcast from England, now practically the last free country in Europe. Josephine sliced potatoes while François and the Laremies clustered around the radio to hear news of the world at war: A German air raid had sunk a ship carrying nearly nine thousand refugees from France to England. Russian troops had marched into Latvia and Estonia. Pétain's government had moved headquarters not to Marseille but to Bordeaux. (Jacques was so nearby!) Several members of the French cabinet had resigned in protest over the government's capitulation, including General Charles de Gaulle, the undersecretary of war. They'd gone to London to set up an alternative French government. Had Jacques gone with them?

"It's about time somebody spoke up about that shameful armistice," Josephine said. "General de Gaulle and his followers are heroes, if you ask me."

"Shhh! *Ecoutez,*" M. Laremie said, turning up the volume. And then, over a faint crackle, came the voice of de Gaulle, measured, confident, strong, telling the people of France not to surrender as their government had done.

"But has the last word been said? Must we abandon all hope? Is our defeat final and irremediable? To those questions I answer — no! Speaking in full knowledge of the facts, I ask you to believe me when I say that the cause of France is not lost."

Josephine put down her chopping knife and, wiping her hands on a dish towel, moved closer to the wooden table where the others sat. Like them, she leaned toward the box, pulled as if by a magnetic force to this speech that, she knew deep in her bones, she was destined to hear. De Gaulle spoke to all of France, but especially to her. She heard him predict that Great Britain and the United States would come to France's aid, their industrial strength helping to defeat the forces of tyranny.

"They will come," she said. "The United States will help us, I know."

M. Laremie pressed a finger to his lips and moved his head closer to the speaker.

General de Gaulle called for all French soldiers on British soil "now or in the future" to contact him. He was calling her, and Jacques, to join him — and the rest of the Maquisards, all, to save France.

"Whatever happens," he said, ending the speech, "the flame of French Resistance must not and shall not die."

"Vive la France!" she cried, pumping her fist in time with her full, beating heart. François stood to join her, *"Vive la France,* Madame Baker," and then the Laremies, *"Vive la flamme de la résistance,"* all crying and embracing one another, enlivened with hope for the first time since the French government had abandoned Paris, a span that seemed like years but which had only been eight days. If only Jacques were here.

It didn't take him long to join them, although it felt, to Josephine, like a century. She was cutting flowers from her garden beds, breathing in petals, blossoms, *fleurs,* such a pretty word, scents of rosemary and thyme washing over her, the sun winking down, life greening and blooming at her feet, the Dordogne glittering past at the base of the hill, birds flitting from branch to leafing branch, the sun warming her arms and throat. Les Milandes — her fortress, her gift from God, her refuge — towered above.

Pétain, not Hitler, ruled this countryside, and de Gaulle from London, his broadcasts swelling her heart more every day. All who wanted freedom for France should join him in London, he said. Josephine wanted to go, but she must wait for Jacques. He would come.

Paulette came up from the river, her dark

curls tied in a red kerchief, her face rosy, a pistol dangling from her right hand. Beside her walked François, touching her waist. When he saw Josephine, he dropped his hand. Aha!

"She is doing very well," François said.

"I shot a bird in flight," Paulette said.

"Poor little creature," Josephine said. Paulette was a better shot than she was. Damn.

The maid shrugged. "If I hadn't finished it off, one of your cats would have done it."

"*Quelle insouciance,*" François said, and the look that passed between them made Josephine wonder if more than guns hadn't been going off in the brush.

The rumble of an automobile froze them in place. François took the pistol from Paulette and tucked it into his pants. "Let's go inside," Josephine said, but the nose of the car appeared: the tilted grill, the extravagant, winglike wheel covers, the headlights rising on posts like the eyes of insects —

"Jacques!" she cried, hands springing to her hair, feet running as the black car pulled up to the house. She stilled herself: Let him come to her. As he approached, his eyes never left hers, as blue as ever, French blue, the Germans had no idea. Love filled her mouth and nose, and she dipped her head before it could reach her eyes. She offered him a kiss, left cheek, right cheek, left cheek, and slipped her arm through his.

"Foxy," she said. "You finally came. When are we going to join de Gaulle?"

But they had to wait for orders. Jacques had absconded from the Deuxième Bureau when de Gaulle left, intending to go with him to London, but the general had other ideas. An intelligence officer would be more useful in France gathering information, he'd said. Jacques told him about Josephine and the other Maquisards, so de Gaulle had sent him to Les Milandes.

"He will call us when we are needed," Jacques said. He shrugged when Josephine said she'd rather go to London, but she could see his disappointment.

One evening in October, a tall, white-haired man came to the door, his eyes darting and wary, asking for Captain Abtey.

"There is no one by that name here," Paulette told him.

He leveled his gaze upon her as though addressing a stupid child.

"Whatever name he is using, then."

He had come from Marseille, sent by Paillole, a captain in the Deuxième Bureau with Jacques and now a leader in de Gaulle's

Free French force. Paulette invited him in, to Josephine's consternation: he might be a spy for the Germans. But his story had seemed plausible to the maid, and he'd even produced a letter of introduction. He left the following day with Jacques's passport, saying Paillole would produce a new one with a different name and an older age, since men under forty were not allowed to leave France. They also requested a passport for Josephine.

A week later, four Nazi soldiers and an officer came to the door, saying someone had reported gunfire coming from her property. Josephine knew it was a ruse: everyone in her home knew to silence their guns during target practice. The Germans wanted to search the château and outbuildings for weapons.

"What do you think of that?" the officer said, narrowing his eyes.

"I think, monsieur, that you cannot be serious." She wondered under whose authority they had come — this was the free zone, after all — but, eyeing their guns, she didn't ask.

"Gunfire? That's probably my old Peugeot somebody heard," she said, gathering her wits. "The engine backfires, can you believe it? I knew I should have bought a German model. How do you like the Mercedes-Benz you're driving?"

She rang for Paulette and asked her to make tea for the visitors, then led them into the sitting room.

"I'll give you a tour of the place first, sure, but what kind of hostess would I be if I didn't offer you something to eat and drink? We raise geese here, and Paulette just cooked one up last night for supper. She made pâté from the liver, you've got to try it."

She heard herself chattering too much, but the Germans didn't seem to notice. The tall one had eyes like a winter sky that lingered on her breasts. She made sure to touch him often as she spoke and smile into his face. The sound of the dumbwaiter trundling down the laundry chute relaxed her nerves a bit: she knew it carried a hammer, the secret signal to her guests — Trotobas, two defected officers from the French army, and the Laremies — to hide themselves. In a moment, they would be scurrying through the secret panel and into the cave that they had dug. Jacques, having heard the car, came up from the river, fishing rod in his hand, and introduced himself in a twang as "Jack Saunders," an American tourist who'd befriended Josephine.

"I'm a mighty big fan," he said in English. "Seen all her pictures."

"Your timing is perfect, Mr. Jack," she said. "I was about to give these men a tour."

"Don't mind if I do," he said. The German officer scowled, as if the American were imposing, as though he might have had a chance at some fun with Josephine after forcing his way into her home and poking around for a reason to arrest her.

"He does not look like an American," the officer said. "Let me see your passport, sir."

"In those waders, he looks more like a sewer inspector," Josephine agreed, her heart clamoring; Jacques had sent his passport to Paillole. He pulled out one of his phony business cards and gave it to the officer, smiling big.

"But I don't think he understands German. You know how it is in the United States: they don't teach foreign languages in school. By the way, *you* don't look like a military officer, you're far too handsome. Have you done any acting? I'm working on a new movie, and we have a part that would be perfect for you."

As she talked, filling their heads with words, she led the men up the stairs to the top floor, Jacques bringing up the rear, ready to defend her if needed, she supposed, although she wished he would disappear — without a passport, the situation was too dangerous for him. She kept her smile big and bright as if the men were dinner guests instead of Nazi thugs. The two soldiers looked around while she talked and flirted with the officer, and Jacques kept everyone occupied with his endless questions to her, in English, about the castle's history and each piece of furniture and every photograph and painting. She regaled them with so many stories that, listening, the Nazis forgot to search very hard, which was just fine with her — they missed the gun in the back of her nightstand drawer. When she said the tour was finished except for the kitchen, no one even asked about the basement.

"We have found no weapons, Frau Baker," one of the soldiers said, beaming at her.

"Of course not," she said. "While it's true that I had red-Indian grandparents, they hung up their tomahawks quite a while ago. The war dance is the only dance I haven't done." She slanted her eyes at the officer. "I prefer love to war, don't you?" And, placing her hand on his arm, let him escort her into the kitchen.

Paulette had fixed a plate of pâté and bread and a pot of tea and set them on the table. Josephine poured tea, continuing to chatter. The officer passed the plate her way and she took only a nibble, saying that, as much as she enjoyed pâté, it was fattening. She had a tour coming up, and must watch her figure.

"I will watch it for you," the officer said.

"Will you? Ha ha! You are so witty, Karl," she said.

When the trio left, each bearing auto-graphed records, she stood at the door waving farewell — and then turned and collapsed into Jacques's arms.

"That was superb," he said. "The most marvelous performance of your life."

His arms around her, holding her, his hands on her back, her waist, his mouth on her mouth — it was nearly worth the ordeal to have him close to her at last. In the months since he had come to Les Milandes, Jacques had hardly slept with her — out of respect, he said, not wanting to stimulate gossip, and also from "a desire not to cause trouble in the group." Knowing he had visited his wife and children before coming to Les Milandes, she'd thought his explanations dubious. But now she saw that old glimmer in his eyes.

Feeling his gaze as she walked to the dumbwaiter and pulled it up. Her body tingling. Paulette came in with François, her eyes wide to see that the Nazis had left, and that she and Jacques were both still there.

"We are safe," Josephine said. How did she sound so strong when her body felt like rubber? "The Germans left satisfied and will not return."

"They will return," Jacques said, glancing at her. "One of them, I am certain, has not been satisfied."

He and Josephine must leave now, he said, to see Captain Paillole in Vichy, tell him what had occurred, and request orders. Paulette would take the Laremies into the village and help them find another residence.

"Then you will remain here until François returns for you," he told Paulette. "If any Nazis come to the door, tell them Josephine has left on her tour."

Trotobas and the officers came into the room. "Pack your belongings. We must all disperse immediately," Jacques said. "Les Milandes is our safe haven no more."

CHAPTER 26

1940, Lisbon

Lisbon was exciting, decadent, filled with life, *free* — everything Paris used to be: a fete of music, bright lights, nightclubs, restaurants, and endless parties. The city was perfect for eavesdropping, the Alfama neighborhood at the base of St. George's Castle a maze of narrow streets teeming with spies, Spaniards, Italians, Germans, Russians, British, Jews, and French — everyone hiding secrets like daggers under their cloaks. Only the Portuguese were neutral, but even some of them were on the take.

Wherever there were spies, so was Josephine, working the crowd, playing dumb, brushing up against the enemy when Jacques wasn't looking. He had warned her against flirting — this was not the Italian embassy with its wet-behind-the-ears attaché — but she thought he might be jealous. At last.

From here, once their visas came through, they could travel to Brazil for a tour, Jacques as her *maître de ballet* — she'd had it inscribed on his passport, "agent to Josephine Baker," increasing his respect for her, for now if he were arrested she would be, too.

"The Germans aren't concerned with you," she'd said with a shrug. It was true. When they had obtained their passports from Paillole along with maps, photographs, and fifty-two documents about the Germans (including the Nazi plan to grab the rest of France), she'd pinned the photos and maps inside her underwear and bra, transcribed all the information in invisible ink onto her sheet music, and walked through the swarm of Nazis as though she were royalty. The Germans hadn't even checked her handbag; they'd wanted only a kiss and her autograph. Of course, she sang, "J'ai Deux Amours," pretending she wasn't sick of the song, and letting them all kiss her again when she had finished. The men hadn't bothered with "Jacques-François Hébert," standing meekly by in his old-man getup, heavy glasses and fake mustache, supposedly forty-one but looking ten years older, so nondescript that nobody paid him any mind. At the other end, in Lisbon, the agent was so smitten with Josephine that he never even glanced at Jacques's papers.

"If you are killed, they can kill me, too," she said to Jacques "I don't want to live without my Fox."

He had warned her against keeping secrets from him, but did he really want to know about the consul she'd seduced to get their visas? Whom did she have to sleep with, now, to get them out of Portugal? Jacques gave Paillole's intelligence to a British air attaché along with a letter asking to meet with de Gaulle in London, but the captain replied, again, that they were to wait.

Neither of them was good at waiting, especially now, when the fate of all they loved hung in the balance. But when Paillole summoned Josephine for a meeting in Marseille, Jacques didn't want her to go.

"Doesn't he realize the danger? The Germans could march south at any time. If you are captured . . ."

"I have my poison," she said. "We must be brave, darling. Please, hold me." Shameless, yes, but who knew when — if — they would see each other again?

In Marseille, she checked in at Le Grand Hôtel Noailles, into a beautiful room overlooking the water, and went to see Paillole.

"Your stability impresses me," he said over coffee. "I had feared otherwise."

"Because I am a woman?"

"Because you are Josephine Baker." He offered sugar and a demitasse spoon. "I have heard tales of your temper. It is the way of the artist, no?"

"I'm confident in our success," she said, changing the subject. "The United States will send troops very soon. When that happens, France will crush the Germans to dust."

"Your optimism is heartening." He smiled. "And very American."

She could have danced back to her hotel. She had made a good impression on a high-ranking member of the Resistance, not with coy looks or flirtations, but with her mind. She relayed the information she had coaxed from an Austrian colonel, at a dinner party the night before: Germany planned another major air raid on London at the end of the month, and would soon move into North Africa. Greece had beaten back the Italians, but the Germans would now invade. As she'd spoken, she'd watched the skeptical Paillole's expression change, and saw him unfold his arms and lean across the table toward her. And not once did he ask for her autograph or to hear her sing "J'ai Deux Amours."

When she left, he shook her hand.

"You have become one of our most valuable agents," he said.

Most valuable — her! And a secret intelligence agent, meaning that *she* was intelligent. She hadn't been called that since grade school, when Mrs. Mason had helped her with her homework and said she was "bright." She floated on that cloud back to her hotel, where the reality of her situation brought her crashing back to earth.

As she headed for the stairs, the hotel manager approached. Although she had already checked in, he now wanted her room payment up front. These were "unpredictable times," he said. Josephine pasted on a smile and told him she was cash-poor and would be until her agent arrived from Lisbon in just a few days. The manager frowned; there were no exceptions to this rule. She took out her purse and showed him the few folded bills inside. Would he take them as a deposit? He shook his head, apologized again, and suggested a more affordable hotel near the train station.

Shivering in the tawdry lobby of the cheaper place with its sagging sofas, dingy carpet, low-class whores, and boozy drunks,

Josephine worried for the first time about her survival. She paid for her room with fingers numbed by the cold, and when she turned to pick up her suitcase saw her old friend Frédéric Rey, her dance partner in *La Créole*.

He was trying to leave France, he said, but had no passport. Years ago, he'd entered the country illegally, sneaked in from Vienna by Mistinguett, who had been seduced by his sensitive face and slender body. She hadn't wanted to wait for him to get papers, so had smuggled him in a trunk of clothes. Now he was stuck.

"The Germans do not like homosexuals," he said, twitching like a rabbit.

"*Il faut!* We will get you out!" Seeing his frightened eyes renewed her strength. She jabbed her fist before her nose like a boxer. "I will help you when my agent arrives. But until then, we're in the same boat. The Germans don't like Negroes, either, and I don't have a sou to my name. But we will prevail, Frédéric. *Il faut!*"

They cooked up a scheme to earn some money. What if they revived *La Créole* for Christmas? Frédéric had already sought work at the Opéra Municipal de Marseille, but they had no performances planned due to the German threat. Before the day was through, they'd sealed a deal with the house manager. They had only two weeks to put it all together: sets, costumes, performers, and rehearsals.

After sleeping in her heatless room — even wrapped in her fur coat, she couldn't get warm — Josephine developed a nagging cough. In the mornings, she bathed herself at the sink in cold water, her teeth chattering, and dressed in a haze, having only skimmed the surface of sleep. Strong coffee alone kept her going — for she could not afford to eat — as well as the telegram from Jacques saying that he would join her by Christmas. At night she lay shivering and, when she dreamed, imagined him beside her, keeping her warm.

The dress rehearsal went better than she had imagined. Somehow she managed not to cough, and her singing brought the audience to its feet. Even the "gods" in the upper tier demanded curtain call after curtain call, tossing flowers and shouting her name. She'd almost forgotten the inner glow that an adoring audience could ignite, their cheers blowing on the spark that always kindled inside her, bursting her into flame, into joy, into life.

Jacques surprised her by showing up in Lisbon a few days early, his hair in need of a cut, his mustache shaggy, his expression glum. Paillole would not send them to London, after all. Germany was about to attack the city, and the Resistance team had scattered. The two of them would go to Morocco, instead, to gather information and pass it to the British in Lisbon.

She didn't know which made her happier, Jacques's embrace or the letter he bought from de Gaulle commending her for her "valorous service" and saying he would like to thank her in person someday. Jacques had another surprise for her, too: he had been authorized to give her the rank of sub-lieutenant in the Women's Auxiliary of the Free French Air Force. He had even brought her a uniform, which she wore even though it hung like a sack on her thin frame. She would fill it out soon, Jacques said between kisses, and of that she had no doubt.

"Let's eat," she said.

All the good meals in the world, though, couldn't undo the damage two weeks of hunger and cold had caused. Josephine could not stop coughing. She coughed in the night, bouts that wracked her like seizures. Mornings, she sputtered coffee on her peignoir. She hacked during warm-ups for *La Créole* — but never during a performance, thank goodness. She coughed in the office of the doctor who diagnosed her with pneumonia and wrote a letter releasing her from her contract with the Opéra Municipal de Marseille just in time to leave for Morocco — narrowly escaping the invading Germans who did not respect armistices, as Pétain should have known.

CHAPTER 27

1941, Morocco

"You are invincible," Jacques said as they walked through the Pasha Thami el-Glaoui's gardens in Tangier, Morocco, the trees heavy with figs and dates, lilies exuding an almost sexual scent, colorful parakeets flitting among the foliage. "I think you can talk any man into giving you anything you want."

"If that were true, I'd be married with a houseful of kids," she said.

"How, for instance, did you convince your pasha to let us live in his palace? Didn't you sleep with him before I came? Does he know that we are lovers?"

"Thami isn't the jealous type," Josephine said, watching him from the corner of her eye to see if *he* was jealous.

"A man with thirty wives cannot afford to be, I suppose."

"Neither can a man with one wife."

"I feel more jealous of your abilities than

your affections," he said. "How do you do it? And now you have gotten news for de Gaulle that no one else could."

Josephine smiled, knowing she had done something important. The latest information she had conveyed was critical to the mission: The deputy führer, Rudolf Hess, traveling to Scotland to "negotiate" peace with the Brits, was going to demand the UK's surrender. Meanwhile, the Germans were slowing their push into North Africa. Hitler now had his eye on Russia.

"I wish I *felt* invincible," she said. They'd settled in Tangier to help her recover from pneumonia. Her cough had finally gone away, but her energy had not returned. Was the baby why? She'd discovered that she was pregnant but hadn't told Jacques; she wasn't sure whether he or Thami was the father. "My spirit is willing, but my body feels weak."

"You exert yourself too much on these missions. You drive yourself like a slave."

"I drive myself to *avoid* slavery. Oh!" The pain hit like a hot knife, doubling her over, toppling her to the ground where she writhed, *the baby, not again,* each stab more brutal than the last, Jacques's voice in the distance crying out for help, the world pulling in, growing smaller, concentrated now in one throbbing spot, the place where her child should be growing, and then, mercy, the thoughts stopped coming and the light disappeared, and so did the pain.

Before she opened her eyes, she heard a woman's voice humming a tune. Hands lifted Josephine's head, and a damp cloth wiped the back of her neck. She sighed with pleasure and heard a gasp, and awakened to bright black eyes on an oval face looking at her as if she had just done something wonderful.

The woman called out in Arabic, running through a door. Josephine eyed the IV drip attached to her arm and the metal rail on the side of her bed, and knew she was in a hospital. A man wearing a stethoscope walked in, his face one big smile.

"Voilà! She has risen."

"Where am I?" Her voice creaked like a rusty hinge, as though it hadn't been used in years. She was in a clinic in Casablanca, he told her. How long had she been here? When she'd fainted in Tangier the weather was hot and it was still hot, the windows to her room open to welcome the steaming breath of morning. Already, the nurse was closing things up, pulling tight the curtains in effort to seal out the heat. Six weeks, the doctor said when she asked. June when she'd fallen; now, it was August.

The door swung open, and Jacques burst in and fell to his knees beside the bed. "My love, you have come back to us, thank God, thank God."

"You're here," she said. *My love!*

"He never left." The nurse's tender look said she'd fallen for Jacques, too. "He slept on this cot every night, waiting for you to revive — praying for it, madame."

"You nearly died," he said. "First the surgery, and then an infection. The pneumonia had poisoned your blood."

Surgery. She slid her hand down her torso, felt a ridge of scar tissue bisecting her belly. No more bikinis, and then she laughed at the crazy thought.

"My baby," she said, remembering.

"Yes, you were pregnant, but the fetus did not survive. I am sorry, Josephine."

"It was a blessing," the doctor said. "Your infected blood — the child would have had mental defects."

Her next question felt too heavy to ask, so she tried something light instead.

"Come on in, then, Foxy, and let's try again."

Jacques's expression crumpled, and tears filled his eyes. "Josephine, I don't know how to tell you this. You — you cannot try again for a child."

"That old song? Fox, you know I've heard it before. But I'll never give up." She brushed a tear from his cheek. "We'll have the most beautiful baby ever made."

"No, my love. That cannot be." *My love* — how often she had longed to hear the words. Jacques loved her at last — but where was her joy? She shifted her gaze to the closed windows behind him as the doctor told her he had performed a hysterectomy.

"The infection was very severe," the doctor said.

"Who gave you permission?" she shouted. Her accusing stare bounced about the room, looking for a target. "Who said it was okay to mutilate me?"

"I signed the form, Josephine." Jacques reached for her hand. "It was the only way to save your life."

"This is true," the doctor said.

"You wasted your time, then." She jerked her hand out of Jacques's clawing grasp and turned her back on all three of them. "If I can't have babies, I don't want to live."

Please, dear Lord, just let me die. The one thing she'd ever wanted in this world she couldn't have. Why? The wail of an infant screeched down the hall and landed in her ear. Somebody else's, always somebody else's. She'd had her chance back in Saint Louis and blown it, and maybe the Lord was punishing her now, but what should she have done, instead? Had a kid at thirteen to end up like her mama scrubbing clothes with one hand and holding a baby to her teat with the other, then go home to a man who'd beat them both at the end of the day?

God had bigger things in mind for her, he'd told her so in that vision, offered her a shining crown like she was the queen of something, and he wasn't talking about some low-rent hole-in-the-wall with the first drunk who'd pay the bills in exchange for nightly nooky. She became a big star, just as the Lord had promised, the Queen of Negro Women, first to dance nude on the Paris stage, first to lead in a movie, she'd even starred in an *opera,* and all that fame had given her the cover she needed to help defeat the most evil man ever born.

She had to remind herself of this every day as she lay in that bed, wishing for a knife to slit her wrists. She'd become a part of something vast and important, bigger than herself. They were going to bring down Hitler, and Mussolini, too, he'd turned out to be a horrible man, and that murderer

481

Stalin, if the lunatics didn't kill each other first. What she'd done in Paris, in Spain, in Marseille, in Portugal — it was all God's work, fighting the devil.

Here, too, she gave cover to the spies who met with Jacques around her bed, murmuring plans and trading notes and, in between, telling jokes with her so that anyone who overheard would think it was just a regular hospital visit. A celebrity like her could get away with having six men in her room. Never mind that she looked like death warmed over, never mind the five surgeries she'd had, sick after sick after sick upon sick, opened up so many times that, she joked, they ought to put a zipper in her stomach.

She put on her bravest face even at night, when the demons of the past tortured her with memories of her visit to a tarpaper shack in the Mississippi River bottom. She was thirteen years old but feeling like a tiny girl as the greasy-haired man snatched with grubby fingers the bills she'd stolen from Mr. Dad and yanked her into the filthy room with its dirt floor and smell of formaldehyde so strong she had to cover her nose to breathe. He'd told her to take off all her clothes below the waist, not even giving her a towel to wrap around herself as she climbed onto a metal table and lay down. His fingers prodded her privates and she flinched.

"What's the matter, honey? Obviously I ain't the first one down here," he said, laughing as he inserted something sharp and cold. She cried out, the pain unlike anything before, a jabbing, jeering ache that made her feel like she was nothing, less than nothing, just a balled-up wad of sorrow thrown in the gutter for rats to chew on, for this man to hurt, snickering, while she lay helpless with her feet up and her knees spread and his fingers and eyes and judgment stabbing her like dirty knives. When he removed his hands, they were covered in blood. He opened a drawer and pulled out a wad of gauze and pushed it inside her like Mrs. Kaiser stuffing poor Tiny Tim for Thanksgiving dinner.

"Now, you stay out of trouble, hear? And keep your legs together from now on." She'd stumbled home and crawled into bed, feverish, doubled over from cramping, chills like fingers of ice scraping her insides. For days, she'd thought she might die. *Why didn't you take me then, Lord? Why?*

She spent two years in the Casablanca clinic asking the same question — Why? — off and on. Up and out only to get sick again and have to return, again and again and again. Jacques stayed with her, but she knew it was killing him to do so while, outside, the war raged on. He bore two years' witness to the foulness and betrayals of her body, two years of listening to her cry and groan and curse and snarl, two years of praying and swabbing and hand-holding and, when possible, lying next to her and pulling her close.

He knew her better, now, than any man ever had, better than all her husbands put together, better even than her own mama had known her. If not for Jacques, she would have died, or if not for God, who refused to let her go. Obviously, the Lord had in mind something more for her, something that didn't involve babies.

Then Jacques told her the latest bad news: the Germans had captured La Besnerais, one of the Maquis, and sent him to Dachau after kicking out his teeth. At the news, Josephine stopped begging God to let her die, and started thanking him for letting her live. So many of their gang had died or disappeared, François gunned down on a boat to London, La Besnerais killed in Dachau, Trotobas ambushed in his lover's home and murdered in a bloody gunfight. Had God sickened her for her own good, and for

Jacques's, too?

The Lord worked in mysterious ways. Maybe he still had things for her to do. He must, since he wouldn't let her die. Why did this surprise her? She'd always known she was born to achieve something great. She'd always thought that, someday, she would change the world.

And then, in November — nearly one and a half years since she'd fallen in that courtyard — Josephine lay on her pillow, windows open to the breeze, listening. In a chair beside her, Jacques rustled the newspaper.

"Hush," Josephine said. "I hear something." The nurse strode in, toward the windows, saying the breeze was too strong, that Josephine must not catch a chill.

Shhh, she and Jacques said in unison. Their heads cocked. Outside: a distant rumble, like a low moan. Doors slamming, people crying out. The smell of dust flew into the room, followed by cheers.

"Here it comes," Josephine said, and lifted herself up as if in a dream and floated to the window. Jacques leapt up to help her but she stood on her own, gripping the railing, watching thousands upon thousands of men in uniform, dripping wet and dirty, smiling, marching through the middle of

Casablanca behind the red, white, and blue flag of the United States of America.

"Praise God, we are free," Josephine said. She staggered across the room to the wardrobe, past the nurse's outstretched arms.

"Madame, what are you doing?" The nurse rushed after her, grasping her shoulders, but Josephine shrugged her off.

"I've got to go and greet them. Help me get dressed."

"You are not well, madame. You need your rest."

She pulled her Free French Air Force uniform from the rack, pressed it to her wild-beating heart. *Free.*

"Rest? Did you see the looks on those boys' faces? They've had hard days and nights of fighting to get here. And now they've arrived, and they're going to need cheering up. I've got to go and greet them. Jacques, come and help me get into this. I've got to go."

And now the show nears its end, her life wrapped neatly and colorfully like a present and presented to the crowd: the Paris show-girls, the lights of New York, Yiddish Klezmer music (which, during her three visits to Jerusa-lem, she never heard), and, to send the spectacle through the roof, a phantasmagori-cal parade of wild floats and costumes and the blast of horns in an orgy of music and dance from Carnaval, the Rio festival un-matched for splendor and decadence and also where Jo Bouillon, her last husband, met another love. But she won't sing about that, she clicks her heels and sweeps her hands upward and sings "Vivre," which means "To Live" — what a perfect song for this perfor-mance, in particular, during which she has not only presented her life to her audience but relived it, the pain and the pleasures, assess-ing whether she has done enough. She could have done more, she realizes, if she hadn't spent so much time and energy grasping for love. If she'd truly focused, instead, on loving.

What a fool she was, chasing all those dreams like rainbows, thinking a husband would make her complete. God tried to tell her when she was seven that she had all she needed to be a queen. She didn't need a man.

And this applause the audience is giving to her, is this love? Would they love her more or less if they knew the truth? *Joséphine à Bobino* leaves out her secret work as a maquisard, the babies she lost, the twelve she adopted in the name of equality and peace, her crusade against hatred.

M. Levasseur couldn't put that stuff in a musical. People didn't want the heartbreak, the suffering, the struggle. Even the awful scene that the whole world witnessed — Josephine on the back step of her castle in her bathrobe in the rain, locked out by the bankers who took all she owned — is missing from this revue.

All the really important things have been omitted, as if written right out of her life's story. What would M. Levasseur have done, sent Hitler dancing across the stage? She has never talked about that part of her life, anyway. The one time she asked Jacques to vouch for her, no one believed him. Josephine Baker, a French patriot? How ridiculous.

The curtain falls and the stagehands swarm like ants to remove all the props, leaving Josephine alone on the stage in her flesh-colored leotard with its racy stripe of silver feathers rippling from chest to crotch, and the fountainous spray of white feathers erupting from the crown of her head. Alone, now, to finish out the story of her life; alone as she entered this world and as she will leave it. This finale always feels poignant to her, but tonight she doesn't mind. It feels right to stand on her own. In her best moments, this is how she lived, relying on herself.

The curtain rises and she sings the final song, a tribute to Paris, and the crowd stands, everyone in the auditorium rising to honor her. But as she accepts the accolades and takes her bows, she knows for the first time this adoration, these glowing faces, the flowers strewn at her feet, none of this is love. They don't even know her.

But, hell, she doesn't know herself. Nearly sixty-nine years old, and she still hasn't figured out the answer to the central question of her life:

How will she become worthy of that crown God promised?

CHAPTER 28

1942, Jerusalem

When her body had healed and the Americans had joined the war, at last, Josephine and Jacques resumed their work for the Resistance, gathering information to help defeat the Nazis and touring to lift the troops' spirits. But still Josephine felt dissatisfied. She wasn't doing enough. And yet, although she prayed for guidance, none came. Was God even listening? Maybe the chaos in Europe had him occupied, too.

It was her idea to go to Jerusalem. She'd always wanted to visit the Holy Land, and she and her band were between gigs. At the end of their tour of the city, they went to the Wailing Wall, where the guide gave them slips of paper on which to write a prayer. Josephine tucked it into a pocket, not knowing what to ask for anymore. God had turned his back on her, and motherhood was lost to her now. What good would it do to pray?

The guide took her to the women's area, where a group of old ladies stood keening, backs hunched and shaking, heads pressed against the stones, and two teenage girls held each other and sobbed. A mother, brown-skinned and lithe, nursed a baby at her breast and rocked silently, tears sliding down her cheeks. She reminded Josephine of herself twenty years ago, before illness had taken her youth and beauty. But that was the least of what she had lost. Never would she hold her own sweet child in her arms; never would she know that devoted, unconditional love. *Why, Lord?* She was barren, her body an unfertile field in which no seed could take root, from which no life would ever spring. Feeling keenly her arms' emptiness, she wrapped them around herself.

The tears that she had held back for so long gushed like waters from a breaking dam, pouring over her nose and into her open mouth as she wailed and shrieked cries from the underworld, giving voice at last to her baby's own scream upon being ripped from her body so that Josephine could escape the fate that had befallen her mother, and her mother's mother, and so many generations before. She'd had no doubt, at the time, that she was doing the right thing. God had promised her a crown, and she meant to claim it.

Joining the crying women, she fell to her knees, filling the air with unearthly song, beseeching God's mercy, begging him to reveal the meaning of that childhood vision. She'd lived only for herself for so many years, basking in adulation and praise, grasping for money, greedy for love — singing and dancing while, across the ocean, her people, the people of her race, suffered and died at the white man's hand as was happening, now, to the Jews and Negroes in Europe. But look at what she had accomplished here, and what she was still doing.

"What have you done for us?" the men had asked at the Red Cross Liberty Club for colored soldiers in Casablanca. Glaring at her like *she* was the enemy, when she'd dragged herself from her hospital bed to watch their victory parade through the streets and, with Jacques's help, dressed to go down and greet them.

But not all had appreciated her efforts. The applause had been scattered, the looks on faces disgruntled. Between performances, she milled through the crowd and heard why: these men had signed up to fight, but instead were made servants to the whites.

"Colored soldiers went back home as heroes after the first world war," said Ollie Stewart, a Negro journalist covering the war, sitting with her at a metal table between shows. "The whites won't make that mistake this time. They aren't letting Negroes fight. Only white soldiers are allowed to carry guns. Our people are digging trenches and driving trucks, hauling supplies and ammo. Hell, they weren't going to let colored men enlist, at first. Afraid they'd come back thinking they're equals."

"This can't continue," she said. "We've got to do something."

"You're a powerful woman, but even you can't change the United States military in the middle of a war." The Negro troops had eyes enough to see what was going on, and she would hand them no favors by getting them all worked up now, he said. To survive, they needed to do as they were told and keep their mouths shut.

And so Josephine tried to lift their spirits rather than stoke their anger — and to cheer herself, as well.

"As for getting mad because of race prejudice, we'll have plenty of time for that," she said during the next show. "I will come back to the States and join you in the fight to break down segregation — but let's win the war first."

"What do you care about us?" somebody shouted. "You got out a long time ago."

She couldn't argue with the truth. She'd never stood up to racial prejudice, not in America, not in Vienna, not in Germany, not in Brazil. She had run away each time. She'd never fought back, not even for herself. But she hadn't known, then, how strong she was.

At the wall, her tears subsided. She rose and dried her face with her hands. God had a plan for her; he had shown her a crown. Whether she deserved it remained to be seen. Josephine took the pencil and paper from her pocket and inscribed her prayer, then tucked it into a crevice in the wall.

Use me.

As she walked away, her answer came, filling her mind like an explosion of quiet.

God helps those who help themselves.

CHAPTER 29

1944, Paris

She rode on a Liberty ship with the other members of the Women's Auxiliary of the Free French Air Force, going home to Paris, the city having freed itself without the help of Americans or anyone else. She endured the excited talk of the war for as long as she could, the rumors of a city in tatters, torn apart in the battle. At last, she stepped out onto the deck to get away. Paris destroyed? It couldn't be true.

She pulled her little dog, Mitraillette, from under her overcoat, looking around to make sure all was clear, let it pee, *rat-ta-tat,* like a little machine gun, then scooped it up to nestle into her bosom while she thought of Paris.

Would anyone remain from the life she'd known? Those who'd tolerated the Nazis would still be there, that snake Maurice Chevalier, for instance. He'd come to the clinic in Morocco but she'd refused him: he'd sung for the Nazis, even traveling to their camps. Mistinguett had kept up her old routine, too; she must be seventy by now, flashing those legs in the music halls where Nazis made up most of the audience and brazenly begging the crowd to send her coal and food like she couldn't support herself on the loot she was pulling in.

Josephine would have to face the traitors. They'd be the only ones left, the rest shipped off to camps and gassed or tortured, Jews and coloreds and — ten days before the liberation — three thousand members of the Resistance. How would the city look? Demolished, as some said? Bereft of charm, its artists and writers having fled to America, anyone with a heart gone? But all those patriots would still be there, those who had fought the Germans in the middle of the city, risking their lives with only sixty guns at first, big-hearted men and women who had shot and killed the Nazis and seized their weapons, taken their trucks and tanks, picked them off one by one, trained, as she had been trained, by shooting rats. They would be there.

Maybe, reunited with those who'd stayed in the city of her heart, she'd feel less alone. Not like here, with no lover, no one to love her. Even Jacques, who loved her, had looked away from the sight of her scarred and puckered belly. Still, he'd done her the biggest favor of all by coming up with a solution to her problems. As she'd mourned the fact that she would never give birth, he'd made a suggestion: why not adopt?

Now, on the ship, she considered the notion. Adoption could be costly, and raising a child more so. After all that time in the hospital and then entertaining the troops for free, she had almost no money left. She could still perform, but would anyone want to see her? Illness had taken a toll on her looks.

But makcup and a bit of glitter could hide the ravages of illness and age. Playing to the soldiers had strengthened her body and her voice again. She was ready for a comeback. Perhaps she'd get back on at the Casino de Paris; if not, she could always go on tour and make records, maybe even another movie. And at the heart of everything she did, now, would be her new mission: to end racial prejudice.

How would children fit into that plan?

Children. She had to laugh at herself. Here she'd gone from adopting a single child to "children." But hadn't she always wanted a houseful? She closed her eyes to imagine it, all her precious little ones playing among the oaks at Le Beau Chêne, black and white and brown children all together, loving one another. And the whole world would see them and realize that prejudice isn't something we're born with, but something we learn.

When she opened her eyes, they were full of tears. "Thank you, Lord, for this vision," she whispered.

She stood, wrapping her coat around Mitraillette. A crewman approached, kerchief ties flapping in the breeze. Holding the dog close, trying to keep it still, Josephine smiled as the sailor saluted her, sweet young thing, look at those ruddy cheeks. She tried to make eye contact, but he moved on, she just an old woman in his eyes, grinning like a fool. Mitraillette barked, and Josephine cried out to cover the sound, lifting a hand toward the melting moon, singing a few bars but he was gone, " 'J'ai deux amours, mon pay est Paris.' "

She had two loves but only one had loved her back, and now she was on her way to win its heart again. And when — if — Paris embraced her again, then . . . No, it *must* embrace her, she must earn the money she needed, and when she was back on her feet, she would start the family she had always wanted, but better, for it wouldn't be just for her but for the world.

And then the ship reached the shore and the Women's Auxiliary stood in formation as the crew lowered the gangplank. Josephine could read excitement on the women's faces, and curiosity, and apprehension, the same as she felt: each wondering, would anyone be there to greet her? As they began their descent, cheers arose, and "La Marseillaise" from a hired band, and confetti raining as, on the shore, they embraced one another.

Josephine bade farewell to her dear friend Catherine before a handsome man swept the woman away and frenzy took over and everyone was running, running into someone's arms. Someone jostled Josephine as she put Mitraillette on the ground and stood to look around, sobs and embraces and cries of joy bouncing off the metal ship as Josephine stood alone, looking around, a lump forming in her throat.

Mitraillette yapped at her feet, anxious, and she bent to pick the poor thing up, but a hand was already there, scratching the dog's ears, a hand wearing a gold ring with a *V* in diamonds. She looked up into the face of M. Henri Varna, her old friend from the Casino de Paris, whom she almost bowled over with kisses.

"Welcome home, *Sous-lieutenant* Josephine," he said, giving her his arm.

"How wonderful of you to come," she said. "I thought for a minute that I wouldn't have anyone."

"Au contraire," he said, and gestured toward the cordon established, he said, for security — all the Nazis had flown the country or been arrested, of course, but sympathizers remained — and she saw behind the rope a banner with her name in purple and a crowd holding their arms out to her, hundreds there with brilliant bouquets, young men and old men and children and women. Josephine's eyes filled with tears.

She saw Colette, now wizened and hunched, shadows in her eyes, the Nazis had left but she was still occupied. And M. Paul Derval of the Folies-Bergère with his wife! So many wonderful friends had come to see her, and behind them, cameras pointed like the eyes of gods and reporters strained against the rope with notepads and recorders, shouting out questions.

Josephine posed and bantered, throwing off danger, throwing off treachery, throwing off death and illness, jutting her hip, forgetting that she was anything but a whole woman and one of courage who had earned her stripes with love for her country.

A journalist asked her to sing "J'ai Deux Amours," the band striking up their accompaniment. How could she have ever complained about having to sing it so many times? She loved this song, it was *her* song, her people wanted this from her and she would never again tire of giving it to them. Feeling the beloved caress of the cameras on her, she threw her arms open and laughed aloud. She had not been forgotten, not at all.

She'd barely had time to settle in Paris again when the French government sent its request: Would she entertain the troops in France as she had done in Morocco? Hitler was retreating, but not completely routed, and her performances would boost morale. Josephine jumped at the chance. Then, because she would need musicians, she went to see the bandleader Jo Bouillon, and fell in love at first sight.

What was it about him that drew her? The soft, feminine mouth, the winsome eyes? He could barely meet her gaze, he was shy with women, she had heard, which was maybe why he'd never married. That was a shame: such a gentle man would be good with children.

"I don't know how I can do it," he said when she invited him to tour with her. "My orchestra is under contract to perform a radio broadcast every day for the rest of the year."

"Contracts were made to be broken," she said. "This is for our boys on the front lines."

But the French government was investigating him, suspecting him of being a Nazi sympathizer, he told her, which she already knew. He'd performed on Radio-Paris after the Germans had taken over, accepting Hitler's dirty money.

"Why did you do it?" she asked.

"One must eat," he said, and now she knew why he couldn't meet her gaze. "Not everyone has the temperament for fighting."

Those soft hands, that slender frame, that smooth skin like white silk. Not a callus on his body, she'd bet. He'd melt like candy under her tongue.

"That's all the better reason why you ought to join me," she said. "Entertaining our troops will make everyone forgive you."

"All right, I will consider it. How much?"

"Pardon?"

"How much are you offering?"

"You'll get paid the same as I'm making. Zero."

He frowned. "I am not a superstar, with unlimited funds."

"If you are found guilty of conspiring with the Germans, you'll have even less than you have now." His reputation ruined, he wouldn't work in France again for a long time. "I can help you — but only if you accept my terms."

"And my orchestra? How will I convince these musicians to work for nothing? They will go elsewhere. What is a bandleader with no band?"

Josephine placed her hand on his; he did not pull away. "You will think of something, Jo. You must. It is time you did your duty for France."

But Jo could not convince his musicians to tour for free, so Josephine scraped together some cash by pawning her jewels and taking out a mortgage on her Paris apartment, and off they went.

Working with Jo was a dream. He and his pianist knew just how to back her, and he adjusted expertly to her last-minute changes, shifting the music to her moods; cueing up songs on request from the audience; even adding his own touches, sounding notes when she tossed candy from her basket, playing a vamp tune when she sat in someone's lap — as in the old days, she sought out the homely men: they were the most grateful and no one got jealous.

After each show, she and the band would have supper and drinks on her dime, Josephine sitting beside Jo. And when everyone else had gone to bed, they'd sit up for hours talking about everything under the sun — except her Rainbow Tribe dream of adoption, no sense scaring him off! One night, she asked the question that had been nagging at her: Why hadn't he made a pass at her, they way other men did?

"Maybe you don't find me attractive?" she said, knowing full well she'd lost some of her allure.

He closed his eyes. Josephine waited, relishing the chance to gaze openly at his beautiful face, that alabaster skin, those high cheekbones, the fine patrician nose. He opened his eyes and saw her admiring him, but instead of smiling, he lowered his gaze, looking like a child caught in some shameful act. Josephine reached for his hand, ready to reassure him — *it's okay* — but nothing could have prepared her for what he would say next.

"You are very attractive, Josephine." Not even for a second did his eyes meet hers.

"More so than any woman I have ever met. Your beauty, your pure heart, even your terrible temper" — at last, he looked at her, and grinned — "they are all irresistible. So why, you wonder, don't I make love to you? The answer, I fear, is not simple." He placed his hands over his face, then rubbed his eyes as if awakening after a long sleep.

"You're married," she blurted, and burst into tears. "Why do I always fall for the married ones? What is wrong with me, that I can't love a man who can love me back?"

"No, *mon amie,* I have never been married. Until now, I have never met a woman who interested me." Josephine perked up: he wanted her. She would have her heart's desires — this man who looked like a dream, the bundle of money they would earn touring together when the war had ended, the castle full of children they would adopt from all over the world, her Rainbow Tribe.

"— why, you may ask, but I cannot explain it. Ever since I can remember, I have been attracted to them. I thought I was a homosexual, but now that I have these feelings for you, I am confused —"

"Wait," she said. "What did you say? You're a what?"

"I am a man," he said. "A man who likes

other men."

Alarm bells went off in her head, but she decided to ignore them. What men did together she did not care to imagine, but it couldn't be as good as what she offered. Of course, if he had never been with a woman, how could he know? One night with her, and he'd be cured of that malady. But look at his beseeching face, hunger for her approval written all over. First she needed to set his mind at ease.

"Is that all?" She gave a carefree laugh. "If you want to shock me, you'll have to work harder. There's nothing that I haven't seen, and very little that I haven't done."

He sighed, and his body relaxed. "Then you are not upset."

"Au contraire, I love a challenge." She leaned toward him and kissed him softly on the lips. His response was as sweet as she'd imagined. Her body humming, she led him up the stairs to her room.

■ ■ ■ ■

ACT V
LA GRANDE FINALE

■ ■ ■ ■

CHAPTER 30

1951, Havana

She'd agreed to meet the club owner Ned Schuyler at his hotel, but insisted they sit on the veranda in spite of the cool weather. He was offering her eight thousand dollars a week to perform in his establishment, the most posh, most sophisticated club in Miami, "and that's saying a lot" — but she knew she had to set the tone right off the bat.

"I'll never step foot inside this place again until they change their policies," she said, shivering in the breeze. When she'd tried to check in here last week, the clerk — a colored man! — had turned her away, saying "whites only" while his eyes darted around like he was sending secret signals to somebody. Of course this exclusive Havana club was owned by, and operated for, white Americans, who, Josephine knew, still hadn't gotten over their fear of catching something nasty from Negroes.

"I understand that Miami is a segregated city," she said.

His eyebrows lifted as though he'd never considered the matter. "Miami is very cosmopolitan."

But were Negroes allowed in his club?

"Of course. You will be on the floor."

"And in the audience? Are they permitted there?"

He puffed from his cigarette and blew four thoughtful smoke rings.

"No colored person has ever tried to attend a Copa City show." He unfolded his legs and sat up.

"I won't perform in your club unless there are Negroes in the audience," she said. She held her breath, knowing what she might be giving up. The money he offered would enable her and Jo to remodel her castle and start their Rainbow Tribe.

"I'll pay you nine thousand a week," he said. "Ten."

"I'll happily take your money if you'll integrate your club."

Annoyance crossed his face. She knew what he was thinking: why did she have to keep harping on about this? She felt tempted to walk away, but the stakes were too high. So she sipped her ice water and hummed "J'ai Deux Amours," and Ned Schuyler, who had been contemplating his empty glass, looked up at her and laughed.

"Hell, why not? If a Negro came to the Copa City I wouldn't refuse him, so why not let them in?" There might be a scandal, he warned: "Cosmopolitan" Miami was not *that* sophisticated, it had a 6 p.m. curfew for domestic servants — meaning colored people — to leave Miami Beach.

"We Jews had similar difficulties during the war," he said. "The hatred was immense. Some businesses hung GENTILES ONLY signs on their doors."

His story did not surprise her. After playing Boston earlier this year, she'd gone down to give a speech at Fisk University in Nashville, traveling incognito for another *Paris Soir* piece. Fear and suspicion of colored folks ran rampant in the South even today. Josephine had been yanked off a "whites only" toilet mid-piss, the owner of the gas station screaming bloody murder like she'd put an end to civilization. The white clientele had raced to the exits at the Savannah Woolworth's just because she'd sat at the lunch counter and ordered a milk shake — and the manager, red-faced, had grabbed her arm and dragged her to the door. The worst, though, had been walking into a coffee shop in Mississippi using the door marked WHITE and coming out to face some of her own people staring like she was some kind of ghost. "Go back to France," someone muttered.

"They looked scared," she told her friend Donald Wyatt, a teacher at Fisk.

"Yes, they are scared," he said.

"But I'm trying to help them."

"And after you're gone? Then what? They're stuck here with the mess you leave behind: their white neighbors saying they're 'uppity,' thinking Negroes need a lesson in who's boss, busting heads, setting houses on fire, stringing people up."

Josephine closed her eyes, remembering the flames and smoke from her childhood, hearing the screams. Smelling the burning bodies.

"This isn't 1917," she said, wiping her tears. She looked at him, lost.

"In the southern United States, it is." He took the apples she'd bought and put them in his coat pockets, and, after a final look around, touched a hand to her elbow and steered her toward their car. "And it always will be."

Now here she was in the Copa City night-club in a strapless black Dior gown, high ponytail pinned to her scalp — *a cross between Carmen Miranda and the Empire State Building,* a critic had written of her new look — glued-on eyelashes so heavy she could barely open her eyes, and a big smile to hide her worry as she listened for the protests that were sure to mar this special occasion. Tonight's would be the first mixed-race nightclub performance in Miami or, possibly, anywhere in the South. It wouldn't be the last, if she had her way. *Lord, let it go well.* But she'd faced down Nazis with guns, and she could deal with picketers.

A group walked in, and Josephine went to greet the celebrities Ned had flown in from New York, colored people as well as whites: the prizefighter Joe Louis; Thelma Carpenter, a jazz singer; Billy Daniels, a white singer headed for the front table with Walter Winchell, the famous white journalist regaling them with the story of how Ned Schuyler had called to ask if he minded that Josephine was now a citizen of France.

"Walter, I know you're a champion for the Negro cause, but we weren't sure that extended to French Negroes," Josephine chimed in.

"French, Swedish, Timbuktu: if they're as easy on the eyes as you are, they've got my

513

backing." He kissed her hand, his fingers lingering on her arm a beat longer than necessary.

Backstage, Sophie Tucker, the "Last of the Red-Hot Mamas," a big, brassy-haired singer in a beaded dress and feathers, helped her scan the room for angry faces.

"Don't worry, honey, honest to God. If they blow the place up, they'll blow me up, too," she said, and took the stage, a white woman opening for a colored one, another first in America, Josephine was willing to bet. She did all right, too, had them laughing and all loosened up by the time Josephine walked out singing "J'ai Deux Amours" and dragging a fur behind her. When she'd finished and the applause and whistles had finally subsided, she opened her mouth to make the speech she had rehearsed. But when she saw twenty-one colored faces mixed among the whites like salt and pepper — a seasoning she had never expected to taste in America — she forgot every word.

"This is really my first appearance in my native land in twenty-six years," she said, improvising. Winchell's eyebrows shot up and he scribbled on his notepad, probably thinking of her previous U.S. tours.

"The other times don't count," she said.

"Now it is different. I am happy to be here and to be performing in this city under these circumstances, when *my people* can be here to see me. This means so much to us, doesn't it?"

Nobody, white or colored, appeared uncomfortable. They all looked happy except for Walter Winchell, who frowned and squinted as if he couldn't understand a word.

"When I say 'us,' I mean my people," she said, looking at him. "And when I say 'my people,' I mean my race. Congratulations — we've done it at last!"

Someone in the back shouted, someone else agreed, and if there was a third response no one heard it over the applause. Joe Louis rose to his feet, and Thelma, and everyone else. Josephine felt like she could fly.

Winchell stayed in Miami for a week, coming to every show, waiting afterward at her dressing room door with roses and champagne, so much like an eager puppy she had to stop herself from scratching behind his ears although it was pretty clear how much he'd like it if she did. He gave her a big write-up, called her *the biggest thing to hit Miami Beach since the hurricane of '35.*

The Copa City sold out every show, and

clubs from all over the country started calling, wanting to book her. Josephine made Ned her agent for a 10 percent cut. But the best part, to her mind, were announcements by two other Miami clubs that they would allow mixed-race audiences, too. *I don't care if they're green, as long as they pay the minimum,* one club owner said in the newspaper. People were finally starting to understand.

"Be nice to Winchell," Ned kept saying, as if she wouldn't be on her best behavior with a syndicated writer publishing in two thousand newspapers and broadcasting a New York City radio show. She drew the line, though, when he made the moves on her. At one time she might have slept with him for the good he might do her career, but those days were long gone. *Variety* loved her, *Ebony,* the *Miami Herald,* the *New York Times:* She didn't need to sleep with anyone. She was finally famous in her own country — but the irony was, she didn't seek fame now except as a means to an end, at forty-five no longer chasing what she had hungered for as a youth.

Winchell didn't like it when she slapped him, but he ought to keep his hands to himself, then. At first she'd thought he might hit her back. She'd balled up her fists, ready to fight, but he'd just left red-faced and muttering something about her being sorry. What had he expected from a newly-wed?

Ned had warned her not to get on his bad side, saying Winchell destroyed careers as easily as he made them — but he couldn't hurt Josephine, she was on a roll! Ned had booked her on a nationwide tour with Warner Brothers. She'd be performing in theaters between films, starting at the Strand in New York: headlining on Broadway at long last. If someone had told her during her Ziegfeld Follies run that this would happen, she'd have laughed in their face. Or she'd have wondered why it would take so long for Josephine Baker to catch on in America, even as, deep in her heart, she knew the reason.

A new socko face on the American scene . . . Her comeback is a signal click, a *Variety* reporter wrote of her Strand performances that consisted of seven songs, seven costume changes, and five curtain calls, four sold-out shows every day between showings of *Storm Warning,* a movie about the Ku Klux Klan that Josephine left the theater to avoid. Between songs, she talked about the heartbreak of being Negro in America, of being reviled for the color of her skin, a hatred she had encountered in only one other place in the world: Nazi Germany. That last point made some white folks squirm, but the nodding of colored heads was all the affirmation she needed. For the first time in America, Negroes and whites watched a movie together. For the first time, musicians of both races played in the orchestra.

In Jackson, Mississippi, she went to the Hinds County Jail to visit Willie McGee, a colored man on death row for raping a white woman in 1945.

"She wanted me, and I wanted her," he told Josephine. A neighbor, seeing Willie leaving her house one night, asked the woman about him. Frightened, she said he had raped her.

"She was scared they would take away her child," he said. "I don't hold it against her, but I wish I didn't have to die." She asked why he didn't just tell the truth, but he'd tried that in his third trial. The jury of Southern men refused to believe that any white woman would consent to sex with a Negro. "They took it as a confession. And sentenced me to death."

Before she'd left him, Willie had asked her to sing "Amazing Grace." The song brought all the inmates to the bars of their cells to reach out to her as she passed. "Be careful," said Ned, who'd accompanied her, but Josephine touched palm to palm to palm, kissing hands, thinking of the cages their ancestors — her ancestors — had come to America in.

"This is a travesty," she said in a press conference outside the jail. Willie McGee was innocent, she said, and a symbol of the plight of the Negro: emancipated long ago but still in chains.

"For almost twenty-five years I have lived in France, where we have legal equality of the races," she said. "And I tell you beyond any doubt that for white women to desire Negro men is not unusual. In fact, it is very common."

She was doing this — the relentless touring, the trials and NAACP events and sit-ins, the interviews and photo sessions, the biographical movie they wanted to make in Hollywood, the musical that still-handsome rascal Ernest Hemingway was writing for her — she did it all in the name of equality. And she did it for the money, of course, to prepare Les Milandes for the babies she would adopt.

Sometimes, though, her dreams of racial harmony seemed hopeless. On May 8, she walked onstage in Detroit to announce the death, by electric chair, of Willie McGee.

"A part of every American Negro died with him," she said, choking out her words, tears smearing her makeup. "I'm going to perform tonight, but I hope you'll understand if my heart isn't in it." She pasted on a smile along with her sequins and feathers and sang. At Willie's funeral, she posed with his wife, Rosalie, but the press wouldn't take the photo, they wanted Josephine alone, so she went to her car and drove away. She didn't want attention for herself, not anymore, couldn't they see that?

Even on "Josephine Baker Day," when one hundred thousand people filled the streets of Harlem to celebrate her work against discrimination, even as she blew kisses from the lead car of a twenty-seven-car motorcade, even when, that evening, a man who had won the Nobel Peace Prize presented her with an honorary lifetime membership to the NAACP and performers paid tribute, singing her songs: Noble and Sissle and members of the *Shuffle Along* chorus, Duke Ellington, Gypsy Rose Lee, Buddy Rogers, Lionel Hampton; even when Walter White, president of the NAACP, gave a speech praising her courage and efforts to end discrimination in America, Josephine never forgot why she was there, and what she was doing. Equality of the races was possible, she told the thousands who packed the auditorium: all they had to do was claim it.

"Claim it?" Her old friend Evelyn Anderson, who'd danced in *La Revue Nègre,* said after the show. "How do you expect us to do that?"

"I'll show you," Josephine said.

In Washington, DC, she went into the whites-only room at a segregated café and ordered a Coca-Cola, then told her audience how the owner had refused to serve her.

In Los Angeles, a white man in the audience shouted at her to "go back where you came from."

"I *am* back where I came from," she said. "And you, sir? Where did you come from?" She got a standing ovation, and a front-page story in the next day's paper. Let her people see, and believe.

When she walked into the Biltmore Hotel dining room that night to meet Ned's attorney Shirley Woolf, a white man in a suit uttered a loud curse.

"I didn't know they allowed niggers in here," he said.

The year 1927 returned to her, then, the celebration of Lucky Lindy's transatlantic flight, the rude American's "nigger" comment. How often had she chastised herself for hanging her head, wishing she could do it over again?

God helps those who help themselves.

Josephine took up her handbag and strode out the door to the police station. In ten minutes she was back, in a car with flashing lights. She walked into the restaurant flanked by officers and stood over the man, who cringed as if fearing she might touch him. She was placing him under citizen's arrest for harassment, she said. The look on that man's face as he was handcuffed and taken away!

"I only wish the press had been here," she said to Shirley.

"Ned will be thrilled. What great publicity!"

Josephine hadn't done it for publicity. But what she wouldn't give for America to see a white man being carted off to jail for insulting a Negro. It had to be a first — and, surely, not the last. When her people understood what was possible, they would rise up.

CHAPTER 31

New York would be a tougher nut to crack.
For all the city's worldliness, it guarded its
institutions carefully, among them the
opulent private rooms reserved exclusively
for "high society," which meant white people.

But that barrier could be broken, too.
When the Stork Club, the city's most
fashionable restaurant — off-limits to
Negroes, of course — sponsored a contest
for the "World's Best-Dressed Woman," its
white patrons voted for Josephine. Walter
Winchell had called with the news, congrat-
ulating her. No one else had even come
close, even though the runners-up included
the actress Marilyn Monroe and Eva Perón,
First Lady of Argentina.

"Evita?" Josephine said. "I adore her."

"You know Mrs. Perón?"

Josephine bit her lip. Ned Schuyler had
warned her last May, after Josephine Baker

Day, to choose her words to the press more carefully. A newsman from the *Daily Worker* had asked for the names of her personal heroes and she had mentioned Evita and why not? The people of Argentina loved Eva Perón; she did so much for the poor and for orphans; she founded hospitals; she was helping her own people. She'd grown up in poverty like Josephine and had also found her escape on the stage. A famous actress when she met her husband, she'd given up the theater to serve her country. Who wouldn't admire her?

"We are like sisters," she'd said then. The reporter had looked surprised for reasons she couldn't fathom. The next day Ned and Shirley were at her door, *Daily Worker* in hand, Ned's brow creased with worry. Didn't Josephine realize that the Peróns were dictators, that Juan Perón had praised Mussolini and Hitler? They were not a good couple to be associated with.

"If you're seen as sympathetic to these dictators, your career will go down in flames," he said. "People are already calling you a communist for speaking out against segregation. If you want to make money, I advise you to tone it down a bit."

"That's the same advice I get," Paul Robeson told her over supper in a Harlem soul-food joint. Josephine was shocked to see how he'd changed in the months since her Miami debut; the once-robust singer had shrunk into a small, tightly wound man.

"In Russia, they use racial prejudice as propaganda against our nation. That upsets the government, they think it makes us look bad. But instead of stopping the genocide against our people, they tell us to change our story."

"What are we supposed to say?"

"That things have improved." Paul slammed his fist on the tabletop. "Like hell they have."

Josephine kept her thoughts to herself. She could see that things *had* improved for her people since she'd come back to America, but she agreed that they had a long way to go. Still, if the lily-white Stork Club had named a Negro the best-dressed woman in the world, who knew what might happen next?

"When is the ceremony?" she asked Winchell, moving the subject away from Eva Perón. "I've never been to the Stork Club."

"Don't hold your breath for that one. To tell you the truth, Sherman Billingsley doesn't like Negroes in the place. It's the worst thing about him, but he's my friend and I'd rather not fight."

So what else could she do but invite her friends Roger and Solange Rico and Bessie Buchanan for drinks and dinner at the Stork Club? Roger, who was white, went there all the time, and made a reservation in the club's super-exclusive Cub Room. Josephine put on a long black gown, elbow-length satin gloves, and a diamond necklace, and took Bessie after her final show out the Strand's front door to wade through the crowd and sign autographs and promise that, yes, she would come back to New York, the city had captured her heart and so had America, and no, she had no plans to return to Europe anytime soon.

She and Bessie took a cab to the Stork Club, the driver doing a double take when Josephine told him where they were going. On the way, Josephine squeezed Bessie's hand so hard the woman cried out. What if the restaurant wouldn't let them in? She was French, Bessie said, she had no reason to worry, it was the American Negroes they wanted to keep out — "people like me" — and besides, it was high time they put a stop to this kind of discrimination. If not Josephine, then who? And besides, what could happen with Walter Winchell there?

"He sits at his own table in the back — table fifty," Bessie said. "Holding court, I've heard. Everybody with a news tip or gossip knows where to find him. The club's owner, Sherman Billingsley, even installed a phone at the table for him. He wouldn't dare treat us badly with Walter around."

When they stepped out of the car and up to the door, however, the doorman shook his head. "We're full up."

"We have a reservation," Bessie said, but the doorman refused until Roger and Solange came up the walk. Roger confirmed the reservation and the doorman let them in, watching them from the corner of his eye as though he expected them to pocket the silverware. Josephine entered with curiosity, wondering what the fuss was all about. The place seemed pretty standard with its chandeliers and red carpet, an abundance of flowers in vases and brocaded walls. The rich smell of grilling meat made Josephine's mouth water; she hadn't eaten in twelve hours. Roger led them to a side room where a uniformed man stood guard before a gold chain. Greeting him as "Saint Peter," as if heaven itself lay beyond, Roger slipped the frowning guard a ten-dollar bill and then another before the man allowed them into the sanctum.

"He's grumpy tonight," Roger said. "I wonder what gives?"

Josephine waved to Walter, sitting in the back corner of the room scribbling notes as the actress Grace Kelly spoke, holding him so enthralled that he only lifted his pen in reply. A waiter came and took Roger's champagne order, but brought flutes for him and his wife only. Roger had to ask three times before Josephine and Bessie got glasses.

"The shows have just let out, and they're swamped," he said. "That's why they're slow."

"That had better be the reason why," Bessie said. "These folks don't want to mess around with Josephine."

"At least there's no WHITES ONLY sign on the door," Josephine said. "I was surprised to see them still in the South."

"Why break the law openly when a doorman can provide the same result?" Bessie said.

Roger flagged a waiter who stopped for their orders: Chicken and pasta for him, salad for his wife, steak for Josephine, and crab cakes for Bessie. Again, the waiter never glanced at either of the colored women. Josephine ordered a bottle of red wine for the table, St. Emilion, Roger's favorite, but the youth acted as though she hadn't spoken until Solange repeated the order.

"He's awfully young to be hard of hearing," she said to her husband.

"Walter Winchell told me the owner doesn't like Negroes coming in," Josephine said. Solange patted her arm and told her not to worry, and refilled her glass. As Josephine drank, a warm buzz rose from her empty stomach and spread across her face and chest. The waiter brought the wine and opened it, pouring into the wine glasses he'd brought for Roger and Solange and, again, neglecting her and Bessie.

"They don't like Negroes, that much is obvious," Bessie said, sipping red wine from her champagne flute.

"I had not thought of it, but you may be right," Roger said. "I have never seen a colored person in this place."

"What's that crashing sound? Another barrier falling?" Josephine said, giggling, the wine having gone to her head.

After a long while, their bottle of wine almost empty, the food arrived at last — or Roger's and Solange's meals did. The waiter spoke only to them as he set down their plates, still acting as though the Ricos were sitting by themselves in a cozy tête-à-tête. The Ricos watched their food cool until Josephine encouraged them to eat. She lifted her hand to ask where her and Bessie's meals were, but no one seemed to see her; eyes slid away as though she were invisible. Roger said he'd never seen the place so busy, but Josephine noticed that the waiters only seemed to hurry when passing their table. Her stomach rumbled. The Ricos were finishing their meals; the wine was gone. Josephine looked across the room at Walter, and pointed to the empty place where her food should be. He frowned and, seeming to realize what had happened, shook his head and averted his gaze.

A waiter rushed past. Josephine called out, but his step never faltered. Roger stood, cursing, and stepped over to the front counter where their waiter stood writing up a tab. He exchanged a few words and the man followed him back to their table.

"We have waited more than an hour for our order," Josephine said.

"Did you hear Mrs. Baker speaking to you?" Roger said.

"I'm sorry," he said, "we are busy tonight. As you can see."

"You're busy feeding everyone else but me and my friend. Folks who came in long after we did have had their meals and left. Where is the steak I ordered ten years ago?

Where are her crab cakes?"

"We have run out of steak," the waiter said. "We are out of crab, as well."

Josephine stood so fast her chair clattered to the floor. "We will see about that. Who has a dime for the phone?"

Roger rose to accompany her to the main dining room, where she called Walter White of the NAACP.

"I've just been refused service at the Stork Club," she said, shouting to be heard over the band. "This is a clear case of racial discrimination."

She hung up and told Roger that they were all invited to Walter White's apartment.

"He wants to have a press conference about this tomorrow. Will you speak, Roger? I'll need witnesses to back me up. We'll talk to Winchell on the way out, he saw what happened." But when they stepped back into the Cub Room, Winchell's table was empty.

"He hightailed it out of here as soon as you left," Bessie said. "Practically ran out the door with his friends."

Their waiter came out and set a plate on the table.

"What is this?" Josephine cried. "A steak or a chunk of wood? Look at this sorry, dried-up thing." Roger demanded the tab,

531

but the manager rushed out waving his hands and saying that Mr. Billingsley did not charge celebrities to dine in the Cub Room.

"Does he think I can be bought for the price of a meal? You've always been happy to take my money before," Roger said, and flung a handful of bills on the table.

"Mr. Billingsley does not want any trouble," the manager said. "Please come and speak with him tomorrow."

"Come back here? You must be crazy. Tell Mr. Billingsley that he'll be hearing from us," Josephine said over her shoulder as she headed out the door. "But we won't ever step foot in this place again. And by the time we're finished, nobody else will, either."

She wore sunglasses, her eyes as puffy as if she'd been crying all night instead of ranting and plotting with Walter White and her friends. She'd hardly slept, having gone to bed in the wee hours and then getting up early for a morning press conference, hoping to make the afternoon newspapers.

They held the event, called by the NAACP, outside the Stork Club, their backdrop the white facade that was, Josephine noted, the perfect color. Walter had called picketers, who circled outside the entrance with signs that read STORK CLUB: COLOR DISCRIMINATION IN AMERICA and FAMOUS NITE SPOT A WHITE SPOT. To Josephine's delight, a crowd of reporters and photographers came — but not Winchell.

After she, Bessie, Roger, and Solange had described the evening's humiliations, the questions began: Were there any witnesses to support their version? Service at the Stork Club was notoriously slow, a reporter said: couldn't this be a mistake?

"There is no misunderstanding about the Stork Club's policy of segregation," Josephine said. To be questioned in this way was infuriating. Did these white journalists doubt her word? Clearly, they didn't want to believe. They'd probably all had dinner in the Stork Club at some point, even while knowing that Negroes weren't allowed inside.

"I witnessed it," Roger said. "My wife and I were served, but Josephine's food never arrived until we made a fuss."

"And then it was inedible," she added.

"So — you were served?" the reporter pressed. Was he a friend of Billingsley's too, like that turncoat Winchell?

"Walter Winchell was there, and he saw the whole thing," Josephine said. "I'm sure he will confirm what we've told you."

But Winchell did not confirm. That afternoon, Walter White and Shirley Woolf came to her suite at the Gladstone Hotel with a stack of newspapers. Walter's jaw clenched as he handed them to her. "Somebody isn't telling the truth," he said.

Josephine could not believe what she read. Sure, Winchell said, he'd seen Josephine Baker in the Stork Club's Cub Room last night, but he didn't know she was having trouble. When she'd gone with Roger into the main dining room to make their call, he'd thought they were going to dance — a whiz-bang Brazilian group was playing samba music, and it sounded like a lot of fun. He'd have gone in to watch, he loved to see Mrs. Baker dance, but he and his friends had to leave for a late-night screening of *The Desert Fox,* the Warner Brothers flick about the Nazi General Rommel. The film was pure propaganda, by the way, this was what they should be talking about instead of some misperceived slight to the notoriously fragile ego of a pampered star who had waited out the war in luxury in a pasha's palace while her fellow Negroes got sent to death camps along with the Jews.

Josephine threw the newspaper across the room, screaming and cursing. Walter

Winchell would pay for those lies. He'd called *her* a coward? Shirley hung up from her call with Ned and rang for the maid to take the newspapers away, saying Josephine had seen enough.

"Ned says to let this drop," she said.

"Never!"

"You don't want to get on Winchell's bad side. He'll destroy you."

"Moi?" Josephine laughed like a maniac. "He's not good enough to lick my shoes." Although he would have given anything if she had let him.

"He is very influential," Shirley said. "And vindictive. Why not just focus on your tour? Ned added three new cities yesterday, including a return to Los Angeles, and a meeting in Hollywood while we're there. You'll make a bundle if you don't blow it. Or if Winchell doesn't blow it, which he is perfectly capable of doing."

"He can blow *me.*"

"Believe me, Jo — I've seen him in action. Get him going, and he won't stop until you lose it all. Everything."

Josephine looked out the window, at the city spread like a smorgasbord below, hers for the taking — the entire, vast country, hers! — or so it had seemed only yesterday. If she did as Shirley advised, she could still have it all, riches beyond anything she had earned so far in her life, more than enough to pay the bills at Les Milandes.

But if she let the Stork Club's discrimination drop, and agreed to forget about Walter's running out the door while she and Bessie got treated like something the cat had dragged in, how would that be helping anyone except Sherman Billingsley and Walter Winchell? The Stork Club could go on telling Negroes that the place was "full" when it wasn't, and Winchell could continue to portray himself as an advocate for the oppressed. And Josephine Baker, by virtue of her silence, would be complicit.

She would not give in to white tyranny. She denounced Winchell to the press as a phony and an egomaniac, and the traitors came crawling out of the woodwork. Valaida Snow from *Shuffle Along* — the Negro sax player arrested in Europe and sent to a concentration camp during the war — wrote a letter praising Winchell for helping her career; a colored newspaper editor lauded Winchell's support for the Negro cause and criticized Josephine as a sham and a fraud "hornswoggling the colored brethren into accepting her as a group heroine and champion."

She talked as fast as she could but she

couldn't keep up, the accusations flew faster and faster until Winchell announced that the FBI had launched an investigation into her "communist ties." An anonymous caller told her to "watch yourself," that they may like "commies" in France, but in America they shot them dead. Josephine called a press conference to announce that she hadn't been afraid of Nazis, and she wasn't afraid of the KKK. Winchell fired off a retort in the next day's newspaper, saying it was easy to thumb your nose at the Nazis while sipping bubbly on a Casablanca beach.

"He doesn't know what in the hell he's talking about," she said. "If Winchell keeps this up, I'll sue his ass."

"It's hard to win a lawsuit against a journalist, especially when you're famous," Shirley said. "You've heard that there's no such thing as bad publicity?"

"Whoever said that was a fool."

"Juries tend to believe it. Hey, don't look at me that way. As an attorney, I'm giving you my professional advice."

It sickened her that the world might think she'd shirked her duties during the war. But how could she set the record straight without breaking her vow of secrecy? She telegraphed Jacques Abtey, asking him to fly to

New York with the citations and letters she had received from de Gaulle and others praising her courage. In the meantime, she did a tour in Montreal, happy to speak French, and told *Le Petit Journal* that she would not succumb to slander.

"I will keep working as a missionary of peace," she said. "I will keep on fighting for Americans because I don't want them separated by prejudice."

How wonderful it felt to see Jacques again, tanned and fit and more handsome than ever, a twinkle in his blue eyes that she didn't remember seeing before — but, back then, they'd been fighting for their lives.

"Foxy, I have never seen you looking so relaxed," she said.

"I wish I could say the same of you. Jo, why did you come here when you swore you never would do so again? The United States is not a good place for you, do you remember?"

"It isn't a good place for a lot of people, especially Negroes. That's why I came back."

She got an interview on Barry Gray's radio show with Jacques, Bessie Buchanan, and Walter White, all of them testifying on her behalf — outraged, they said, that anyone would attack a woman of such courage and strength.

"Josephine Baker is a credit to the Negro race," Bessie said. "And Walter Winchell is an insult to the human one."

Winchell retaliated by publishing a quote, in English, from Marcel Sauvage's biography of Josephine — written when she was an ignorant child — in which she'd said that Harlem's Negroes were victims of the Jews. Josephine didn't remember saying it: was it another of Marcel's distortions? She held another press conference denying that she was anti-Semitic, but the damage could not be undone. In her room, as she and Jacques toasted in the New Year at midnight, she received a telegram. Her next venue, in Tampa, had canceled her engagement. She shrugged and laughed, but then another cancellation came in, and another, along with a notification from Ned Schuyler that her film deal was off.

"What are you going to do, Josephine?" Jacques said, pity all over his face, like he thought she might cry. For a moment, she thought she might, too, as her hopes and dreams for America toppled over like falling dominoes. She would not win the love of her country. She would not end racial segregation. She would not earn the money she needed to transform Les Milandes into a world-class resort where she could raise her Rainbow Tribe and continue her work for equality. She would not be able, even, to start adopting babies. Yet.

But God had called her to the work she had done here, and she had heeded that call. She had given it her best. The rest was up to him, and she knew he would not let her down. Her tour of America would end, but Josephine Baker was just beginning.

She filled their glasses, and they lifted them in a toast.

"To Paris," she said. "To Les Milandes. To freedom. I've had it with the United States of America, Jacqui. It's time to go home."

Chapter 32

1954, Tokyo

Surrounded by babies, Josephine blinked her eyes, bedazzled. Her eyes full of soft, warm, beautiful, sweet-smelling babies. Except the one in her arms, who suddenly didn't smell sweet any more. Josephine handed the child to a nun, who took it away speaking in a rapid Japanese that sounded to her ears like scolding. The poor little thing! She couldn't help herself. Nor could Josephine help her, though: she hadn't come for a girl.

"Our staff gets overwhelmed sometimes," Miki Sawada was saying. "We have so many children, with more coming in all the time." Miki's orphanage, in Kagawa, a tiny prefecture north of Tokyo, had opened after World War II. It cared for mixed-race children, at first the offspring of Japanese women and American soldiers, but now that the United States had troops in a different war, it took in Korean-American children, as well. "Like this little boy," she said of the toddler who had wrapped his arms around Josephine's leg.

Josephine reached down to take him into her arms, but he wriggled from her grasp like a slippery fish, laughing and chattering. She clapped her hands, feeling like a child, herself — in a toy store.

"I want to take them all," she told her friend. Of course, she could not: filling her castle with oriental babies would ruin her plans, and Jo had agreed to adopt only one.

Coaxing him to let her start their tribe was easier than she'd expected. She'd greeted him in a slinky gown when he came home and suggested he go upstairs and dress for dinner. When he came down, she had a romantic record on the stereo, a coupe in her hand, and his favorite dinner waiting to be served, duck cassoulet with green beans and a salad. After dining, they'd danced, slow, the way they used to do. The feel of his strong, lean body next to hers aroused a thrill in her that she'd almost forgotten, so long had it been since Jo had slept with her.

She'd thought she could change him? Boy, was she ever wrong. He preferred the boys who worked in the gardens, and didn't bother to hide it anymore. Josephine couldn't help feeling neglected, but she consoled herself with the knowledge that Jo's guilt worked in her favor. He would do anything for her.

Who needed all the fuss and worry of sex, anyway, at her age? She was too old for that, going on fifty now and every year showing on her face, in her hips and waist and arms.

"I love you," she said. "But — it isn't enough, Jo. I need more."

"You know I do not mind if you have lovers, too."

"That phase in my life is long gone. I want a husband —"

"Until death do we part, remember?" Clearly thinking she was about to ask for a divorce, he grabbed her hand like a drowning man. Good.

"I want a husband *and* a family. I've never made a secret of this. We've talked about it from the beginning. It's not the love of a man I'm missing, but children."

His face lifted in a smile. "Yes, of course, we will adopt as soon as the castle is ready."

"It's good enough now, isn't it? A baby won't know the difference. Look, Jo." She opened a desk drawer and pulled out her letter from her friend Miki, who had moved back to Japan with her husband when he'd retired. "She has invited me to visit her new orphanage. I could bring a child back with me!"

He burst into laughter.

"So that is what you are up to." He gestured toward the table, the flowers, the music, the wine. "You didn't have to go to so much trouble. You didn't need to play the vamp. You need only to ask me for anything you desire."

She moved over to the champagne bucket and refilled their glasses. "How could any gown be too beautiful for this occasion?" She handed him his coupe, and raised her own for a toast. "Here's to our new baby boy. The first of many, I hope."

"Here's to our family." He touched his glass to hers. "I had thought such a thing was impossible for me. But now, thanks to you, I will at last have a son."

"Many sons. We're going to adopt an entire tribe, remember?"

"A tribe, yes," he said. "And a tribe needs a chief. I wonder which of us that will be?"

Josephine was the one in charge today, here in Miki's orphanage surrounded by precious children, including the cute slippery little Korean fish now climbing into her lap and then, when she tried to get hold of him, sliding down again and running away.

"Just like every man I've ever known, he slips right through my fingers," she told Miki.

"I think he's more clever than any of your men," Miki said. The boy's name was Akio, meaning "autumn." He'd been found under an open umbrella, a small red pouch around his neck, a talisman inside inscribed with his name and the precepts of Buddhism.

"But of course, you could baptize him as a Christian," Miki said. "He is only about eighteen months old."

"Buddhism is perfect," Josephine said.

By the time she said goodbye, the older children had grown bored with her and run outside to play. Carrying little Akio, her arms full at last, she walked alongside Miki to enjoy the afternoon sun — and spied an infant sitting under a tree wearing only a diaper and a frown.

"Now, that's a sad-looking baby," she said.

"Yes, but not as sad as when he has to go indoors. You should hear him cry. How funny that he is named Teruya, which means 'shining house' in Japanese."

Josephine asked if he were Buddhist, too, and Miki said, no, this child was Shinto, whose eight million gods were found everywhere, even among the dead. Josephine put

Akio on the ground beside him and peered into the baby's face. He returned her gaze with such gravity that *he* might be a god, too. Josephine wavered, almost regretting her hasty choice of Akio — until her baby put his arms around Teruya and kissed him, making him smile.

"Look at that! These two were made to be together. I'll take them both," she said. After all, she had two arms.

"Two babies? Won't your husband mind?"

"Who knows?" Josephine said, wiping the tears from her eyes. "Who cares? They're my damned children, not his."

On the flight home, juggling the crying babies with the help of her maid, Josephine wondered what she'd done. Akio and Teruya — whom she'd renamed Janot, which means "serious" — had seemed so happy and peaceful in the orphanage. But now, nothing could quiet them. As with dogs, the howls of one set off the other and back again, until Josephine wanted to throw them both out the window. All her life wanting babies, she'd never thought about the squalls or the stink.

She had never felt so glad to feel wheels touch pavement. As soon as it happened, the babies calmed down. Josephine could hardly believe her ears, which continued to ring.

"They must know they're going home," she said. "Maybe they feel Jo's presence nearby."

"I think they have finally exhausted themselves," the maid said, and it was true. Both had fallen asleep.

Disembarking from the plane, Janot in her arms, Josephine beamed at Jo, who reached tenderly for the child.

"Be careful, he's asleep."

"And he will sleep again, later. This is an important moment, when I hold my son for the first time." Janot did indeed wake up, but instead of crying he gazed into Jo's face as gravely as the first time Josephine had seen him.

The maid came over with Akio, who had also awakened.

"Give him to Jo," Josephine said. "He wants to hold his son."

With one baby in each arm, he furrowed his brows. "Which is ours, *chérie*?"

"Both. Aren't they wonderful? Just pretend that we were expecting a child, and that I had twins."

Seeing his annoyance, she turned on her heel and began walking toward the terminal, her heart thumping. Jo would come around.

The important part was not to show any weakness, or how desperately she wanted him to love the babies.

And then he called out her name and she stopped, and he caught up to her, one baby in each arm. She reached for Janot, worried that Jo might drop him on the tarmac, remembering her mama's bitter words hurled so often in anger: *I wish that doctor had let you fall on your head, right on the concrete floor. You'd be dead, and I'd be free.*

She hadn't meant it, Josephine knew that now. But she would never say that to her babies, because it wouldn't be true. *I was so afraid he might drop you that I shouted at him not to run, to stop where he was, and I walked up and took you out of his arms. My only thought was to keep you safe.*

"Don't drop one just to get rid of him," she snapped.

Jo looked confused for a moment but then, when she'd taken Janot, he kissed her cheek.

"You were right to adopt two children," he said. "This way, we will be twice as happy."

After each night's performance of *Joséphine à Bobino,* Josephine feels energized — but tonight is different. Tonight, she brims with life, popping and spritzing with it like the bubbles in her glass. She cannot sit still, but hops onto the table and begins to dance, kicking plates to the floor and laughing like there's no sorrow and no tomorrow. From the floor, her costar commands her to come down, his eyes snapping with French contempt, his thin mustache twitching over a trying-to-be-patient smile. She will injure herself in those heels, he says, she will fall and break her neck and they will have to perform twenty-two sold-out shows without her. They will have to hire a replacement — ha! As if anyone could take the place of Josephine Baker, the most famous woman in the world, fifty years on the Paris stage and still dancing like a girl.

"Have some dignity, don't be a bouffe, you are embarrassing us all." With each admonition his voice rises, hammering, insistent, crackling with indignation over the attention she commands, over the fact that every pair of eyes in the room watches her shake and twist her body, which remains, even at sixty-eight, magnificent.

Giggles bubble from Josephine's mouth. He folds his arms and narrows his eyes, playing the stern father but reminding her of one of her children — twelve in all, her Rainbow Tribe — pouting when he didn't get his way. She slows her dance and reaches toward him, *"Mon cher,"* she mouths, beckoning; she would caress that handsome face and kiss those pursing lips until they smiled, but he isn't interested in her, none of them are, not anymore, not that she cares. She wouldn't want him, anyway, pretty mouth or not, baguette in his tight pants or not, torso muscles rippling under her hands or not. She renounced all that years ago, tired of giving herself to men who pressed their mouths to hers and sucked out her vigor and her love, and never gave enough in return. She was made to do so much more, and, by God, she did it all.

And she has relived it all tonight, flooded by memories throughout *Joséphine à Bobino,* not the stage life but the real, which is, she understands now, better than any show could

550

ever be, even with the hunger and the ill-nesses and the ghosts. Josephine Baker is unstoppable! Even the US government couldn't, ultimately, defeat her. Even this petulant child in the body of a man cannot subdue her.

"We have all had a long day," he says. She kicks off her shoes and slaps her feet on the wood, flaps her arms like wings, arches her back and hitches up her bottom. *Shake-shake, thrust-shake, shimmy-shammy kick-kick.* What does he know about long days? Has he sung thirty-three songs, danced his way from toddler to twelve to nineteen to sixty-eight, zoomed a shuddering Harley-Davidson across the stage, and held two straining dogs on leashes while wobbling in four-inch heels down a staircase, all while his head throbbed from having his face stretched tight and pinned under a sweating, stinking wig, and from the recorded music pumping from the enormous speakers on either side of him? Yet Josephine never faltered even a single step, never tripped over a single note.

A professional, that's what she is, fifty years of experience — no, more than that, for she has been dancing since she was in the womb. "Wore me out with all that kicking, like she was doing the Charleston in my insides," Mama used to say. The Charleston, the Mess-

Around, the Black Bottom, the splits: she was born with dancing in her bones.

And what about him? What has he done that he should be so tired? Has he risked his life for the country he loved, risked his career for the people he loved, risked anything at all that mattered for something bigger than himself?

She whoops and spins again, and then someone plays the Charleston on the jukebox and her knees and elbows start flying, her arms crossing and uncrossing and her eyes crossing, too, at the dancers turning their faces away and laughing, not because she is funny, but because she is old.

"Sit down, Grandma," somebody mutters. "My God, it's embarrassing. One hundred and four years old, and she behaves like a child." How can they speak of her this way, she who has lived in ways they have not even begun to comprehend?

"One hundred and four?" She laughs and lifts her hands into the air, shakes and shimmies her body, the table, the whole damned joint. "Look again — I'm seventeen!"

"All right, Josephine," the costar says, advancing toward her, extending his hand, "we believe you." Smirking like a sullen teen, he'll roll his eyes at her next. "We believe you are seventeen. You have convinced us. Now come down from that table — please" — there it is, the eye roll! — "before you revert all the way to infancy."

CHAPTER 33

1975, Paris

Now she's tired, so tired. She feels like she's been dancing all night and she has been: on the stage in *Josephine à Bobino;* in the café, dancing on tables; and now, in bed, reading reviews while dancing and living and loving in dreams that really aren't dreams but memories, the events of her life unspooling like a film whose plot she cannot understand. What does it all mean?

She's been tested so many times that she doesn't know what she was supposed to learn or what good she has been or done. It seems like every time she tried to make a difference, something got in the way.

And now, in her mind's eye, another scene: 1963, two hundred fifty thousand people, many "Afro-American," as her people came to call themselves, and white people, too, and brown and yellow and red, a vast sea of brothers and sisters converged in Washington, DC, in a mighty protest to demand an end to racial prejudice and discrimination, and, in their place, equality. See the humanity filling the streets, waving signs, holding hands, embracing one another, singing "We Shall Overcome"; chanting "Freedom"; everyone peaceful, altogether, all together, the ultimate Rainbow Tribe.

She starts to cry at the sight of Dr. King leading the march, wearing a suit and tie as always in spite of the brutal August heat, his kind face shining and serene, the picture of pure love. If only she could warn him — *Be careful, Martin, or you'll be dead within the year.* But if he had known, would he have done anything differently? Would he have stopped preaching, exhorting, demanding, talking, daring the world to dream?

And there is Josephine, in her Free French Air Force uniform, taking the podium just before the great man himself, the only woman to speak on that day. She has flown in from Paris for the occasion, honored to be invited, and also a bit surprised.

After the performers sing their protest songs — Joan Baez; Peter, Paul and Mary; Bob Dylan — Josephine steps up to the mic, not a performer today but something more: a woman who has lived the horrors of oppression, hatred, and fear, and yet speaks of love. All she ever wanted to do was wake the world up to this reality: We are all human. She beat relentlessly against prejudice like waves breaking against a stone wall and taking it away piece by piece, and now she stands before her people to bear witness.

"This is the happiest day of my life," she says, and it was, she knows that now as she watches herself at that podium addressing the crowd with dignity, with grace, with love. It all came together in those perfect moments: her own past full of travails; the present when so many gathered together in the name of equality and sang that they were not afraid; and the future that looked — to her, to them all — filled with possibility.

"I am not a young woman now, friends. My life is behind me. There is not too much fire burning inside me.

"And before it goes out, I want you to use what is left to light that fire in you, so that you can carry on, and so that you can do those things that I have done. Then, when my fires have burned out, and I go where we all go someday, I can be happy.

"You know, I have always taken the rocky path. I never took the easy one, but as I got older, and as I knew I had the power and the strength, I took that rocky path, and I tried to smooth it out a little. I wanted to make it easier for you. I want you to have a chance at what I had. And we know that that time is not someday. We know that that time is now."

And the crowd lifts its voice as she puts the coda on her own protest song, the cheers of two hundred fifty thousand people arising from the earth as though the earth itself exults, but Josephine hears only her own self crying out, understanding, now, the measure of her life.

And in her bedroom, the robed figure from her childhood, the man with the beard like a white flame and eyes of pure love, appears before her with a sound like the wind, his hands reaching toward her with a gleaming golden crown, placing it on her head, pinning it there with a star. At last. Elation fills her, and light, shooting from her fingertips, pouring from her mouth as she finishes.

Thank you, and may God bless you. And may he continue to bless you long after I am gone.

ACKNOWLEDGMENTS

Thanks to my literary agent, Natasha Kern, for her unflagging and enthusiastic support over more than a decade; my good friends Mark Allen Williams, Karlee Etter Turner, Trish Hoard, and Richard Myers for all the time spent listening to me talk about Josephine Baker and providing your valuable insights; to Gwen Moore at the Missouri History Museum in Saint Louis for driving me in the rain on a fruitless search for any intact residence where Josephine lived as a child, for telling me about the demolition of her entire neighborhood, and for taking me to the Soulard Market; to author and radio host Dennis Owler of Saint Louis for regaling me with tales of the golden age of jazz in that city; to Olivia Lahs-Gonzales at the Sheldon Art Galleries in Saint Louis for her information and conversation about Josephine's life and work; to Charles E. Brown at the Saint Louis Mercantile Library and

William "Zelli" Fischetti at the State Historical Society of Missouri library for their help researching old Saint Louis; to Tomy Rouleau and Ophélie Lachaux in Paris for opening the wonderful Theatre des Champs-Élysées to me for a private tour of the theater where Josephine Baker made her debut and, at 19, became a star; to the documentary filmmaker David Burke in Paris for talking with me about African-American life and music in the city during the 1920s and '30s, and, as always, to the members of my wonderful street team, Sherry's Sirens.

ABOUT THE AUTHOR

Author and journalist **Sherry Jones** is best known for her international bestseller *The Jewel of Medina.* She is also the author of *The Sword of Medina, Four Sisters, All Queens, The Sharp Hook of Love,* and the novella *White Heart.* She lives in Spokane, WA, where, like Josephine Baker, she enjoys dancing, singing, eating, advocating for equality, and drinking champagne. Visit her online at AuthorSherryJones.com and at Facebook.com/SherryJonesFanpage.